# Bold Lies

Rachel Lynch grew up in Cumbria and the lakes and fells are never far away from her. London pulled her away to teach History and marry an Army Officer, whom she followed around the globe for thirteen years. A change of career after children led to personal training and sports therapy, but writing was always the overwhelming force driving the future. The human capacity for compassion as well as its descent into the brutal and murky world of crime are fundamental to her work.

# Also by Rachel Lynch

*The Rift*

## Detective Kelly Porter

# BOLD LIES

## RACHEL LYNCH

CANELO CRIME

First published in the United Kingdom in 2019 by Canelo

This edition published in the United Kingdom in 2019 by

Canelo Digital Publishing Limited
31 Helen Road
Oxford OX2 0DF
United Kingdom

A CIP catalogue record for this book is available from the British Library.

Print ISBN 978 1 78863 552 3
Ebook ISBN 978 1 78863 268 3

Look for more great books at www.canelo.co

Printed and bound in Great Britain by Clays Ltd, Elcograf S.p.A.

# Chapter 1

George looked across the lake. It was a beauty. Like all of them, it sat serene and calm, like a feline at rest, waiting to pounce; driven by cloud and pressure from above. He peered skywards but was satisfied that he had time to catch one more fish. His permit had always been sorted by his dear friend Alan, but that was no longer possible. The old man had enjoyed a good innings, as they say. The cricketing reference would have pleased him; that was how they'd met, after all.

The boat rocked gently and he heard the screams of children kayaking in the distance. Derwent Water was fairly quiet out of season, and large enough to cater for all tastes. The big house had its own private beach, but no one owned the lake; that belonged to everyone, and rightly so. He smiled, thinking of his daughter's laugh. He still hadn't forgotten.

His line tugged and his concentration was taken to the crystal-clear depths, and a fuss under the gentle ebb and flow of the water lapping at the side of his boat. He allowed some line to be yanked away and then reeled it in a little: whatever it was wasn't large. The poor thing also didn't give him much of a scrap, coming to the surface straight away and practically rolling over exhausted after a minor scuffle: snowflake generation, thought George.

His mouth fell open.

He'd only gone and caught a bloody vendace! The freshwater herring was supposed to be extinct, but he'd heard rumours of a revival. He reached gently into the water and cupped the wriggling silver body: she was beautiful. He admired the colours shining off her skin, and was almost tempted to keep her. He'd been using a hook for fish much bigger than this little mite, but it had only caught the side of her mouth, and he removed it with ease, lowering her back into the water for her to revive and dart away.

His day couldn't have gone better, but then he remembered that he'd forgotten to take a photograph; now no one would believe him. He had no idea if he'd even brought his damn phone with him.

He packed away his gear, then picked up the oars, and headed for the private beach. There was a motorboat, of course, but he couldn't understand why anyone would want to chug toxic fumes into the clear air in this wonderful place. He gave thanks to his old friend; he would toast his memory tonight, as he always did when he came here to keep an eye on the place. The burden was not insignificant, but he understood the motives behind the decision. It had made him unpopular, but that wasn't a first and it certainly didn't put him off. The most important thing was that he was honouring the dying wish of an old gentleman.

George couldn't imagine moving here. Well, not yet, anyway. There was too much invested in London. It would take years to transfer everything and make it ready. And it was a pipe dream anyhow.

By the time he eased his small boat onto the shingle beach, the sky was getting dark. Even though it was June, the mountains could make everything turn to night if they wanted to. He glanced up at the peaks behind the house: they were covered in thick grey cloud that showed no signs of clearing. It was time to go in and make sure he had a fire lit. The kitchen was always warm, thanks to the Aga. But the main fire in the sitting room was magnificent and George had lit it every night in remembrance of nights with Alan, sitting in front of it sipping a fifty-year-old Janneau Napoleon. The cellar in the old pile was Alan's pride and joy, and George couldn't bring himself to clear it out just yet. Apart from to open the odd bottle of red with dinner, of course. He never was very good at telling the difference between a bottle worth a thousand pounds and one from Tesco, but they all tasted good from Alan's collection.

He left the boat on the beach and walked up to the house, stopping when he saw that he had a visitor. It wasn't entirely a surprise, and he held out his hand in greeting.

'Come in, I'm just about to put a lasagne in the oven,' he said. Their feet made scraping noises in the gravel and George stopped outside the kitchen door to take off his wellington boots. His visitor didn't bother.

'Who were those men?' he asked.

'What men?'

'They drove past me on their way out. Don't tell me you've got plans for the place already?'

## Chapter 2

Derwent Marina was quiet. The small building, set back from the beach, with seats outside and at least fifty boats and vessels for hire, was a modest operation. The car park catered for about ten cars. The place ticked along during the winter but saw a steady trade build from the spring onwards. There were boats and kayaks available to buy, but mainly it was rentals that brought in the steady flow of cash that enabled Graeme Millar to pay his mortgage and live a comfortable life. He paid a few locals to fit buoyancy aids, size up wetsuits and generally keep the place clean and tidy, but he ran the business and was responsible for the upkeep of the plot. The land didn't belong to him; he paid rent to a landlord who refused to sell up. In fact, most of Derwent Water's coastline was privately owned by wealthy families desperate to cling on to illustrious histories but unsure of how to maintain their enormous estates. Most had been turned into luxury holiday homes, or water sports centres.

Allerdale House was no different. It stood huddled behind trees on the lake's western shore, away from the prying eyes of the tourists crammed onto the steamer puffing between Keswick and Lodore every day. But a kayaker, strong of arm and curious to boot, might catch a glimpse of the grand slate facade, slightly up a hill and facing east. The trees shielding the residence from nosy visitors had been planted over two hundred years ago, and the only indication that they guarded something special was a sign on the beach that read: *Private: Keep Out! No landing on the beach.* Graeme Millar told every customer the same, and even supplied a map showing which beaches they were allowed to paddle up to. The red lines denoted no-go areas, and there were plenty of them. With Allerdale House's owner passing away after Christmas, who knew what would become of the place.

At 9 a.m. the wind was insignificant, and Graeme knew that it would be a good day for business. It was Whitsun week and the kids were on half-term. Sure enough, two cars pulled into the car park and children got out, looking at the water and approaching the kayaks with delight. He always recommended two hours for families with small kids, because he knew that it would take them at least an hour to make it out of the marina. Derwent Water was just under three miles long, but an inexperienced kayaker would be lucky to get halfway down before having to turn back again, either through cold or exertion. There were a few islands in between to keep them occupied, including the one where *Swallows and Amazons* was set, though Graeme reckoned that the majority of kids hauled to the Lake District on holiday these days hadn't even heard of the book.

He called one of his staff over to get the families booked in while he checked the boathouse to see if the three rowing boats he'd had to pull from the water last week were repaired and varnished yet. Major repairs were carried out in the winter, and the wooden vessels had only needed a tweak or two. The boats were his livelihood and they needed looking after properly.

To an outsider, the boatyard looked like a tip; a junk-yard of detritus and bits of wood. In fact it churned out new boats every year, and a launch was currently being renovated in the shed. *The Lady of the Lake* was a stunning ninety-seater, a 1929 model; once a dayboat on the Amsterdam canals, then a tourist tripper on Lake Windermere, she'd made her debut on Derwent Water in 1985. She'd needed a season out of the water and a loving refurbishment. Graeme swung open the doors of the main shed and admired the gleaming mahogany and oak panelling. Her name had been repainted and she looked glorious and ready for action. He sucked in the morning air tinged with varnish and cleaning chemicals. But something else caught his attention.

'Damn cats!' Graeme was a dog lover, and to him, cats were vermin, killing local wildlife and scavenging from the campsite two hundred yards down the shore. Today one of them had obviously caught a bird and brought it in here to rot, or perhaps something bigger, like a rat. He made a cursory circuit of the boat, finding nothing but noting that the smell was worse near the stern, especially by the cabin. He tutted. He'd have to climb up there to make sure. The last thing they needed was the *Lady* being put back into service with an animal carcass somewhere on board.

He went back out into the morning sunshine and towards the smaller shed, where the rowing boats were upended and ready to be carried back to the marina. Two were six-seaters and one a four-seater. They took a good hammering during the peak season, but they were sturdy craft and had been in service since before the 1950s. All the wooden vessels in the marina were way older than Graeme, and they'd no doubt outlive him too.

It wasn't until lunchtime that he got the opportunity to tackle the problem of the *Lady*'s suspected passenger. He ate his sandwich before venturing back to the shed with a ladder, thinking that whatever he might have to dispose of could well put him off his food. Trade had been steady throughout the morning and he pushed aside the worries that plagued him throughout the long, quiet winter, as he did every year. His was essentially a seasonal income, and he'd been through some tight scrapes.

Walking back to the shed through the trees, he avoided the wettest parts of the ground, which lay exposed and unpaved just as they had a hundred years ago. Patches of gravel had been laid, but not on the shortcut that he took. He looked south and whistled to himself, stopping and smiling as the clouds parted over Cat Bells. It was probably the most iconic of the spines around here, and when the sun shone, there was nowhere more breath-taking. He made out a snaking stream of walkers trudging up to the summit, their bright coats looking like a line of tacks on a map. It was the busiest Wainwright in the whole National Park.

When he opened the shed door, his heart sank. The smell had worsened. He sighed and set the ladder up, climbing onto the vessel and pulling back the tarpaulin. She looked exquisite. He hopped over the edge and his stomach turned over. Something had definitely died up here and it was creating an eye-watering stench.

He bent down and peered under the seats, which were warm and reminiscent of boatyards of long ago, when steam and beam was the only way to travel. He covered his mouth: nothing. Following his nose, he walked back to the cabin. Twenty-five of the launch's seats were under cover, an essential arrangement in the Lake District. On rainy days, scuffles for shelter sometimes caused moments of rage between passengers. The smell was definitely worse back here and he knelt down again. Nothing. He stood up, puzzled, and walked towards the bridge, covering his mouth again as he neared the control panel. Another tarp covered the helm.

'Bloody hell!' This was no bird, he thought. He wondered if a dog had crawled in here to die. The stench was reminiscent of a dead sheep on the fells, covered in maggots and sweet with rot. His hand shook and he felt foolish for being so apprehensive. He'd seen dead animals all his life. It was unpleasant, that was all.

He pulled back the tarp.

An adrenalin rush took hold of his body. He ran to the ladder, leaping onto it before his brain could even process what he'd seen. He stumbled on the slippery rungs and jumped from halfway to the gravel below. His legs shook and he retched as he left the shed and ran to the water's edge to be sick.

Slowly his senses returned to him, and he took his mobile phone from his pocket and dialled 999.

# Chapter 3

In a rented garage in Bethnal Green, ten minutes from the Tube station and five from the best Thai restaurant in east London, Emily Wilson closed her computer. Mike was finishing up with the incubators that housed flasks containing the proteins of brain cells, and he'd already locked the two sterile cabinets containing their most dangerous compounds. From the inside, they could have been in a maximum-security laboratory in a slick facility in Washington, under top-secret instructions from the White House to find a cure for all pathogens. As it was, the lab was home-made from top to bottom, and no one apart from four people knew it existed.

The four scientists had worked in the industry for a total of over a hundred years. They knew what they were doing.

But that was the point. And that was why they'd told no one. They were close to finalising eleven years of research.

George was on holiday, and Alexandros had left early to call his mother in Cyprus. Alex was thirty-nine years old, but his mother treated him like he was still ten. She checked that he'd eaten, that he'd slept well, and that he'd booked his flights home for the summer. Today she'd texted him to say that the family cat, Aphrodite, had finally passed away peacefully after eighteen years of idleness and luxury. She had been distraught. Alex had made his apologies before he left, and Mike and Emily had poked fun at him, pretending to be offended. But it had been a good day, and they were going out to celebrate later that evening. George was on his way back, and was due to join them in the Thai restaurant. He had told them that he had some exciting news to share with them.

They all felt an excitement that they hadn't felt for a long time, something akin to the birth of a new baby, or a daughter getting married, or, they assumed, winning the lottery. George was the father figure to them all; the project had been his idea, and his conception. His whole life's work was invested in this little lab in the middle of a council estate near the Regent's Canal, where they'd worked like moles in the dark for years, testing, retesting, dedicating hours after a full-time shift at their day jobs to come here and look at one more slide, observe one more alteration, discard one more compound. Often they worked into the night, but it had all been worth it. George's condition was showing signs of coming under control, and sometimes they couldn't quite believe what they were on the verge of achieving. Emily and Mike both had families to attend to, but they still committed way more time than they should, and George was grateful.

A clatter outside made Emily look up and peer through her goggles. Mike did the same and caught her eye, shrugging. They were used to the odd scrap outside between teenagers, or a drunken brawl involving bottles and brawn. She took off her goggles and stretched. The four of them were friends as well as colleagues, all employed by the pharmaceutical giant Ravensword. The lab in Bethnal

Green was an extracurricular activity. They didn't get paid. They did it because they believed in it.

Their clandestine meeting room was affectionately known as the Squash Club, because that was where Emily and Mike told their respective spouses they were when they spent hours away from home. George wasn't married any more, and his only child had tragically passed away. Alex was a free spirit, with no shortage of interested girls but no desire to commit just yet. His dark good looks made him hugely popular in the bars and clubs he frequented, and it gave him an exotic edge. He shared his various encounters with the others in the Squash Club, garnering advice from his elders and envy from George, who looked back nostalgically on his own youth. They were a tight unit. Like family.

There was a checklist to adhere to every evening when they shut the lab, and Mike ran through it now with Emily, who yawned again. The last job on the list was to lock the inner facility and turn off all the lights. A generator kept the incubators going, as well as the dimmed lights inside the cabinets.

The lab was like a skin inside the garage walls, and once outside, they both felt the rush of cold air. They were like lab rats themselves when they were locked inside, methodically transferring compounds from one plate to another, looking for changes that might indicate a match. Mike locked the door and secured the bolt. There was perhaps three feet of space between the outer garage and the inner lab, and they barely had room to fasten coats and pull up hoods. Despite it being June, it was late, and the sun had long disappeared.

Neither heard the main door open.

Mike was the first to be hit. A large instrument slammed into his head, splitting his skull apart and dropping him to his knees. Before Emily could scream, two hands grabbed her throat and twisted her head to one side before forcing it the other way with such force that it tore the skin around her throat, snapping her cervical spine and severing her spinal column. She fell on top of Mike.

The two attackers closed the outer door and got to work. First they stripped the couple and bagged their clothes. Garments were taken from a suitcase and scattered on the floor, as though left there in haste by a pair of lovers. Next the inner lab was unlocked and the bodies dragged inside. One of the men answered his mobile phone and nodded. 'Only two,' he said.

The van was waiting outside. Three more men came in and began stripping the lab. Everything was to go: the cabinets, the benches, the fridges, the Flexi chairs bought by George as a treat last Christmas; the rats, two mini pigs, one cyno monkey – which was quickly subdued by injection – as well as the pictures on the walls of grandparents, children, holidays and weddings.

After the lab was emptied, the men disappeared for a few minutes and came back dressed in white protective suits, carrying cleaning equipment. They began scrubbing the floor and walls. Finally, when the place looked more like a garage again, the bodies were positioned. The men opened Emily's legs and placed Mike on top of her. One of them pulled his trousers down and simulated anal sex with Mike. Another took a picture on his iPhone. Finally, a scrap of paper was placed on the bodies. On it was written in blue pen: *Bitch*.

A groan caught their attention and they were startled to realise that Mike was still alive. One of the men pulled his foot back and kicked his head like a football. Mike fell silent, and the man who'd kicked him bent over and put his fingers to his throat: nothing.

The men left and got back in the van. It was fully dark now, and there was no one about. Another man, who hadn't been part of the tidy-up, came into the garage and looked around. Satisfied, he nodded and took out his phone, snapping a few pictures to prove that the job had been done and done well. Then he left, locking both the inner and outer doors using the keys he'd been provided with.

Inside the lab, Mike's mobile phone began to ring.

# Chapter 4

Detective Inspector Kelly Porter stared at her computer screen. The office was undergoing a quasi-refurbishment: a few new chairs, a new carpet and a paint job. HR had ruled the old stiff chairs ergonomically unsound, and the whole force was getting replacements that could be set at the user's preferred angle. Kelly had to admit they were comfortable. Some of her colleagues had spent the morning racing up and down the corridor on them. DC Rob Shawcross had just beaten DC Emma Hide three to two, and she was refusing to shake his hand. As a responsible senior officer, Kelly should have admonished them, but it was highly entertaining to watch. No blood or coffee had been spilled and it had taken mere minutes out of their day. On top of that, it had lifted the spirits of everyone who'd worked on the Tombday case three years ago. David Crawley had appealed his sentence, and the Old Bailey had delivered its verdict this morning.

Tombday had been a complex web of money-laundering and trafficking, run by businessmen in the Lakes and reaching way beyond the UK borders. David Crawley had only been one cog in the wheel, but he was a childhood friend of Kelly's and an ex-boyfriend. It was a touchy subject. The Court of Appeal had argued that it was never proved that he had obtained material benefit from the people he'd carried in his lorries, and that he was unaware of the transactions made in order to get them there. It was also ruled that the persons had come willingly rather than being coerced, and it was questionable that he had ever intentionally planned to exploit them. In fact, there were so many sections of the Trafficking Act that the original case failed to satisfy that Crawley's offences were reduced to aiding and abetting, carrying a five-year sentence. On account of his impeccable record sheet in prison, and the fact that he'd served almost three years already, he had been freed this morning.

It was a huge blow.

DC Emma Hide brought Kelly a coffee and placed it on her desk. Kelly looked up and smiled at her junior. Her iPad pinged and she flipped it open to notifications from HQ. A 999 call had been transferred to the serious crime unit for North Lakes, and Kelly was expected to move on it straight away. She toyed with sending Emma along, but decided against it because she wanted some fresh air. Try as she might, she couldn't keep herself tied to her chair, and this was a serious crime scene. She'd handed out plenty of domestics, illegal hunting and burglaries to her team. But this was different. A body had been found at Derwent Marina. As yet, it was unidentified. The only information she had was that it was male, and had been found by Graeme Millar, who ran the marina. If Graeme hadn't recognised the victim, then chances were he wasn't local. That raised a flag for Kelly. It meant that he was either a tourist or a traveller. A forensic officer was already at the scene.

'Emma, I've got to go out. Are you working on the burglary at Allerdale House?'

'Yes, guv. I think Kate said she was in between paper-work, though.'

'How's it going?'

A local call early this morning had alerted police to something suspicious at Allerdale House's boatshed. People knew one another round the lake, and apparently a kayaker had spotted that the doors were open and passed the information on to the police. Upon inspection, the first uniforms on the scene discovered that a crime had occurred.

Old Lord Allerdale was dead, but his grandson and heir, Sebastian Montague-Roland, had been tracked down in London, and had supplied a list of items stored in the shed. The house had been standing empty for the last six months, but there were rumours that building work was due to start there to renovate the place and turn it into a luxury leisure complex.

At first glance, the robbery looked like an opportunist break-in. An old pile like that with no one living in it was tempting for the criminal-minded, but apparently some of the equipment taken from the boathouse was valuable. This raised Kelly's interest, as it meant that the place could have been targeted.

'The site is still being processed, guv.' Emma was dressed in casual gear and could have been planning to sprint out of the door for a run at any moment: but then she always looked like that, and carried it off. Kelly glanced down at her feet, and sure enough, she was wearing trainers. Kelly was relaxed about dress, up to a point. If they were driving round Cumbria, in and out of sheds and boat huts, then formal gear just wasn't practical.

'Can you ask Kate to come in here?' she asked. Emma nodded and disappeared. Kelly sipped her coffee and scanned the few details she'd been given about the body found at the marina. Male, over fifty, Caucasian and naked. That was it. She knew Graeme Millar through Johnny; they drank in the same watering holes after a fell race or a lake swim. The Keswick area was extensive to an outsider, but the fell-racing world was an exclusive and tiny club, one that Johnny had only recently become part of. He and Graeme had much in common, in that Graeme had spent five years as an infantry officer around the same time as Johnny had been serving. They had an instant connection. It was the beginning of weekends of sailing lessons, and the inspiration behind Johnny's boat purchase. *Wendy* had been transferred to Derwent Marina from Pooley Bridge in the spring, and Graeme turned a blind eye to the mooring fee.

DS Kate Umshaw came into Kelly's office and sat down. 'I do like these chairs.'

'I know. I think they're a bit too comfortable, though. We need to take a drive to Keswick.'

Kate raised an eyebrow. Everybody knew she preferred paperwork. This was one of the reasons Kelly wanted to get her out of the office for a change.

'What's happened?' she asked.

'Body. Derwent Marina.' Kelly shared the sparse details she had so far, and grabbed her coat. Kate did the same.

'Forensics are there. Let's hope it's just a drunk who found somewhere to shelter and stripped off.'

'Did he die of exposure? In June?'

'Might be a suicide. How are the nicotine patches going?' Kelly asked.

17

'Dull. It's the worst decision of my life,' Kate said. Kelly shook her head. Kate was one of those smokers who would choose a fag over a life jacket.

They checked in with the rest of the team before they left, then headed to the lift. Eden House had several floors, and their office was at the top. Uniforms manned the lower floors, and the two women acknowledged nods as they filed out of the building towards Kelly's car.

They'd only gone a few hundred yards when Kelly began to feel the benefits of being out of the office. The thought of bumping into Dave Crawley was pushed to the back of her mind, and she concentrated on the drive. With a bit of luck, the body would keep them busy all day. There might be a perfectly innocent explanation, but the Murder Investigation Manual dictated that the first rule of inquiry into a deceased body without an obvious cause of death was to treat it suspiciously.

Derwent Marina was past the town of Keswick, at the end of a tiny road just beyond the village of Portinscale. Kelly had spent many school trips learning to kayak down there, and memories flashed back as she parked up outside the main office. Business had been suspended for the day, and uniforms were on the scene interviewing various groups and individuals. She spotted Graeme, and he waved. Kate got a bag out of the boot that contained all they needed to oversee the processing of a crime scene, and they walked over to him.

'Hi, Kelly. I hoped it would be you they called.'

Graeme looked ashen, and Kelly realised that it was easy to forget what the sight of a dead body did to people, even an ex-army man. Graeme hadn't seen active service, though, not like Johnny, and so it was possible that he'd never encountered a corpse before, at least not one that had expired outdoors with no clothes on.

'You all right?' she asked. He was sitting on an upturned canoe.

'It was the smell.'

'Ah, I get it. That's not something you'll forget in a hurry.'

He ran his fingers through his hair.

'I understand you've given a statement?'

He nodded.

'Thanks, you can go then. Maybe go home and distract yourself with something else.'

He hesitated. 'When do you think they'll take him away?'

Kelly looked towards the boatshed, which was now cordoned off with police tape. She felt Graeme's anxiety. This was a cash business and his livelihood depended upon it.

'I won't know that until I've seen him. I'm sorry.' It was all she could say. There were no guarantees. His brow knitted and he got up slowly.

Kelly and Kate walked through the trees towards the large shed. A uniformed officer standing outside moved aside for them. The tape extended around the back and down to the shoreline, but already campers from the neighbouring site were gathered, taking pictures with mobile phones. At least the cover of the shed meant the body was protected from exposure on social media.

As soon as they stepped inside, Kelly appreciated what Graeme had said about the smell. Kate handed her a bottle of perfume and she rubbed some under her nose. She also heard flies. She climbed a ladder and made her way to the stern of the launch. Another smell caught her attention: recently varnished wood. It was in stark contrast and was rather beautiful. The forensic officer, in full kit, was clicking away with a camera.

The dead man was slumped over the captain's chair. Kelly reckoned he was in his late fifties, and apart from a huge wound to his temple, he looked as though he was asleep. It was an undignified way to go. His skin hung off his body in saggy rolls. He wasn't fat, just not used to exercise. He was pale, almost white, apart from his arms and face, which were tanned from outdoor life. Kelly wondered if he was on holiday. He wasn't malnourished or prematurely aged, which indicated a certain amount of prosperity; that ruled out vagrancy or homelessness. There was a watch mark on his wrist and an indentation on his wedding finger: the body had been stripped of every piece of clothing and jewellery.

'Gunshot wound?' she asked the forensic officer. He nodded. Kelly raised her eyebrows. It wasn't what she'd expected to find on a Monday morning on the shores of Derwent Water. It would be difficult to keep this one out of the press; that was for sure.

'We've got two entry wounds, but, so far all I can find is one exit, unless they came through the same mess. That's one for the Coroner.'

She didn't need to get too close to recognise the wound pattern. On his left temple, two entry wounds had crusted over, and she could see that flies had laid their eggs already. On the other side, a massive exit wound had ripped his skull apart. It was something Kelly had witnessed a few times before, but never here in the Lakes. What was less obvious was why somebody had gone to all the trouble of removing clothes and jewellery to conceal the identity, but left the body in an obvious place. A cursory glance confirmed the absence of blood splatter or matter adhering to the surrounding panels of the cabin: he hadn't been shot here.

The man had been shot through the brain, execution style. If he'd done it himself, the gun would have fallen from his dead hand and would still be on site. He also probably wouldn't be naked. And it would be messy.

'Weapon?' she asked.

'Feel free to look around. I haven't found anything.'

With no weapon and no crime scene, just a dump site, and no name, Kelly knew that today would indeed be a busy day. Happy Monday, she thought.

# Chapter 5

Alexandros Skarparis drove into the immense car park owned by Ravensword on the labyrinthine Dockland Industrial Estate. He hadn't slept well, and it had little to do with Aphrodite the cat. He appreciated his mother's grief, but he had other, more pressing matters to worry about. Last night he'd gone to the Thai Orchid on Bethnal Green Road, admittedly later than arranged, only to be told that his party hadn't turned up. He'd tried the mobile numbers of all three of his colleagues, and each had gone to voicemail.

He'd driven to the garage in Bethnal Green, parking on Old Ford Road, just short of the canal. The garage was in darkness, the bolt double padlocked, and there were no cars parked in their usual spots. He'd never come across this sort of dilemma before, and they'd never discussed it. He'd had no choice but to go home and eat fish and chips in front of the TV, alone and puzzled. Vexation soon turned to concern as he tried his friends' mobile numbers over and over again. He called work colleagues, trying to find the whereabouts of his three co-workers by asking banal questions that could wait until their next shift together at Ravensword. He'd even been so bold as to call Emily's husband, pretending that he'd misplaced his work pass to the gym, wondering if Emily had picked it up. The call had been returned at midnight, when Emily's husband had begun to panic and rang the police. He couldn't get hold of her either.

All Alex's efforts had come to nothing, and now when he tried their numbers, the calls didn't even go through to voicemail anymore; their phones were simply dead. He tried the garage once again, but it remained locked up like before. They shared responsibility for the keys, and he racked his brain for ways to get hold of a spare. Perhaps one of their lockers at work might yield what he wanted. Then he remembered that George always kept a key in a toolbox in his garden shed at home. He sat in his car looking at the factory where he'd worked for the last nine years, never taking a day sick, and decided that today was the day to break that record. He needed to know why his friends had disappeared off the face of the earth. He told himself that George had hit traffic on the way back from his holiday in the Lake District, and that Emily had taken her dog to the vet, and that Mike had a relative to visit in hospital. But it didn't shift the feeling in his gut.

He rang the lab inside the gargantuan facility, just in case one of them had arrived for work before him. None of them had. All four of them worked in the neurocellular research section, investigating the neurotransmitters responsible for reward pathways. Their lab was affectionately known as the Happy Bus, because part of their work involved creating newer and better antidepressant drugs. The irony, which wasn't lost on their associates, was that it was indeed a happy lab. Alex realised with a painful pang of panic that he was growing more perturbed by the minute for his friends.

'Have any of them checked in at all overnight?' he asked the lab coordinator.

'No, Alex. I haven't seen them at all. I thought George was on holiday.'

'He was due back yesterday. It's just that I think I'm coming down with flu, and I wanted to let them know I won't be in today.'

'Ah, no worries, I'll tell them as soon as they come in. Get well soon. Take care of yourself, there's a lot going around…'

Alex started up the engine again and swung out of the car park, directly underneath a CCTV camera.

George lived in Wanstead, in a town house tucked away behind mature trees and a stone wall. Alex had been to dinner there many times. George lived alone, and had done since his divorce. The death of his daughter had driven a wedge between him and his wife that could never be removed. But that was a long time ago, and George had never remarried.

Alex parked along the street and walked to the house, going straight around the back. The gate was unlocked and he peered through a few windows, seeing nothing. There were no lights on, or any movement of any kind. The back garden was George's pride and joy. Blooms exploded all over as the plants and trees sucked the goodness out of the June light, thriving in their well-chosen plots. A pond glimmered in the early-morning sun, and the sound of rushing water over the rocks and reeds made Alex smile. He imagined George sitting here reading *The Lancet* or some medical tome, with his cup of tea and a couple of ginger biscuits.

The shed was at the bottom of the garden, and he followed the path to it. It was locked. Birds chirped, and bees flitted between lavender and jasmine. Alex knew that the key was kept under a pot behind the pump for the pond's water feature. He took it out and unlocked the shed door. It didn't take long to locate the bunch of keys for the lab.

He heard voices at the front of the property and thought it might be the postman, or even George himself. But something made him stay in the shed, out of sight. He reached out to the wooden door and eased it closed, then craned his neck to peer through the small window.

Three men walked around the side of the house into the garden. They went to the back door and opened it with keys, slamming it behind them. Alex was gripped with fear. The men didn't look the type to be dropping in on his friend for a coffee. They had the appearance of thugs: black jumpers, scruffy jackets, bald heads and bare-faced arrogance. They weren't the sort of folk that Alex would associate with his friend. He waited, uncertain what to do. His heart pounded in his chest as he heard crashes from inside the house. Dismay flooded over him in hot sweat and he had no idea what to do next. Should he call the police?

Before he could make his mind up, the back door opened again and the men reappeared carrying various items: a computer, some files and a suitcase. One of them looked directly at the shed and Alex ducked down beneath the window. He thought he might wet himself, and he was sure his racing heart was as loud as the thundering of horses' hooves. He pinned himself against the wall and held his breath.

Ten minutes passed and Alex tried to stand up, but his knees had locked. He knelt forwards and rubbed the back of his legs. They'd gone into cramp and he wanted to cry out, but he daren't. When he was able to stand, he looked through the window again. There was no sign of the men.

Fifteen minutes later, he was driving towards his own flat in Stratford. As he approached, he saw that one of the men he'd seen at George's house was talking to his neighbour outside on the street. Alex threw his hood over his head and dipped down as far as he could without losing sight of the road and crashing. He prayed that his non-descript Vauxhall hadn't been spotted. Looking back in the rear-view mirror, he satisfied himself that he was in the clear. He drove straight to Bethnal Green.

He left his car in one of the car parks below a high-rise and sprinted through the alleyways towards the garages. His heart pumped in his chest and sweat collected on his brow, running into his eyes. He kept his hood up and glanced over his shoulder.

His hands shook as he unlocked the padlocks on the outside of the garage. He quickly closed the outer door behind him and opened the one to the inner lab. Once in, he closed the door behind him and sighed. A coughing fit seized him as the smell assailed him, and he groped for the light switch, holding his breath. His mind whirred as he desperately tried to figure out what the hell was going on. The roof vents were open.

The room was stripped completely bare except for two naked bodies, one on top of the other, flies landing on the bloated parts and dancing in the blood. Alex sank to his knees and looked into Emily's eyes. She stared straight up, her mouth open as if in ecstasy at her lover's prowess above

26

her. Mike's body straddled hers in an obscene embrace, and Alex knew that the scene was staged.

He bent his head and a sob escaped from his mouth. His dear friends had been abused and their bodies defiled after their lives had been snuffed out. He couldn't look at their injuries.

Adrenalin shocked his body into action and clarified his brain. He took one last look at the corpses of the colleagues with whom he'd shared so much time, knowledge, love and laughter. Then he wiped his eyes, stood up and flicked the light switch off. He left both doors slightly ajar before running as fast as he could away from the garage. He wanted justice, he wanted revenge, but he wouldn't get it hanging around waiting for the police to turn up. It would take them weeks to ask questions and wait for lab results. He knew how these things worked. He'd started in forensics many years ago. He'd be the prime suspect, and he was pretty sure that George was dead too. No, the only way to get what he was looking for was to command the scene from afar, electronically. He had all he needed.

He couldn't go back to his flat, but he didn't have to. He drove to Bethnal Green Road and dumped his car outside Kentucky Fried Chicken. Then he walked to the Tube station and took the Central Line to Holborn, changing to the Piccadilly Line for Heathrow, where he bought a one-way ticket to Larnaca. Perhaps he'd make poor Aphrodite's funeral after all.

# Chapter 6

Kelly called her father.

'Can I hitch a lift with Cumbria's most eminent semi-retired coroner?' she asked.

Ted Wallis had bought a town house in Keswick to be nearer to his daughter. He'd told her that Carlisle wasn't particularly offensive as cities went, but he'd never had a reason to live there, apart from his work at the mortuary in the bowels of the university hospital. It was convenient and logical, like most of his life had been. Now, at almost seventy, he'd begun to think about what might make him happy, and it was a new experience. He confided his innermost thoughts to Kelly, and she enjoyed listening. It was a new and intimate experience, and she wondered if he experienced it with his other daughters.

He'd told her that he wanted to live inside the National Park, close to Kelly and the memory of her mother, Wendy. The house was a charming stone cottage-like dwelling, built for the well-to-do during the time of the booming pencil industry. Cumbrian lead was the finest in the country, but the mines, like all the others, had ceased to trade decades ago, before Ted was even born. Greenside lead mine was on one of the descent routes from Helvellyn, and Kelly had walked past it many times, peering into the windows of the abandoned sheds along the Glenridding Beck, which was popular with gorge walkers and made for a refreshing dip after a long hike. Ted told her that the Helvellyn range was beyond him now, but she disagreed, vowing to get him up there one of these days.

The house's most valuable feature was the off-road parking, and Kelly pulled in to the space and tapped on the door. It was open, and she went inside. Ted was waiting for her and they embraced. She'd accompany him alone today, leaving her team back at Eden House to work on the identity of the dead man. There was no reason for her to witness the autopsy – it was quite obvious that the bloke had died from a gunshot wound to his head – but this was an opportunity to see Ted at work, and learn from him, as well as to catch up.

The fact that she had believed for forty years that her father was John Porter was something Kelly didn't dwell on. After her mother's death, she had decided that life was too short to squander on what-ifs and wherefores. When she'd first found out about Wendy's illicit affair with the dashing pathologist, she'd acted like a petulant toddler. But after some soul-searching, she had grown out of the straitjacket of resentment and self-pity and now spent as much time with Ted as she could.

It had been her idea for him to house-hunt in Keswick. He'd even joined a rambling group. Part of her wanted him to fully retire, but the thought of forging a relationship with a new coroner was something she wanted to put off for as long as possible. Plus, the work kept him sharp, and he was a young sixty-nine; still vital and shrewd. Semi-retirement for Ted actually meant training up junior pathologists, not necessarily a drastic reduction in hours, and so he was generally to be found either at his desk at home or staring through a microscope in Carlisle. His working life hadn't changed all that much, but his personal life had reawakened. Kelly had made sure of that. His step was lighter, his eyes clearer and his face more open. He'd made new friends in the drinking establishments of Keswick, and he'd been on walks that he'd forgotten existed. Kelly was in fact a little envious of his free time.

She noticed the photograph of her mother on the side. It had been taken forty years ago, before Kelly was born, and Wendy was wearing her emerald-green ball gown. Ted followed her gaze.

'She was beautiful. Just like you, Kelly.'

She waved her hand in front of her, batting away the praise.

'Don't worry, I'm not going to let your head get too big,' he added.

Kelly smiled at him. She could see that he missed Wendy terribly; they all did. Her nieces, her sister; all of them. She felt a pang of guilt that she had stopped checking in on Nikki. Her head told her that it was out of her hands: her sister didn't appreciate her poking her nose in. But her compassion (and the voice of her mother) told her otherwise. With Dave Crawley out of prison, though, and his wife best friends with Nikki, she reckoned that now more than ever she wouldn't be welcomed. As always, prevarication won.

'Did you say gunshot wound?' Ted asked, shaking her from her musings.

Kelly nodded. 'I know, unusual round here or what?'

Gun crime was the preserve of the Manchester ghettos, not the Lake District. Obviously Kelly had seen plenty of gunshot wounds in London, and Ted had worked and trained all over the world. But here in the Lakes, it was unheard of.

'Weapon?' he asked.

'Nope, no sign of it, and we used gun dogs. They're clean shots, from what I saw: and look professional. The stripping of the body was cool and calculated, not leaving us much to go on. Whoever did it doesn't mind so much that we find out who the victim is, but he doesn't want us to know exactly where and how he came to welcome a couple of bullets in his brain.'

'Let's hope that one is still in there, it's possible. The trajectory of the first could cause the damage and the resultant force could slow the second and stop it dead.' Ted said.

'That's what I'm counting on.'

'Casing?'

'Nope.'

He picked up his briefcase and they left the cottage. Kelly drove towards the M6. In Carlisle, a body waited for them in a fridge. She already knew that the man hadn't been in the boatshed long, because fly activity was in its earliest stages. He was post-rigor, but that only meant he'd been there for around eight hours. The corpse still stank, though, and she'd brought a handkerchief and perfume with her. It didn't matter how cold a body was; it still radiated the sweet aroma of rot.

'How's Johnny?' Ted asked. He glanced at her ring, bought by Kelly's boyfriend last Christmas. It suited her, and was the only ring she wore. The rubies and bright yellow Indian gold complimented her dark brown hair, which was just becoming sun-kissed as summer approached.

'He's good. He just missed out on doing sub-twenty-four hours on the Lakeland 100, but he did bloody brilliantly.'

'I'll say. I hope he's going to put some weight back on now.'

'That's what I said. I've been feeding him butter and cream.'

'He's not going to make a habit of it, is he, these ultra-marathons? It's not good for the body.' Ted grew serious.

'But the butter and cream's all right? I know. I think he's proved a point, and that'll be it. It's sailing next.'

Next year would be Johnny's fiftieth and her fortieth, and they wanted to do something spectacularly different. Perhaps the Florida Keys. That was why they were taking lessons with Graeme. It wasn't lost on her that it would be Ted's seventieth next year too.

Traffic was light on the motorway, and they arrived at the hospital in under an hour. No one would guess that the smart father-and-daughter couple who strode into the main entrance were on their way to the mortuary to examine a corpse.

Kelly was familiar with the layout – she'd been there before – and she watched as Ted scrubbed up and gave out instructions to assistants. His energy and professionalism hadn't flagged, despite his age, and it made an impression on her every time she saw him work. She didn't reckon she'd still be a copper at that age; she'd have burnt out by then and would hopefully be living in a cottage at the foot of a fell, maybe with a partner, maybe not. The cadaver was wheeled into the room and placed on the slab.

Kelly took out her perfumed handkerchief, Ted placed his glasses on the end of his nose, and they fell silent, apart from Ted's dictation and the click of the camera.

There was nothing unusual about the body apart from the gaping hole in the skull. No defensive wounds, nor any other injuries or haemorrhages. The guy had been taken out. X-rays showed that one single bullet was left inside the brain. Ted took a pair of long tweezers that looked like they belonged in a museum and began fiddling inside the man's head, pausing occasionally to check the apparent paths of the bullets. Kelly watched as he pulled, but nothing came out so he tried again. He tutted and attached a camera to the instrument, then flicked on a monitor. Kelly knew that bullets did extraordinary things inside the human body: they rarely travelled predictably. This time, with the minuscule accuracy of technology, he located the small slug of metal, and pulled it out.

'Bingo. Nine millimetre. Probably a Glock. It's all I ever saw on cases like this in Manchester. Pistol for sure.'

Kelly agreed that a Glock would be the weapon of choice for a criminal in the UK, but they'd still need to send it away for analysis. One day they might find the weapon, and no two bullets left a ballistic chamber in the same way. Each firing of a shot in its entirety caused a different configuration of damage. It was as solid as a fingerprint or a drop of semen, but without the gun, it was useless.

'I'll do toxicology and histology. You never know, he could have been drugged,' Ted said. 'Can I buy you lunch?' he added.

Kelly nodded, staring down at the man on the slab. She hadn't really looked at his face when he'd been slumped over the captain's wheel of *The Lady of the Lake*. He had a kind face; he looked like somebody's grandfather. X-rays had already been taken of the jaw, and they were hoping for a name any time soon. For now, he was known as Mr Launch.

## Chapter 7

Kelly read DC Emma Hide's report on the Allerdale House burglary. Everything had to come past her for a signature. It was still a live case, and photographs of what the owner thought had gone missing had been distributed to forces up and down Cumbria. Specialist websites and magazines, as well as known criminals, were usually the first ports of call. The list included several sail cloths, two trailers, one small solid mahogany and oak support launch, a prized two-man sweep oar boat made in 1919 that had hung from the ceiling, three brand new engines, and an array of diving kit worth over two grand on its own. It was more than they had anticipated; the value of the stolen goods was inching up to half a million pounds, and that only included those with a price tag: one of the antique boats was priceless.

Tyre tracks had been taken, but there were no witnesses and no CCTV on the private road leading to the house. The owner, with big plans to turn the property into a high-end leisure facility, wasn't overly concerned about the money, just the fact that the oar boat had belonged to his grandfather, who had rowed it on the River Cam as a coxless pair for Magdalene College in the 1930s. However, the unusual nature of such a piece of craftsmanship would make it more difficult to conceal and sell, which worked in their favour.

Kelly read that Allerdale House had passed to its current owner in March, after a long probate, but she also noticed that it wouldn't entirely belong to him until a period of trust had elapsed. What really grabbed her attention, though, was Sebastian Montague-Roland's comment that it was a shame that a visitor to the house had left earlier than scheduled, otherwise the burglars might have been interrupted and fled. Apparently, an old friend of his grandfather's, George Murphy, had been staying there on his annual fishing trip.

Kelly left her office and went into the incident room.

'Emma? The Allerdale case. Have you managed to get in touch with George Murphy yet?'

'No, guv, he's not answering his phone.'

'Do we know who he is, and how long he stayed there?'

'He was there a week and scheduled to return home yesterday, but presumably he left a day early. We've sent local uniforms to his address in Wanstead, east London, but there's no answer. He isn't at work either.'

'Was he due to return to work today?'

'Yup.'

'I wonder why no one saw him around the lake. He must have gone shopping, or bought a paper.'

'None of the folk interviewed have mentioned it so far, guv.'

'I would have thought Graeme would have known. He's always sailing past, rubbernecking to get a glimpse of the place.'

'Guv?'

'It doesn't matter. I'll ask him about it. I don't suppose we have a photo of George Murphy?'

'Not to hand, but he should be on the Ravensword website.'

'Ravensword? Why have I heard of that?'

'It's a massive pharmaceutical company in the East End of London. That's where he works; he's a scientist.'

Kelly's heart sank. She was reminded of when she lived on Old Ford Road with Matt. Lazy Sunday afternoons in the pub in Bow Wharf on the Regent's Canal. She squeezed her eyes shut and massaged her temples.

'You all right, guv?'

Kelly smiled and nodded. Matt Carter came into her head again. Matt the twat.

Emma went back to her computer and typed quickly. The Ravensword website came on the screen, and Kelly recognised the logo of a black raven sitting on top of the pommel of a golden sword and realised why she was familiar with the company. She'd never thought much of it before when choosing a bottle of shampoo or mosquito spray for her holidays.

Diagrams of cells and brightly coloured strings of DNA, website forums, excerpts from learned journals, and photographs of starving Africans, presumably being helped by Ravensword medicines, flooded the home screen.

'What the hell is that?' Kelly pointed to a bright turquoise spiky ball being invaded by orange slugs. Emma tapped on the play icon and they watched an animation of how one particular virus attacked liver cells.

'I was rubbish at science at school,' Emma said.

'But amazing at poetry,' Kelly reminded her. 'I was crap at science too. Let's find George.'

Emma deftly navigated her way to the staff area. She scrolled through pages of mug shots until she came to a man in a white coat, beaming into the camera. He'd begun working for Ravensword fifteen years ago, in the neurocellular section. It sounded extremely grand and mystifying at the same time. Kelly craned her neck.

'What is it, guv?'

'Come out of that and bring up my emails.'

'You'll have to put your password in.'

Kelly tapped her code in and her emails came up on screen. She opened one from Ted from earlier in the afternoon. It contained the initial coroner's report and a selection of photographs from the autopsy. It was the first time Emma had seen the body found at the marina.

'Wow, that's clean, isn't it?' she said, studying the wound. Kelly nodded. She scrolled through the photographs. Ted was thorough and had taken close-ups of everything he'd flagged for analysis. They looked at fingernails, nostrils, skin colour, teeth, lip contour, and eye fluid. Then they came to one of his whole face.

'What do you think?' Kelly asked. 'Maybe he hadn't left when the burglars came after all. I'd bet my life that we're looking at George Murphy.'

# Chapter 8

Tilly Knight called George's number again. It was well and truly dead. It wasn't uncommon for a man of his age to let his mobile phone run out of juice; her dad did it all the time. But she was frustrated. When she got wind of a new story, it wasn't only her professional interest that was piqued, it was also her livelihood. A freelance journalist's income was random at the best of times, and she never knew how long she'd have to wait in between jobs until her next cheque. She'd registered as self-employed rather than as a limited company because she didn't earn enough.

She tutted angrily and ended the call, then grabbed her sweater and left the flat to go to the corner shop for cigarettes. She had dreams of making a splash in cutting-edge investigative journalism. She envisaged awards, accolades, and documentary-makers begging her to sell her stories to them for million-pound productions snapped up by the big TV networks. At this rate, she'd remain a nobody, shopping at Lidl, wearing the same pair of trainers she'd had for three years and shaving her legs instead of waxing. It wasn't just about the money, although she did wonder if she'd forever live in a rented two-bedroom flat in Leyton. She was thirty years old, and she had no idea what tomorrow would bring. It wasn't supposed to be like this; she should have a husband and a couple of kids in a semi-detached house in Hampstead by now, but that life hadn't come knocking.

The shop was a mere five-minute walk, as was the Tube station, which was why she'd chosen the flat. The traffic was incessant. It felt sometimes like she lived in the middle of a movie set and she was an extra; the frame went round on a loop of buses, cabs, four-by-fours, commuter shares and police vehicles choking the A12 artery into London, with an action hero about to pop up from behind a red bus, chasing a villain, frustrated by the thick jam of obstacles in his way. Leyton was like that, a concrete suburb dissected by an A road, and it saw its fair share of gun and knife crime. But Tilly kept herself to herself.

She was well known to the shop proprietor, and he reached for her brand of cigarettes automatically. She picked up some milk and a chocolate bar, paid and left.

Before George had gone off the radar, he'd given her a few nuggets of information, and it was her intention to pursue those today. She had nothing else in the pipeline for the time being. A women's magazine had commissioned a piece on the spate of stabbings in the city, but they'd put a tragic spin on it from the point of view of one mother in particular who'd lost her son. It wasn't a broadsheet, but it paid some bills.

George had given her an outline of why he wanted to speak to her, as well as his home and work addresses and some concerns he had about the impact his research might have. It could be an interesting piece, but without George, it was dead in the water before she even got her pen out. It might well be a merry dance, but when she'd spoken to him, he hadn't sounded deceitful in the slightest. He'd come across as genuine, ethical and a little bit scared. To

Tilly, investigative journalism at its best revealed some kind of cover-up by the big boys, and an effort to silence the minions. George Murphy believed that he'd been, if not threatened, at least nudged to stop what he was doing.

The other thing that endeared him to her was that when she'd asked him how he'd found her, he'd replied that he liked one of her articles on Irish abortion legislation. It had touched her. She'd written three articles on the subject and each one had been published online only. When she asked George how he'd come across them, he'd said that he had once been involved in research into the morning-after pill, and it was a subject that he followed closely. The guy knew his stuff. It made sense when she later found out that he worked for Ravensword.

She walked back to her flat, smoking a cigarette. The nicotine entered her bloodstream and she calmed a little. It was a filthy habit and she wished she could stop, but every time she tried, her craving for the tobacco hit took over and she caved. She sucked hard to finish the damn thing before she reached her flat. She rarely smoked indoors, as per her tenancy agreement, but her bedroom had a tiny balcony for just that purpose, and she used an old catering-size tomato tin as her ashtray. It must have contained hundreds, if not thousands of butts.

The thought of what she'd put into her lungs was quickly dismissed as she went out onto the balcony and lit another. She sat on the single metal chair and looked at her notes. The sun was high in the sky and the summer promised to be a belter. The noise of the streets below, ever present in her life, buzzed and beeped. She was used to the racket. She'd chosen a second-floor flat to at least be a little farther away from the traffic, but the fumes and dust from the road still drifted upwards, and some days it was too much to have a window open. Today, though, was fairly pleasant.

She stubbed out the second cigarette and stood up to stretch. She needed a shower before she began to chase the few leads that she'd been given by George. Her first stop would be the library, where she could dig out old copies of medical journals relating to Ravensword's research. She also wanted to check a few newspaper articles, especially to do with what George had told her about the death of his daughter, fifteen years ago. It was what had got him into his independent pursuit of a ground-breaking cure for her condition. Medical science had tried to save her, but the problem was that they were limited in their outlook.

Tilly was easily carried away into a rabbit hole of unidentified depths when researching something that stoked her interest. Part of what she loved about her job was that she was forever learning about new subjects, and this was no different. That was why she'd agreed to speak to George again. The case had led her into a labyrinthine world of illness and cure, and what might motivate the acceptance of one drug over another. She'd made a list of specific things to investigate, as she always did, otherwise she'd find herself spending a whole day chasing something to a minute level that wasn't perhaps needed just now. And there was a lot to cover. George had said that he could supply her with everything she needed, and that was why he'd given her his address.

'Why do you trust me?' she'd asked him. It was quite clear that he trusted very few people, and she was puzzled as to why he'd share so much in their first conversation.

'You have a kind face,' was all he'd said. The reply had sent all sorts of alarm bells ringing in Tilly's head. Firstly, how did he know what she looked like? That was easy: it must be her photograph at the bottom of her articles. Secondly, who had a kind face any more? That one stumped her.

'And you remind me of my daughter.'

At that point, Tilly had nearly hung up. But she was curious. As always, her inquisitive nature led her on, regardless of the danger she might become embroiled in. The need to seek answers was like a drug; it filled her every waking moment when she was pursuing a story. And she wouldn't give up until she had what she wanted.

'I can pay you well,' he said.

'How much?'

'Fifty thousand pounds if it's published.'

It really was a no-brainer. Images of her hitting the headlines, discussing the case on BBC Breakfast and penning a book flooded her mind. It was that big, George told her.

'Why now?'

'I think they're on to me.'

'Who's they?'

'I'm not sure yet.'

Which was another reason why Tilly felt uneasy. She'd seen too many people disappear in the midst of ongoing controversies to not take him seriously. She knew, and she thought George did too, that it was easier to get rid of someone – essentially to rub them out – than it was to get a new store card. She'd seen it before. It was something she'd never discussed, and she'd never personally investigated, but she knew without any doubt that it went on, every day, every year, even though no one could prove it. The thought of penetrating a world where that happened was too thrilling an offer for her to resist.

If George was uncontactable, then she had to consider that, given his story, something alarming might have happened to him. It wouldn't take a genius to work out that he'd been researching investigative journalists and possibly blowing the whistle. Tilly might already have an expiry date on her head. She tried his number again, and this time it didn't even give a signal. It simply went silent, as if the phone was no longer in service.

Before she left for the library, Tilly did something that she hadn't done in a long time. She wrote to her mother. She figured that a letter was the safest way. She knew she was being melodramatic, but she managed to pen something satisfactory in the end. It was informative enough to give a clue to where she might be found if she went missing, but protected her family from knowing too much.

After her shower, she smoked another cigarette on her balcony and tied her hair up above her head. Her friends told her that her skin was still so taut and clear because she had no kids waking her up in the middle of the night like they did, sucking the life out of them and ageing them like automatons in a baby factory. It was true: she didn't look thirty. She applied a little make-up and checked her outfit in the mirror: jeans, T-shirt and a short summer jacket. It wasn't showy, fashionable or particularly alluring, and that was the point. Miss Ordinary. She put the envelope for her mother in her bag and left the flat.

# Chapter 9

Kelly was in the middle of eating a sandwich when Ted called with news about the identity of Mr Launch. His dental records had revealed a match to fifty-nine-year-old George Murphy of Wanstead, London E11.

'Thought so,' she said.

'Really?' Ted sounded disappointed that somebody had beaten him to the information, and Kelly appreciated his keenness. She explained about the burglary at Allerdale House, and how she'd recognised the man from his photograph on the Ravensword website.

'Oh dear, I suppose you'll have to go to London then?'

'That's what I was thinking. We'll see.' The thought of returning to her old constabulary filled her with anxiety. It wasn't something that could be explained, and it wasn't tangible, in as much that it wasn't justified, but the thought of seeing former colleagues and meeting acquaintances she'd rather forget was unsettling. The problem was that the man had been murdered on her patch, and so somebody would have to go, and she couldn't imagine sending anyone else. It was protocol in such circumstances for the SIO to lead or at least support an investigation into the man's life before they could establish the circumstances surrounding his death.

But first they had to visit Allerdale House.

'So, are you thinking burglary goes wrong? That this man disturbed them? It certainly was a nice little pile of valuables that was taken,' Ted said.

'The best part of half a million, I reckon.'

He whistled. 'Unusual for here. Why do you think he was moved?'

'To clean up forensically. Crime scenes are much more helpful to the police than dump scenes. It's quite clever really, and indicates further that we're dealing with professionals rather than just a bungled burglary. Could you establish time of death?'

'Definitely some time on Sunday night.'

They hung up. Now that Kelly had final proof of George's ID, they could proceed with haste. She wanted to know the relationship between the dead man and the owner of Allerdale House, and why he was here in the Lakes, so far away from home. An annual fishing trip sounded too convenient. DC Hide's investigation into the robbery had already established that there was no sign of forced entry to the main house and nothing was missing, but the doors were unlocked.

Kelly welcomed the distraction of a new case. Her mother's house had finally been sold, and she didn't know how she felt about it. It was a relief in some ways, but it had been her family home, where she'd grown up, and it was as if a piece of her would be forever gone when the cheque was cashed. Wendy hadn't had a mortgage, or any debt, so Kelly's half of the money would be in her account in around three week's time. She was suddenly a wealthy woman. Her mind wandered back to the idea of an extravagant celebration for her and Johnny's birthdays next year, and she knew that her mother would approve.

She sighed and went to get Emma Hide from next door. Sebastian Montague-Roland was newly arrived from London and she wanted to meet him. His family had owned Allerdale for seven generations. The house had been built before the First World War with money from the British Empire. The first Montague-Roland was a Scot who pioneered a sand-proof locomotive engine in South Africa, invaluable to Cecil Rhodes' mining kingdom. From there, he'd invested in shipping and the first jet engines, both lucrative trades after 1914. Clever deals and traditional Scottish frugality meant that by the depression of the thirties, the Montague-Rolands were able to ride the wave and emerge unscathed.

It was an unusual coupling – a scientist from the East End and a man of Montague-Roland's connections – and Kelly was ruling nothing out. There was money to be made in science, and she wondered how far Sebastian's investments had taken him into that world. All they knew at the moment was that George Murphy had been a family friend, who'd loved fishing and escaping the city. It was a long way to come for clean air, unless he had other connections to Cumbria, perhaps. A search of his background told them nothing new. He was divorced and had no surviving children. His fifteen-year-old daughter had died tragically from complications arising from drug addiction fifteen years ago: about the time George had started to work for Ravensword. He'd left no will, and a sizeable pension, so there was money to be had from his death. But for whom? She wanted to visit Ravensword herself right away, but that would have to wait. A phone call had confirmed that George had an impeccable history at the pharmaceutical giant, and that he was well liked there.

Allerdale House was remote, but they were still hoping for sightings of vehicles capable of removing the missing items. It would have taken more than one, as well as more than one pair of hands.

It was a pleasant drive to Derwent Water. Emma drove while Kelly updated her iPad and stole glances at the countryside and the lake. It was a serene lake, but busier than Ullswater and more accessible. She'd seen more of it this year than ever, thanks to Graeme's sailing lessons. Which reminded her, she needed to call him. She dialled his number and he answered quickly.

'Hi, Graeme, how are you doing?'

Emma remained quiet and listened to the conversation.

'We have a name,' Kelly told him. 'George Murphy. He was staying at Allerdale House. I'm surprised no one saw him, he was there for a week.'

Graeme agreed that it was strange that no one had spotted the visitor, but pointed out that the estate was large enough for someone to remain there undetected. Kelly thanked him and hung up.

'That's odd,' she said out loud.

Emma looked at her boss. 'What, guv?'

'The 999 call for the burglary came in pretty rapidly considering no one had spotted a man staying there for a week. Who made the original call, do we know?'

'I don't believe they gave a name, guv.'

Emma turned off the main road and entered the single track that led to the car park for Cat Bells. The tiny peak was a favourite with families, and the route was busy already. Kelly could see the snaking line of bright jackets making its way up to the top: the best view of Derwent and beyond. It was a good training run for Johnny, because it had a path all the way up, it was usually clear, and it was a sharp ascent. She'd been up there a few times with him, and tourists had stared at them as if they were lunatics. They turned off again, down a private lane, and came to large wooden gates and a slate sign reading: *Allerdale House. Private.*

There was an intercom and Kelly rang it, introducing herself. Sebastian Montague-Roland was expecting them. The gates opened and Emma drove through slowly.

'Christ, there's some money around here, guv.'

Most of the tourists visiting the National Park never saw this side of the Lakes and had no idea that a lot of the land was privately owned, dished out by nobles since the time of William the Conqueror and maintained by the mining of stone and valuable minerals until there was none left. Allerdale House was resplendent in its surety. The grey slate gave an austere feel, but the grandeur of the design itself said otherwise. Beams, gables and sloping roofs framed the vast house, surrounded by pretty gardens and thoughtful features. The place stank of money. Many of the notable houses in the Lakes had been sold to rich bankers from London, or royalty from the Middle East, but a few, like this one, had remained in the hands of the original owners. It must cost a fortune to maintain.

They went to the main door, which was answered before they were able to knock. A man in his forties stood there, and they could see police uniforms behind him. He held out his hand.

'Sebastian Montague-Roland. Come inside and join the Cumbria Constabulary party, Detective Porter.' It was a peculiar welcome, given the severity of the circumstances.

Montague-Roland was immaculately dressed and, like the house itself, finely styled and richly adorned. He wore an expensive watch and his skin was tanned. His hair was greying at the temples and his teeth were straight and white. Kelly peered at his shoes, which were clearly hand-made. He walked into the house and Kelly and Emma followed him, looking up at the grand rafters. Light shafted in from every angle; the architecture was nothing short of genius. The floors were of highly polished wood, with elaborate heavy rugs scattered around; Kelly thought them to be Persian. The decor was sparse because the walls were mostly exposed, but the furniture and upholstery were lavish.

'It's a beautiful house,' she said.

Montague-Roland turned around and flashed a smile. 'Thank you. My grandfather had very good taste. Can I offer you tea?'

'No thank you. We'd like to ask you some questions. I apologise in advance if you feel you've been over it a thousand times before.'

'It's only to be expected. Let's go into Grandfather's study.'

He led them through a hallway and they passed several uniforms checking off inventories. Kelly spotted two forensic officers chatting in a doorway and held up her hand in greeting. Cumbria wasn't a large constabulary, and forensic officers were few and far between. She'd worked with both of them before. She paused as Emma went on ahead.

'Anything?' she asked.

'The owner says nothing was touched in here, but we're checking the rooms used by the deceased. We're finishing up now. It's surprisingly clean and tidy. We know the fire was used because there're dead embers and a recent copy of the *Gazette* for kindling.'

Kelly thanked them and caught up. Mr Montague-Roland looked impatiently at his watch, appearing slightly miffed that she had made a detour. He was clearly a man who thought himself in charge.

The room they entered was panelled, with wooden cupboards, a desk and walls of books. It was like a study photographed for a high-end magazine, languishing in its perfection. Several computers sat on tables, switched off and dusty. There must be thousands of pounds' worth of kit in this one room alone. Kelly couldn't figure out why burglars would have targeted the boathouse and not the main house, given the obvious opulence of the property.

'Please sit down.' Sebastian sat behind the grand desk, looking every inch the heir to an empire. Kelly made a mental note to contact the solicitors for the estate to see who the trustee was.

'How did you know George Murphy?' she began, and Emma took out her notebook.

'Straight to the point, eh?' It was a cold response from a man whose property had been violated. Kelly said nothing.

'He was actually a friend of my grandfather's. They met at a cricket match, I believe, a freebie laid on at Lord's by Ravensword, and clicked over their shared enthusiasm for English sports that have had their day. Grandfather was a lonely man and I found out that he invited all sorts of people here, to fish, to hunt, to dine and to provide company. That's my understanding. The invitation was further extended to George after my grandfather's death as a goodwill gesture. He knew the old place well, and always looked after it. I asked him to check a few things out before I came up myself to finalise building plans. I was too late.' He looked at his hands. It was the first sign of emotion.

'Sorry, I'm confused, Mr Montague-Roland,' Kelly said.

'You can call me Sebastian.'

'Sebastian. I thought the estate was left in trust; are you saying that you own it outright?'

'Oh, that business is all sorted now. Grandfather was worried that I'd turn it into a debauched party cave. It was always meant to be mine, and now it is.'

Kelly looked at Emma. A thought occurred to her that had been sitting on her shoulder since they had arrived. *Debauched party cave?* The late Lord Allerdale had not approved of his grandson's lifestyle. She looked at his hands, and then at his socks, noting the way he occasionally glanced at the male uniforms. He was either a homosexual or a dandy, and the latter had died out decades ago. Was there a family skeleton here?

'Right. You said that you thought George had left a day earlier than scheduled. What made you think that?'

'I called the house several times and he didn't answer, that's all. It was just a presumption. I should have raised the alarm then; he might still be alive.' Another flash of grief came and went.

'It's vitally important that we create a picture of George's life so we can get to know him better. I've asked for any paperwork left by your grandfather to be collected, mainly to see if their relationship was anything more than friendship. For example, whether they had business dealings together, or if they knew the same people.'

'Well, I kept a lot of his things. I haven't really been up here much; business keeps me in the capital. Still, we'll make something of the place yet. My plan is an exclusive resort, with a Michelin-starred restaurant and a luxury spa – that's all the rage now...' He had wandered into his own world of money-making, and Kelly brought him back to the present.

'Would anybody else have known that George was here?'

Sebastian's demeanour shifted, but he shook his head. He also folded his arms.

'I doubt they knew the same people. George was a salt-of-the-earth East End lad. My grandfather was a philanthropist; he brought all sorts of waifs and strays home.'

The condescension struck Kelly as curious. She got the impression that Sebastian didn't appreciate his grandfather's penchant for friends with less money or status than himself.

'So, you don't think the friendship was genuine?' she asked.

'I'm sure George got a lot out of it.'

'Can you elaborate? Did Mr Murphy gain financially from the relationship?'

'I have no idea, but I think my grandfather was too generous to everyone, and towards the end, he'd let anyone in.'

'How long had they known each other?'

'I'm not sure. Best part of ten years, I think.'

'Could you show us where George slept?'

'They've already been over everything with their sticky tape and plastic bags.'

'I'd still like you to show us,' Kelly said.

Sebastian sighed and stood up, leading them back to the hall and upstairs to a bedroom. Kelly flicked on her iPad and scrolled to the forensic reports that they had so far. Some genetic material had been collected from the en-suite bathroom adjoining George's room and sent to the lab for testing. A few usable prints had also been lifted from a water glass by the bed and a bottle of medicine in the bathroom. She noted from the report that the bathroom seemed to have been cleaned thoroughly and had smelt heavily of bleach when forensics first entered. Kelly still didn't have a murder scene, and she was on the lookout for one. Dogs had been used to search the area around the boathouse for anything indicating the smell of death, but had turned up nothing. It was a puzzle.

The bedroom was tidy. She walked towards the bathroom and opened the door. The aroma of bleach was still present. She knew from the report that the use of fluorescein by forensics had indicated that blood residue could have been cleaned from the shower, but only the lab could confirm that. They'd have a long wait to determine whether George had merely cut himself shaving or whether there was enough blood to cause suspicion.

'Do you have a cleaner?' she asked.

'No. There's no point. All of this will be ripped out as part of the refurbishment.'

'Can't you smell bleach? But there isn't any in here.' She opened various cupboards and checked her notes for items removed. Cleaning products were not on the list.

Sebastian sniffed. 'I'm not sure. It could be the wild garlic outside the window.'

'Did you speak to George when he was here?'

'No. Like I said, I rang but he didn't answer. The key was left in a lockup and he knew where to find it. Not that he needed it round here; the doors are always left open. He knew about my plans to convert the house to a business and he said he wanted to stay here for one last time.'

'When was this?'

'It was by email. A couple of months ago, I think.'

'Do you know how he got here? There's no sign of a car, and it's a remote location.'

'I did notice that. He always drove.'

'So, we've probably got a missing vehicle too,' Kelly glanced at Emma, who made a note. 'It's curious that the burglary occurred at the boathouse but they didn't bother to come inside the house, don't you think?'

'It's a disappointing start to a new venture,' Sebastian said. Kelly stared at him and Emma looked away.

'Why were you calling him on Sunday?'

'I wanted to ask him if the builders had arrived to start work. They're notoriously lazy.'

'Which building firm are you using? It's our understanding that there have been no sightings of work vans in the area.' She was thinking how builders' vans would be perfect to transport the heavy and sizeable stolen goods.

'I can't remember off the top of my head. I'll have to ask my PA and get back to you.'

'What is your occupation in London?'

'I don't have a job as such. I look after several invest-ments, and I manage this.' He swept his hand around, indicating the house.

Kelly took one last look at the bedroom. It was too neat for a man in his fifties with no wife to tidy up after him and no one to impress on his mini-break. Nothing was scattered across chairs; there were no toiletries on shelves, no newspapers and no luggage. Perhaps George had already packed to leave, but she knew from experience that men didn't normally leave a bed that well made or fail to throw the odd dirty sock into a corner.

'Thank you for your time. We'll be staying for a while to chat to some of our officers. Thank you.'

'Yes, help yourself.'

They went back downstairs to the study, and Sebastian asked if he could leave. Kelly watched out of the window as he walked towards the lake, his hands in his pockets.

Several box files and envelopes containing bank state-ments had already been packed away, and Kelly ordered the computers to be removed as well. The affairs of the old Lord Allerdale were in immaculate condition, but she knew instantly from the volume of them that they'd need weeks to trawl through it all. She peered out of the window and watched Sebastian. Beyond him, across the lake, she could make out the Keswick Launch, and she called to Emma, who followed her gaze.

'The easiest way to get a body over to the marina would be by boat,' she said.

'Which is why there were no witnesses to vehicles in the middle of the night.'

'It also indicates local knowledge.'

Kelly's phone rang; it was DS Kate Umshaw from Eden House.

'Guv, we've just had the Met on the phone. Two of George Murphy's colleagues have turned up dead in a garage in Bethnal Green, and another has gone missing. All four worked in the same lab.'

# Chapter 10

Johnny helped Kelly pack, or rather, more accurately, watched her place items in a suitcase and take them out again. He lay on her bed eating a steak baguette in an attempt to put on weight. So far he had no new plans for any more crazy fell races.

Kelly was antsy. HQ had given her a week to visit the Met, working alongside the team investigating the deaths of George's two colleagues. She was to take one officer with her, and she chose DC Emma Hide, who could do with the exposure. It was a victim information-gathering exercise as well as a collaboration, and she explained to Johnny that she intended to be back before the weekend. The Met's SIO was essentially in charge of the case in London, with her as consort. George had been killed on her patch, but the fact that his whole lab had been wiped out moved the inquiry to a new level, and the SIO in London was a DCI. There was a potential foreign element to add to the mix, as the fourth member of the team was a Greek Cypriot national.

In the background the TV blurted out the appeal for information about George Murphy and his colleagues. It was a small news segment, as murders in the capital were all too common; even double homicides. Some information had been kept from the press as a matter of strategy – such as the significance of Allerdale House, and the murder weapon – and the report concentrated on the fact that the scientists all worked for Ravensword.

In Kelly's absence, DS Kate Umshaw would be in charge, and Kelly had left clear instructions for her team to investigate the burglary and George's last movements. Had anyone seen him fishing? Where had he bought his groceries? Who had he called? Had the phantom workmen turned up? None of their inquiries so far had picked up any of the items stolen from the sheds, so they were still chasing the vehicle tracks and CCTV on the roads out of Keswick. The burglars could have gone east to the M6, then to Scotland or south. Or they could have gone west to Workington and Whitehaven, then on to Barrow-in-Furness.

Kelly's brief from HQ was to work with the Met to gain an understanding of George Murphy's life, but she was acutely aware of a growing tug of anxiety in her stomach. She hadn't been back to London since she'd quit the Met, and from what she could gather, Matt still worked the murder squad in Hendon.

'How long will you be?' asked Johnny. She knew he'd sensed her anxiety; Johnny wasn't stupid, and he'd often asked her if she missed the city. She looked at him and saw tension in him too. It softened her.

'No longer than a week.'

'I'll miss you. This is weird.'

'I know. I feel as though I'm wading into the unknown. I lived there, for Christ's sake. I don't know why I'm so worried.'

'How do you feel about bumping into old colleagues?'

Johnny didn't know about Matt. She'd never felt the need to discuss the fact that she'd been shat on by a colleague who just happened to be her lover.

'Mixed.' She concentrated on what clothes to take. Work was easily covered by suits and jackets, but the city was almost ten degrees hotter than Cumbria this week, and she toyed with how many jumpers to pack, if any.

'Where are you staying?'

'Apparently we've got a Premier Inn near Hendon.'

'At least you know the area.'

Kelly nodded and fiddled with the ruby ring that Johnny had bought for her. She'd miss him too. He was the first man she'd found herself trusting. He hadn't hurt her, he hadn't taken anything from her, and he meant what he said. She'd miss her house too; she'd become used to living here, and her routines had grown out of the stillness of the lakes and mountains. The doors to the decking were open and the breeze blew in gently. She'd been back in the Lakes for three years, but it seemed like five minutes. The thrill of the city had left her long ago, and she dreaded the assault of traffic fumes, sirens, drunks, litter and stifling air, toxic with dirt.

Johnny finished eating and placed his plate on the side, then propped himself up and watched her. He looked down at his hands and picked at his nails; it was out of character.

'What if you need to stay longer?'

She stopped what she was doing. 'That won't be necessary. I'm not going to solve the case, I'm just going to get to know my opposite number. It's a joint inquiry now.'

'I got a call yesterday from my mate at the hospice in Hertfordshire: they need guides to take groups up the Three Peaks for a fund-raising challenge.'

Kelly smiled. She knew he'd do it. Not just because he loved it, but because he couldn't say no. Just like she couldn't.

'Do it with me?' he said. 'I haven't done all three in years. I'd only be a guide on Scafell Pike; you and I could go on and do Ben Nevis and Snowdon on our own.'

'Why not? Getting away for a weekend doing that would be great. I'm in.'

'You already packed that three times.' He nodded at the green Jack Wolfskin fleece she wore for walking.

'I'm not a city girl any more,' she said.

'I hope you don't turn into one either. You might get the bug back and decide to stay.'

'Don't be stupid. I've got too much here to keep me. The only reason I'm going myself and not sending a junior is because I can't get George Murphy out of my head.'

'I know. You're hooked, and until you find out what happened, you won't let go.'

'It sounds so dramatic when you say it like that. Why can't I just let someone else have a go?'

'You do. All the time. But this one's complicated. I could tell that when you first told me about it.'

'Look after Ted for me.'

'I've arranged to take him for a pint, and I'm walking with him tomorrow. I've got something in mind that ends up at a pub.' Johnny winked. 'Anyway, why so maudlin? You're talking as if you're going to be away a lot longer than a week. Is there something you're not telling me?'

'No. Not at all. I just don't like leaving. I didn't think it would be this hard.'

Johnny got up and took the fleece out of her hands. When he held her, her body went limp and she breathed deeply. She could smell the river and the mountain air and she sucked it in, storing it for the week ahead to keep her sane. He ran his fingers up her skull, gently but firmly, and she arched her back. What to pack for a trip to London became suddenly irrelevant as he undid her blouse and she pulled his T-shirt over his head. He didn't have the body of a fifty-year-old. It was hard and smooth, and much younger. His face showed signs of wisdom that could be seen as age, but it was insignificant. He led her to the bed and she kicked off the clothes waiting to be packed. They landed on the floor, along with her bra and pants.

It didn't matter how many times Johnny took her to bed; each time she was surprised. She expected to grow bored, or at least crave some kind of new thrill, but it never happened. She was satisfied every time. The longer she knew him, the safer she felt, and the more natural it became to fall into bed on a midweek afternoon without worrying about who thought what or what might happen tomorrow. If she were ten years younger, she'd want to have babies with this man in her bed, making her laugh, making her gasp. But they were too old, and the world had enough kids.

She didn't want to get out of bed, and neither did he. Their bodies fitted together perfectly, and they lay like spoons listening to the steamer puffing in from Glenridding.

'I'll be here waiting.'

'I know.'

'What time do you go?'

'I've told you already, the car comes at five. We're hoping to miss the M6 traffic.'

'I'll make you something to eat. I'm still hungry.' He got out of bed and dressed quickly. He was tanning already from his work on the fells for mountain rescue. Men who spent a serious amount of time outdoors aged differently, Kelly thought. His eyes were bright and his skin glowed. She couldn't help think of Matt Carter, and how all the time she'd been in his bed, she'd never felt like this.

She got up and pulled on sweatpants and a T-shirt. She'd change into her plain-clothes garb at five minutes to five and not a minute earlier. Her hair was washed and dried, though a bit tousled now, and her make-up relatively intact. A quick shower would freshen her up later.

A call from Ted interrupted her. He'd breathed down the necks of a lab in Carlisle for the best part of twelve hours and they had the results from the en suite bathroom at Allerdale House. The pattern of smudges and smearing, along with the protein analysis of the specimens, was consistent with somebody being killed inside the shower unit. Kelly had her crime scene, though they'd have to wait for workable DNA to prove that the person who died in there was George.

However, it blew any previous motives out of the park. If George had been killed inside the house, and nothing had been stolen, that only left one conclusion: that the scientist had been deliberately targeted.

# Chapter 11

Kelly spent the drive to London studying the report from the double homicide in the garage in Bethnal Green. She'd walked home with fish and chips through that alleyway – a shortcut between Bethnal Green Road and Old Ford Road – more times than she cared to remember. It was ten minutes from her old flat. The landscape was one of high-rises and car parks, as well as rented garages. She looked at the photographs of George Murphy's two colleagues. It would appear that Emily Wilson and Mike Hudson had been pursuing some kind of torrid affair, and had been caught in flagrante.

Kelly didn't like coincidences.

Emma was the perfect travel companion. She assessed documents and data, and didn't make small talk. The driver was silent throughout, apart from to ask if either detective wanted to stop for a comfort break. The answer was negative; they wanted to get to London as soon as possible to meet the SIO in charge of the double murder. And they wanted to find out what George had been like in life.

Darkness descended as they sped through the Midlands and around Birmingham via the M6 toll. The mountains of the Lake District were a lingering memory; housing estates, high-rises and choked roads replaced the clear air of lakes and rivers. Kelly felt slightly claustrophobic, but Emma was entranced. As they approached the outskirts of London, thousands of lights bounced off the windows from cars, cafés, shops, phones, aeroplanes and trains. They were surrounded by neon and noise, assaulting them in a wave of electrical pulses. Kelly closed her laptop, as well as her eyes.

She was back.

Her heart rate increased and she felt the familiar pump of adrenalin flood her veins. Her life was so different now. Three years in the Lake District had softened her. Not that she'd lost her edge professionally, but her environment was no longer filled with testosterone junkies, dawn raids and stab vests. She'd had her fair share of danger in the Lakes, but that came with the job. If you apprehended bastards for a living, then some harm had to be expected. But in London, there was scum on every corner, on every street, in every office and behind every shadow. It was as if the city was a giant organism with an underbelly of seediness and crime, and the officers pursuing truth were constantly battling against it. Homicide detectives no longer worked alongside colleagues at local stations. Now, murder was a specialism, and they had their own headquarters. Three control centres ran the whole of London, regardless of which borough the crime was committed in. Scotland Yard was the mother ship, but pods existed around the city, usually in the areas where it was cheapest to rent large office complexes. The one they were making for was in Hendon.

The car stopped in front of a huge glass building with all the lights still burning. Murder wasn't nine-to-five. Kelly read the sign outside, emblazoned with the Met's badge: *Middleton House. Specialist Crime and Operations Command.* The size of the office block denoted how busy they were: death kept this whole premises in operation. A flutter of intimidation disturbed her, but she heard Johnny's voice in her head, reassuring and supportive. Her internal dialogue pulled her this way and that, between failure and success. She looked sideways at Emma, who was transfixed.

'Come on, we're here,' she said.

They thanked the driver and told him they hoped they wouldn't be too late. He'd likely grab a coffee and catch up with colleagues as he waited to drive them to their hotel. He was on the night shift, so he had hours to kill.

Kelly gathered her briefcase, notes and various screens, leaving her personal items in the boot. Emma did the same. They both stretched, and straightened their clothes – they'd been sitting in the back of the car for almost five hours – before entering the building. Their ID was checked and their names entered on the system, then they were allowed through the glass barrier and upstairs to level five, where the SIO was expecting them. Kelly fiddled with her ponytail and her collar, trying not to look nervous in front of her junior. She hoped their welcome would be as smooth as possible, and that there would be no subtle one-upmanship from their elite colleagues. They were here to work on the same page.

They were escorted to one of the many incident rooms, and Kelly saw Emma glancing around, taking in the sheer vastness of the operation. In Penrith, Kelly's office and one incident room, boasting some new chairs and a knackered old radiator, was the sum of Serious

Crime for the Northern Lakes. Her colleague and friend DI Lockwood took care of the south.

She scanned the corridors and the desks through the glass walls to see if she could spot any old colleagues. She had no idea how she would react if she did. On the one hand, it would be wonderful to catch up with people with whom she'd shared countless lunches, office hours and after-work drinks. But on the other, she couldn't shake the feeling that they'd look down on her because she'd run away to the provinces. She drew a deep breath and they entered the room.

She counted nine officers, and she knew that there'd be another nineteen in bed, ready to take up the reins in the morning. But at least the SIO was there, and they could get an up-to-date picture on how the investigation was progressing.

'Boss,' their escort said.

A man in dark trousers and a white shirt turned around and ran his hands through his hair. He had no tie on, and he looked as though he'd put in twenty-four hours straight already.

'DI Kelly Porter, boss. Cumbria Constabulary.'

'I know who our guests are, thank you. We've been expecting you, DI Porter.'

Kelly held out her hand. When their skin touched, it was like a thousand knives shot into her sticky palm and up to her shoulder. With an effort, she kept her grip firm as she stared into the eyes of DCI Matt Carter.

Whatever happened from here on in, it couldn't get any worse.

# Chapter 12

Tilly Knight parked around the corner from George's address, as she knew full well that the main road was a nightmare for traffic. She'd never visited his home before, but she knew the area well. She gathered her notes and her bag from the passenger seat and got out. Perhaps he was ill, she thought.

She'd spent all morning in the library, researching Ravensword, the theories behind George's calculations, and a few names that he had supplied her with during their only phone call. It was all good background, but she couldn't help the nagging feeling that she was wasting her time. If he wasn't home, and he didn't answer her calls this afternoon, then she'd move on. He'd specifically asked her not to call him at Ravensword, and she'd honoured that, though she could always pretend to be somebody else: it went with the territory.

Wanstead High Street was full of kids from the local high school eating chips, pies and other unhealthy fare. They were, for the main part, well behaved, with the odd joker jostling a pensioner or shaking up a Coke bottle and spraying his mates with it. Tilly walked away from the centre of town and under the railway bridge, taking a left turn. Ahead of her she saw police. Her footsteps slowed and she looked left and right but kept walking, not wanting to attract suspicion. She got her sunglasses out of her bag and put them on. A patrol car sat outside George's address, and police tape cordoned off the property. Two uniforms stood outside the front gate, looking straight ahead with the intermittent side glance. Occasionally one or other of them spoke into their radios.

It was perfectly normal for members of the public to rubberneck under such circumstances, and Tilly paused as she approached.

'Ma'am,' one of the officers said.

'Good morning. I know the man who lives here. Is everything all right?'

One of the officers reached into his pocket for a notepad.

'I'm afraid I'm not at liberty to say, ma'am, but if you'd like to give us your details, we can get back to you. Did you know him well?'

'Not really, just to say hello to, but it looks a bit worrying, if you know what I mean. Is George all right?'

The officer spoke into his radio, off to the side, nodding and pressing buttons. The radio crackled but Tilly didn't catch what was said. He turned back to her.

'The occupant is deceased, ma'am. An investigation is under way. When was the last time you saw him?'

Tilly touched her hand to her mouth in genuine shock. Adrenalin flooded her system and she remembered George telling her how serious he thought his story was. Surely it couldn't be a coincidence?

'Oh, about two weeks ago,' she said. 'Before he went on holiday.'

'Right, ma'am, and did he mention that he was meeting anyone on holiday?'

'No, he said he was fishing as always, and couldn't wait to get away. He didn't mention anyone to me.'

'Very good, ma'am. Can I take a name and contact number? The detective in charge of the case might like to contact you. It's part of a routine line of questioning.'

'Of course. It's Madeleine Cromer. I live on the other side of town.' She racked her brain for a random street in Wanstead, and remembered Redbridge Lane West. She was fully aware that she was committing a crime, but the likelihood of them remembering her face after a three-minute exchange, when their focus was on the property behind them, was slim. It might raise questions when no Madeleine Cromer lived at the address she was supplying, but if they let her go on her way now, she need never set foot in Wanstead again.

'When did he die?' she asked.

'On holiday, ma'am.'

Tilly returned to her car and drove as fast as she could back to Leyton. She referred to her notes and dialled the number for Ravensword.

'Oh, hello there. I'm sorry, I'm a bit teary, I…' She broke off for authenticity before carrying on.

'Do you know the extension you need?' The woman on the other end wasn't in the best of moods, but Tilly persevered.

'Well, it's the neurocellular lab. You see, I just found out about George, and I…' She paused again.

'Oh Christ, I'm sorry. Yes, we're all in shock here too. How can I help? Are you a relative of George's?'

'Yes, he is… he was my uncle, my only relative really. He was like a father to me, and I just don't know who to turn to. I can't get to London, and I need to do something.

Can I at least talk to his colleagues? I know Emily quite well – I met her kids once, when I was down seeing George. Or perhaps Alexandros? I know he was like a son to George.' It was an Oscar-worthy performance and she thought the mention of George's colleagues added a touch of class.

'Oh, gosh, miss, I… Wait a moment, please.'

Tilly was put on hold for a few minutes. When the woman came back on the line, her voice was conspiratorial.

'Look, I really shouldn't be telling you this, but there's been a terrible incident. You need to contact the police.'

'Why? What's happened? I'm due to meet with lawyers and the police when I get to London. Please tell me what's going on.'

'You say you're his niece?'

'Yes, he had no children.'

'Can I take your name, miss, in case I have to call you back?'

Shit.

'Of course, it's Carrie Law. Mike knows me too.' She hoped that would do the trick.

'You need to call the officer in charge, Miss Law. His name is DCI Carter. The investigation is ongoing, but Emily and Mike were found dead too.'

'What?' The panic in Tilly's voice was genuine. 'What about Alexandros?'

'He's…' The woman coughed. 'I've said too much. I could lose my job.'

'Please,' Tilly pleaded.

'He's gone missing.'

Tilly couldn't speak, but she didn't need to. The woman had hung up. She double-checked that her caller ID was off. Some clever dick might be able to trace the call sometime in the future, but by that point Tilly hoped she'd have got to the bottom of what was happening. Huge companies like Ravensword had the facility to record calls, of course, but she was confident the receptionist wouldn't have taken that risk.

She sat at her kitchen table staring into space, then reached for her bag. She went out onto the balcony with her cigarettes and lit one shakily before bringing a news site up on her phone. The report about the murders made no mention of Alexandros. What the hell did it mean? George had told her that he was staying in a pal's pad on some lake up north. She went inside to get her notes, not caring that cigarette smoke followed her. When she first had contact with a source, she wrote everything down, from their favourite takeaway to their pet's name. It was there: he'd said he'd be staying at Allerdale House, on the shore of Derwent Water, owned by the Montague-Roland family. Christ. Montague-Roland was the name of some lord, she was certain of it. It was the kind of name that, once heard, never went away.

She googled the local news for the Derwent area and found what she was looking for straight away: *London man found murdered at Lakes marina*. Within a few minutes, she had learned all she needed to know about the death of her new source. A man who'd told her that he'd spent months trying to find the right journalist for the job, and that he was sitting on something that might cause him harm. The article was to be his insurance.

Next she googled Montague-Roland. A photograph of a slimy-looking City type came up, alongside one of a much older man. The older man had died late last year; the slimeball was his grandson and heir. She clicked on related searches and learned that Sebastian Montague-Roland intended to create a leisure empire out of the pile on the shores of Derwent Water, and that building work was due to start soon. She also read of the recent burglary, in which hundreds of thousands of pounds worth of items had disappeared from the boathouse. The dates matched: George had been there.

Some story.

Tilly felt her heart rate increase and knew she was on to something.

She contemplated her next move. She'd already lied to the police, and George had very likely been killed for whatever it was he knew. Perhaps so too had his colleagues. She had several options. She could forget about the whole thing and concentrate on something else, but the problem with that was that she had nothing else solid at the moment. She could continue nosing about here and find out more about George Murphy. Or she could book a hotel in Keswick, three hundred miles away, and snoop around up there.

She googled the small town and studied the photographs of the quaint market, the lake and the fells. She was enchanted. She knew enough about murder investigations to be aware that the body would be kept *in situ* until all the tests were complete. She googled the chief coroner in Carlisle, and Ted Wallis popped up. He looked like the kind of man she could have a pint with. She checked her bank balance: she had five hundred quid left or thereabouts, but she had a credit card. It was reckless, it was foolish, and it was utterly impulsive, but that was what she was in this game for. Something about it felt right. Something inside her made her want to find out what had happened to George Murphy. She brought up the Ravensword website and stared at his photo on the staff page. He had a kind face. There were photos of his colleagues on the same page, and she shivered as she looked at them.

As she sat staring at the screen, her bank balance changed. A sum from her pending transactions had just cleared into her account. The amount was ten thousand pounds, and it had been paid by George Murphy.

Tilly went to pack.

# Chapter 13

It was an unusually choppy day on Derwent Water, and no one was on the lake. Not even the launch was keeping to its timetable. At the marina, all the kayaks, canoes and rowing boats were out of the water and stored in the shed, and Graeme sat behind the counter reading a book. If he had no customers by noon, he'd shut up shop. The stormy weather was forecast to last for three days, but in the Lakes, weather forecasts meant nothing. Yachts and Lasers bobbed up and down on the swell, and tarps flapped with the wind.

Graeme had given his staff the day off. Should anyone venture to rent a rowing boat on a day like this, he was capable of fitting them with a life jacket, giving them a map and reading them the rules. The office was warm, heated by a powerful portable radiator that Graeme had pulled close to him as he lounged on a comfy chair.

At eleven o'clock, a man opened the door and strode in. He didn't look local. He wore red chinos, a blue shirt open at the collar with a brightly coloured cravat, a tweed jacket, and a tan, certainly not gained in Keswick. Perhaps he was lost. It happened often. The marina was a dead end, and people were usually looking for the beginning of the Cat Bells walk. The man didn't look like a hiker, though, and it didn't take Graeme long to work out that he was eyeing him as if he wanted more than directions. Graeme had had his fair share of homosexual interest down the years, and it didn't bother him in the slightest, though he knew plenty of people that it did offend, especially in the army.

He wondered idly what the man was doing here. He just didn't fit. Perhaps he was a journalist. The story of the body in *The Lady of the Lake* had not died down, and Graeme had had visits from reporters as far away as Manchester. He had followed the story in the papers, and he also knew plenty of people who were reliable purveyors of local gossip. The poor bloke had been killed by a single gunshot wound to the head – a detail that had been kept out of the press – and a buzz had begun to circulate around Keswick about the similarity to an execution-style killing. Graeme had shared a few pints with Johnny Frietze, who wasn't at liberty to say too much. Everybody knew that Johnny was DI Kelly Porter's boyfriend, and that Kelly had been called to London.

Graeme liked Kelly, but then most people did. She was fiercely private, but once you got to know her, she was good company. He'd taught them both to sail, though Johnny was by far the more interested. Kelly was one of those people whose job filled far more hours than her leisure pursuits. Johnny was the opposite. He'd come to the Lakes to find a life after serving in the army. Graeme's own short stint hadn't involved any active duty, but he had trained – and been stood down – for Iraq once. He had no medals, but great memories. It had never been a long-term goal anyhow; it just looked good on his CV. It was ironic that after all that he'd ended up back at home, running a quiet marina, and he wouldn't want it any other way.

'Morning, mate. Can I help?' he said.

'Bracing weather. What a lovely spot. I came here as a child occasionally, but never ventured down this way.'

'Where are you staying? Walking holiday?' Graeme peered at the man's shoes; they were impractical and expensive. He looked like a City type on the hunt for a posh weekend hideaway that he'd never use. The guy clearly had too much money.

'Sebastian Montague-Roland, Allerdale House. You probably knew my grandfather; everybody seemed to.'

The man spoke of the late Lord Allerdale with a side portion of resentment. Graeme had seen it before many times, especially within the officer class. It was the paradox, he assumed, of getting to one's station in life because of Daddy's status, but at the same time feeling acrimony over the fact.

'Your grandfather was a great man; I was sorry to hear of his passing. He was a gentleman and you don't see a lot of those these days.'

'Quite.'

'How can I help you today?' Graeme asked once more.

Sebastian looked around the cabin and picked up a few brochures. 'Well, you might have heard that I'm refurbishing the estate, and I'm after a few select sailing items that are quite difficult to get hold of.'

Graeme nodded. That was his trade. 'Such as?'

'Antique racing shells.'

'Composite?'

'Good heavens, no. Spanish cedar.'

Graeme raised his eyebrows. 'Like rocking horse shit, I imagine.'

'I beg your pardon?'

'I deal in plastic, mate. If I rented Spanish cedar boats, I'd be out of business in a week.'

'I was clearly mistaken. I could have sworn that my grandfather said you knew your racing shells.'

'Of course, I admire them from afar, but I don't deal in them. You need a specialist for that, someone like Pocock.'

'I was hoping to circumnavigate the obvious dealers. I want it to be unique. It's for decorative purposes, obviously. I'm planning a high-end restaurant as part of the leisure complex at Allerdale Estate.'

Last time Graeme checked, the property was called Allerdale House, but the guy had aspirations, he gave him that.

'I can have a look and ask around,' he said.

'That's what I was hoping. I am most grateful. I'm interested in any decorative oars, rigging and boat paraphernalia as well. I'm going for a classical look; think roaring twenties.'

He passed Graeme a card with a phone number on, brushing his hand and lingering just a little too long. Graeme took the card and flicked it between his thumb and forefinger.

'Righty-ho,' Sebastian said. 'I'm about all summer – well, apart from looking after business in London, of course. I'll be up and down, so to speak.'

Graeme ignored the blatant flirting. 'You got yourself a project manager, have you? I'm handy as they come and know all the local trades.' He might as well use the man's obvious interest to his advantage.

'Are you applying for a job?'

'If you put it like that.' He smiled his best and widest grin, holding Sebastian's gaze. 'We could negotiate the use of the beach in return for me sending custom your way. There's plenty of wealthy Americans come here asking about good food and facilities.'

'Perhaps you'd come over to the house this evening for a chat? We can discuss it then.'

'Sure.'

Sebastian looked pleased and turned to leave. Graeme watched him go. He found the man odd, for sure, and certainly couldn't see him fitting in around these parts. He was definitely in need of a local manager if his vision was to succeed, and Graeme fitted the bill perfectly: local knowledge, good business sense, a passion for water sports, an already trusted relationship with the community and, of course, the perfect balance between customer service and a head for profit.

He laid the card on the counter and went to his computer. There were a few dealers he'd come to know over the years, and he had a good idea where to start his search for an antique Spanish cedar racing shell.

# Chapter 14

Kelly had forgotten where she was until she heard the traffic. She'd slept fitfully and she felt anything but refreshed. Her dreams had been vivid and unsettling, replicating dreams she hadn't had in years. They were brief, intense, and generally placed her in danger, with no backup and the life of an innocent at stake. Just before the dream ended, great violence threatened the victim she was supposed to be protecting, but she never knew what happened to them. The point was that she was alone. And vulnerable.

She sighed. She felt as though she'd tossed and turned all night, and her vest and pants were soaked in sweat. Light poured through the thin curtains, as it had all night. Sirens, drunken arguments, aeroplanes in holding patterns, car horns and thumping music all conspired to make her first full day in the capital an uphill struggle. She decided that lots of coffee and Emma's excitement might dull the edges. She'd packed her running kit, but knew deep down that it would stay in her bag. She could pound the streets after dark, but that would only serve to heighten her anxiety, not soothe it. She felt tension in her shoulder blades and realised that she was carrying within her a sense of dread, and she knew exactly why.

She sat up and got out of bed. The room was sparse, with no tea and coffee facilities, and a modest shower room. It was all she needed. She washed her hair under the hot water and already felt herself becoming more alive. The towel was fluffy and large and she rubbed herself briskly. Now all she needed was coffee. She had flashbacks of grabbing a pastry before work, years ago, outside a Tube station. It was a pleasant memory but she was glad that it was behind her. The thought of how much sugar and caffeine she'd flooded her system with was enough to make her shudder, but funnily enough, that was exactly what she wanted this morning.

She'd arranged to meet Emma at eight downstairs. Her junior was already waiting. A car had been organised to transport them to the office every day for as long as they were here in the city, and Kelly winced at the waste of money. Looking at Emma, it would also be a lot more fun to see her on a Tube train. Her colleague was starry-eyed and couldn't wait to get started.

'There's a Starbucks on the corner. I'm not going anywhere without one.'

'How do you know, guv?'

'It's a wild guess. I'm joking; this is where I used to work.'

Emma followed her. There was indeed a Starbucks on the corner, and their driver was instructed to wait. The streets were rammed, and Emma gaped around her, hypnotised by the sheer volume of busy people on the move, determined and focused, barking into mobile phones and gulping coffee. Kelly smiled. The queue in the coffee shop was long and made up of impatient, sullen, stressed individuals, shifting from foot to foot, peering round the person in front, like cars trying to find a way through a traffic jam.

Emma said hello to a few people, but soon stopped doing it when she received only glares in return.

'Why is everyone so angry?' she whispered.

Kelly shrugged her shoulders. It was true. She'd never seen it from an outsider's point of view, because she'd always been in the thick of it. But it was glaringly obvious now. Rudeness, impatience and tetchiness were commonplace and normal. Finally they reached the front of the queue and placed their orders. Emma picked up a Danish pastry with apricot, and Kelly chose a pain au chocolat. It was a lethal habit to slide into, and she kept telling herself that they'd be home in Cumbria soon, and she could run it off.

Armed with their sustenance, they got into the waiting car and it set off. They hit traffic straight away, and didn't arrive in Hendon until almost 8.50. They could have walked quicker; in fact, Kelly would suggest it tomorrow.

DCI Matt Carter had briefed them with an update last night, and today would be their first day of actual lead-chasing. The array of screens, audio equipment, PNC access points, interactive whiteboards and bodies dashing from one office to the next startled Emma, and Kelly strode in front of her, showing her the way. She knew the building well, and it was already beginning to feel like home again.

Their priority was finding Alexandros Skarparis. After all, he was the only one of the foursome working in the neurocellular lab who might still be alive, and he was also, so far, their prime suspect. He was the common denominator between the three colleagues and had mysteriously disappeared around the time Emily Wilson and Mike Hudson were brutally killed in the garage in Bethnal Green. Matt was already in the office, despite being the last to leave last night. Kelly recognised the look behind his eyes: hunger. He'd begin a period of twenty-hour days if he had to, and wouldn't let up until he had answers. That was the way he operated, and Kelly had learned from him. She felt her stomach tense. He smiled broadly at his visitors and took their hands warmly, lingering on Kelly's. She dropped her hand and looked away.

They got down to business, first discussing George.

'His body was moved to the dump site,' Kelly said, 'and we have forensic evidence that someone was killed in one of the bathrooms in Allerdale House – DNA to be confirmed. That's the same property that was burgled for some pretty expensive kit, we believe on the same day. But nothing inside the house was missing and there's some valuable equipment and belongings in there.'

'Do you think the burglary was connected in some way to his death?' Matt asked.

'Definitely, either as a bonus or planned. It could have been a smoke screen to throw us off, or the intended target; the high-end sailing market is small but worth millions. George would have been collateral damage if the burglars stumbled across him unwittingly, to prevent him raising the alarm, which would explain why they perhaps panicked and decided not to burgle the house, despite having access to both the boathouse and the main house.'

'Do we know who had keys?'

'The owner said that doors generally weren't locked.'

Matt rolled his eyes.

'Did you manage to establish motive?' he asked, knowing that she hadn't yet had the luxury of clarifying that one. The execution MO suggested convenience, and that usually meant money. The blunt-force trauma MO in the killing of George's colleagues also suggested a lack of compassion seen in business-like killings.

Matt delivered the sparse updates about the Bethnal Green murders that had come in overnight, and then they headed to the morning briefing. It was conducted in a vast incident room, and was attended by around thirty officers, with pads, screens, phones and radios at the ready. Kelly knew she wouldn't be anywhere near boots on the ground in this investigation, but it was still invigorating watching the uniforms, DCs and DSs go about their business and report real-time, sometimes in the form of live CCTV or tracking computer software. Matt was at the helm and would remain in his ivory tower commanding the troops. For Emma, it was an incredible opportunity to learn from the best.

'DI Porter and DC Hide are familiar with the area of Derwent, and I'm going to hand you over to them now,' he said. 'We're lucky to have them with us and I want everyone to give them absolute cooperation as long as they're here.' He sat commandingly on the edge of a table and an officer tapped notes next to him. Kelly looked around and met a sea of eyes, all on her. She spoke from where she sat.

She'd been assigned her own lap-top computer, which she referred to along with the maps on the whiteboard and the slides she'd hastily constructed in her hotel room the night before. It was a struggle to concentrate with Matt's eyes boring into her. She couldn't work out if he was willing her on or willing her to trip up. Their relationship had been kept secretive, and, to her knowledge, no one in the room knew about it. A sudden flashback to him naked jumped into her head and she closed her eyes, willing it to leave. She wondered if he still slept with a knife in his bedside cabinet. In London, detectives received death threats all the time. They put a lot of people behind bars, and criminals who'd already crossed the line wanted to punish those responsible for getting them caught. All killers thought they were clever and believed they'd get away with it, but in reality few did.

'These are the items stolen from Allerdale House. As you can see, it's a specific market and we need to pursue all known dealers. The insurance money is substantial. DC Hide and I have interviewed the owner, but I haven't worked him out yet. He's a cross between shifty and plain awkward. I didn't get the immediate impression that he was withholding, and equally I wasn't sure I would trust him either. My initial summary is that he was a disappointment to his grandfather: the old man didn't name him as heir straight away, leaving his fortune in trust initially. I've got solicitors calling me back to tell me the details of that arrangement. He could have had a grudge. His name is Sebastian Montague-Roland; some of you might remember the name from the colantropine scandal back in 1995. Alan Montague-Roland – Lord Allerdale – exposed an aide of Margaret Thatcher's, which led to two lords being stripped of their titles, and three MPs and a smattering of CEOs of large pharmaceuticals being sacked. One of those companies was Ravensword.'

'Where all our victims worked,' Matt interjected. The room was silent, with everybody paying attention. Kelly was impressed: Matt ran a tight ship.

'For background,' she continued, 'colantropine was an additive in breakfast cereal – it aided the absorption of vitamin D added to the cereal during fortification. It passed all its safety tests, but the problem was that the results of lab tests showing that it burned lesions in rats' brains were buried under a pile of top-secret documents, only accessible by a few in the know.'

'I don't like coincidences.' Matt stole Kelly's line.

'Neither do I,' she agreed. She chided herself for playing his game and blushed a little. He was as wily as a fox and she needed to concentrate. 'We need a warrant for the neurocellular lab at Ravensword, and I want to go through the place carefully. We're looking for anything that might have got George Murphy into trouble.'

Matt took over. 'Our next lead is the pellet found in George's skull. Ballistics confirmed it's a Glock, which narrows it down.' That got a few laughs. 'I want all the gun amnesties alerted, major cities on board and known contacts pushed for anyone trying to get rid of a handgun. Long shot, excuse the pun. If they have any sense, they'd have dumped it in the lake up there.'

Matt spoke about the Lake District as if it was make-believe and separate from the rest of the UK – which consisted primarily of London – and it irked Kelly. She'd grown protective of her county, and its reputation for being backwards and in the sticks was something that infuriated her. She also noticed that, despite introducing her to deliver what she knew on George Murphy, Matt had taken over. He just couldn't help himself. She decided to let it go. Let him sweat over the detail. A young officer caught her eye and a tiny curl of his mouth indicated to her that his boss did this a lot. She gave him an imperceptible nod, and they both went back to concentrating on the DCI.

'What's next?' Matt looked at Kelly and waited. *Now* he wanted her to speak!

'Like I said, the burgled items include some very specialist sailing equipment. We need to contact as many dealers as we can. These are few and far between, due to the high value and antique nature of the artefacts. I want to include overseas interest.'

She waited for people to take notes.

'Sebastian Montague-Roland.' His picture came up on screen. 'His business is mainly in London. He dabbles in stocks and told me that the trust issue had been "sorted"; he's now worth a handsome sum. I think we need to treat him as a person of interest. Only he and George had access to Allerdale House on the night in question, though it is highly likely that the doors were unlocked. There's no cleaner, and an expensive refurb planned for later this year hasn't yet started. The place should have been deserted, though we are looking into a building company who'd made some initial plans. Montague-Roland informed us that he tried to contact George on Sunday evening to see if any workmen had been to the property, but he didn't answer the phone. He supplied us with a number for the builders and they told us that they hadn't yet got round to sending anyone. So that rules them out of our inquiry for the time being.

'Now we come to George's colleagues. DCI Carter?'

Matt stood up and put his hands in his pockets. He didn't use notes.

'The note left with the victims firmly places the blame on Emily Wilson. Was it a plant? A diversion?'

The note came up on the screen. *Bitch*. It was brutally jarring. The female officers visibly shifted in their seats.

'It implies an affair with Mike Hudson, but this is vociferously denied by next of kin. It's a touchy subject. Sometimes nobody knows that a sexual liaison is in full swing.' There was a pause, and Kelly felt herself blush again.

'The garage. We know it was rented by George. Why? Forensics have been through it and reported traces of chemicals not designed for anything other than a controlled environment. There was also residue of faeces of an animal not native to the UK. Namely the cyno monkey.'

Baffled glances travelled around the room and a photograph of a monkey came up on the board. The caption underneath read: *Cynomolgus monkey, native to south-east Asia. Commonly known as the crab-eating macaque.*

'They were running a lab?' An officer correctly deduced where Matt was leading them. He nodded.

'I want to know why. Perhaps they found something lucrative, and Skarparis has run off to sell it to the Russians, killing his colleagues for good measure?'

'But why steal an antique rowing boat, and why travel to the Lake District in the first place? Why not wait until George returned home?' Kelly asked. She couldn't help herself. Matt had drawn them all in, and she was taken back to years ago, when she'd found it as awe-inspiring as Emma did now.

'A lab coordinator at Ravensword said she had a call from Skarparis yesterday morning enquiring about his colleagues. She said he sounded stressed. We're checking the company's CCTV and I think we go with releasing his photograph to the press. He's Cypriot, isn't he? Monitor the airports.'

'Who found the bodies of Emily Wilson and Mike Hudson?' Kelly asked.

'A dog. The garage doors were ajar and it was attracted by the smell. When the owner went to look, he saw them.'

'I used to live near there. There's CCTV all over the place.'

'Correct. It's being checked. As is ANPR for both George's road movements before he went up north, and Skarparis's. We're looking at the routes between all the victims' residences and the available routes to Ravensword and the garage over the last six months.'

'That's a huge undertaking.' Kelly appreciated the scale of such a task. It could take months. Matt nodded, as if to say: *What did you expect?* An irrational thought entered her head, and she stared back at him: was he hoping that she'd be in London for more than a week?

Four photographs of cars flashed up above them. Identical models to those owned by the lab colleagues. All of them were what Kelly termed grey leads: bog-standard, dull-coloured makes that were probably among hundreds of thousands of identical vehicles produced in the same year. Skarparis owned a black three-door Vauxhall Corsa. George drove a slightly more notable VW Touran in navy blue, while Emily had a silver Nissan Micra. Mike owned the most interesting set of wheels: he drove a new Seat Tarraco, but it looked like all other showy four-by-fours out there, and was dark grey. Kelly knew that some poor sod would spend the next few weeks trawling through ANPR footage looking for standard-coloured, non-descript cars. They all had to do it when they cut their teeth, but it could be mind-numbingly boring.

'DI Porter agrees that we're looking for a group for the murder of George Murphy, due to the scale of the burglary. A double murder is not usually carried out by a single perp, so we're applying that to the garage too. Speaking to Alexandros Skarparis is of utmost importance, because he ties them all together. It's perfectly plausible that he's terrified and in hiding. He hasn't been to his home address since Monday.'

An officer came into the room and handed Matt a piece of paper. He read it, folded it and closed his eyes. When he opened them, he looked at Kelly.

'Alexandros Skarparis boarded a flight to his native Cyprus yesterday evening. We'll have to get the Home Office involved.'

## Chapter 15

Tilly was enjoying her drive north, and the comfort of knowing that her bank account was not a source of constant worry for the first time in three years. It was like a weight lifting off her shoulders. She turned the radio up full blast and tapped on the steering wheel, but every few minutes her body reminded her where she was headed to, and why, and her stomach tightened, making her nauseous. She'd set off early, wanting to miss the build-up of traffic around Birmingham.

At Lancaster University, the radio went dead and she couldn't get any reception – not even a farming channel – so she switched on her Bluetooth. The sky, so dark and grim in the Midlands, shone bright blue, and in the distance she could see the peaks of mountains. Beyond the turning for Kendal, the landscape changed dramatically and she couldn't help looking to her left every other minute to stare at the dark mountains. They were way in the distance, but she could tell that the scale of them up close would be incredible.

She'd ventured north only twice before: once to Leeds to visit the university when she was choosing her course, and on another occasion to Liverpool on a kind of music pilgrimage when she was a student. Two things stood out from both trips: the cold and the rain. She remembered the people as charming but curious about her accent, and she found it ludicrous that they assumed she was posh. She'd gone to a local co-ed in north Hertfordshire, then on to Bristol University. She was what she considered normal.

She'd booked a B&B online in Portinscale, near Keswick. The town looked quaint on the internet photos. All the houses were built of slate, and stunning views of the mountains could be had everywhere. It felt rather indulgent to be acting so extravagantly, but then she realised that if George was advancing such a generous sum so early on, the topic was serious: enough to die for. She might never see the rest of the agreed fee, but for now her interest was piqued. She also realised that the transfer, given how long it took for such transactions to process, was likely to be the last George ever made. Police profiling of murder victims was thorough and detailed, but also slow, so she knew they'd examine George's bank accounts at some point, but she guessed she had a week or so to stay one step ahead. It wasn't that she was worried about acquiring the money illegally or unfairly – she had everything recorded, including his offer of fifty thousand pounds on publication – it was more that she wanted to find out more about George before they did. And before whoever killed him found out who he'd been talking to.

She followed the navigation instructions and pulled off the motorway at Junction 40. As she drove closer to the mountains, she gawped more and concentrated less. She'd had no idea that the Lake District was quite so extraordinary. The fells were literally just there, behind the houses and hotels. At the B&B, she parked in a space on the driveway and got out. She could see a lake, but she didn't know which one it was. It was framed with fells and forest either side and she was instantly drawn to it. Her task for the evening was to orientate herself and get to know the area where George had stayed and died, but she decided to take a walk to the lake as soon as she'd checked in.

The woman at the reception desk was friendly and interested in her southern accent.

'First time?'

Tilly nodded, beaming. The woman had red cheeks and bright eyes and told her where and when breakfast was served. Her voice was reminiscent of *Coronation Street*, though much gentler. She gave Tilly advice on how to get to the lake, where was good to eat and the location of the nearest shop. She also showed her to her room. It was clean and overlooked the lake.

'Which lake is that?'

The woman smiled patiently. 'It's Derwent Water.'

'Derwent Lake? It's beautiful.'

'No, it's called Derwent Water. There's only one that's called a lake and that's Bassenthwaite; the others are all meres, tarns or waters.'

'Right, thank you! I'll remember that. Derwent Water.'

'Enjoy your stay. I lock the office at ten; after that, there's an emergency number to call on the door. I only live three doors down, so I'm always here.'

Once the woman had left, Tilly went to her car to get her bags. She dumped them in her room, then decided to explore rather than unpack properly. She followed the directions given to her, and within a matter of minutes she found herself at the edge of the lake, on a pebbly shingle beach, watching the water lap the shore. There was no one else about and she looked both ways, uncertain of which way to go. She decided to follow the shore back towards a town that she presumed was Keswick, which she saw not far in the distance. A wooden steamer crowded with people was pulling away from a jetty. A pathway left the shoreline and skirted around a campsite, leading to a park. Soon the way was fairly crowded with people, and she figured she must be in Keswick itself.

She was now at the jetty that she'd seen the boat leave from, and she watched as children fed ducks, people hired rowing boats and families bought ice creams. She remembered that it was half-term week for schools. She fancied an ice cream herself and queued with the others. As she waited, she looked across the lake to see where the steamer had gone, but she couldn't spot it. There were plenty of people in boats and kayaks and on paddle boards, and she suddenly understood how shocking the events of earlier in the week must have been for such a small community. The place was idyllic.

'Lovely day!' a woman in front of her commented in a local accent. That was another thing she'd forgotten about the north: people talked to one another.

'It's gorgeous,' she replied. The woman was elderly but appeared sprightly. 'Do you live around here?' Tilly asked.

'I do, I've been here all my life.'

'You're so lucky,' Tilly said, and she meant it. 'Although did I read in the newspaper that there was a man killed near here this week?'

The woman became animated, leaning in and covering her mouth with her hand as she launched into a detailed description of what Tilly had read in the newspaper. By the time it was their turn to order, Tilly knew exactly where George had been found, by whom, and what the locals were saying. She also knew where he had been staying, and that the man who owned the place, Allerdale House, was an outsider who was arrogant and reclusive. She had a photographic memory and she logged every detail as the woman talked.

'Let me get these,' she insisted.

'Well, that's kind of you, miss.' The woman smiled broadly and Tilly paid.

'Is there a public toilet here?' she asked. The woman gave her directions, and it was a neat ending to their conversation. As Tilly walked away, she wrote notes on her phone and googled Derwent Marina. She looked up and orientated herself, calculating that she could probably walk there in five minutes.

## Chapter 16

'DC Hide, I've allocated you to DS Compton and you'll spend the rest of the day with him.' An officer stepped forward and shook hands with Emma. Emma glanced at Kelly, who nodded reassurance. This was what she'd come for, and she was about to see the coal face. It was invaluable experience. Emma's grin was wide. Matt barked out jobs for his remaining officers, who left the room promptly. He and Kelly were left alone.

He got off the bench and approached her. She held her breath. Her heart rate elevated and she could feel her skin flushing. She regretted the decision she'd made to come to London. She could have sent Kate Umshaw, who'd have chewed Matt up and spat him out.

He walked straight past her and closed the door. Her nerves settled and she sat down.

'You look really well, Kelly. I wanted to talk last night, but, you know.' He swept his hand around the incident room, indicating that this wasn't the place to discuss their messy break-up.

'I am really well, Matt. Let's not dwell on the past. I'm here for a reason.'

'I just wanted to say sorry,' he persevered.

'Don't you dare.' She kept her back to the glass wall, so any onlookers couldn't lip-read. She glared at him but kept quiet. She couldn't have this argument now; they had work to do.

'I didn't mean to—'

'Stop. Forget this or I'll walk now. If I have to work with you, everything has to be straight. No lingering conversations about the past. No after-work drinks.'

'No hotel rooms?'

'Fuck off. I'm seeing someone.'

'So am I.'

'Oh, for Christ's sake, Matt. We're adults.'

'And?'

'We've got work to do. Stop being an arsehole.'

'God, I've missed you.'

'Give me a job, or I'm out of here in a patrol car taking statements from Emily Wilson's cleaner.'

'You're beautiful.'

Before she could retaliate, he'd walked away and switched on several screens and radio frequencies.

'Live action this morning, from Ravensword mainly. We can keep an eye on all other inquiries as they happen. Do you have this rig up north?'

'Fuck off.'

'You still say that a lot.'

'With good reason.'

The radio crackled. 'Patrol car 247, boss. Approaching Ravensword. Will report further when inside building.'

Kelly wished she did indeed have this rig. She chastised herself. Actually, nothing beat meeting suspects face to face, and if she had to drive the length of the Lake District, then all the better.

Simultaneously officers checked in from all over the city, giving updates and sending images for their SIO to collate. Not that he had much to do, because it all happened automatically, but it meant that a human being was watching events unfold as one big picture, and, more importantly, making the decisions that a computer could not.

Several pods were working on Ravensword. One focused on George's lab and his work, another on the board of directors. A third was looking at ongoing research projects, currently involving the House of Lords, and yet another was investigating the neurocellular lab. Other pods were studying CCTV and recordings made by the switchboard.

Kelly tapped her foot. She was unaccustomed to the inertia. She wanted to be on the ground with them, asking questions, looking into people's eyes, making split-second decisions and evaluating on the move.

'Fidgety?' Matt asked rhetorically.

She got up and walked around the room. 'I need to get out and do something, Matt. I can't stay tucked away in here just waiting for stuff to happen.'

'Why don't you go and find out where Alexandros Skarparis's family home is? And phone the Home Office to see if we can get him flown back. I know a girl who works in visas.'

'I bet you do.' She left the room and logged on to her computer, where she entered Skarparis's name, flight number, work permit details and address. It didn't take long to find out that his mother lived in Larnaca, and there was a phone number. She dialled it.

'*Yassou!*'

Kelly heard a cacophony of noise and chaos. 'Alexandros, *parakalo*?'

The woman hung up. So, he'd gone home for sure. Next she got in touch with the Home Office Border Force and explained her predicament. After forty-five minutes, she was finally put through to somebody who told her that to request a foreign witness to return to the UK, there first had to be a letter from the Crown Prosecution Service confirming the need for that person to be in the country, and the charges. They were more than willing to give advice on a particular case, but authority from a chief commander was required. She wandered back to the incident room.

'Do we really think Alexandros is a suspect? I mean, an authentic one.'

'I don't know anything about the guy, do you? Regardless of what initial inquiries make of him – and I know he's got no previous – he has to be investigated. Anyone who runs raises questions.'

Kelly nodded. 'Who's your chief commander? We need his permission to request Alexandros back.'

Matt nodded. 'Look, this was sent from one of our teams at Ravensword.' Kelly glanced at the screen. 'It's the staff car park on Tuesday morning.'

'Is that Alexandros's Corsa?'

'Same.'

'Can we identify him as the driver?'

'Wait!' Matt chided her. 'Impatient as always.' Kelly didn't like the way he acted as though he was her best pal, intimately knowledgeable of all her little habits. But he did. And he had been.

'There he is!' she said. 'So he parked up at 9.29 a.m. and made a phone call. Then he left. Zoom in,' she said. 'He looks pretty downcast.'

'Let's check the ANPR from Ravensword to his address,' Matt said.

They got four more hits, proving that Alexandros Skarparis had left the car park, without clocking on, and then driven in the direction of Wanstead before seeming to take known routes back to central London an hour later.

'Can we get in touch with the team at George's house and check the witness statements for any sighting of a Greek Cypriot man?'

Matt nodded. They were aligned and it felt non-aggressive. Kelly was relieved. The thing she'd most dreaded when she'd found out the identity of the SIO was that they would come to loggerheads over minor details. They still had the same thought processes after all these years, and she didn't need to explain her motivators and theories. He'd already thought of them.

Matt contacted the relevant team and had an officer trawl through the statements. Meanwhile, they were able to track the Corsa across east London to Bethnal Green. Footage from Bethnal Green Tube station caught Alexandros accessing the Central Line. They'd figured he must have caught the Tube to Heathrow and it was confirmed by one of the ticket office cameras. It had taken them almost an hour, but they now had his last movements in the UK, and the times added up. A further hit came in from the Highways Agency: Skarparis's Vauxhall Corsa had been clamped outside Kentucky Fried Chicken in Bethnal Green Road.

A witness statement from one of George's neighbours also had a sighting of a dark-skinned man in George's garden on Tuesday. The same neighbour also said that a white van had parked outside around the same time. Nosy neighbours could be the best friend of the police sometimes. Three men got out of the van and entered the garden, but the dark-skinned man hid in the shed, which was why the occurrence had stuck in the neighbour's brain.

'Did the white van men leave with anything?' Kelly asked.

'She said a few suitcases, and she added that the men looked "rough".'

'Ballsy. Not fazed about the daylight, and a white van isn't exactly covert. How did they gain access to the property?'

Matt had already asked the same question. 'No sign of forced entry,' he confirmed.

'I wonder what Alexandros was doing in the shed. Has it been searched?' Kelly scrolled through information on several screens.

'Yes, and there was a key rack with one empty hook.'

'The garage?' she guessed.

'That's what I'm thinking.'

'So, Alexandros panics because he knows that George is dead. Then he goes to the garage and finds Emily and Mike.'

'He left the door open so they'd be found.'

Another call came through; it was from the general appeal for Alexandros Skarparis.

'Guv, I'm at a Thai restaurant on Bethnal Green Road. There was a table booked for four under the name of Mike Hudson for Monday night at 7 p.m. They were regulars, but didn't show. Mr Skarparis turned up late and was surprised to find that his colleagues weren't there. He waited for about half an hour and then left.'

Kelly turned to Matt. 'Time of death for Emily and Mike?'

'Early Monday evening, between 4 and 8 p.m.'

'Where was Alexandros before that?'

'He knocked off work at midday.'

Matt called the team at Ravensword and asked them to check the footage for Monday afternoon. Perhaps they could work out where Alexandros had gone.

After twenty minutes, they had a trace on him leaving Ravensword, heading to Bethnal Green. The trail went dead somewhere in Bethnal Green, and they lost him.

'Let's check the CCTV for the estate where the garage is.'

Matt contacted yet another team, which was sitting inside the Tower Hamlets council building. So far, they'd found no CCTV camera facing in the direction of the garage, but there was one facing the car park opposite. They had positives on three of the four cars for Monday afternoon. Emily had arrived at 11 a.m., Mike at midday and Alexandros just before 1 p.m. Alexandros left at 3.10, and it was confirmed that Mike and Emily's vehicles were still there, wheel-locked, and complete with parking warnings.

It was a great result.

'So, George was renting the garage and he and three colleagues were working on something private. If they had a primate, they must have been testing something.'

'Let's find out if Ravensword knew about it.' Matt grabbed his jacket. Finally they were going out.

# Chapter 17

The patrol car that took them across the city to the London Docklands was even more technologically resonant of something built by NASA than the incident room. Kelly had been inside plenty of vehicles kitted out with multiple radios, blues, computers and coffee stands; but this was something else. Three TV screens were set up so they could carry on their work from the back seat. The leather interior was reminiscent of a top-end night club, and she couldn't even hear the engine. The thing was a beast.

'Is it armour-plated? It feels heavy.'

Matt nodded. There was a glass barrier between them and the driver, and she felt as though she were in a mobile conference suite.

'You're missed, Kelly. Why don't you come back?'

'Don't start, Matt. I'm not in the mood.'

He smiled. 'You haven't lost your fire. That's why you're an amazing officer. You're wasted in the sticks. I'm impressed by your track record. I did ring when you exposed that trafficking circle, and that weirdo serial killer – "the Teacher", was it?'

'I know you did. I ignored your calls. And stop calling Cumbria "the sticks". It's three hours from here on the train.'

'Sorry. Why did you ignore me? I just wanted to offer my congratulations; they were massive cases. I actually wanted your advice about a killer in London around the same time.'

She turned away from the screens and looked at him properly for the first time. He was well built and she knew he worked out. His brown hair was thinning on top and greying at the sides. His skin was lifeless and his eyes were vacant, as if harbouring great sadness. He was nowhere near as attractive as she remembered, and she knew she must have been in love with the thrill of working cases together in a super-heated environment. She thought of Johnny: his bright, open eyes, his fell-kissed skin, and what he looked like when he stepped out of a lake. She stared out of the window and prayed the journey would be quick.

The factory was as colossal as she'd expected it to be. Companies like Ravensword turned over billions of dollars per year, and Kelly surmised that much of their profit went into the upkeep of these vast buildings across the planet. They parked in the same car park where Alexandros had made his phone call to the switchboard on Tuesday. They still had a walk of half a kilometre to the main entrance, and once inside, they showed their badges. The staff were clearly aware that the investigation into their colleagues' deaths was in full swing, and the place was crawling with uniformed and plain-clothes police. The atmosphere was sombre.

The arrival of the SIO always caused a stir, and the uniforms who recognised Matt stopped what they were doing to greet him. Matt acknowledged them officially and swiftly. Kelly, bringing up the rear, admired the respect he commanded. He'd done well.

They were shown into an office and greeted by a man in a suit, who asked them to sit down. They declined. The suit identified himself as the head of media relations. It really wasn't helpful.

'We're not journalists,' Matt said.

'I have several hats, I—'

'We need to have a serious conversation with somebody who knew the work of the neurocellular lab well. We'll wait here.'

'I can answer any questions you might have. We're being as transparent as we can be, and your officers are in the neurocellular lab now.'

'Somebody from HR would be a good start.' Matt wasn't giving in.

'I'm going for a walk,' Kelly said quietly. Matt understood.

She left, watched by the suit, and wandered down the corridor. She was aware straight away that somebody had followed her out of the media office, and she turned around.

'I can find my own way, thank you,' she said. The young man who had obviously been detailed to watch her nodded and dropped back.

Kelly made her way back to reception and studied a map on the wall. When asked who she was, she flashed her badge and the enquirer backed off. She didn't make a fuss, and didn't stand out. These pharmaceuticals were too secretive, and she needed to talk to the scientists who oiled the machine, not the suits who looked after the money. She gained a quick understanding of how the factory was laid out: it consisted of several lift shafts serving different floors. It reminded her of MI5. The labs were all in the bowels of the building. She made her way to HR, which she knew would be run by women. This could go either way: she'd find either solidarity or bare hostility.

Luckily it was the former. She accepted a coffee and chatted to the three staff on duty. She was open about who she was and made the women comfortable. A printout of a cartoon stuck on the wall titled *Human Remains Department* depicted a conspiratorial gaggle of women picking over limbs. Kelly thought it amusing. It was supposed to be.

'What were they like?' she eased in.

'So nice! All of them!'

Kelly heard stories of how George gave people lifts home, and Emily brought in cakes, and Mike spoke about his teenagers all the time. The women were unanimous in their verdict that Alexandros was the company heart-throb, although this was informal and in the strictest confidence. Kelly laughed companionably and listened to them pouring their hearts out. It was a position that very few people found themselves in: having to speak to a police officer about the murder of work colleagues, and dear ones at that, or so it sounded.

'Was there any company gossip about them? I know how it is – I used to work for the Met. Stories fly about.' She waited.

'Nothing at all. Apart from everybody wanting to sit next to Alexandros at the Christmas party.'

'Ah, the Christmas party!' Kelly echoed. 'And do you think Mike and Emily were both happily married? I know that's a weird question – how would you know, right? But anything at all is a help at this stage.' She had begun her real line of questioning, but the women hadn't noticed.

'They brought their partners and kids in on family days, and they were just lovely. George never remarried.'

'After his daughter died and he divorced?'

The women were impressed that she knew so much.

'Yes. It was so sad. He was such a lovely man, he would have made a fantastic husband.' One of the women passed her colleague a tissue and she blew her nose.

'Do you think we're safe? No one is telling us.'

'I'm sure you are. I can't tell you our lines of inquiry, but I have faith that Ravensword has in place more than adequate security procedures for staff.' It was true but bullshit at the same time. Every company had procedures, but that didn't mean they worked, otherwise they wouldn't have three bodies, one still in Ted's freezer in Carlisle. She felt an instant pang for home and couldn't believe that this was only her first full day here.

'Did the team keep themselves to themselves, or did they have other close colleagues? Do you all socialise separately?'

'No, we're quite a close bunch. I know each lab is a bit territorial, but we're all friendly.'

'What about management?'

The women looked at one another.

'Something juicy?' Kelly asked. Two of the women giggled.

'It's nothing,' the other said sternly.

'Really? It might not be,' Kelly said.

'It's well known that the biggest budgets go to the biggest tits.'

'Ida!'

'And the biggest tits are in which department? I know George didn't have any.' Kelly raised her eyebrows conspiratorially and the women all smiled.

'You might want to check out the head of primates, Professor Cooper. She's very close to the current CEO.'

'And the last one.'

'Thank you,' Kelly said. 'And thank you for the coffee.' She asked where the head of primates might be located and left.

She already knew from inquiries that the company's CEO, Philip Tooting, was in Bermuda on holiday. Three employees killed and one missing should have brought him home, but apparently he was seeing out the remaining five days. Kelly thought it odd, callous even.

Tooting's offices were, of course, on the top floor, overlooking the Docklands. The view from the vast reception area was breath-taking. It was a megalomaniac's paradise, and Kelly imagined that the CEO must stand up here and find it difficult not to congratulate himself frequently on his astounding success. She chatted to some of the reception staff and left with the feeling that the semblance of respect she had detected was in fact more accurately fear. It was in the body language, the fake laughs, the furtive eyes, as well as the fact that they had little knowledge of Tooting the man, but an encyclopaedic understanding of his expectations. They logged on to computers to tell her his mission statement, they paused when asked if they found him easy to work for, and they peered around before sharing even minor details. It was disturbing, to say the least.

Her visit to the primate lab was equally unconvincing. The technicians not only seemed harassed by the noise of the place, with monkeys screaming from their cages and metal rattling and echoing around the sterile room; they also appeared to be overworked.

'They sound distressed,' Kelly said, nodding at the animals, and it was true. It was like a zoo.

'Not at all. Monkeys are noisy creatures. They're well cared for; we have strict guidelines and inspections. They're not keen on new faces, that's all. They have amazing senses and can probably perceive your unease.'

'I'm not uneasy.'

'Let's take you somewhere quieter.'

Kelly asked three staff about the neurocellular lab and the answers were all the same: George, Emily, Mike and Alexandros were well liked, and there was no one who might want to hurt them.

'They weren't the most high-profile section in the complex at the moment, but they played a very prominent role in the company's success.'

'So which section *is* high profile?'

'Malaria is hot right now, but asthma and cancer are the big earners. It's all political.'

Kelly appreciated their candour, but when she asked where Professor Cooper was, a perceptible iciness crept into their demeanour. Apparently the professor left her lab whenever she pleased for as long as she fancied. Kelly was getting the distinct impression that neither the CEO nor the head of primates was particularly well liked.

Her next stop was the neuro-cellular lab. If the mood about the place as a whole was gloomy, then the atmosphere where the victims had worked was wretched. Two technicians packed belongings into boxes, and both had to stop occasionally to blow their noses. A few uniforms were working on computers; Kelly recognised two young detectives from Matt's team.

'Hi, guys, any luck?'

They shook their heads. 'We've had five different scientists helping us translate all of this stuff into English. Apart from experiments, tables and results, it's just time sheets, shift patterns and pay grades.'

'All as it should be then?'

'Yes, guv.'

'So what exactly *were* they working on?'

'Mood disorders.'

'Mental illness?'

One of the technicians looked up. 'No, I'm sorry, I need to explain.' Kelly got the impression that the detectives had already had the lecture that she was about to become privy to. 'Mental illness is like a long-term acute mis-wiring, but mood swings are short-term chronic episodes. For example, depression isn't a mental illness, it's a mood disorder. Being drunk isn't a mental illness, but intoxication makes one act like a lunatic.'

Kelly nodded. 'Carry on.'

'George's team was working on neurotransmitters, and the chemicals that switch them on and off.'

'I'm sorry, you've lost me.'

'It's probably best if I show you the diagram I drew for your colleagues.'

The two detectives looked at Kelly and signalled their approval; it had clearly helped them, so she decided to give it a go. The diagram looked like a sketch of a broken rope. The technician explained that since every event in the body was electrical, pulses needed to jump the gaps in nerve endings known as synapses. He pointed to the broken rope and Kelly tried to imagine the size of a nerve.

'Hold out your hand.'

She did so.

'If I was to hold a naked flame underneath your hand, you'd feel pain, but quicker than that, you'd have an overwhelming instinct to pull away. That's an electrical message. The same is true for feelings: they're just messages travelling around the body, acting upon what we know and have learned already. So toddlers know very little and act in predictable ways. Adults are trickier because we've probably been hurt in love, we know what it's like to make a prat of ourselves drunk, and we also know that happiness might be round the next corner even though today is awful. So we use past experience to make decisions.'

All three detectives were mesmerised by the technician and nodded along like puppies.

'George's team was working on how we can make those electrical connections less or more intense, depending on the need.'

'I think I get it. Do you mean like antidepressants?' Kelly asked.

'Kind of, but something more complex that could actually train the brain into remembering. Antidepressants simply mask stuff, like a magic trick, but they're not a long-term cure. I could go into reward pathways and the dopamine highway, but I think that's probably a bit too much.'

They all nodded.

'Thank you for your explanation,' Kelly said. 'It's been really helpful. Is it a big budget? I know the highest earner for the company is asthma drugs, but what's the business of depression like?'

'Controversial.'

'Meaning?'

'If we found a long-term cure, the money made from the short-term magic trick wouldn't be as impressive, but that's just my cynical opinion, and cynicism isn't really appreciated round here. I'm sorry, it's been an upsetting couple of days.'

'Are you aware of George perhaps working elsewhere apart from Ravensword? Did he mention a private lab to you? What about Emily and Mike?'

The technician hesitated. 'Actually, that's really strange. A couple of weeks ago, Emily said something a bit odd. I was standing right behind her. They were going to play squash and then go for a meal: they regularly did that, the four of them. Emily said to George, "I'll see you at the lab." When I took a double take, she said it was a mistake and we laughed it off. I never thought anything of it. Were they working somewhere else?'

'We don't know, it's something we have to investigate. Did George ever mention the garage he rented in Bethnal Green?'

'No.'

'Do you know where they played squash?'

'I think it was Bethnal Green, because they raved about the Thai restaurant there.'

As Kelly made her way out of the lab, she googled squash clubs in Bethnal Green. As she suspected, there were none. Next she uploaded HOLMES onto her iPad; the dynamic reasoning software was accessible to anyone working the case, and she could see updates coming in live. She cross-referenced the controlled drugs residues found at the garage with what was available in George's lab, and got a match. She put a call through to the detectives in the lab and asked if drugs used in the developmental phase could be easily stolen, or was it like in a hospital where every minute vial had to be signed for. She had a reply straight away from the technician: before drugs became manufactured in combinations they knew were safe, all lab workers had free access to them, though it would be difficult to steal large amounts and he didn't know anyone who would.

Perhaps he didn't know his colleagues as well as he thought.

# Chapter 18

The police had gone from Allerdale House by the time Graeme arrived for his meeting with Sebastian Montague-Roland, but blue and white tape remained across various gateways and windows. He parked in the lane and buzzed the intercom. He'd toyed with not coming, because it was blindingly obvious that the guy was after a liaison. There were thousands of gay men out there who you'd swear blind were straight, and it was perfectly clear that Mr Montague-Roland was hoping Graeme was one of them.

He hoped things didn't become tricky. He'd been propositioned before: most of his girlfriends had loved cruising gay bars and nightclubs when they were at university together – they had the best ambience apparently. He hoped he hadn't led Montague-Roland on. He had a moment of conflict, but reassured himself that he had only shown interest in a job.

The house was a fine example of Lakeland materials: wood, slate and stone. It was the first time he'd been here and he couldn't wait to have a nosy around inside. He drove through the gate and stopped outside a huge front door just as Montague-Roland came out with an outstretched hand. Graeme shook it. 'Mr Montague-Roland,' he said.

'Oh please, it's Sebastian. Come in, I've put some pasties in the Aga and I've got a rather marvellous bottle of Chablis on the go.' He said *pasty* as if it had an 'r' in it. Southerners stood out like sore thumbs up here.

'I'm driving,' Graeme said.

'Pity. I'll have to drink it all myself.'

Sebastian closed the huge oak door behind them. The furnishings, lighting and decor were all arresting. Graeme appreciated good design and stared around at the sumptuous interior.

'Impressive, isn't it?' Sebastian said.

Graeme nodded. 'Perfect.'

'Well, I wouldn't go that far. I've got my own ideas and I think Grandfather will turn in his grave when I fix the place up my way.'

Graeme was examining the artwork on the walls. Every painting was an original. 'Did you ever consider opening as a museum?' he asked. 'Tourists love walking round these old stately homes, and pay a fortune for it.'

'Imagine how much they'll pay to stay here,' Sebastian grinned.

'So, you said you've already tried some building companies? I did see some surveyors up here.' Graeme was aware that his information could be seen as prying. 'I sail past the beach a lot.'

'I've tried several people: all unreliable. That's where you come in; you're local, you know the area, and you're already a stone's throw away.'

Graeme rubbed his chin. 'Absolutely. I'd be happy to. When do I start?'

'Let me share my ideas first, and you can start giving me some figures.'

As they walked through the house, Sebastian regaled Graeme with snippets of family history and stories of how certain priceless artworks had got here from all over the world. He never mentioned his grandfather unless it was to repeat a valuation or an opinion. There was no affection, no memories and no stories of a blissful childhood spent swimming in the lake.

'Did you come here as a child?' Graeme asked. They'd finished downstairs and Sebastian was taking him up the grand double staircase.

'I was sent off to boarding school at the age of five. Grandfather preferred older children who could understand facts and figures. He invited me a lot later on, but by then, my tastes had changed.'

'How many guests will you be able to accommodate?'

'I'm thinking intimacy: probably twenty-five maximum. They'll be paying in the region of a thousand a night, so that'll do.'

'Nice.'

'Pocket money.'

Graeme had never been near money like that, and it made him uneasy.

'How did you know George Murphy?' he asked. It was an innocent enough question, but Sebastian's demeanour changed.

'I beg your pardon?'

'The man who was staying here; the guy who—'

'I know who you mean. What type of question is that?'

Graeme could see that he'd offended Sebastian, but he didn't know how.

'I'm sorry, I didn't mean to be rude. It's just that I didn't see him around. No one knew he was here. If any of us

116

had realised he was staying, we could have kept an eye on him. It's a close community. That's what your guests will love.'

'I'm not sure you follow my idea. My guests won't be little Englanders looking for a twee boat ride over to get an ice cream; they'll have impeccable standards and will be expecting the best. In everything.'

'Of course. There are many exclusive resorts in the Lakes, and I'm sure yours will be one of the finest. I know everybody you need to make your dream come true. The most important feature is the privacy. You can give them anything they want.'

'Quite.'

Graeme had managed to calm his host down and dared to breathe easier for now. They carried on with the tour. He wouldn't mention the murder victim again. But Sebastian did.

'What do you know about George? What are people saying? I know they talk. What am I up against?'

Graeme thought very carefully about his response. It could be instrumental in him landing a lucrative position here at Allerdale House. He certainly wasn't about to tell Sebastian about his particularly intimate knowledge of the crime, or his relationship with the detective in charge. He was in a precarious yet oddly satisfying position.

'Very little. People are saying that it was a bungled robbery. Wrong place, wrong time. Poor man.' He lied easily.

'Quite.'

Sebastian led him back downstairs to the kitchen. The smell from the Aga was wondrous, but Graeme toyed with leaving right away. Did he really need the job? He decided that he did. Managing a project of this size could change his life, and that of his kids. Sebastian opened the Aga and placed a pasty on each of two plates. They sat at the kitchen table, without ceremony.

'Let's talk money,' Sebastian said.

'What's your budget?'

'Name your price.'

'I'm not after your cash. I'd expect a project manager's wage. The rest would be costs.'

'Project managers are on a thousand a day in London, but this is Cumbria.'

Graeme wondered how a man like Sebastian would know that kind of thing. He had no clue what type of project management could possibly pay a thousand quid a day, but he chanced his arm.

'I'd only want seven hundred.'

'Done. I might ask your advice on other matters. I need to learn about my neighbours.'

'Of course you do.'

They ate. The pasty was decent, but not local.

'I'm going to London tomorrow,' Sebastian said. 'Here's a key: come and go as you please. Don't spend a penny without my say-so, and keep me informed about what's being said about that nasty business with George, will you?'

'Of course. I know most folk round here.'

'You can be my eyes and ears, then.' Sebastian held his gaze.

'Thank you for the pasty. It was a good one. I must be getting back now. I won't let you down.'

'Family to go back to?'

'Divorced.'

'I like all sorts of pasties – meat, veg, fish… How about you?'

'I only like the traditional ones, I'm afraid. That fancy stuff isn't for me.'

He'd made himself clear. Sebastian smiled.

'Perhaps I can change your mind.'

Graeme stood up. 'God loves a trier,' he said. Sebastian laughed. The line in the sand had been drawn.

They shook hands and Graeme left Sebastian with his bottle of wine, next to the warmth of the Aga. The same Aga where George Murphy had cooked his meals for a whole week without anyone knowing he was there. As he left by the back door and walked around the front, Graeme looked up at the smoking chimney and the lights burning upstairs. Had George existed in the dark and not lit a fire? It was a curious set of puzzle pieces that rattled around in his head. Next time he saw Kelly Porter, he'd ask her for sure.

# Chapter 19

Kelly watched the taped interviews with Emily Wilson's husband and Mike Hudson's wife. It was harrowing viewing. After her years of experience on the force, interrogating witnesses – some serious dead certs, others mere question marks – she knew sincerity when she saw it. The psychologist agreed. Emily Wilson's husband had three children under the age of six to look after, and he was like a man lost inside a hell of pain and never-ending torment. His eyes were red and puffy, he looked thin and undernourished, and he was unkempt. They had stock photos to compare, and he was a shadow of his former self. He was adamant that his wife had not been having an affair with Mike Hudson, but they'd worked that out already. Whoever had staged the scene had bought time and that was all.

Mike Hudson's wife had two teenagers. Kelly remembered her own teenage years, and how, no matter how bad the rebellion and the angst, every teenager deep down needed a loving parent. Just one would do, but these kids clearly used to have two, and now they didn't. Mike's wife was equally dismissive of the idea of a torrid love affair. Both Emily and Mike had been in happy marriages, albeit with their usual dramas and dips. The squash club came up

120

again, and Kelly and Matt agreed that it was undoubtedly a code for whatever was being researched in the garage.

Neither spouse knew about the garage and what went on there.

Kelly and Matt were also coming to the conclusion that the organisation of the murder was fairly sloppy. Not forensically, but the obvious staging and effort involved indicated that several people had been involved, and they both knew that when you had a crew of criminals, they were rarely loyal. It was just a matter of finding them. They were desperate to follow up on the white van lead spotted at George's house. It was the strongest suggestion of foul play and they needed to rule it in or out.

They sat in the staff café at Ravensword and spoke quietly. It had been a long morning, but HOLMES had been updated a total of seventeen times, and that was promising progress. Matt explained that a lot of their work in murder inquiries increasingly involved checking CCTV, and Kelly told him of her frustration at the lack of it in Cumbria. No one installed CCTV on country lanes. Matt said he'd have to come and check her operation out one day. Kelly changed the subject.

George's neighbour who'd spotted the van hadn't managed to get a number plate, and there were probably twenty thousand white vans cruising the streets of London, legitimately or otherwise. But they both knew it was only a matter of time. They'd already had a result from one of Alexandros's neighbours. Alexandros's flat had been abandoned just like his car, but this time possibly with good reason. The place had been turned over, and forensics were busy processing for fingerprints and clues as to who had been frantically and destructively searching it.

The neighbour reported that he'd actually had a chat to some workmen in a white van parked outside at around midday; the same time Alexandros was in the area but seemed to drive through. The neighbour had given some good descriptions but he hadn't taken the number plate either: law abiding citizens rarely did. Stratford boasted many CCTV cameras, being effectively an A road through a residential area, and they got a hit from some traffic lights close to Alexandros's address at 12.40 p.m., but it would have to be cross-referenced; they needed more sightings to follow the lead.

In all, between the hours of 11 a.m. and 1 p.m., seven white vans were recorded in the area. Four contained only a driver. Two contained a driver and a passenger, but one had three men squashed into the front. Usually the demeanour of workmen ticked one of three boxes: eating, hunched over the wheel looking tired and bored, or shouting and gesticulating at the driver in front. These three didn't fit in any of those categories. They looked sullen and uncommunicative. The number plate was put into the ANPR, and the van came up as unregistered. However, hit after hit came back from CCTV around London, and they were able to begin to map out possible routes for the trio.

Matt tapped instructions into his iPad to send the details to the PNC for every force to be on the lookout but not to approach the vehicle or the men.

'I'd forgotten how much of a whirlwind city investigations are,' Kelly said.

'What's it like up north?'

Kelly rolled her eyes; she'd let her guard down again.

'I'm serious, I want to know. You're famous down here. That trafficking case was mind-blowing.' Matt put his iPad down and sipped his coffee. He wouldn't let it go.

'It's beautiful for a start, and I wish I didn't have so much to investigate. There are obstacles – tiny single-lane roads where you can get stuck behind sheep, tortuous journeys through mountains – but local gossip is always handy. There are also a million places to hide, like the city, though instead of glass and concrete you have lakes and fells.'

She was aware that she'd become animated and was surprised by her own passion. It was curious how, now that she was away, she felt like she belonged in the Lakes. It was a moment of true comfort and she smiled to herself.

'What are you grinning at? You look ridiculously happy, Kelly, what's his name?'

'God, you men! I don't need a man, Matt.'

He sat back and feigned defence with his arms. 'Whoa, sorry. Still a touchy subject then, Boadicea?'

Kelly got up.

'Shit, Kelly, I'm sorry. I'm just trying to make conversation. I want us to get on.'

A few people looked over at them and Kelly realised that it wouldn't look good to make a scene. She sat down. She wasn't ready to tell Matt about Johnny. She felt it would be some kind of betrayal to let him into her private life, and anyway, it was none of his goddamn business.

'I'm happy there, Matt. Let's get back to work, please.'

Matt sighed. 'All right.'

'I have to say that if I was in Cumbria now, and we had sightings of a white van, I'd be out in a patrol car looking for it. I think it was Mike Harding, the comedian, who called one of the roads up there the longest cul-de-sac in Britain.'

'Good for trapping perps, then?'

'Exactly.'

They smiled at each other and carried on their assessment of what they had learned this morning.

'I was thinking about the men who were seen going into George's house, and who potentially ransacked Alexandros's flat,' Kelly said. 'What were they looking for? And what about Mike and Emily's houses?'

'Do you think it might be connected to the garage?' Matt asked.

'More importantly, are Emily and Mike's families safe?'

Matt tapped his phone and spoke to somebody to check. Family liaison teams were with both families and would remain with them for the foreseeable future.

'Find out if they had computers at home,' Kelly whispered. Matt nodded.

Routine searches of both properties had taken place, as was normal with murder victims, but not all the items had been thoroughly processed yet. Personal computers could provide a wealth of knowledge, and if somebody wanted to gain access to what was going on at the garage, they might not stop until all the loose ends were tied up.

'All good, apparently. The personal items, including family laptops, are being searched: nothing of interest has been found so far. If anyone's watching the houses, they'll know that our presence is round the clock, and we've got no evidence to suggest that they're in danger at the moment. The liaison teams are used to handling situations like this. So, what else? I haven't had any information coming through to link any of the neurocellular team to the colantropine scandal.'

'Any news on the Cypriot authorities speaking to Alexandros?'

'Nothing so far. I guess it's stuck in the Home Office. Come on, let's go and visit Philip Tooting's secretary and see when he's back from gallivanting around Bermuda.'

'Do you think it's odd that he hasn't flown back?'

'Odd? Yes. But you know what these corporate types are like. The thing that worries me is that George and the others kept the garage such a fierce secret, yet somebody else knew.'

'The other thing I've been thinking about is funding; it's not easy or cheap to build and run a private lab.'

Kelly's phone buzzed with a call from Kate Umshaw in Penrith.

'Kate. News?'

'How's the big smoke, guv?'

'Crowded.' Kelly glanced sideways at Matt. 'What have you got?'

'We've got George Murphy's VW Touran, abandoned in the Brandelhow car park.'

'Underneath Cat Bells?'

'Yup. And it's in perfect condition, almost sterile.'

'To be expected, I suppose.'

'But if someone was cleaning up, they missed something: a USB stick in an envelope, inside a toilet bag in the spare wheel housing. The car has been processed forensically: no prints, and the USB contents have been sent for examination. There's something else. I've got a list of phone calls made to and from Allerdale House the week George was there. Several came in from

Montague-Roland's number, but there was only one outgoing call. It was to a mobile registered to one Matilda Knight. She's a journalist.'

## Chapter 20

Back at her hotel, Kelly stretched her legs and undressed. They'd been at it for eleven hours, and she needed a shower and to curl up in lazy joggers and a sweater. Emma was still not back, and Kelly knew that the young DC would probably only sleep when someone actually ordered her to. She used to be like that herself. It was different as an SIO, though, more mentally demanding. All the graphs and indices and links she had flowing around her brain made her dizzy, and there was only so much information she could retain before she needed to recharge. Philip Tooting's secretary had been told that his presence would be helpful, and she'd finally got the message through to him. He wasn't pleased, apparently, but he also wasn't above the law. Not only had his neuro-cellular section been decimated; they were potentially running an illegal lab. The USB stick from George's car had been sent to a sterile lab environment in Carlisle to be examined in detail. Unfortunately, they couldn't just stick it into a computer and look for themselves, because whatever they found might not stand up in court unless certain procedures had been followed.

Kelly padded to the bathroom and turned on the shower. The water was hot and she stepped straight in. She couldn't still her mind, but washing her hair helped a little. The city was grimy and her skin felt deeply unclean. Even her nostrils had dirt in them.

After she'd finished, she wrapped herself in a thick towel and lay on the bed to call Johnny.

'Hey,' she said, grateful for the sound of his voice.

'Kelly? How's it going? When can you come home?' He got straight to the point, but it was just what she needed to hear. The close proximity to Matt in such an intense environment was challenging, and more than once she'd questioned her motives for coming.

'Soon, I hope. There's so much still to do, but I think there are a few developments up there as well that might bring me back. It's just good to get to know what I'm dealing with down here, face to face. What have you been up to?'

'I took Ted to Tarn Hows. The weather was spectacular. We cracked open a flask of tea and chewed over his younger days, when he first set eyes on your mum.'

'He can talk once he gets going.'

'I don't mind. It's good for both of us. We appreciate the same things.'

Kelly nodded, though Johnny couldn't see it. She knew what he meant, and in her small, clinical hotel room, she pictured the two of them sitting on a picnic rug drinking tea.

'When's the last time you saw Graeme?' she asked.

'Millar?'

'Hmm.'

'Our last session, probably, so you were there. Why?'

'It's just I think finding the murder victim shook him. Could you check on him? See if he's ok? Why don't you ask him out for a pint while I'm away?'

'Of course, I will. Is this as a friend or do you want me to pry?'

'Come on, Johnny, you're so good at it. It's not as if I'm asking you to spy on him.'

'All right. Anyway, are you naked?'

'I've just got out of the shower.'

'Oh Jesus. Don't tell me that.'

She lay back on the bed and smiled, closing her eyes. She sighed deeply and realised that the tension in her shoulder blades had returned, something that hadn't bothered her in ages. She tried rubbing it, but she couldn't reach. 'I need a massage.'

'You'd better come home, then. Have you finished for the day?'

'For the day, yes, but I'm going back in after I've had a floppy sandwich from the corner shop.'

'Nice. Can't you find something better in our capital city?'

'I'm not really hungry.'

'If you stay down there longer than three days, I'm coming to camp in your room. I don't think Premier Inn would notice an impostor. And they wouldn't challenge a cop; I could be vital to the investigation.'

'We'd get away with it, I'm sure.'

When they'd said goodnight and hung up, Kelly imagined Johnny meeting Matt, and wondered what they'd make of each other. They were so different. She pictured Matt staring at Johnny's flip-flops, but also at his broad shoulders and assured eyes, and she knew she was with the right man. She closed her eyes and her mind floated to what Johnny had said. His daughter, Josie, was more than capable of looking after herself, and he was due some time off from mountain rescue volunteering. It might not be such a bad idea, having him to come home to after a day in the office with a man who constantly seemed to be pushing her buttons. Every time they got a quiet moment, Matt tried to fill it with some reference to how cosy they'd once been, and how well he knew her. It irritated the fuck out of her, but he was right about the latter.

Her phone went off again. Matt. Ears burning, she thought.

'There've been no major developments, Kelly, though an artist has produced a good picture of one of the workmen who spoke to Alexandros's neighbour, and we've got a close-up of all three men from the front view of the van, which I've sent nationwide. I was calling to see if you wanted to meet me for a nightcap, just to throw a few ideas round; maybe grab a bite to eat?'

Kelly stared at her phone. It was an innocent enough request. They were colleagues, working the same case, facing the same headaches – not to mention growing hunger – and she didn't want any animosity to disrupt that. It had been easier than she'd thought, seeing him again; how could a few pints hurt?

'Sure. The Premier Inn isn't exactly fine dining, and I think their vending machine is out of egg mayo.'

'Which one are you at?'

He could have accessed the information himself; after all, his force were paying for it.

'Just under the North Circular at Brent Cross.'

'I know it. I can be there in twenty minutes.'

'Christ, give me a chance. Thirty?'

They hung up and Kelly looked in the mirror. She couldn't be bothered drying her hair. The sun was shining through her curtains and it looked like a warm city evening. She slipped on a pair of jeans and a thin-knit V-neck, then slid her feet into some pumps and grabbed a jacket, just in case. At the last minute she applied a little make-up, simply because of her age – or at least that was what she told herself.

He was waiting for her downstairs. He was wearing the same shirt and trousers as earlier, and looked like a knackered copper after a fuck of a day.

'You haven't been home?'

'Nah. I should have a bed in the office really. We've got this army cot thing, and I have been known to bed down for the night. Don't worry, there's a shower room and I've got a locker.'

'So, where is home now?' She had no idea why she asked. She supposed it was her turn to make polite conversation.

'About ten minutes that way this time of night, and an hour in the morning.' He nodded towards Hampstead Heath.

'Nice.'

'It's about as nice as I could afford.'

'I don't know; with London weighting, you can't be struggling.' She nodded to the iPad under his arm. 'Do you ever turn that off?'

He shook his head, and Kelly knew they were bedfellows of habit: she never turned hers off either.

'Come on, there's a great Japanese place along here.' He pointed down the main road, which to Kelly looked like every other road in the capital, the skyline dominated by high-rises and office blocks. She couldn't remember feeling this claustrophobic when she'd worked here.

Matt slipped his iPad inside a smart black mini briefcase with a shoulder strap, and they began to walk, passing high-end restaurants, dive snooker halls, deserted parks, gleaming Bentleys, and people asleep under cardboard in doorways, all cohabiting in disharmonious harmony.

The restaurant looked busy and the buzz flowed out onto the street when he held the door open for her. The music was a chilled mix, more appropriate to a beach hut, but super-relaxing. They were shown to a booth and handed menus. Kelly had clocked the sushi as she walked in and it stimulated her taste buds. A few beers and some sweet-savoury fish, along with delicate salads and noodles, was a treat indeed. There was a new sushi place in Keswick, but she and Johnny hadn't tried it yet. She felt a pang of guilt, but she was dining out with a work colleague, that was all.

'It sounds like you've got a solid team up there, Kelly.'

'I have. We're tight. I don't know how you remember everybody's names in that place.' It was true: the number of daily assigned officers was phenomenal, and then there were the regulars who worked shifts. 'There are only five of us, and I like it.'

'You seemed to cope all right when you were here. Has your memory slipped?'

She glared at him.

'So, what sort of things have you investigated since the trafficking case?'

'A few punchy cases. We tick along.' She wasn't about to be pulled into a cock-off. She studied the menu.

'I heard about your mother. I'm sorry.'

Kelly looked down at her hands, at the ruby ring Johnny had given her, and was taken back to her last Christmas with Wendy.

'Hello.' Matt waved across her face. 'Earth to Kelly. I'm trying to get in and maybe clear up a few things, but you're as cold as a dead body, Kell.'

'Don't call me Kell. I thought we were sharing a meal and throwing ideas around?'

He spread his hands. 'I just want to get to know you again after what happened, that's all. Come on. Open up a bit, you're so serious.'

She smiled coldly and put her menu down.

'I'm going to say this only once. You're a twat and you sold me down the river to get promotion. The Coryn Boulder case was not my fault; you knew what I knew. I've moved on and I think you should too. There's no way in. I'm not that person I was three years ago, and neither should you be.'

'We almost got married.'

'Thank God we didn't!'

'You're so sexy when you're mad.'

'You're lucky that I'm hungry or I'd walk out right now. And I need a beer.' She raised the menu to cover her face and stared at the pictures of the prawn, salmon and avocado uramaki.

## Chapter 21

Philip Tooting was catching up on the goings-on in the business world since he'd been away. He reclined comfortably in the back of the Mercedes S-Class saloon. It would drop him off at his favourite London club, where he'd checked in for one night only. His wife had no idea he was back in town.

The sun glowed orange on the great whitish-grey Portland stone facades so typical of the area. Colossal chunks of the stuff had been dragged from Dorset to construct most of Regency London. The car left the bustle of tourists outside the BAFTA and the Royal Academy and entered the quieter, more understated class of Mayfair. Tucked behind the exclusive clubs and fancy restaurants of Piccadilly, Berkeley Square was a haven of elegance, where even the air seemed fresher away from the rush and intensity of ordinary people pursuing regular business. Nothing about the square was common. The central garden was the largest of its kind in London, and Georgian architecture still dominated the quadrangle.

The Montague Club occupied one corner of the prestigious W1 footprint, rising up five storeys, with a further two beneath street level. In the eighteenth century, it had been the family home of one of the wealthiest families of the era. It was a typical Georgian town house: a geometric arrangement of large sash windows in rows of threes, with each side reflecting the other in perfect symmetry. Decorative pediments completed the doll's-house charm. The club had undergone renovation over the past couple of years, and its membership – by invitation only – had been refreshed with a younger, hipper generation made up of fashion designers and pop stars. But the old guard remained, still frequenting the Regency-style saloon (ladies were asked politely to socialise elsewhere, in any one of the rooms more appropriately designed for their delicate sex), leaving the younger ones to inhabit the bohemian rooftop bar, or the soundproof glass room in the basement, which served Michelin-star canapés and belted out cool jazz.

The immense black wooden door was guarded by two innocuous porters in subtle attire, who were in the know about every single one of the club's current members and their guests. Philip adjusted his tie and brushed fluff from his dinner jacket before folding the newspaper away. There was no rush to get into work tomorrow, despite the police breathing down his neck about two lab technicians who'd been caught with their bloody pants down. Then there was George. Philip had liked the man. It was a tragedy. A burglary gone wrong, they were saying. He was a damn good scientist too and would be sorely missed by the company. But what the police thought Philip could do about any of it was a mystery. He was in no position to shed light on their inquiries. They were just being awkward, which was their job, he supposed. Well, they could wait.

The car slowed and pulled up outside the club, and the driver got out and walked around to open Philip's door.

He thanked him and they confirmed his pick-up time for tomorrow.

One of the porters acknowledged him with a nod and opened the door of the club for him. As he stepped inside, it was like coming home. There was nowhere on earth quite like it. No one else could match the understated English hospitality, learned over centuries of history and decorum. Dubai had the money, but no antiquity. America had the space, but no finesse. Paris had the quality, but no manners. Asia had the precision, but no charm.

This was perfect.

Bermuda was a regular bolthole, the ideal place to let off steam and get some serious work done without the nagging irritations of his office. The house belonged to a friend, of course, but he was at liberty to use it any time. His first-class airline tickets were also the product of a long-standing bond between old buddies here at the club. Philip's basic salary was a modest million, before benefits, of course, but there were members here whose money couldn't be counted. And it was never discussed. Friends helped one another, that was all. And that was why he was here.

The members of the Cambridge rowing alumni association ranged in age from twenty-nine to eighty-two, and they met once a year to do what boys did best: smoke cigars, catch up, and perhaps gain a few more contacts. Of course, there were fabulous female rowers too, but this club was exclusively male, and mostly white.

Straight away he spotted a few old chums walking up the grand staircase to their private room, and they shook hands and exchanged pleasantries, chatting about wives, children, jobs and the weather. The serious stuff would come later, over port and cheese. Handshakes and booming exclamations rattled through the marble halls, and the portraits of ancient members stared down at them, listening in, still attendant to the festivity. Apparently Churchill used to play here as a little boy, when he lived across the square, and his impressive likeness cast its eye over them with gloriously rotund approval.

Philip carried very little with him; he was in what the military members called 'fighting order': a credit card, his yellow original Café Crèmes, a lighter and his room key. The men were distinguishable only by the colour of their hair or the thinness on top; otherwise, they formed a steady stream of dinner-jacketed gentlemen with highly polished shoes, hands in pockets and healthy belly laughs, snaking towards the dining room that awaited them. There would be speeches, and acknowledgements of members no longer with them but not forgotten. The older portion would trail off around midnight, with a few diehards propping up the private bar until the early hours, brandy in hand, money and politics in mind. Most of the attendees lived in or around London, employed either by banks or government offices, but a sizeable number travelled there for the weekend, enjoying the club's hospitality and catching up with old friends.

The dining room glowed softly, lamplight warming the claret walls and bouncing off silver and crystal. It was a good turnout, with over a hundred expected, and the bar was busy and loud. Philip lost the men he'd walked in with and greeted other alumni on his way to the bar. Around twenty of those attending tonight were Montague Club members like himself, including the man who approached him from the other side of the room.

'Philip. How the hell are you?' It was a familiar voice, and one he'd been hoping to hear tonight. Christopher Slater was a rarity: an ex-CEO who people actually liked. Sometimes he was mistaken for a civil servant, something that encouraged his wrath. In his eyes, there was nothing worse. He was a non-executive adviser for DEFRA, he told people, *not* a civil servant. Philip had learned this early on in their friendship.

'Christopher, how good to see you. I trust the old girl is in good spirits.' Philip always referred to the Permanent Under-Secretary for DEFRA in the same way. It was irreverent and rude, and that was the point. Philip went back a long way with Robyn Hastings and disliked her intensely. She was one of the breed of female senior civil servants, like Dame Charlotte Cross from the Department of Health, who strutted about the halls once dominated by men, decrying the sins of their male counterparts while at the same time sticking fingers into as many illicit pies as possible. It was the ultimate ruse: the new wave of female power politicians could be trusted like none other, couldn't they?

'Chugging along like a vintage locomotive, all piss and wind.'

Both men chuckled.

'Drink?' Christopher asked.

'Absolutely. I'll have a pint. I managed to get a room here tonight, so I have a free pass from Lady Tooting.'

Christopher raised his eyebrows in knowing approval. 'She doesn't know you're here.'

Philip only had time for two pints before the bell rang for guests to take their seats for dinner. As always, he was sitting with Christopher, and they made their way to their usual table. The Colonel was already there, sporting a red nose, glass of claret in hand, and telling his neighbour a long but no doubt very entertaining anecdote. Sure enough, the man laughed out loud at the punchline and the Colonel was able to turn to greet his old friends. Journeys, accommodation and the weather were discussed. The latter was an apt talking point because London was heating up to record levels for June, and they were all thankful for the air conditioning.

The clamour of voices from the bar stilled to a steady chatter as men took their seats and shook more hands, recognising faces from adjacent tables. Menus were perused; the Montague Club never let them down. The head chef knew that tonight's gathering required meat in all its guises, and plenty of it, alongside gutsy sides and artery-clogging desserts. The bar staff were also aware that this was one of the busiest events of the year (excepting the military officers' reunions), and they stood ready to pour wine and take bar orders.

There was only one late arrival to their table, excepting the late smokers, and he was a singularly distinguished addition to the dinner; his family had owned this chunk of Berkeley Square for centuries. He was stopped several times on his way to the table, to shake outstretched hands and exchange pleasantries. Philip watched him lavish attention on certain guests and remembered what his grandfather had said about him. Alan Montague-Roland had declared that no poof would ever get their hands on his fortune, and the young man had been forced to promise that he was cured of his evil lust. Even then, the empire had been put in trust. Philip himself didn't much care which side a man batted for; he just wanted a job done and done well.

The noise died down as the diners looked forward to their first course. Wine was poured and several tables asked for more bottles before the food had even appeared. The last-minute smokers entered the room and took their seats. As part of the refurbishment, every reception room had been furnished with an adjoining sheltered area – in this case a balcony – where guests and members could smoke, happily oblivious of the ban. The aim was to make the spaces like extensions of the building itself. Awnings, heaters and planted walls all helped to keep the smokers happy.

The new arrival finally reached their table and greeted Philip, Christopher and the Colonel with enthusiasm. 'That will be my chair then,' he laughed. He took his seat happily, fussed over by a waiter, who poured his wine. He made a point of thanking the man, slipping something into his pocket.

'Good to see you made it, Sebastian,' said Philip.

# Chapter 22

Tilly tried to act composed as she got up off the ground. It was only her second day in the area, and she'd wandered down to the marina where the body of George Murphy had been found. But so far she'd only managed to trip over a buoy rope and land on a canoe. The man coming towards her to help had his wetsuit rolled down to his waist, exposing his chest, and she couldn't help but admire his taut and chiselled torso. Her eyes went to his face, which was kind and handsome, in an outdoor, worn sort of way. He was much older than she was, but the hardness of his body and the way his wet hair fell about his face caused such a flutter inside her that she blushed. She felt like a fawning teenager.

'Are you all right?' He held out his hand to help her and she took it. His skin was warm.

'I think I'll live, though the embarrassment might kill me.'

'You on holiday? That's not a local accent.' He let go of her hand once she was on her feet and put his hands on his hips. His voice was soft and the accent not too thick. He looked at her with confident assurance and it made her feel that she'd like to spend time with him. Her eyes wandered to his chest again.

'Yes. I've just come up for a couple of days from London.'

'No one comes from London for a couple of days! Stay longer. It's going to be perfect this weekend.'

'It is beautiful. I've just been walking round the lake.' She was lying; this was her first stop.

'You rise early. Do you sail?'

'No! God, I wouldn't have the first clue.'

'So are you lost? This is a boatyard.' He laughed, and she watched him.

'I thought I might start small and rent a kayak or something. That's easy, isn't it? I got your details from the Keswick Launch.'

He glanced over his shoulder, then back to her. 'The paddle boards are more fun if you don't mind getting wet.'

'Can you show me?'

'They do instruction in the shop, but we're not busy yet, so why not? Come on, let's get you into a wetsuit. Have you got a costume under there?' He eyed her clothes. She returned his glance with a puzzled look and he smiled again. 'No lakes in London, eh?'

He walked towards the shop and went into a shed to the side of the entrance, speaking over his shoulder.

'You came at the right time; it's going to get busy later.'

She really wanted to find out where *The Lady of the Lake* was kept, but this was a good start. She followed him inside.

'What's your name?' he asked.

'Tilly, pleased to meet you, I think. Do you work here?'

'I own the business. I'm Graeme, pleased to meet you too.' He smiled and took her hand again. This would do very nicely, she thought. It was a local boat owner who'd found the body, according to the woman at the ice cream parlour. This guy must know all the boat owners around here.

'I think this will fit; you're slim and in good shape. You should be fine. You can change in there.' He pointed to a curtained changing room.

'What do I wear underneath?'

'I'll go and get you a costume, on the house. I won't tell if you don't.'

He returned with a Speedo swimsuit and she changed behind the curtain. She saw him admiring her when she re-emerged. This afternoon's research might turn out to be a real perk of the job.

As they made their way to the water, people said hello to Graeme, and Tilly worked out that he was a popular fixture here. He brought a buoyancy aid and put it on her, fastening it tight. He had to lean around her and put his arms round her waist. He smelled clean. He didn't wear one himself and she guessed he'd been on the water all his life. After that, he went to collect two paddle boards from a rack, carrying both of them with ease, and put them into the water next to where she was standing.

'Graeme!' They looked round. Graeme waved. A teenager ran towards him and gabbled something about one of the wood sheds. Graeme gave him instructions and told him he was taking a student out for an hour or so. The kid ran off and Graeme returned his attention to his new pupil. He gave her a step-by-step account of what they were going to do, then waded into the water, which was flat and peaceful. Tilly reckoned it couldn't be that hard to master.

'It's easier to kneel at first, and then, when we get past the river mouth over there, we'll try and stand, OK?'

'Right!'

They waded out as far as Tilly's waist and he helped her onto the board. She knelt up carefully, and after a few minutes of feeling wobbly and out of control managed to take her first strokes. It involved a lot of hands-on instruction from Graeme, but his touch quickly felt normal.

'Brilliant! Keep that up and follow me.' He got onto his own board and paddled briskly towards lots of little boats moored up on the water. Tilly found her rhythm and tried to concentrate without staring too much at the scenery, which was breath-taking. On one side a serenely sloping mountainside bore down upon them; ahead, probably five miles away, a disappearing valley sat under cloud, and to the other side was a great untouched forest. She couldn't quite remember seeing anything so perfect: the weather, the water, and the peace and tranquillity.

Graeme paddled towards her.

'Do you want to try and stand?'

'Of course!'

He held her board and told her to be bold and do it one leg at a time, steadying herself in between. She accomplished it the first time and watched as Graeme effortlessly stood up too. He showed her how to go forward and turn, and she was able to negotiate her board around the moored boats and closer to the middle of the lake. He took her around a tiny island, where she thought they might stop, but he continued paddling towards a beach.

As they drew closer, it was quite obvious that the beach was private: there were signs erected, and the shingle was deserted, but Graeme carried on confidently towards it. Tilly's curiosity made her follow.

'What's this?'

'It's private land, but it's also my new job. Come on, I'll show you. You're a natural at this! You shouldn't live in a city.'

Graeme got off his board and showed her that he was waist deep, so Tilly did the same. They pulled their boards to the beach and dragged them ashore. She was surprisingly breathless from the exertion and she made a mental note to try to get back in shape.

'What is it? Your new job?' she asked.

'This is the largest surviving private estate on Derwent Water, and I've been put in charge of the refurbishment. It's going to be an amazing project: a huge leisure complex for high-end visitors.'

'Who owns it?'

'Some rich family from London, of course. The Montague-Rolands. My guess is they won't spend too much time here, though; it's purely a business venture.'

Butterflies tickled her tummy as she realised where she was. She also noticed the police tape.

'What's that here for?'

'Ah, we had a nasty incident here at the weekend, but don't let it put you off, it's totally out of character for the area.'

'I did hear something about a man dying in a boat?'

'That's where he was found. Apparently this is where he actually died.' He pointed up at the house.

'I heard he was murdered.'

'Yeah, he was. I found him.'

Tilly stared at him. 'Really? Oh my God! That's awful!' The joy in her voice emanated from the pure stroke of luck; luckily, it also made her horror seem more genuine.

'I've had better days.' He turned his back on her and Tilly realised she would have to tread carefully. This was where George had stayed; where he'd called her from. She hadn't read anywhere that he'd been killed in this house, and she wondered how Graeme knew so much.

'I'm sorry, I don't know what to say. Do you want to talk about it? You seem to know a lot about what happened. I'm guessing this sort of thing is very rare here. In London it's a different story.'

'Sure. I didn't know the guy. I found him in one of our beautiful refurbished launches; he was slumped over with a massive hole in his skull. But he was staying here – old family friend apparently. People talk, and I also know the detective in charge.'

Tilly shivered. A faint, disturbing thought passed over her head like a shadow: she was on a deserted beach with a guy she didn't know, right next to a crime scene, and she had no idea why she'd been so stupid. Then Graeme smiled at her and she knew exactly what had led to her poor judgement. But it didn't change the fact that what she'd thought might be a bit of fun had turned out to be intense and potentially dangerous.

'Is it public knowledge how he died?' She needed to keep him distracted.

'No, I don't think so. I shouldn't really be telling you, I guess, but the guy is dead after all. You're right, this sort of thing just doesn't happen round here. It was a burglary and they panicked. That boatshed was completely emptied of antiques and kit totalling half a million quid.'

'Bloody hell.'

'I know,' he said, misunderstanding her.

'No, the house.' He followed her gaze and nodded realisation.

'That's what most people say. The owner wants guests to arrive from the water for exactly this type of effect; you've just tested it out for me.'

Tilly gawped at the grandeur and majesty of the house. It was hidden perfectly, and only when you'd begun to walk away from the beach was a full view possible.

'We'll build a car park at Portinscale, or the marina, and ferry guests across privately.'

Graeme climbed some wooden steps and Tilly followed him, her worries forgotten.

'The owner has returned to London; would you like to see inside?'

'I'm soaking wet!'

'There's a cloakroom next to the kitchen, and anyway, downstairs is all slate and wood flooring. I'll make us a hot drink.'

The cold water, fresh from the fells, had lowered Tilly's temperature considerably, and she shivered.

'Come on, you're getting cold.' Graeme took her arm and led her up the steps and around the back of the stunning property. He opened a door and stood back to let her in.

Tilly frowned. 'Why isn't the place locked up?'

He laughed. 'We don't lock doors as a rule here. Of course, we will when it's up and running.'

'Do you think he disturbed them then? The burglars?'

'Yep. That's exactly what I think. Poor bloke.'

'Why did they go to the trouble of moving him to the boatyard if he was dead?'

'I suppose they could have panicked and tried to throw the police off the trail. He was completely naked; I guess that takes away a lot of the evidence, doesn't it?'

'Have you been offered counselling?'

'I don't need any of that!'

'What about what you saw?'

'I'm used to it. I was in the army, I know a gunshot wound when I see one.'

'It was a gunshot wound?' Tilly tried to contain her excitement.

'Yeah, I know. Bloody place is turning into the OK Corral.' He closed the door behind them and showed her into a large room with towels, slippers and ponchos freely available.

'This will all be smartened up. Guests will be able to grab some walking kit or wet-weather kit and go off for a morning hike, coming back to hot chocolate or a cheeky whisky.'

'Are you a designer?' Tilly asked.

'No, but I know all the tradespeople round here. Someone from London could get ripped off if he talks to the wrong people.'

'It's a massive project.'

Once Tilly had dried her hair and wrapped herself in a robe, Graeme took her to a large kitchen and put an old iron kettle on the Aga. He opened a few cupboards and found two mugs.

'Tea?'

Tilly nodded. Their damp neoprene pumps made prints on the stone floor.

It was a welcome comfort to sip the steaming liquid. Graeme took her into the hallway and she gazed around her in wonder. It was extraordinary; she felt as though she was inside a museum.

'Wow,' was all she could say.

'I know, it's pretty impressive, isn't it? Come and look at the view out here.'

She followed him and stared out of the largest single pane of glass she thought she'd ever seen. Derwent Water stretched out in front of them, and beyond the treeline there were mountains and woodland. The image made her feel at peace. George must have loved it here. She lowered her gaze and felt an overwhelming sense of tragedy, but also niggling unease. A gunshot wound. Burglars who carried guns were not usually after a load of sailing kit.

'If the doors are all left unlocked, why wasn't the house burgled? There's stuff in here worth millions: look at that painting, it's a Cézanne and I bet it's an original.'

'Who?'

'French post-impressionist.'

'I'll take your word for it. You're not just a pretty face, are you?'

'Do you think he was alone up here? The victim, I mean.'

'I saw a few workmen in the garden.'

'What? Did you tell the police?'

'No, I—'

'Why? They could have been the burglars!'

Graeme ran his hands through his hair. 'You're right. I'd forgotten all about it. I'd just found the body and this place wasn't even mentioned.'

'Because they moved him; that was the whole idea, wasn't it?'

'You're right. Between you and me, the officer assigned the case knows her stuff. I teach her how to sail. She's amazing, and she'll get whoever did it and find out why.'

'I'm sure she will. What's her name?'

# Chapter 23

Kelly had left a note under Emma's door last night, telling her she'd popped out to meet a friend. It was true. Kind of. But now she felt guilty. It was an anxiety that crept up beneath her ribs and made her feel unsure of herself. All she needed was a strong coffee and a croissant and she'd be all right, she thought.

Memories of the previous evening flooded back and she stopped to wince several times on her way around the room, gathering clothes and finding what she needed for today. She remembered coming back to the hotel, but the timing was hazy. She'd known it was late, and that Matt thought himself in with a chance of getting her into bed, but she'd still had the wherewithal to make it distinctly clear that that wasn't on the cards. Not last night. Not ever.

She tutted loudly and shook her head, hoping in vain to clear it. What had started as a drink between colleagues had ended with Matt being rejected, and from past experience, he didn't take that well. She wondered how it might change the mood in the office and tutted again: she'd been stupid to accept dinner in the first place. It made her miss Johnny even more.

The last thing she needed was a hangover; long days in the massive office block in Hendon were bad enough without feeling lacklustre and sapped of energy before she even got there. She searched her bag and found paracetamol and ibuprofen and downed two of each with water. A shower would wake her up, she told herself.

By the time she'd finished and dressed, slapping on more make-up than usual, she felt semi-human. She'd said she'd knock for Emma, but her junior was already standing outside in the corridor waiting for her.

'Morning, Emma! Did you enjoy yesterday?'

'Guv, it was amazing!'

'Good, that's why I chose you. Where did you go?'

Emma recounted the details of her investigation the previous day, enthusing about the technology and her temporary colleagues. She reminded Kelly of herself twenty years ago.

They walked to the lift and Emma pressed the button. Kelly felt nauseous. All she had to do was get through the day and drink plenty of water, then she could fall into bed later and sleep the sleep of the dead. Unless something kept them working into the night.

'Why did you leave London, guv?' Emma blushed. 'Sorry, I shouldn't have asked, it's none of my business.'

People talked, Kelly knew, and rumours flew around; probably about some poor decision-making. She looked at Emma and smiled as the lift doors opened.

'Not at all.' They strode out of the main entrance and towards the waiting car that Kelly had forgotten to cancel so they could walk. They'd follow the same pattern as yesterday and stop at the Starbucks to grab some sustenance. 'It's intense. I learned a lot, and it was time for a change. I missed home.'

'How long did you work down here?'

'Ten years.'

'Wow.'

They joined the long breakfast queue in Starbucks. Kelly picked up three packs of egg sandwiches.

'I used to work with DCI Carter,' she said.

'Without speaking out of turn, guv, I think I prefer working for you.'

'I appreciate your honesty. He's good, but everybody has their own style. I'm a bit more casual. Today, listen to how officers communicate, and think about what we do at home. The bedrock of any investigation is people talking. I'd rather be in a noisy office than a quiet one.'

'Yes, guv.'

Kelly's stomach tightened as she thought ahead to seeing Matt again. She wished she'd spent her evening with a takeaway and a bottle of wine, watching crap TV. It would certainly have made things easier this morning. The alcohol from last night mingled with her anxiety and teased her consciousness into a sense of doom: a classic hangover. She'd made a great start to the visit, and had Matt firmly under control, but she'd been weak and he knew it; now he'd be sniffing around even more, and she could do without the added pressure.

The coffee hit her bloodstream and she felt instantly stimulated and less tired. They got back into the car and she opened one of the sandwiches and devoured the calories. If Emma thought her choice of break-fast unusual, she didn't show it. When she'd stopped chomping, she screwed up the rubbish, wiped her mouth and flipped open her iPad, scanning the investigative notes and opening emails.

When they arrived, Matt was already in the incident room and greeted his visitors warmly. He acted professional and busy, and to Kelly's relief showed no indication of being frustrated or embarrassed by her rejection last night. People filed into the room, and she took a seat and listened to the game plan for the day. The investigation was becoming complex and everyone knew this was standard. Cases usually began like a spider's web: small and contained, eventually spiralling out to different points, all needing hard work, eventually spanning a whole empire.

Matt barked out a whirlwind of instructions, and dozens of people took notes and input information on laptops. The entire floor was run with precision, and Kelly felt dizzy already, and desperate to reach for her second sandwich. Her style at home was more relaxed and deliberate. Matt, by contrast, was a man possessed, and he sniffed a few good leads from yesterday and gave out jobs as if his life depended on it. He was far removed from the man who'd eaten sushi with her last night. She pushed the thought away.

The office cleared, and they were left alone again. Kelly opened her can of Coke and guzzled it.

'Hangover?'

'Yup. I never learn.'

'Have you had an egg sandwich yet?'

'This is my second,' she said, taking another out of her bag and opening it.

'Not in here! God, that stinks!'

'Oh stop whining. It's only eggs.' She chewed and closed her eyes. Her headache was fading. She'd read somewhere years ago that the best thing for a hangover was eggs, and she'd stuck by it ever since. Matt's memory of the fact only served to threaten intimacy once more, so she changed the subject.

'Plan for today? Is it really necessary for the two of us to spend so much time together? Alone?'

'Technically you're my deputy SIO, and we're on the same investigation, so long periods of time spent assessing progress is professionally necessary. We need to cooperate.'

He'd perched on the edge of a desk. Kelly could tell that he enjoyed getting under her skin, and she toyed with going home early. She'd learned so much already about George Murphy, about Ravensword and his colleagues. She could liaise with Matt over the net, hourly if need be. His constant angling was becoming tiresome, and she knew he wouldn't give up.

'I thought I'd go back to Ravensword today and see if I can get to see Philip Tooting. His secretary kindly let me know that he's due in around midday,' he said.

Work mode awarded her relief. 'What are you going to ask him?'

'I want to gauge the man. I'll be looking for signs of infighting between the departments, and I want to know if his affair with Professor Cooper is ethical.'

'I think the white van lead is more important,' she said.

'It's *as* important. We'll do both. I need you. You saw what happened yesterday; it's better if we're together. We get twice the number of decisions pushed out, in real time, to officers on the ground.'

'Bullshit,' Kelly said under her breath. Matt grinned. 'Matt, you've been SIO on how many cases? Fifty? How many times did you share that role with a junior rank? I'm guessing never. Why now? Last night—'

'We covered a lot of ground.'

'I'm not here to rekindle our relationship; it's not going to happen.'

'Don't you remember how much of a flirt you were last night?'

'What?'

'I don't want to rekindle anything, Kell. You're safe. I just thought, after your friendly advances yesterday, that a congenial, for-old-times'-sake shag might be up for grabs. Obviously I was wrong. It won't happen again.'

'Do you really have to talk like that? Look, I can't work with you if you keep smudging the edges. I'll be better off going home and letting you take over fully. I can just liaise and carry on the investigation into George's death.'

'No, you can't!' There was panic in his voice. 'I'm sorry. I'm toying with you, I admit that. I don't want you to go. You're just as capable as you always were and the buzz I get working with you is making me feel alive. Come with me to Ravensword. We can interview the CEO and the Primate Professor together. Let the troops investigate the white van; our business is analysis, not nuts and bolts.'

'Only if you promise to stop playing games. Otherwise I really am going home.'

'All right, you have a deal.'

'Done. Did all that come in overnight?' Kelly nodded to the screen behind Matt, which was constantly updating itself with names, addresses, sightings, statements, number plates and photo composites.

Matt nodded. 'I thought you might have read it this morning before work. That's what I usually do.'

'Absolutely, me too. But I… Well, to be honest, I needed caffeine. I caught up on emails on the way here.'

'Come on, let's go.'

They talked about the case as they walked to the car.

'Nothing from the journalist?' she asked.

'We have an address, and officers are visiting there today. We've got a previous employment record, but she's freelance now. There's been no answer on her mobile phone so far. The response from the artist's impression of white van man has been incredible. It was on the evening news last night. These things usually get lost amongst all the other public appeals and can have low productivity, but this one has given us loads to go on.'

'Do you have endless resources?'

'No, believe it or not, I get officers burning out every week because they can't keep their eyes open. I've got two men working the artist's impression. I wish I could call every single lead back myself, but I can only work with what I've got. It might look smooth, but it certainly isn't. I reckon from what you've told me that up there in the sticks you have every advantage: good old-fashioned police work in a limited geographical area, thinly populated, with a loyal, dedicated small team.'

'Bloody hell, can you please stop calling it "up there in the sticks"?'

'What do I call it then?'

'The Lake District. You should see it. It's stunning.' As the words slid out of her mouth, she regretted them.

'Maybe I will one day.'

# Chapter 24

Philip Tooting welcomed his esteemed lunch guest. The times she'd visited the club, she always used the back entrance. It was common for members and their guests to be discreet. The tabloids had photographers everywhere, and not only that, every person with an iPhone thought it their God-given right to poke it in people's faces and press 'play'.

Dame Charlotte was a hefty woman, as the most senior female civil servants were wont to be. His theory was that to get to the top of the slippery pole as a woman, you had to be either a lesbian, infertile or both. Either way, femininity had to be absent, and that included giving birth, cooking and taking care of one's figure. Robyn Hastings was the same: lovely shoes and handbags, but bulging arse and wobbly neck.

Charlotte had been awarded her damehood for services to charitable organisations abroad, when she'd been a thrusting young dynamo in the Foreign Office back in the day. She'd chased FCO postings from China to Peru, and made her mark as a person to back. She'd never married.

'It's always a pleasure, Philip. I hope the marvellous chef here has worked his magic once again.'

He went to pour her wine. She put her hand over the top of the glass.

'Never mix business with pleasure, Philip.'

He poured himself a large glass of expensive red. She watched him sip it, and he was reminded of a programme he'd watched with his son years ago, about two pythons squaring up to one another over a rat in the desert.

'It's not all business, is it, Charlotte?'

She threw him a wry smile and perused the menu. They were in a private room, as always, and the lighting was low, with gentle classics playing through the hidden speakers in the ceiling.

They'd met six years ago, introduced by the late Lord Allerdale, who'd brought Charlotte as his guest to a dinner here at the club. Philip had been Sebastian's guest. He'd known from the offset that old Allerdale didn't like him; probably something to do with his line of work. The old man was a philanthropist, and he saw big pharmaceuticals as parasites, feeding off the poor and afflicted. Charlotte was more of a pragmatist, and they'd got talking about the terrible plight of street kids in India. She was still in the Foreign Office at the time, and in a unique position, as ambassador to the UN in New York, to raise awareness and beg the pharmaceuticals to develop and donate drugs to vaccinate children. There was no money in it, of course, but, politically it was worth a stab, and Philip promised to look into it. His board of directors dismissed it outright in the end – they were tied up in a huge investment at the time – but he sought out the ear of the civil servant from then on when he needed to, and they'd formed a bond of sorts.

Tonight, they were here to discuss the progress of a project that was still in its infancy.

'I liked Lord Allerdale,' Charlotte said.

Tooting laughed.

'No, I really did. He always gave me a good scrap. One night we argued about the Tories until the small hours over a bottle of 1800 tequila.'

'I never had you down as a tequila girl.'

'The colour of gold, that stuff, and smoother than cognac, trust me. No headache the next day either. He sank bottles of it.'

'It's amazing that he lasted so long.'

'Indeed.'

'I'll never get my head around philanthropy. I mean, it's all right caring for the poor, but handing them a way out on a plate, as if they somehow deserve a free ticket when the rest of us have to fend for ourselves, is a puzzle to me.'

'Now wait a moment, Philip, that's my livelihood you're talking about.'

'I know, Charlotte, and I love it when you get cross.'

'I suppose I do live up to my name. I believe in what I do, though, unlike you snakes over there at Ravensword, who market the cheapest product for the highest profit margins.'

'Oh, I'm truly offended! We Pharmas get a bad press. Our business is to save lives.'

'Only if it makes a profit.'

'Malaria?'

'You're forced to do that because it looks good and you can sell on the back of your good deeds; it's a win-win.'

'Shall we order?' Philip asked. Charlotte smiled and nodded.

'I was chatting to my opposite number in Afghanistan yesterday,' she said when the waiter had gone.

'How's it all going? Department of Health still in Kabul?'

'Just about. A car bomb exploded outside three weeks ago, killing thirty-five people, two of those were government officials, but it wasn't reported here, of course.'

'And you think a shift in economic dominance would tip the balance of power?'

'Of course. Look at 2002, when the Taliban was almost decimated, farming destroyed, ISIS not even a table of men in a dark room, and Afghanistan on its knees begging for help. Fast-forward fifteen years, and the thriving opium yield, together with a desperate and hungry population, means we can't get a lever in any more. It's pure mathematics.'

'Can you bring maths into government?'

'The only maths you care about.'

'Money?' He smiled and raised his glass.

'Quite. I'll have a glass of that wine now, please.'

'I think I'll order another bottle. Before you get plastered, Under-Secretary, I have a few printouts for you. Things have moved faster than we thought, and I've got some projections of cost.'

'We've already discussed that, Philip. My role here isn't – and never will be – about funding. There's no way I could possibly get away with it and you damn well know that. I'm your legitimacy.'

'Well, that's where we have a problem, Charlotte. Because George was our fund-raiser. And Alan was more generous than his grandson.'

'Sebastian? He could fund a small failing African nation!'

'I'm not sure he can. You see, the inheritance is tied up in some trust: his lawyers have been fighting on his behalf for months.'

'Wait a minute. Are you expecting *me* to find the money?' She pushed back her chair and glared at him. 'Who do you think you're talking to? A few fancy meals are not going to buy me, Philip.'

'Well that's the thing, Charlotte. I have it on good authority that your Damehood was… shall we say not entirely merited.'

'I beg your…' She stood up.

'I'd sit down if I were you. Your food's about to arrive. My source tells me that you – amongst others – were on the take from a certain children's charity based out of Nairobi at the time.'

'Slater,' she hissed.

'Oh don't go throwing mud, Charlotte. Let's just say that what I have in my possession could be as big as Haiti.'

'You bastard. I absolutely never—'

'Yes you did.' He stared at her, and her face twitched. 'Now, about the gap in funding for the project…'

# Chapter 25

Johnny was showering after a particularly gruelling hike up to Broad Stand, between Scafell Pike and Scafell, just after dawn. It didn't matter how many warnings they put out about the sheer rock face straddling the two peaks; people always thought they could do it without ropes. Every year, some dozen or so folk got stuck on the series of rocky steps that made up the Mickledore col, each the height of a man; hence the permanent stretcher box instalment up there. Johnny didn't usually get drafted in by the Wasdale crew, but they'd been inundated with calls in the area and were short of volunteers.

It was always a pleasure hiking up the Scafell range, but never when it was to bring down a body. It happened. Falls from Broad Stand were usually fatal. When he guided the Three Peaks later in the year, he'd stick to the corridor route.

He'd had a call from Graeme Millar, who wanted to share a pint and a chat. It was a welcome diversion with Kelly away, and just what she had requested. He'd been taken by surprise at how much he missed her. He'd even slept at hers a few nights, and lit the fire, curling up on the sofa with a glass of red – though only one, in case he got a call for a rescue. Josie was becoming ever more the independent young woman, and she only came to

163

him when she needed something – usually money. He'd suggested going out on the boat, but she always had better things to do, like Instagram. In fact, he'd spent more time with Ted than with his own daughter.

The old man was bloody good company, and they chatted about cricket, rugby and the army. Ted was fascinated by the operational tours Johnny had done, and he asked about his medals. Johnny didn't wear his medals, not even on Armistice Day, and he didn't talk about them much either, but an enthusiasm he hadn't experienced in years had crept back when he answered Ted's questions about his role in Iraq and Afghanistan. Old wounds that he'd fled from suddenly didn't seem so threatening for some odd reason. Last night, they'd ended up sleeping on the boat after a full bottle of whisky and tales of Baghdad. They also talked about Kelly, and Ted's other two daughters from his marriage to Mary.

The weather had been sublime this week, and they both felt sorry for Kelly, holed up in some city hotel, choked with traffic fumes and angry commuters. Johnny had spent his fair share of time in London when he was a young subaltern, looking for a break from gruelling exercises in Wales. He'd grown up near Lincoln but hadn't been back for years. Army postings had taken him all over the world, so he couldn't say he belonged anywhere really. Until he came here. This was the first time he'd felt he could stay somewhere for ever, and now he had even more reason to. Kelly Porter had got under his skin and he didn't want that to change. It wasn't that he wanted to marry again, but he liked the idea of being with her for a long time to come. It felt right.

He dressed and walked into town, where he'd arranged to meet Graeme. He'd offered to drive to Keswick, but Graeme said he was happy to come over to Pooley Bridge, which was less crowded with tourists, though they were getting to the time of year when that would all change. For two crazy months, the whole county was choked with millions of visitors, all trying to eat at the same time, buy ice cream at the same time, and board a steamer at the same time. It was manic and often led to episodes of what might be termed nowadays 'holiday rage'. He and Kelly avoided the hot spots during peak season, and they weren't short of hideaways. If you knew where to look, it was easy to find a deserted waterfall, a silent dale or a hidden tarn. But nothing beat winter, when the visitors were fewer and the skies clearer.

Graeme was sitting with a young woman when Johnny walked into the pub.

'This is Tilly Knight – Tilly, this is my pal Johnny Frietze. He works for the mountain rescue round here. Tilly's on holiday from London and I'm showing her around.'

Johnny shook Tilly's hand and went to order a pint. He was off duty for the rest of the day. He was a little disappointed; he had been looking forward to catching up with Graeme alone: they usually talked about the army, ex-wives, their love of the outdoors, and their advancing age. They both turned fifty next year.

He went back to the table and sat down.

'You know the Allerdale place on Derwent Water?' Graeme asked him.

'Of course. Didn't old Lord Allerdale die recently?'

'He did. The place has now been taken over by his grandson, who wants to turn it into some posh hotel, and he's asked me to manage the project.'

'Congratulations, mate! That's fantastic news.' The marina was a precarious venture, and Johnny knew that Graeme was never sure where his next mortgage payment was coming from, never mind the maintenance for his two daughters. He didn't know what sort of a man the new owner was, but he had no doubt that Graeme would deliver for him. Once the landowner realised his worth, perhaps it would lead to bigger things, like managing the whole estate. Johnny raised his glass and clinked it against Graeme's.

They fell into comfortable conversation, with Johnny asking Tilly polite questions about her holiday. Something about the way she paused before answering stuck in his mind; he found her charming, but a little out of place. He told them about the incident on Scafell this morning. Graeme agreed that the classification should be changed from a Grade 1 scramble to an official climb with ropes. It wasn't that the people who became stuck there were incompetent; simply that one trip could lead to serious injury because of the terrain. It was the same on Helvellyn's Striding Edge. Most of the fatalities there were as a result of losing one's footing, but it was a bit like a Great White taking a test bite: it never ended well. Any fall onto sheer rock could kill, and trips and accidents happened even to professionals, but they just couldn't get it across that inexperienced walkers shouldn't attempt certain routes.

'How's Kelly getting on down south?' Graeme asked.

'She's doing all right. I'm not sure she was too keen, but the case has turned into something national, I think.'

'That's what I wanted to talk to you about.'

'Kelly?'

'No. Her case. Is she still looking into the Allerdale House burglary?'

Johnny nodded. 'It's all part of it.' He watched Tilly, uncomfortable about saying too much in front of a total stranger.

'Well, I saw some workmen hanging about one day when I'd pulled up to the beach to see what was going on. I've had my eye on the place for a while, wondering what was going to happen to it since old Lord Allerdale died. I had no idea that someone was staying there.'

Johnny took a sip of beer and paused. 'Look, I don't mean to be rude, but I've only just met your friend, and you know I'm in a difficult position here.'

'Oh, of course, you're right. I should have explained. I was giving Tilly a paddle board lesson this morning and thought it wouldn't do any harm if I took her up to show her the house.'

'Mate, it's a crime scene.'

'I know, but while we were there, she said I should tell the police what I'd seen.'

'So why are you telling me?'

'Because you're Kelly's boyfriend.'

'Thanks, but Kelly's job is none of my business.' Johnny glanced at Tilly, who stiffened slightly.

'Gosh, I don't want to cause any problems between you two. Would you like me to leave?'

'Yes,' Johnny said.

'No.' Graeme spoke at the same time. They looked at one another. Johnny put his hands up.

'All right, sorry. Look, can you just give us a minute?' he asked Tilly.

'Of course. Graeme, honestly, I don't mind. I need the loo anyway.' She picked up her bag and walked away.

'When did you meet her?' Johnny asked.

'Why?'

'I could get into so much shit for discussing this with you.'

'Who from? Kelly?'

'Yes, Kelly. What have you told her? The complete stranger.'

'Oh come on, Johnny, she's not special forces. She's a fucking tourist.'

'She's a honey trap.'

Graeme burst out laughing. 'Mate, you're paranoid.'

'Tell me what you saw, and I'll pass it on to Kelly.'

Graeme nodded. 'Thanks. Look, I never saw the guy who was killed before. I thought the place was empty and it couldn't hurt having a look around. It was last Friday, I think. I rowed up to the beach. There were three blokes in the garden. I jumped out of my skin and so did they. When I asked who they were, they said they were surveyors, but they didn't look like surveyors. They said I was trespassing and to leave – you know, aggressively. I'd never seen them before and they weren't local. They were shifty. Up to no good.'

'And you didn't mention this to Kelly?'

'I didn't speak to her about the house, just about finding the body in the boatyard; the two weren't connected then. Anyway, I didn't really think about it until I went back there and saw the police tape. It set me thinking about the burglary, and how they'd need a vehicle to take away all the stuff.'

'Between you and me, I think they'd need more than one, and something with a trailer mount. Can you remember what the men looked like? You might have to go in and give a description.'

'I can certainly have a go. Why has Kelly gone to London? Is that where George Murphy lived?'

'It's a bit more than that. Two of his colleagues have been killed as well.' Johnny wasn't speaking out of turn; anyone could get the information off the internet. Besides, he trusted Graeme, just not the girl he'd known for five minutes, who was now on her way back from the toilet.

'Where did he work?' Graeme asked.

'Big pharmaceutical company in London.'

'No wonder he liked coming up here.'

'Do you remember the vehicle those men were driving?' Johnny asked.

'I didn't see it; I was beach side, remember? But I did see a van parked in Portinscale, outside the shop. I only remember because I couldn't park there as the damn thing was blocking the whole road.'

'I don't suppose you got the number plate?'

'Are you kidding? I didn't apply for special forces for nothing. Of course I did.'

'Do you mind if I rejoin you?' Tilly asked.

'Please do,' Johnny replied.

## Chapter 26

Marine Light Nautical Antiques had traded since 1912, and had seen better days. The former triple facade, adorned with awnings, silks and clever lighting, was now reduced to a small window at the front of a single plot, with various curiosities in the window and a worn sail hanging across the door. The bell clattered when the man opened it then closed it again, locking it behind him.

A small woman wearing a colourful house coat, glasses perched on the end of her nose, and woollen gloves to compensate for the lack of heat in the dingy shop, tottered towards the counter. She was around seventy years old and had a kind, enquiring face, but piercing, no-bullshit eyes. Her red lips smiled at her visitor and she nodded to the door.

'Locked,' he confirmed.

'No funny business,' she warned. 'Follow me.'

The back of the shop was a mess. He was led into some kind of office strewn with papers. He didn't touch anything.

The woman pointed to the door. The man turned and closed it. They faced one another. She indicated a camera in the corner and he rolled his eyes.

'Look, lady, if I wanted to get rid of you, I would have done it by now, maybe when you were visiting your daughter yesterday, or dropping your grandkids at school on Tuesday.'

The woman's face froze in horror. 'You bastard.'

'Whatever. You got the bonds? The goods are all set, and here's the key. You get the whole damn lot on sale, bar thirty per cent. I'd stop whingeing if I were you.' He opened his jacket and showed her a pistol in his inside pocket. It was just out of view of the camera.

'No money up front. You touch my grandkids and I'll rip your balls off.'

The man laughed. 'I bet you would, Brenda. Now stop pissing around.'

She smiled and reached into a drawer, handing him an envelope containing fifty grand's worth of saleable investment bonds in the name of her dead husband. It was his insurance. Hers was the camera he couldn't see.

'Think you can shift it?'

'Of course! Have I ever let you down?'

'No, Aunt Brenda, you haven't. How are the kids anyway?'

'Ah, I can spoil them and hand them back. It's been a long time; come for supper soon.'

'I need to lie low for a bit.'

'You made a mistake? You get too cocky?'

He squirmed uncomfortably. He had indeed made a mistake. He'd got greedy and now he needed to disappear for a bit, and that was where his aunt's money came in. If anyone could shift stolen sailing antiques, it was her; she'd been doing it for fifty years and he'd learned the trade alongside her. He hadn't been tasked with the boatshed burglary, but he couldn't resist once he'd seen what was in there. And now he was in the shit.

'How can I find you?' she asked.

He handed her a mobile phone. 'It's a pay-as-you-go, completely untraceable. Don't go calling your friends for a chat, there's a good girl. Only use it for me, or I might rip your balls off.'

'They're bigger than yours, Leo.'

They smiled at one another and he stepped forward to embrace her.

'You're a good boy, Leo. Did you bring the photos?'

He nodded and took an envelope out of his jacket. She emptied the photos across her desk.

'You weren't toying with me. There it is. Is it really 1929 cedar?'

'How the fuck do I know?'

'Don't you swear in front of me, I'll put you over my knee, you're never too big for that. You got your potty mouth after your mother died.'

'Sorry.'

'It's beautiful.' She studied the photo of the wooden two-man boat.

'Whatever.'

'You have no taste or class, so I'm not surprised you don't appreciate it.'

'I spotted it, didn't I?'

'Now you want a medal? Have you got time for a nip?' Her eyes twinkled and she pulled a half-bottle of bourbon out of a drawer. She reached for two shot glasses and filled them, handing one to her nephew. They both gulped the liquor in one.

'So. What do I do when they come knocking?' the old lady asked.

'Do you still have the gun I gave you?'

'Of course.'

'Tell them that I'm a good-for-nothing, and you haven't seen me in years.'

'And what if it's not the coppers who find me first?'

'Use the gun. These are serious guys, Brenda, they've done it many, many times before and they use hired thugs – ex-convicts, ex-army and the like, you know the type.'

'Sounds like family.'

'I'm not kidding around.'

'I know you're not. Don't worry, I can handle myself.'

## Chapter 27

'Kelly, how are you?'

'Hi, Ted, this is a welcome call.' She still couldn't bring herself to call him Dad, but it was a minor point and one that didn't seem to bother him. She was genuinely pleased to hear from him, as her day was turning out to be just like the last one: professionally productive but personally precarious. Matt was angling to get inside her head at every opportunity, and she was on the verge of throwing in the towel and sending a junior officer in her place. But actually, even that wasn't necessary: she could just leave Emma, and keep in touch via iPad. It was mind-boggling that you could solve a crime these days without ever leaving your chair.

'I'm coming home soon.'

'That's great news. Johnny will be pleased, and so am I.'

Always the gentleman, she thought. 'Did you ever work in London?'

'That's where I trained. It's where I met Mary. She was an Essex girl and I the dashing doctor. We lived off the Edgware Road. I decided on the pathology route after I saw a murder victim's bite marks develop post-mortem, can you believe. I was hooked.'

'Normal people get hooked on shopping, or origami.'

'Quite. I never did take to London, and the employment opportunities were better up north, so I took the Carlisle job and learned my trade. The rest, as they say, is history.'

'I'm not suited to it either. I don't know how I lived here for ten years.'

'The Lakes get into your blood, Kelly, and they're already in yours. Can't you do everything via computer these days anyway? I have people call me from Canada asking how to measure contusions they've never seen before.'

'Did the bite mark really develop post-mortem?'

'It did. I've never forgotten it. That's how he was caught in the end. It was the brother all along. Usually is, isn't it?'

'Family? Yes. Not in this case, though.'

'What have you found?'

Kelly walked along the corridor; she'd excused herself from Matt to take the call. They'd met in the canteen at Ravensword, just like yesterday, to swap some interesting information. She looked around to make sure she was out of earshot.

'Professional.'

'Have you thought of drug deals going wrong?'

'Why do you say that?' Kelly was taken aback.

'Because the toxicology results are back. George Murphy was a cocaine and opioid addict.'

'What?' Something that the CEO of Ravensword, Philip Tooting, had mentioned earlier in the day came back to her.

'He had levels in him that a non-addict couldn't tolerate.'

'But there was no paraphernalia found at Allerdale House.'

'Did you use narcotic dogs?'

'I had no need to.' Kelly frowned. This was entirely unexpected and threw her way off the scent. It even made her question whether the murders were connected at all. She felt a fool. And she'd have to break it to Matt. 'Are you sure?'

'One hundred per cent.'

'It still stinks. Why were the three victims killed within hours of one another? Plus they not only worked together, but were working on some clandestine project of their own. And why has Alexandros fled to Cyprus?'

'Greed? Perhaps he knew how valuable their findings were and wanted to cash in himself.'

'No. The bodies were set up. Drug dealers usually love to scatter paraphernalia around, because it gets them off the hook. And it doesn't explain moving George's body. Dealers can't be bothered to do that. Unless...'

'What?'

'The bathroom George died in was cleaned. What if it wasn't to hide evidence from the police, but to conceal it from the owner?'

'Lord Allerdale's grandson? Why?'

'I don't know, but when something like that happens, it's usually to protect the person who lives there. That makes it personal.'

'Who's the coroner doing the autopsy on the two victims found in the garage?'

'I'll email the details to you. Why?'

'They were stripped as well, weren't they?'

'Yes.'

Kelly could see Matt staring at her and looking at his watch. She really had to get away from him. Especially after last night. She turned back to her phone.

'Tidy,' Ted said. 'Rare for murder.'

'I agree. Look, I have to go. I've made my mind up, I'm coming home tomorrow. I'll see you soon.'

Kelly walked back to where Matt was sitting. He had some news. Not only was Matilda Knight not answering her phone, but her flat had been turned over, and ten thousand pounds had been transferred to her account by George Murphy before he died.

'Does she have a car?'

'We're already on it. She drove up the M6 on Tuesday.'

'She's gone to do her own homework.'

'Exactly.'

# Chapter 28

Professor Cooper stormed into the CEO's offices. The admin staff were used to it. Not all heads of sections could get away with it, but with Cooper, it was different. Tooting never seemed to complain, and while he would impose an informal ban on letting other scientists into his office, the same was never true for her.

Gossip pointed to two reasons: one on the left side of her chest, and the other on the right.

Glances were shared across the room as she waltzed past Tooting's personal assistant and into his office, slamming the door.

'Miranda!'

'Don't Miranda me! What's going on? I could lose my licence, Philip. You said you'd cover my arse, and so far all you've covered is afternoon tea and a shag at the Ritz.'

Philip Tooting sat back in his leather recliner and smiled. He placed the tips of his fingers together and rocked back and forth. He had never been a looker, but money and status had left the indelible mark of success, and it proved irresistible to gold-diggers like Miranda.

'I've told you before, everything is accounted for; you just need to hold your nerve. If you haven't got the balls, then maybe I'll have to take someone else to the Ritz next time.'

'Are you threatening me?'

Philip laughed. 'Good God, no. That's not how I operate.'

'Has this got anything to do with those poor fuckers in the neurocellular section? Because if it does, I'll make your life hell. I've got receipts, I've got photos, I've got—'

Philip sat up, the smirk wiped off his face.

'Are *you* threatening *me*?' he asked. He stood up and walked to his desk, perching on the edge. He was a tall man and towered over Miranda. He looked her up and down with a snarl. He'd bedded a hundred women like Miranda Cooper, and he had just signed off her cash cow. Suddenly he didn't find her attractive any more, and the implants he'd paid for looked sluttish. He studied her face and realised that she was ageing badly. He'd only fancied her because of the thrill of bending her over the desk, watched by screaming primates: it was high risk, and that was the turn-on. The woman who cowered before him now had outgrown her worth.

He used to quite like her temper and her demands for more funding for the primate section, as long as his accounts department could make it work. Now he saw the panic in her eyes as she realised she would have been better off not mentioning blackmail. He could tell that she was trying to find a way to retract what she'd said, at the same time as knowing it was too late.

'I've got meetings, Professor Cooper; put your complaint in an email and send it to my secretary.'

'But—'

'That's all, Professor.'

Her shoulders sagged and she turned and walked to the door, holding her coat around her chest.

Philip buzzed his PA and asked for Professor Cooper to be added to the list of scientists who'd need an appointment in future. Then he walked to the huge window that took up a whole wall and peered across London. He'd told Miranda she'd have to hold her nerve, and that was exactly what was required. If Ravensword was to be implicated in anything illegal, a full-blown lengthy inquiry would have to be launched. Yes, they might have massaged a few figures, but the detectives weren't looking for numbers that didn't add up, or exaggerated findings, or expense accounts used to schmooze clients. They were merely after what old George was doing in his garage in Bethnal Green.

The two detectives had played their good cop, bad cop routine earlier this afternoon and Philip had almost laughed out loud. The male wore a cheap suit and fancied himself as some hotshot saving the world, one nasty pharmaceutical at a time. The female, on the other hand: now she was one to watch. She reminded Philip of himself: eagle-eyed, alert to every movement and eye twitch. She was good. He'd seen her studying his hands and his legs, as well as his face. Body language was important for business too, and Philip had learned the art well. He could always tell if one of his juniors was up to something, and DI Kelly Porter had the same nose. He liked her.

But she was batting for the other team, sadly.

'Why do you think the crimes are connected, Detective?' he'd asked.

'Occam's razor, Mr Tooting. I'm sure you've heard of it.'

Philip's eyes had flicked to his vast book cabinet, where a copy of Professor Nuttall's tome on problem-solving sat.

He had no idea how she'd spotted it, but his secretary did say that she'd been here snooping around before. She shouldn't have been able to get into his office, but maybe she had.

'No, I haven't,' he lied. He wanted to have a little fun.

'I'm sure you can google it. Or look in one of your books. Or are they there just for show?' she'd asked.

'Yes, they were left here by the last CEO. I think they look nice.'

The detectives had stayed for almost half an hour, asking questions about his staff, procedures, access to research and other files, and if he knew what George Murphy had been up to in his garage.

'Murphy was formally reminded of his restrictive covenant last year; why was that?'

'You'd have to ask HR. Ravensword is very much like the police, Miss Porter, we have departments for different jobs. I oversee, and I don't read everything I sign.'

'Isn't that a little remiss?'

'I think that's a fairly immature question. I have to trust and delegate. I can't see everything.'

'So who did you trust to threaten a valued member of staff?'

'The name escapes me; again, HR can help.'

'And who gave you cause to worry that George might be working elsewhere?'

Philip had spread his hands and sat back in his leather recliner at this point, fingers together, groin on display. He'd watched as Kelly Porter's expression changed imperceptibly from mistrust to disgust.

'Again, HR will tell you.'

'Well that's our problem, Mr Tooting, HR can't tell us. The signature on the letter is yours, and it was generated in this office by your secretary – her initials are on it – so it must have been dictated by you.'

'Sometimes letters that are not dictated by me bear my title.'

'Is that ethical?'

'Of course. It's business.'

'There's no file in HR that tells us what George Murphy was suspected of doing, and I have to say that my conclusion is that you're being obstructive.'

The male had joined in at that point, and Philip had realised with a thrill that Porter's colleague was mesmerised by her too. He looked between them and decided to throw her a bone.

'Look, George was a much-respected colleague. He was part of the furniture here. I seem to remember some talk – and that was probably all it was – that he was looking to move on. We wanted to keep him. His contract said that he couldn't work for a competitor for a year after leaving us. It's standard.'

'So what about the garage in Bethnal Green?'

'I had no idea about that, and I'm trying to keep it quiet to preserve George's reputation. There were rumours that he suffered the same affliction as his daughter. He was a drug addict, and I think he was stealing from his lab to support his habit.'

That had shut her up. From then on in, the meeting had grown tiresome, and the detectives had given him their cards and asked him to call with anything he might remember: all standard stuff. They'd left unhappy, of course; coppers were never anything but. However, something told Philip that he needed to make a few phone calls after they left, because he knew that DI Kelly Porter had only been pushed off the scent in the short term. She'd be back. He'd noticed a tension between the two detectives that was more than professional, and he reckoned that might be something to use.

# Chapter 29

Christopher Slater entered the headquarters of the Department for Environment, Food & Rural Affairs shortly after ten o'clock in the morning. His role as a respected non-executive director was keenly sought after in business circles, and to the civil servants coming and going through the foyer, this particular adviser always wore a smug grin. His duties brought him to London perhaps two days a week, where he was expected to sit at his desk, review documents, check and challenge. It was a dry affair, and sometimes he longed for something meaty to get his teeth into. Everybody remembered the colantropine scandal, of course, even though it was over twenty years ago. He didn't necessarily want something on that scale – heavens, nobody wanted breakfast cereal to cause brain damage; no, something just a little controversial would suffice.

The job paid, not well, but enough to maintain his six-bedroom pad in Surrey, keep his wife happy, and allow him to have the odd Arturo Fuente cigar at the Montague Club. More importantly, it afforded him status. It was the natural order of things that the further one climbed up the slippery pole of success, the wealthier one became. He hardly paid for a thing these days, with people falling over themselves to take him to lunch or fly him out to their villa. Nowadays, it had to all be above board, with every receipt ticked off by the Permanent Under-Secretary, but she was easily circumnavigated. Proof and accountability: it just got harder, that was all.

His evening at the club had been thoroughly enjoyable, and so had his one-night stay. His favourite doorman turned a blind eye to young ladies arriving in the early hours, staying a mere hour or so and tipping generously. Reflecting to himself on his walk to the lift, Christopher decided that he had pretty much everything he needed. Life hadn't turned out badly. Of course, it was only when one embarked on one's second half-century that the awful realisation dawned that this was it: no trial run, no serum to resurrect youth, and no pause button. Yesterday would never come around again. He'd learned to say fuck it to just about everything, and found that it was a pleasing way to exist. If he could do it all again, he'd make different choices, but then so would everyone. All those conformities and goals that humans strived for in their little organised cages of propriety would go out of the window, and he'd be the first in the queue. He rather fancied living naked on an island with a tall Texan blonde, fishing, fucking and frolicking. He knew that was never going to happen. Even with all the billions invested in reversing ageing, eternal youth was a pipe dream.

He had a fairly full timetable today, and he took the lift up to the third floor, striding through yet more busy offices (damn open plan) and finally reaching his own (enclosed). He shut the door. He hadn't been inside two minutes when his secretary poked her head in asking if he'd like his coffee. He'd attended enough meetings on equal rights, the gender pay gap and throwing jobs at anyone not male, over forty and white that he could recite every policy going. But his secretary still made him coffee in the morning. Gone were the days when he could pat her bottom for it, but all good things came to an end eventually.

'PUS is pissed and after your head,' she said, and went to make the coffee.

Christopher realised that Charlotte must have seen Philip and grassed him up to his boss, Robyn Hastings. Being a non-executive director of several companies had its uses. If one wanted to gather sensitive information and sit on it, one could make a tidy fortune. As a NED over ten years ago to The World Cares, a children's charitable organisation in Nairobi, he'd met Charlotte Cross, then a young thruster hoping to get her hands on a decoration or three. Kids' charities were the easiest screens to hide behind, especially in countries like Kenya, where money flooded in and disappeared. Charlotte's world was catching up with her. He chuckled to himself. He couldn't wait to see Robyn's face.

He turned on his computer and waited for the shit to hit the fan. He was untouchable. They couldn't sack him: he knew too much.

He creased his brow. When he was at the office, he made a point of only attending to DEFRA business. He had his own Mac at home, and any other affairs were dealt with there. So he was puzzled, and a little perturbed, that the Colonel had emailed his work address. He sighed and forwarded the message to his home email.

After opening various drawers, arranging pens and switching on his iPad, he settled down to read. Most of his work here was spent looking for the devil in the detail.

That was what caught everyone out. Whole departments were employed to sift through millions of pages of information looking for mistakes, liabilities and inaccuracies. His background as CEO of a large multinational made him perfect for the job, and it was a way to keep his mind active, as well as get away from his wife and pop into London occasionally. His reputation meant that he was a NED for three different departments.

Another new email from the Colonel popped into his inbox, and he tutted. He forwarded that one too and contemplated calling his friend. Then he considered that it might be important. Once was a mistake; twice was a warning. He retrieved the message and opened it. It read, simply: *Dinner venue located.*

Instinctively he looked up and around his office. He was verging on irritation now. He grabbed his mobile phone, intending to leave the office and head back downstairs. One never knew if government offices were bugged. He had two very important tenets in life, which he'd learned in his forties: trust no one; and if something is plausible, it's been done already. He liked the Colonel very much, but he couldn't trust a man who was capable of ordering bombs the size of a small caravan to be dropped on children in Iraq. Before he allowed anybody into his life, he found out what their limits were, so he knew what he was dealing with. If he accepted a person's failures, anything more was a bonus.

People always let you down.

Before he got to his door, it opened and Robyn Hastings strode in.

'Under-Secretary, I'm just popping out—'

'No you're not. I know exactly what you've done.' She glared at him.

'With respect, I have no idea what you mean. I have a job to do.'

'Blackmail, that's what it is.'

'You must be mistaken, Under-Secretary.' He held her scowl.

'I'll tell you now, Slater, I'm on to you.'

'No you're not.' He smiled and saw a tiny muscle in her neck throb. 'Shut the door on your way out, will you.'

His secretary stared at him as he strode towards the lift. She went to say something, but, reading his expression, thought better of it. It was well known that Robyn Hastings was gay, but few knew that she'd been seeing Charlotte Cross for five years. The love-struck bitch was defending her mate, and it touched him momentarily. Charlotte Cross had been on the take from The World Cares for years, and back in the day, when no one checked expenses, she'd lived a lavish life as an expat. She'd got the taste for it and moved on to other charitable organisations, which was how she'd wound up on the Queen's Birthday Honours list three years ago. There'd been a distinct shift in wind direction recently, however, and scandals like this were becoming more prominent. An ambassador in South Africa could barely chuck a few diamonds onto his household expenditure these days without someone snooping around.

Christopher's own record was clean: Philip had taken care of that.

He took the lift back downstairs and walked lightly out into the sunshine to find a bench in the square. It was a beautiful day. He jabbed the Colonel's number into his phone and listened to the ringtone.

The Colonel answered quickly and began to gush joyous greetings.

'Benjamin, why the hell are you emailing me at work?' Christopher listened impatiently to the reply. 'I don't give a monkey's arse. I've told you enough times that's completely out of the question. You, more than anyone, should appreciate what some nerdy little civil servant can do with a computer. Remember that sergeant who retrieved deleted emails from you to some corporal about bending her over your desk?' He listened again before interrupting. 'Benji, I'm going to have to wipe my whole hard drive clean. Can you please keep to your side of the bargain?'

Finally Christopher got an apology, and they briefly discussed the meaning of the email. Time was of the essence, but the officer who had led over a thousand men through one of the most brutal campaigns of the whole Afghan war needed bloody reassurance. He was losing his edge.

'Benji, why are you even asking me this, man? Get a bloody grip. And make sure you tidy up as well.'

But Christopher had noted something else in his friend's voice.

'There's an article about to break in the tabloids,' the Colonel admitted. 'It comes out tomorrow. I've been accused of raping two female soldiers. One in Bosnia in 1999, and the other in Iraq in 2005.'

'Christ, man. Can't you pay someone to shut up?'

'The wife's just bought a villa in Barbados, and I'm strapped.'

'Strapped? What the hell do you do with it all?'

'I don't know.'

Christopher did know. The Colonel was an alcoholic, and very generous when intoxicated, which was most of the time.

'How the hell can you be prosecuted so long after the event? And which publications have got the story? I'll see if I can have a word with someone my end.'

It was possible to stop stories from going to press, but usually only when a member of the royal family was involved. However, the editor of the *Herald* was an old pal of Christopher's, and he'd been obliging in the past.

'Look, one thing at a time. Get this other business sorted out and let him know. Keep a low profile tomorrow, and for God's sake, Benji, if you get pissed, don't talk to the press. It won't end well.'

The fall of a decorated senior officer was juicy news indeed, and to get it buried would take the pulling of some very long strings. Christopher hung up and shook his head. The Colonel had just ruined a perfectly good day.

## Chapter 30

Tilly woke up and rolled over, straight into the tanned back of Graeme Millar. She recoiled and put her hand over her mouth. It wasn't that she'd forgotten what had happened. It was just that, in her dreams, she'd been elsewhere; that, as well as the fact that she hadn't woken up with a man for a long time. She took her hand away from her mouth and thought carefully about how to play the situation.

After they'd parted company with Graeme's very suspicious friend, they'd spent the afternoon together and he'd asked her out for dinner. She figured that being with the man who'd found George's body was about the best place to be for her research. When he drove her home – probably over the limit, but she guessed that was what people did in tiny towns up here – she'd invited him in. It had happened naturally, and she told herself she hadn't done it for her work. But now she felt a bit uneasy. She'd created a whole fake identity, and every minute she spent with this lovely man, who'd been so generous and great fun, was another minute lying. She'd thought initially that a man his age must have a wife and kids, but she'd been wrong, about the wife at least: she'd left him five years ago for a local builder who Graeme drank with in the pub. It was all very cosy. He did have two daughters with his ex, and their arrangement was amicable. He hadn't had a relationship since though and that surprised her, because he was extremely good-looking, funny and fit.

She watched his back move as he breathed and considered her next move. She actually liked the guy. She loved how laid-back he was, and she'd been pleasantly surprised by how much she'd enjoyed the end of the evening as well. He was confident in bed, and took everything slowly, making sure he pleased her as well as himself. It was, in her limited experience, a rarity.

He rolled over. To begin with he seemed to suffer the same disorientation, but when he realised where he was, he smiled and drew her close.

'I'm taking today off. Fancy going sailing?'

'You take a lot of time off.' The idea sounded fabulous, but she needed to work. She wanted to see where George had died, and where he'd been dumped, and she was with the right person to describe both scenes to her. But she couldn't help thinking that she could be pursuing other angles, such as why the house hadn't been burgled. She knew damn well why: because George's death had been planned. He didn't disturb a few burglars. Still, she figured Graeme could help her with those queries as well. She really had hit the jackpot. The missed calls on her phone bothered her only slightly. She never answered calls from unknown numbers, but there'd been five. There was also one from a foreign number.

Graeme had told her last night that the police had been pretty thorough in their search of Allerdale House, and she knew that meant they'd check the phone records. She'd flicked through her phone, and sure enough, George had called her from a landline with a Cumbria dialling code.

She asked herself why he would be so stupid, but then she realised that he'd done it on purpose, because he knew he was being pursued.

She had decisions to make: act nonchalant and come up with a good excuse as to why he'd called her, or trust the police to take her theories on board. Fuck that, she thought. It was too risky. She had to find out exactly what George had been hiding, and prove it.

She was brought out of her thoughts by Graeme kissing her neck. He was almost fifty, but he didn't seem to mind the age gap, though what man did if he was getting what he wanted? She knew she was a mature thirty, mainly due to the nature of her job. She didn't go out clubbing and she didn't have a gaggle of girls she swapped gossip with. She preferred the company of older people. Graeme was in extremely good shape. He was naked already and didn't seem to mind the morning light illuminating the fact. Before she knew it, he was on top of her, moving up and down again. She certainly hadn't factored this into her Lake District itinerary, but she wasn't complaining.

She allowed herself to be carried away with it: his body, the moment, the delicious craziness of it. Her mind emptied and she clung onto him. They fell off the bed and he picked her up, wrapping her legs around him and pushing her up against the wall. She had no idea if these bedrooms were soundproof, but she couldn't help herself, and her sighs mingled with his, accompanying the rhythmic thuds on the wall. He gasped and she felt his body go weak. He managed to take her back to the bed, where they fell beside one another, panting and sweaty.

'I need a shower,' she said eventually.

'So do I.'

'I'll go first.' She went into the bathroom and left him on the bed. He shouted to her asking if she'd like a coffee from the tiny shop in the village. She said yes and heard the door slam. By the time she was finished, he was back with two takeaway coffees and a selection of pastries.

'I know you girls like to stay slim, so I didn't know what to buy.'

'It looks wonderful, thank you. There's another towel in there for you.'

She dressed quickly, suddenly bashful, and devoured a croissant, sipping the warm, creamy coffee as she looked out of the window. The day was clear. People said it always rained up here, but so far all she'd seen was sunshine, though this was only her second day.

Graeme strode naked out of the bathroom and wrapped himself in the towel he was holding, taking a coffee and a Danish roll.

'So, Tilly Knight, why are you here on your own?'

'I like travelling alone. I had a few days off, and my grandmother loved it up here; she was from somewhere called Kendal?'

Graeme nodded.

'Anyway, she died last year, and I thought I'd come and see what all the fuss was about.'

'I'm glad.'

'Do you think it might affect business up at the big house – you know, the murder?'

If Graeme was taken aback by the question, he didn't show it.

'It's on your mind, huh?'

'Well, I never thought a place like this would ever see anything like that.'

'I agree. It's really out of character for the area. I heard that poor man came every year, staying at the house with his pal, Lord Allerdale. Like I said, the old man died after Christmas and his grandson inherited the lot.'

'Was there no son?'

'No, he died in a boating accident when the boy was ten years old. Sebastian was essentially raised by his house master at school.'

'What about his mother?'

'Raging alcoholic. She committed suicide a year after her husband died.'

'You know a lot about them.'

'They were like minor celebs up here. Everybody knows the story, it's nothing new. The boy didn't have the best start in life.'

'Was he not close to his grandfather?'

'No idea. He's all right, though, for a southerner.'

Tilly slapped his arm.

'Did the grandson know George well?'

'George? You're making it sound like he was an old friend of yours.'

Tilly smiled. 'Sorry, I'm not used to talking about dead people. I thought it would sound better if I called him by his name.'

'Good point. I have no idea; my relationship with Sebastian is purely business, though he was interviewed by the police.'

They finished their coffees and each took another pastry.

'I like a woman who eats properly. So you're not on a diet all the time like all those supermodel types down there in London?'

'No! I love food. The robbers would need a van for all the stuff, wouldn't they? And you saw one, and you saw workmen.'

'Hold on! Bloody hell, you're hurting my head. Why are you so obsessed with this? I suppose you're right, though, and someone had to drive George to *The Lady of the Lake* and dump him there.'

'You use that yard a lot, don't you, yet you heard nothing.'

'Maybe they used a boat.'

'Why take the time to do that if it was just a burglary gone wrong? What exactly was stolen?'

'Oh, all sorts of stuff. I know the old man's antique racing boat from his Cambridge days was taken, because Sebastian was asking me to look out for a replica recently.'

'Oh. That must have been stolen for a specialist buyer, surely?'

'Guess so.'

Tilly's phone rang; it was the foreign number again.

'Aren't you going to answer that?'

She put the phone to her ear.

'Tilly Knight?'

She didn't recognise the voice. She hesitated, then took a deep breath.

'Yes.'

'George gave me your number. This is Alexandros Skarparis. I'm calling you from Cyprus.'

'Oh, hello, could I ask you to hold for one second? I'll just get my bank details.'

She turned to Graeme. 'Bloody Amazon, my card ran out and they need my new one. I think it's in the car.' She rolled her eyes and left the room, closing the door behind her.

'Alexandros?' she whispered. 'Oh my God! You're all right! You know about the others?'

'Of course I do.'

'Look, I can't talk. Can I call back in an hour?'

## Chapter 31

Alexandros walked barefoot along the beach. His home was a quiet town on the southern shores of the island, close to a British army base. It boasted the best fish and chip café outside of the UK. He climbed over the rocks that separated the main beach at Larnaca from that of Dhekelia military garrison. He'd never minded the British, but his mother and grandmother remembered the war in 1974, when the Turks had come and neighbour turned on neighbour. Communities had slaughtered one another while the British remained in barracks. There was bad blood, but Alex remained torn. Britain was now his home, and that was why he was melancholy. He had no idea if he'd ever be able to go back there. He also grieved for his friends. Images of Mike and Emily's bodies invaded his thoughts in the middle of the night, when his defences were low and the dark was pregnant with threat.

His only hope was Tilly Knight. George had told him he trusted her. She'd said she'd call back in an hour and he'd suggested Skype. He wanted to see her face. Speaking to somebody about something as grave as his situation wasn't something he wanted to do without feeling a connection. He was taking a huge risk and he wanted to get to know her a little.

He thought about his colleagues. They'd always promised to keep the lab a secret, and Alex tried to think who else knew about it. The only thing he could come up with that might be vaguely important was the letter George had received from Ravensword reminding him of his employment covenant, which stated he shouldn't engage in work elsewhere. They'd discussed it and George had reassured them that he'd sort it. When asked if anyone at Ravensword knew about the garage, he had told them no. But did they? Then there was the funding. Only George knew where it came from; could that have been important? But why would the person who gave George money kill him?

Alex's head hurt, which was why he'd come to the beach. He'd made the call as he walked along the warm sand. June was a beautiful month on the island: not too hot. It was difficult to believe that he was in the middle of such a crisis. He was at a loss and didn't know what to do. He couldn't hide for ever.

No matter how much his mind went round and around in circles, he knew that Ravensword must be involved somehow. He'd have to prove it before even thinking about handing himself in. He was aware that he was a plausible suspect, and that was why he'd fled. Nothing and no one could protect him in London; only the mountains and hidden beaches of his beloved island could do that.

He knew it was only a matter of time before the British authorities would impose enough leverage to get him sent back, and then he was as good as dead. His mother still thought he was avoiding a clingy girlfriend – hence why she'd hung up on the British woman – but she was also thrilled to have him home, and he was constantly pampered. It had crossed his mind that anyone who was able to take out three of his colleagues without trace was also capable of boarding a BA flight to Larnaca, but he tried not to think in those terms.

Sometimes he forgot why he was home – in the few days he'd been here, he'd swum at the beach and visited old friends – but in the middle of the night, as he lay sweating with only a ceiling fan for comfort, it hit him: his friends were dead, and he should be too. It was pure serendipity that he'd left the lab on Monday afternoon to speak to his mother.

Emily and Mike hadn't been privy to the finer details of what they were doing, and so they'd had less to hide. They'd been drafted in to share the workload and carry out the tests that technicians would in any lab, while George collated and made decisions. They were keen to lend a few hours to the Squash Club for George's sake, and in memory of his daughter. Their respect for their department head was such that they took payment sporadically and sometimes in kind. George once paid Mike's credit card off after rifling through his wallet to find it, knowing he was over £8,000 in debt. Other than that, they worked for free.

The process was the same for any developmental drug: identify a need, then a target, then test drugs in test plates by the thousand until they got some positive results. But that was only after endorsements, reviews and approved investment. The process could take decades, and several million pounds. And that was just the beginning. After the discovery of a positive result, they had to find out why; and that was where the animals came in. They were that far down the line at the Squash Club, without the patent and approval, of course. Generally two species had to be tested, and they'd chosen rodents and a cyno monkey. The Thai meal was supposed to celebrate reaching the stage where the drug could be tested on human control groups. They all knew they had no such thing, and that George was their control group. The tests were to start officially this week, but Alex knew that George had been testing himself for weeks.

The sand on Dhekelia beach was fine and brown, and it stuck to his feet. He carried his shoes in his hand and waved to people he knew. He took a table close to the beach and kept his shoes off. The café was rammed with tourists and everybody spoke English. The owner waved at him and shouted, 'Two minutes, Alex!'

He always had the same meal. He'd developed a taste for mushy peas in England, and Lambros prepared them in exactly the same way, including baking soda. That was why the café was such a hit with the soldiers. The barracks had changed over the years and now the soldiers came mainly unaccompanied, the British government no longer able to afford to send their families with them.

It was cool under the shade of the umbrellas, and Alex watched the world go by beyond his sunglasses. Despite his apprehension, he had a good feeling about Tilly Knight.

Her call came through as his fish, chips and mushy peas arrived. They'd be boiling hot anyway, and he put them to one side. A lovely, open face filled the screen and Alex smiled.

'Tilly?'

'Alex?'

There was a time lag, but after they'd got used to that, Tilly told Alex about what she'd discovered in the Lake District, and they fell into a conversation about what they might do next. They had several options, one of which was going to the press.

'Historically, cases like this get squashed before they even reach print, because they'll have someone working on the inside,' Tilly said. 'As soon as we press "send" on the computer, there'll be some kind of encryption to flag up sensitive words and phrases, and they've got the money to employ someone full-time to do it. It's as sophisticated as what the Met has at its disposal.'

'Really?' Alex was shocked.

'I'm afraid people can always be bought. Or killed.'

It was brutal. Alex stared at her.

'I'm sorry. I don't need to remind you of that.'

'I found their bodies.' There was a silence. 'I think I'm next.'

'They've probably worked out where you are. I'm sorry, that's the truth. However, killing someone abroad is always tricky. Have you got a property that no one else knows about?'

'We have a house in the Troodos Mountains. But what about my family?'

'Can you convince them to go with you?'

'I have thirty-two cousins.'

'Right. It could protect them if you can't be found. It might be your only hope. Don't tell anyone you're going.'

Alex put his sunglasses on his head and wiped his eyes. 'Tilly, the man who found George. Did he say he suffered?'

'It was a gunshot to the head, Alex. It was quick.'

'But he knew it was coming.'

'Yes, that's why he called me that evening. I think the police have traced my number.'

'What will you do? You can always come here. We can hide together.'

'Tempting.' Tilly bit her lip and Alex watched her. She was beautiful, and he wondered how George had found her.

'We need to be able to talk at short notice. As for the documents and data, I think the only safe way to do it is if you hold each page up to the screen and I photograph it on my phone. I've bought a new one without a contract. I paid cash.'

'You're quite the detective.'

'Well that's the other interesting thing, Alex. The man who found George knows the detective in charge person-ally, and he swears she's a good egg. If I could get to her, then I think we might have a chance. She's gone all the way to London to pursue the case.'

'How can she protect me?'

'I don't know; maybe she can get you an escort to fly back, or you can give evidence to her over the phone. Do you want me to contact her?'

'All right. I'll pack and go to the mountains tonight. When can we do the documents?'

'When will you be there?'

'Eight o'clock? Six your time.'

'Done. Stay safe. Look over your shoulder, Alex. They'll come in twos and they'll be English.'

'You too. There's a British army base here. Should I go there and hand myself in?'

Tilly thought about it and played scenarios forward. 'Not yet.'

Alex ended the call and began to eat. He hoped Tilly was who she said she was.

# Chapter 32

Graeme called the number of a guy he'd gone to university with. He was a rowing nut, and if anyone could source an antique rig, it would be him.

When Sebastian had asked him to source a replica shell, like the one belonging to his Grandfather, which had been stolen; he hadn't actually referred to the burglary as such, and had told Graeme that he was simply after the replacement antique for decoration. Graeme thought it odd, but it was none of his business. When he'd been in the house, he'd seen an old photo of Lord Allerdale in his youth, sitting in the shell, beaming at the camera, wearing a flat cap and a white shirt and clutching his oar. He'd been a fit and handsome man. Graeme had looked at the photograph for a long time and thought it was a good job the old man was dead; he figured the theft of such an item would break his heart. Perhaps Sebastian hadn't mentioned the loss because he wasn't a lover of boats and saw the rig simply as decoration, but Graeme had some knowledge of what a piece of kit like that might be worth.

His friend answered the phone and they chatted like people did who no longer saw one another and wondered why. Distance was the bugbear. His friend lived in Cornwall; they were at opposite ends of the country. Graeme promised to go and stay down there sometime, but he knew he wouldn't.

His friend whistled when he heard the description of the stolen shell. He promised to stay on the lookout for something similar and get back to Graeme in the next couple of weeks.

Graeme went out to the jetty with the intention of carrying on working for a bit before taking Tilly out for a sail. *The Lady of the Lake* was being launched today, and they could watch from the water. The police had said they had everything they needed, and had allowed the boatyard and the boat herself to be released back to their original duties. Few people knew exactly where the body had been found, but these things always had a nasty habit of leaking out. It could actually turn the *Lady* into a tourist attraction, who knew?

Tilly looked tense when she strolled into the yard. Graeme had only known her for two days, but he knew anxiety when he saw it, and instinct warned him to tread carefully. It was time to have a proper conversation, but he didn't want to scare her off. He'd been through her handbag when she was asleep; he'd also tried to log into her computer, but had found nothing. Johnny had a point: he had been completely sucked in. He needed to find out more about her. His brain screamed at him to walk away, but he couldn't. He was too fascinated by her. And he liked her.

He smiled warmly and the tension left her brow. She was beginning to dress like a local, the jeans and pretty blouse of the day he'd met her replaced by shorts, flip-flops and a warm gilet. She had great legs. He signalled to her that he wouldn't be long. The occasion of a launch was always a spectacle and Tilly had shown more interest than he'd thought she might. She'd said she'd love to go out on the boat to watch, but that she had to make a few calls first. He'd arranged to meet her at the marina and left her room. Whatever it was she was up to, he was sure it wasn't what she said it was.

Finally, he finished what he was doing and strode over to her.

'Did you bring your smart camera?' he asked.

'Oh fuck!'

'How could you forget that? It's massive!'

'I'll go back for it.'

'Are you all right? You seem jumpy.'

Up close, she looked pale. Several members of staff glanced over at their boss's new focus of attention. Tilly kept glancing over her shoulder.

'Actually, could you come with me?'

'Of course. What is it?'

'There were two men hanging about this morning close to the guest house.'

Graeme laughed. 'Some of the locals are a bit odd.'

She ignored him. They left the marina and walked along the road towards the village.

'Don't you think it's about time you told me what this is all about?' Graeme said. 'I mean, I've only known you for a day or two, but I think you should just come clean.'

She stopped and looked at him.

'Oh God, is it that obvious?'

He saw relief on her face, but the fear still sat heavily in her eyes. She was scared of something.

'Bloody hell, that's them!' she gasped. 'Turn around!'

'What? Wait.' He hurried after her in the direction they'd come from. When he glanced back over his shoulder, two men were standing on the corner, talking to each other. They didn't look suspicious to him, but he also didn't recognise them.

'Tilly!' He jogged to catch up with her and grabbed her arm. 'Slow down!'

'Not here.' She looked terrified now.

'Where then? What about your room?'

'Will you go and get my stuff? I can't go back there. Please!' She was crying now.

'Come on, I'll take you to the office and then I'll come back and collect your stuff.'

'Oh shit, my computer's in there. I need to get it.'

They looked back. The men had gone. Graeme put an arm round her, and they turned and headed in the direction of her accommodation. When they got there, he told her to wait while he went to her room.

'Be careful!'

'You can explain everything to me when I come back. Go into the shop; there's CCTV in there. If you're really sure that somebody's out to hurt you, that's the best place for you to be.'

She did as she was told and walked towards the small convenience store. Graeme went up the stone steps outside the B&B and up to her room, but stopped when he found the door open. He peered around it, and only when he was satisfied that no one was in there did he go in.

The place had been turned over. He searched for her laptop but couldn't find it. Then it hit him: whoever had done this could now be searching for Tilly herself. He sprinted back to the shop and was relieved to find her peering at the canned goods aisle. She saw that he was empty-handed, but before she could question him, he took her by the arm and led her out of the shop.

'You've got a lot of explaining to do, Tilly Knight. I've got a place out of town, I'll take you there.'

# Chapter 33

The animal had rotted pretty well. The police tape kept onlookers away but it wasn't a dead body, just a monkey, so the crowds hadn't lasted long. News of the find, in the Regent's Canal, near Bow, had got back to Kelly and Matt, and it had been identified as a cynomolgus primate. It didn't take a rocket scientist to work out where it might have come from. The poor thing was being autopsied by a vet. Toxicology and histology might indicate what the scientists were working on when the animal had lived.

Matt had spent the whole of last night trying to convince Kelly that she was needed here in London, but she was adamant that she wanted to go home. She'd got what she'd come for, and HQ in Penrith certainly weren't going to complain about her returning to the constabulary and saving them a bit of cash. Having her visit the Met under the circumstances was justifiable, and she'd learned a tremendous amount about the case. Not least this morning, as more sightings of the white van spotted at George Murphy's house flooded in.

After a phone call from Johnny telling her about Graeme Millar's information, they'd also checked out the vehicle number plate for the white van he'd seen in Portinscale. It turned out to be uninsured and unregistered. The absence of a record raised more red flags: if it belonged to a legitimate building company, the van would be traceable. The plate was given to the ANPR computer to see if they could clock it entering or departing the Lake District. Graeme's information further puzzled them because Montague-Roland had said that he was unsure if anyone was at the property.

The office thronged with noise and moving bodies, all anxious to finish their current task and move on to the next. It was dizzying but thrilling at the same time. Kelly read an email from a parole officer in central London. A circular had been sent to all the Met's current databases for criminals recently out of prison or on parole for burglary and aggravated violent assault or murder. It was a size-able list, but the officer had noted that one of his wards had missed an appointment, and when he was tracked down and warned, the man in question became angry and agitated. It was a common sign that an offender was in trouble, and one that parole officers were taught to look out for, so when the officer heard about a brutal crime involving violence and theft, he thought of his perp.

It was worth checking out. Kelly took it to Matt.

'Leo Brown? Never heard of him. Who is he?'

'He has a long record of burglary and assault. He's ex-army, dishonourably discharged for being tested positive for Class A drugs. He's a general rogue, always on the lookout to make a few quid – and his aunt owns a nautical antiques warehouse in Islington.'

'You are pulling my leg?' Matt grinned. 'Do we have a photo?'

Kelly nodded and used his computer screen to bring one up. In it, Leo Brown sported a black eye.

'Where is he now?'

'He missed another appointment with his parole officer.'

'I bet he did. Go public with it, let's smoke him out. Do we have prints and DNA from his prison file?'

'Yup.'

'It needs to be shown ASAP to the witness at George's address. Let's look at the photo of the geezers in the white van again.' He brought the images up on screen, but they were too grainy to be sure. 'Address of the antiques place?'

Kelly gave it to him, and he barked an order through the microphone attached to his computer. A car was instantly on its way to the warehouse.

'What about the van sighting and the men seen by Graeme Millar at Allerdale House?'

'No number plate match.'

'Who is this Graeme Millar?'

'He's ex-army. Owns a boatyard, and he's just been hired by Sebastian Montague-Roland to renovate Allerdale House.' Johnny was a source of valuable information at times.

'Ex-army?'

'Matt, it's impossible. I know him! He's a friend.'

'That counts for nothing, Kell, and you know it.'

'Stop calling me that! He has no motive.' She found herself defending somebody just because she liked him, and it felt unethical.

'Anybody can be bought, and these killings were unemotional.' He raised his voice. 'He knows how to handle a weapon, and he was snooping about Allerdale House. What regiment was he in?'

'I don't know. You've got this wrong, Matt.'

'You're too close to a suspect. I wonder if Leo Brown ever served with Graeme Millar.'

Kelly sat down heavily. She needed some fresh air. Being in the office with Matt was suffocating. She looked at her watch. She'd asked the driver to pick her up at 5 p.m. and it was 4.30 now. Her case was all packed and in the boot of the car, and she'd checked out of her room.

'You can't leave,' Matt said.

'Jesus, Matt. Stop it. It's even more important for me to get back there now, seeing as you're hell-bent on the idea of Graeme Millar masterminding the whole thing with a load of army mates.'

They glared at one another. Neither of them realised that a small crowd had gathered in the adjoining office to watch them argue. No one had seen anyone stand up to the DCI before, and it was good viewing.

'As SIO, I think I'll have to visit the scenes in the north myself.'

'What? You would really be that childish, in the middle of a multiple murder investigation?' Kelly went to walk out, but he held her arm. 'Let me go, Matt.'

He looked past her through the window to the other offices, and the crowd quickly dispersed. He dropped her arm and she walked towards the door. When she reached it, she turned around.

'I'll have my phone and my iPad switched on the whole journey home, and we can work together on updates.' It was weak and she had a momentary prick of guilt. He looked very alone there in his engine room, with no one to bounce ideas off. He said nothing.

As she walked to the lift, the self-reproach turned to excitement as it dawned on her that not only had she resolved the past in her own head, she was also going to see Johnny very soon. It put a spring in her step and she didn't look back as she entered the lift. She grabbed a coffee on her way out, and saw that the car was waiting for her, with Emma inside.

It had been a productive trip and she'd achieved what she'd set out to do: namely to give context to the two cases and ensure consistency between the forces. Sometimes, working with the Met could turn into a David and Goliath situation, and she hoped Matt wouldn't veer away from what they'd agreed now that she'd left. Surely not even he would be that immature. She mulled over his parting words and closed her eyes, willing them to be desperation to get her to stay. She couldn't believe he'd come all the way to Cumbria just to make a point.

She greeted the driver and her colleague and popped her coffee into a holder. Once she was settled in the back of the car, she arranged her notes and various screens around her so she could keep up to date, and they set off.

So far no one had been able to get hold of Matilda Knight. She had been seen up to now as merely a person of interest, but after her car was caught on the ANPR travelling north, she had moved closer to the top of Kelly's list. If her journalistic nose had got the better of her, it made perfect sense to check out George's last days in the Lake District. More worrying was what had happened to her flat. If the woman was in danger, they only had limited time to find her. Kelly put a call through to DS Umshaw and told her to release Knight's photograph to local units. They needed to find her. She was perhaps the last person to speak to George. It was looking more and more likely that it was his controversial work that he'd been killed for, and speaking to a journalist before a homicide was something that needed investigation. Perhaps she'd gone off radar on purpose. Someone could have easily called her to tell her what had happened to her flat; it was big news in the apartment block where she lived.

Updates popped up on HOLMES. The USB stick found in George Murphy's car had been examined, and she opened the report. The stick had contained three files. One was a bank statement relating to a private account in the name of George Murphy, held at a Lloyds branch along Wanstead High Street. The only transactions were payments into the account, and transfers presumably made by George to another account they knew to be his primary account. But it was the payments that caught Kelly's eye. Over ten years, more than one million pounds had come into the account, and every payment was made by the late Lord Allerdale. They'd stopped in January, a month after his death.

She sent a message to Matt asking if they knew where Montague-Roland was. There were several things that needed clearing up, not least the fact that people had been spotted on his property while George was there, and now they also needed to know if he was aware of funding from his grandfather to George. Remembering the last time she'd spoken to him, Kelly guessed he wouldn't be happy about it, but with the dispute over the will, perhaps he knew already but had chosen not to tell them.

The second file contained scientific data that might as well be written in Icelandic. Kelly didn't have a clue what it all meant, but she knew that Matt would be finding someone who did as she sat there in the car, still stuck in traffic. There were equations, sums, diagrams and names she'd never heard of, though she did spot a phrase she'd heard before: 'reward pathways'.

The third file contained the autopsy report on George Murphy's daughter. Kelly read it carefully, and by the time she'd finished, tears were rolling down her face. She thought of all the autopsies she'd studied, and how George's daughter might have looked when she'd been cut open and examined. The girl was only fifteen years old, and the report said that she'd been revived success-fully after an overdose of heroin, only to suffer a huge myocardial infarction.

Kelly was confused. She found a tissue in her bag and wiped her eyes. Did addiction run in the family? Did George feel guilty about the death of his daughter because he was himself an addict? Ted had been adamant that the amount of drugs in the man's system when he'd died ruled out one-off use. But that didn't explain the money invested by Lord Allerdale. No business interests between the old peer and George Murphy had been flagged up by the heir to the estate, so Kelly assumed it was a private arrangement. A phone call to the family solicitors had already confirmed that the original trust arrange-ment in Alan Montague-Roland's will had been success-fully contested in a lengthy court case and a settlement was being drawn up to amend the terms. His grandson wouldn't have to wait for the funds after all.

Money.

George was being funded by Lord Allerdale. The funding stops. The millions go into trust. Who controlled the trust?

She rang the solicitors and stared outside. They were stuck in traffic and going nowhere. It'd be a long journey.

Finally a senior partner came on the phone and explained that they were no longer at liberty to disclose the details of the estate of Lord Allerdale because of the new settlement.

'On what grounds did Lord Allerdale's grandson contest the will?' she asked.

'Oh, he didn't. Well, not exactly. It was the executors.'

'And who are they?'

'I'm not at liberty to say.'

'I'm a police officer!'

'Perhaps you could send me a letter on headed paper?'

She stared into her phone. 'Are you serious?' she asked.

'Of course, madam.'

She hung up. The paperwork involved in getting a warrant for such information was tedious and irritating, but it would have to be done; she tasked Emma, who was doing nothing else.

She sat back in her seat, closed her eyes and wondered what George had been up to. If he was trying to understand the chemistry of addiction, surely that was a good thing and not something that would end up getting him killed, along with his colleagues. It also struck her that Alan Montague-Roland had been an extremely moral man: maybe they should look into him more closely. He had been a champion of dozens of good causes and an active, well-liked member of the House of Lords, campaigning on issues close to his heart, such as education and health.

But he obviously didn't trust his grandson.

## Chapter 34

Professor Miranda Cooper was supposed to have left her office by now. She had no idea how Philip had managed to do it, but the snake had obviously pulled in some favours and massaged some files, because she'd been well and truly sacked. She could appeal, of course, but that would take months, and lots of cash. It was a huge risk to take with money she didn't have, and to go up against a big corporation like Ravensword was practically suicide. She'd never win against their army of lawyers.

But she could do some digging while she still had access to his office. As well as studying anthropology, she took a keen interest in IT and had always been something of a nerd. When Philip had asked her for a favour a couple of years ago, she'd been more than happy to accommodate him. He'd wanted a private computer set up in his office. The tech department at Ravensword was enormous, led by an eminent professor with a Cambridge degree, so she assumed that whatever he wanted the computer for, it wasn't legitimate. Who was she to care? She was bedding a married man; ethics had been left at the bedroom door on this one.

Tooting's penthouse suite was deserted and she let herself in to his office. Whenever the boss was away, his staff couldn't wait to get the hell out of there and left at five o'clock sharp. She was hoping he hadn't got round to changing the door code yet, and she was relieved when it clicked open. She edged round the enormous mahogany desk, shuddering as she pictured him sitting behind it like a king, barking orders and making little people squirm. She was curious to see what nuggets he was storing on the computer. Of course, it could just be porn, but she had a hunch that a man like Philip Tooting might have his hands dirty elsewhere.

She would love to get hold of something she could use. It didn't have to be much. Just enough to turn the partners off him for a change. Just enough to make him hurt a little.

She jumped as she heard a noise behind her, but it was only a blind flapping in the breeze from an open window.

She suffered a sudden crisis of faith, realising that Philip would be an idiot to leave incriminating information at his office. Then she remembered that the arrogant idiot would think that no one could get in here without his knowledge. And she'd promised him that her firewalls were bulletproof, and different to those used by Ravensword.

She looked at the screen. He was so predictable. His icons were pedestrian and familiar, all except two. One was a smiley face, which was odd for someone who lacked any type of gaiety to speak of, except dark humour. The other looked to her like a family crest. She was sure she'd seen it before. It was a shield, with three flowers on one side and two swords on the other.

Bingo. She knew where she'd seen it: on the entrance placard to a swanky club that Philip had taken her to in Berkeley Square. She'd been impressed. It was exclusive, opulent, and obscenely indulgent. It was called the Montague Club, and Philip had said he was a life member there because he knew the owner.

She clicked on the icon. It asked for a password, and she searched her memory for words that Philip liked to use. One sprang immediately to mind. He said it when he orgasmed, and the first time she'd heard it, she'd almost laughed. It was his favourite word. He'd muttered it under his breath once when he was angry with George. Poor George. He was obsessed with addiction and how to cure it. Any father would do the same, and not stop until he found peace over the death of his child. She genuinely felt for him. Which was why she'd agreed to help him. She'd doubted he'd get far on his own.

Over the last ten years, George had had three monkeys and one chimp out of the primate lab. Miranda had asked him for updates – tactfully, of course – and he'd always said the same thing: 'I'm quietly confident.' She'd felt affection for him, and was cross with Philip when it became company knowledge that George had been effectively threatened over his restrictive covenant. That was when she'd let it slip about what she suspected he was up to. She'd wanted to protect the old man and his pursuit of his pipe dream that would never come to anything, but Philip had taken an unusual level of interest in her revelation.

Revenge was a beautiful thing, and Miranda checked her phone for the number of the detective who'd been nosing around her lab. Rumours circulated quickly at Ravensword, and Philip had a loose tongue when he was in her bed with a whisky inside him. As soon as she found out that George had been killed, she'd begun to see Philip in a new light. Of course, he'd have had nothing to do with it – some thug far removed from the CEO of the multinational would take the rap – but Miranda reckoned she could hazard a guess at why George was no longer with them. The deaths of Emily and Mike had thrown her until she'd realised that they were helping George too. It made complete sense.

It also told her that he had finally done it. She'd love to see his work. She'd searched the inventories of all the labs, and anything signed by George, and was piecing together a loose picture of what he'd achieved. What she couldn't understand was why Ravensword wasn't biting his arm off. Surely a drug like that would sell for billions. Maybe it was unsafe. But they were scientists: if something was unsafe, you made it safe. Perhaps he was trying to sell it abroad, though that theory didn't really hold either, because he wasn't doing it for the money, and Ravensword was global anyway.

She wondered if he had shared his findings with someone and they'd betrayed him, but it was well known that the neurocellular lab were a close-knit bunch, and besides, Emily and Mike had lost their lives too. That just left Alexandros bumping everyone off to steal the data, but that was ludicrous. She'd come on to him at an office party once, and he'd turned her down then spent six months apologising. His decency was as authentic as his moussaka.

No, Philip was behind it. She knew it.

The password worked and she let out a tiny squeak. She opened documents and scanned information, her photographic memory picking out words and phrases of significance. After ten minutes, she knew she would have to take the whole file. She downloaded it onto a USB stick, then shut down the computer and looked round the room one last time. It had crossed her mind that Philip might go so far as to shut her up as well, but that would be downright dumb, given the amount of police attention around the building lately. She'd flag it up when she called the detective, because it was a concern, even if not an immediate one.

She returned briefly to her own office, then left her large bunch of keys at the main desk with her badge. The car park was deserted, and she looked around her, trying to calm her paranoia. She laughed to herself when she started the engine and her car didn't explode. Steadying her nerves, she locked all the doors. It would only take half an hour to get to her flat, and then she'd call the detective. As she pulled out of her parking place, she changed her mind, unable to contain her excitement, and dialled the number she'd been given on hands-free.

The main gate was open and manned by night staff.

'Fucking good riddance,' she muttered under her breath, smiling sweetly at the guard.

Taking the slip road through the industrial estate that led to the busy main road into the city, she pulled up and waited for a break in the traffic. The call went through to a switchboard and she told them she was trying to get hold of DI Kelly Porter. The other detective – DCI Carter– hadn't looked as savvy, and Miranda wanted to speak to the female officer. She realised that the DI might already know what she was about to tell her, but it would feel good anyway.

She was put on hold.

She pulled out onto the main road. Three cars behind her, a lorry moved into the middle lane and overtook, slipping back in behind Miranda. She had no idea it was there until it slammed into the back of her car, crushing it against the buffer wall on the left-hand side of the road. She heard herself screaming and felt her hands come off the steering wheel. The only pain was in her feet, and she guessed that they were trapped by the weight of the mangled engine that had shunted backwards with the impact. She felt curiously detached; she knew deep down inside that this was it, that she was not going to make it. Her head spun in slow motion and banged against hard surfaces, but she couldn't reach up. She saw only blackness.

The first person on the scene was a driver who'd witnessed the whole thing unfold from four cars back. The scene was carnage, but Miranda's car was the worst. He approached the driver's side and peered in, but instantly regretted it. The sight of the woman forced him to bend over and vomit. He was shaking so badly that he couldn't dial the correct digits on his phone. Another driver did it instead.

The whole section of road came to a standstill. In the distance, the sound of sirens could be heard. Somebody went to the cabin of the lorry that had completely crushed the front of the woman's car.

It was empty.

## Chapter 35

Colonel Benjamin Dansford scrolled through an email from a private tour operator in Dubrovnik. He'd served there during the nineties, but it was quite the tourist destination again after being bombed to shit two decades ago. He was planning a cruise, taking in Montenegro, and was finalising details of the hotels. His choice was usually based around the wine cellar.

His hands shook. He regretted opening a third bottle of red last night. A cigarette would sort him out, he decided, and he left his office to walk to the end of the street. In the MoD building he didn't wear uniform, and so he was anonymous, blending in with all the other office workers and tourists filling the pavements of London.

He had considered Cyprus again for his summer break. He and his family had enjoyed three postings to the Mediterranean island, and had toyed with buying property there. Lots of army families bought in the north, where it was cheaper, but it was a precarious venture and many of his colleagues had lost money doing it. He'd decided they'd have to give Cyprus a miss this year, though. He'd faced whining from the wife and kids, but he was adamant. It was too risky.

He lit a cigarette and puffed deeply. He felt like shit. His last medical had revealed the early signs of Type

2 diabetes: high cholesterol, raised blood pressure and reduced oxygen levels in his lung capacity. He knew he had let himself go years ago. He never was the fittest in the drawer, and he'd always scraped through his annual military tests, but being a gunner wasn't physically taxing, and sitting behind desks even less so. He'd been at the MoD now for six years, managing to avoid active postings to please the wife and keep her in her Putney army quarters, which were highly sought after and prized.

He was planning to take the next available early retirement, though the army was now kicking itself for getting rid of so many officers back in 2013. Even old-timers like him could be expected to hang on until their late fifties now. He was done. He was knackered, and had an alternative plan. He had money stashed away all over the place; so much that he sometimes lost track of it. He didn't need any more, that was for sure. But he could never say no; that's why he'd lied to Christopher. Besides, it was none of his business. Nowadays, with banks snooping around and asking questions about where large sums of money came from, he had to deal in cash a lot of the time. It wasn't too much of a headache, especially knowing so many contacts abroad. But it was becoming trickier, and there was a dwindling source of those willing to risk everything.

He planned to stay in his room at the Montague Club later, and that was when he'd meet Christopher to propose his idea. That buffoon Sebastian Montague-Roland would also be attending, and he knew that he faced a long, dull evening ahead. But the benefits were worth it. He'd never paid for his membership at the club, and his wife didn't know about it. He settled all bills in cash, and kept a safe in his permanent room full of the stuff.

He didn't much like Christopher Slater, if the truth be told; after all, business was rarely advisable with friends. If he liked the guy, it wouldn't work; he'd feel too wretchedly guilty about the deceit. Philip Tooting was more his cup of tea. At least he possessed a sense of humour similar to his own, unlike the aristocratic brat or the dour civil servants' lackey. Evenings at the club were always more pleasurable when Philip was involved. He'd made noises recently that they needed to tidy up their affairs somewhat, until the business at Ravensword had died down. Benjamin had laughed at him, convinced of their infallibility, but Philip had been deadly serious.

'Some care is needed when paying for services,' he'd said cryptically. He always spoke like this, in code, and it made Benjamin chuckle, knowing that Philip fancied himself in the secret services. It was a common occurrence: people finding out that you were in the army and assuming they could have joined too, as if it was some kind of stint as a lollipop lady. No one gave a thought about the shit you went through to reach a rank of substance. The weeks of sleeping in a wet bivouac in Scotland, the months away from loved ones, the brutal marches with fifty kilos on your back, not to mention the sight of war. He didn't know anyone who'd served their country who, by his age, had healthy knees and ankles, and his back killed him all day long. His mind was as broken as his limbs. He would deserve his pension when it finally came, though it was a pittance. And that was why he'd sought other employment.

He stubbed out his fag and went back inside, aware that he smelled strongly of tobacco. His wife hated it, and wouldn't kiss him until he'd brushed his teeth, but he didn't much miss her affection, since he'd started paying for it elsewhere. A woman put her hand to her mouth as he walked past. Cheeky bitch, he thought. Entitled women: they were everywhere. Next thing, they'd be on the front line, whingeing about long hours and sleeping arrangements.

The world was going mad.

He looked at his watch. It was only two o'clock, but he had little to do. He'd become stale and bored in his job; it was time for a transfer. He'd avoided one for long enough, and he knew that any time soon he'd be relocated again. His desk telephone rang. It was some Brigadier upstairs, wanting to know who he knew in the Ayios Nikolaos garrison in Cyprus: the intelligence wing of Dhekelia Garrison. A detective wanted to speak to a local by the name of Alexandros Skarparis.

'Can you deal with this one, Ben? The commander's preparing for the Jordan exercise and he really hasn't got time for this shit. Just find out who liaises with the authorities from the garrison, will you, and get someone sent to his address as a matter of urgency.'

'Of course, Brigadier. Leave it with me.'

## Chapter 36

As the sun disappeared behind the Pennines, Kelly allowed herself to enjoy the moment and try to find some space in her head. She was almost home. The last time she'd made this journey, she'd been travelling to the Lakes for very different reasons, her tail between her legs, dishonoured by a colleague and unsure of her career and her future.

She'd been going to see her mother that day, and she wished she could talk to her now. It happened a lot. She heard her mother's voice every day. She missed her warmth, her wisdom and her peace. Wendy had exuded a constancy that Kelly could only strive for. Perhaps everyone compared themselves to their mother, and always fell short. As usual, her thoughts turned to regret. She'd been assured by many people, including Johnny, that it was normal. When someone so central to your life died, you yearned to make things right. She'd asked herself if she thought they would have been friends had they not been mother and daughter.

She tutted and crossed her legs: her attempt at peace wasn't going well. The car was quiet. Emma had secured the warrant for information to be supplied by the late Lord Allerdale's solicitors, and it was being prepared. Kelly stared out of the window at the dying day and willed herself home. The last part of the journey, once past

Manchester and Liverpool on the M6, was the quickest and most satisfying. She could see the mountains to the west and wished she was on top of one right now. It was a peculiar sensation, standing on the highest point of land and turning three hundred and sixty degrees, taking it all in, soaking up the awe. That was about the only thing that could truly clear her head, and she yearned for it now.

Finally the car pulled off the motorway. They'd soon be home. The prospect of sitting on her wooden terrace, listening to the stillness of the river, sipping a glass of wine, calmed her. In the five hours it had taken them to get here, the investigation had grown yet bigger and more complex. They always did. The worst part wasn't wondering what was coming next; it was worrying that the leads would start to dry up before the case had been closed. She'd worked on unsolved cases before, and they left an indelible mark. They were excruciatingly unsatisfying for everyone involved: families, officers, witnesses and the SIO.

She mulled over the moving parts, her mind refusing to still. In all three murders, the motive seemed to be to silence the victims. The staging had been done for kicks, and that churned her stomach.

Before leaving London, she'd called Johnny and asked him about Leo Brown, the young corporal kicked out of the army for drugs twenty years ago. He'd rung round a few old pals and learned that Leo Brown had spent two years at Catterick, and was in and out of trouble for minor misdemeanours all the time: fighting, drunken behaviour, assault on a girlfriend and keeping his sleeping area in rag order. Usually the army straightened out messed-up kids prone to violence and flouting authority, but not so with Leo. His reports were poor, and it was a miracle he made corporal. His only redeeming feature was his fitness. Apparently the lad was memorable because he'd shagged the company commander's daughter.

None of Johnny's contacts knew what had become of Brown after he was discharged in 1998, but it was quite obvious that he hadn't turned his life around. Kelly hoped he'd be brought in quickly. His photo had been released, and by now he should know that he was wanted for questioning. If he didn't turn up soon, it would be obvious that he was avoiding detection.

By the time the car pulled up in front of her house, the sky was fully dark. She thanked the driver and gathered her belongings. The house was lit with lamps and there was wine in the fridge. She smiled. It must have been Johnny. She dialled his number and heard a phone ringing upstairs. She pressed end call and threw her own phone onto the kitchen counter.

'You took your time.' He was in bed.

'I'm filthy.'

'Perfect, you've come to the right place.'

She went to him and sat on the edge of the bed. His body was warm and she allowed herself to be held. For the first time in almost three years, it really was like coming home.

# Chapter 37

Kelly toyed with the idea of going in late. It had been a delicious surprise waking up next to Johnny. Her first thought was that the bed smelled different to the one in the Premier Inn, and it was more comfortable. Then she felt his body and knew where she was. When she put her arms around him, she could tell he was beginning to put on a little bit of the muscle that he'd lost, and she liked it. One day, though, he'd have to give up the fried breakfasts, or take on another challenge.

She tore herself out of bed and he made her coffee. They made plans to meet for lunch and drive to Wendy's house. She'd been putting it off for months.

It was as she was getting dressed that she spotted a WhatsApp from her sister. At first she was worried that she'd missed one of her nieces' birthdays. Then she read the late-night rant about the Crawleys being her dear friends, and how Kelly had tried to ruin them. She showed Johnny. Nikki and Dave Crawley's wife had gone to school together, and she'd never forgiven Kelly for putting Dave behind bars, despite the fact that his lorries were full of sex workers.

'Do you want me to speak to her?' he asked. Johnny had been the one who'd been there for Nikki when the darkness drove her to the edge. He'd arranged PTSD counselling, but he could only go so far.

'Why should you?' Kelly said.

He shrugged his shoulders. 'Because I don't want you to and I'm not involved. It's not a problem, really.'

'To be honest, I think she's worked out by now that you're on my side. Don't bother. If she does it again, I'll block her.' It was the end of the conversation. She was determined not to let it sour her good mood, and she pushed Dave Crawley and his self-pity out of her mind.

She said goodbye to Johnny, who planned to take Josie shopping for the morning in Kendal. It wasn't Bond Street, but it had some cute boutiques, and he'd be back in time for lunch.

She was given the news about Miranda Cooper's fatal car accident on her way to see Graeme Millar. She could have brought him in, but they were supposed to be friends. It was Saturday, so she'd given herself a luxurious lie-in until 8.30. Matt had probably slept in the office again; she'd had two missed calls from him before her alarm even went off.

She seriously couldn't get her head around Graeme being somehow involved, but the facts indicated differently, and Matt seemed hell-bent on the new angle. She'd toyed with Philip Tooting about Occam's law, but now it was staring her in the face: the simplest explanation was usually the correct one, and Graeme Millar had been in too many convenient (or inconvenient) places during the inquiry. Last night Johnny had told her that Graeme had brought a girl to the pub who'd been asking all sorts of questions about the case. He thought she was called Millie until she showed him a picture and he confirmed it. Tilly Knight was cleverer than anyone gave her credit for. A journo would have done her homework, and there was no reason why she couldn't have found out about the boatyard and got to know Graeme. She was young and attractive: what single man could resist? Graeme had some explaining to do. And Kelly wanted to know if he'd ever served with Leo Brown.

What Matt had told her about Professor Cooper sat heavily on her mind. 'She was trying to get hold of you, Kelly. We don't know yet if she was on hands-free, or whether the accident had anything to do with loss of concentration.'

An onerous knot had sat in her stomach since that moment, and she couldn't shake it. She'd found Miranda Cooper aloof and arrogant, and she couldn't think why she might be trying to make contact with her, unless she had some information. Matt also mentioned that the driver of the lorry involved had scarpered, scared to death, no doubt, and they had no idea if he was injured.

'Number plate check?'

'Done. It was a Ravensword vehicle that had been out for most of the day. The driver was returning it to the yard and we got a name, but when we checked his address, he was asleep at home. He hadn't been in to work, and his alibi checks out: he and his wife had been up with their daughter for most of the night; she'd kept them awake with a vomiting bug.'

'Shit,' Kelly said.

'Quite.'

'CCTV?' she asked.

'None. And no witnesses. Plenty of people saw the pile-up and the aftermath, but everyone was concentrating

233

on the state of her car, and no one saw the driver leave, or whether he was injured. What are you up to today?' he added, as if she might be meeting a friend for tea and cake. It was a weird situation. She'd been in Matt's company for three long days, shoulder to shoulder, living and breathing a joint investigation, and it was surreal being on the phone to him every five minutes now. She knew she should tell Johnny, but she didn't know when to do it, and how, or even why. It was irrelevant, but not.

'I'm interviewing Graeme Millar. What did Leo Brown's aunt say?'

'She hasn't seen him in years. We did a cursory search: no antique racing shells or anything worth anywhere near half a million quid. How is it up there in the sticks?'

'Fuck off.'

She stopped at some traffic lights close to Keswick and glanced sideways. Her heart stopped as she recognised Dave Crawley in the driver's seat of a Land Rover. He was staring at her, and she froze. Her exes seemed to be crawling out of every crack at the moment. She felt vulnerable and shifted in her seat. The lights changed and she willed the traffic in front of her to move forward. His gaze was still fixed on her in a hateful scowl; she was glad of the protection of the car.

He'd gone to prison because of her, but he deserved to be there. She was only doing her job. Still, the look on his face made her question her sanity. The traffic freed up and she pulled away. He turned off in a different direction and she breathed a sigh of relief, but she noticed that her hands were shaking. Adrenalin hitting her stomach made her feel queasy, and she pulled off the road at the next petrol station to buy a full-sugar Lucozade to calm her nerves. Her armpits were sweaty and she looked over her shoulder several times.

The first slug of the cold, sugary liquid soothed her, and she put her head against the steering wheel and closed her eyes. She knew that her job made her a target for irate criminals. Being banged up was the end of the game for somebody like Dave. She was also acutely aware of how going against the tide of ingrained belief and hearsay in a small community like theirs took balls. To an outsider, or a criminal pinned down by the wealth of evidence she threw at them, she came across as just that: ballsy and indomitable. But inside, she was just a normal human being. Sometimes she hated finding out the things she did, but it didn't change the fact that bad people should be held accountable. She told herself to hold her nerve. She could always get a restraining order against him; any magistrate would do that for her. It was common in cases like this where perps were released early, vowing revenge. Not that Dave had done that, but he'd looked at her like somebody who wanted to kill her, and she knew it would ruin the rest of her day.

Graeme was waiting for her at the marina. His demeanour had changed dramatically since the last time she'd seen him. It looked like all the humour had drained from him: he wasn't his usual happy, casual self at all.

'Hi, Kelly. Do you want a cuppa?' He smiled, but not with his eyes.

'No thanks, Graeme, I'm good. Can we go somewhere private?'

He nodded and led her through the back entrance to a yard that his staff used for smoking. There was a tin ashtray, full of fag butts. They sat on plastic chairs. The yard was in sunshine, and it was pleasantly warm.

Kelly got out a pad and pencil. 'Do you mind if I take notes?'

'Is it formal?'

'I'm afraid the detective in charge of the case is breathing down my neck about some unanswered questions, and I've got some of my own too.'

'Right. What about?'

'I'm not going to lie to you, Graeme, it looks bad. If I have to take you in, I will. At the moment, no one is requesting your arrest, but it stinks.'

'What? What the hell are you talking about?'

'I believe you're working for Sebastian Montague-Roland?'

'He asked if I could project-manage the refurbishment of Allerdale House.'

'The place doesn't even belong to him.' It was a slight massaging of the facts, but up until recently – and perhaps not until she read the documents – it was true.

'What?' It was genuine shock.

Dave Crawley's face came back to her. She hoped Graeme wouldn't let her down like Dave had. She studied him and tried to find signs of truth or deceit; she could detect neither.

'How many times have you been to the house?'

'I can't remember.'

'Isn't it a little convenient that you saw some men posing as surveyors? Why didn't you tell me before?'

'I found a dead body; it was nothing to do with the house then.'

'Do you know Leo Brown?'

'No.'

'Do you know Tilly Knight?'

He opened his mouth.

'I see. Where is she, Graeme?'

'How do you know her?' he asked, avoiding the question.

'She was the last person George spoke to from Allerdale House before he was killed.'

'She didn't tell me that.'

'What else did she forget to tell you? Do you know where she is now?'

'Safe.'

'What?'

'There were some suspicious guys hanging around her guest house, and when I went up to her room, it had been turned over. They took her laptop; it has everything on it that she was working on.'

'What did George tell her?'

'I'm not really sure. All I know is that she's terrified, and it has something to do with what they were doing in some lab in London. She said that Alex told her—'

'Alex? She's been in contact with Alexandros Skarparis, in Cyprus?'

'Yes.

'Jesus. You have to tell me where she is, Graeme. If you withhold the information, you could get into a lot of trouble.'

'It sounds like I'm in trouble already. I'm quite happy to be hauled into a cell if it means she's safe.'

'Don't be an idiot. You've only known her for five minutes.'

'So what?'

Kelly saw then that he really cared for her. Perhaps their relationship was genuine, on his part at least. It was touching, and she softened.

They sat in silence for long minutes.

'I asked an old sailing pal of mine to look out for some of the goods that were stolen from the boathouse up at Allerdale House.'

'How do you know about that?'

'Everybody knows! Anyway, Sebastian said he wants to replace the antique oar boat, though not in not so many words. He's not the sharpest tool in the drawer. I think he genuinely thought I wouldn't put two and two together. I know quite a lot of people in the sailing industry; he asked me to source a replica, without actually telling me that his Grandfather's had been stolen.'

'Do you think he was involved with what happened to George?'

Graeme looked away, then back to her. 'He's difficult to work out, you know? He acts like the dim laird, but he's shrewd. He lives and breathes money. I've never seen him show interest in anything else other than acquisition.'

'You know he wasn't even supposed to get the money. It was all put in trust.' She watched Graeme's face.

'Jesus.'

'You seem shocked. Why is that?'

'He's never really shown any... you know... emotion about what happened to George. It's as if it was an inconvenience. I also get the impression that his grandfather didn't approve of his lifestyle, so it's perhaps not surprising to anyone but him that he'd be cut out of his inheritance.'

'What do you mean?'

'He's gay, Kelly.'

'Really? I hadn't noticed.' She made a note to look into the old peer's voting history on homosexual legislation. 'Has your sailing friend got back to you yet?'

'Yes. He gave me the name of a small business in London.' He looked at his phone. 'The name meant nothing to me, so I saved it for you.'

He showed her the screen, and she jotted down the name, not letting on that it was familiar to her. 'Have you made contact?' she asked. He shook his head.

'You know Sebastian never locks the doors up there? I told him he should, but he still doesn't, not even after the burglary and murder. That's odd, don't you think?'

'In what way?'

'Do you know any homeowner who takes violation like that so lightly? It's his property – well, at least that's what everyone thinks – and George Murphy was supposedly a friend of his grandfather's.'

She shook her head.

'So. Where is she?'

He didn't reply.

'George paid her ten thousand pounds.'

'What?'

'You heard me.'

'Then she's definitely better off staying where she is.'

'Let me talk to her,' Kelly said. 'Go on, call her and tell her who you're with. She should have worked out by now that we want to speak to her.'

'But you can't protect her.'

'Of course we can, and if she puts me in touch with Alexandros, I can protect him too.'

He made the call.

While Kelly waited, Matt called and she answered. He told her that Tilly Knight had been positively ID'd by a uniform stationed outside George's house on Tuesday, but she'd given her name as Madeleine Cromer and had done a very good impression of a concerned friend.

'I think I might have found her,' Kelly said.

'Let me know when she's in custody.'

'We have a problem. She's terrified, and I'll need to set up some kind of house protection.'

'Do it.'

She hung up and listened to Graeme speaking. He passed her his phone.

'Tilly?'

'Yes.'

'This is DI Kelly Porter. You've caused us some headaches trying to find you. I need to speak to you.'

'I know. I don't feel safe. Did Graeme tell you what happened?'

'Yes, and I've just spoken to my boss about getting you some protection. I need to make contact with Alex as well. He's likely in danger too and he has nothing to fear by speaking to me. I can fly him out of the military base and have him safe by the morning.'

'Will Graeme bring you to me?'

'I'll arrange it. Thank you.'

She handed the phone back to Graeme, then closed her notepad. The name she'd jotted down from his phone regarding the racing equipment was Brenda Light, from Marine Light Nautical Antiques. Leo Brown's aunt. She also knew that Leo had served with Graeme, albeit very briefly, in 1997. Graeme had been a young and inex- perienced second lieutenant back then. He'd also been

240

Brown's platoon commander. She would discuss that with him in the car.

But first she tasked Eden House with an alert to all units to look out for the two men suspected of turning over Tilly Knight's hotel room, who could possibly still be in the area.

## Chapter 38

Kelly used the journey to get more information out of Graeme. She was confident that he wasn't involved with George's murder, though she had no proof for that just yet. But what he'd said about Sebastian had stoked her interest and she wondered if he'd been pinned down in London yet. It was only a matter of hours since she'd last spoken to Matt about it. She dialled Rob Shawcross at Eden House and asked if the warrant that had been secured by Emma Hide was ready yet.

The answer was not what she wanted to hear. The firm of solicitors was now saying that the dispute was no longer company business and they'd have to speak to a separate legal department. It was maddening. All they needed was a copy of the original will.

She listened to Graeme talking about his little cottage, and why he'd chosen to take Tilly there. After his divorce, he had taken some of the equity from the family home and bought a tiny stone dwelling in Bampton Grange, just north of Haweswater. It was miles away from anywhere, but an epic base for the best walks in the National Park, and it was all his. It had two open floors, a range in the kitchen, and one bedroom. He said the solitude had provided therapy at the time as he'd pondered what to do with his life. Eventually he'd worked through his feelings of grief and betrayal and had seen a vision of what his future might look like, but even though he'd bought a flat in Portinscale, he couldn't bear to get rid of the cottage. Now, when he didn't have the girls staying with him, he went there to think and to walk quiet trails. He'd nearly told his ex-wife about it, but had second thoughts. It was as if it was somehow symbolic of how he'd survived without her.

It was a lengthy explanation and it made Kelly re-evaluate Graeme. The depth and confidence he showed impressed her. He spoke like a survivor, and she guessed the divorce had been extremely painful.

'You must trust her,' he said.

'Tilly?'

He nodded. 'You'll understand when you meet her. I've never met anyone so passionate and driven.'

It was what Johnny said about Kelly.

She drove expertly along the tiny twisting lanes, passing Haweswater reservoir. She felt a pang as she thought of little Lottie Davis, who'd gone missing there so many years ago. The family had been walking along the gnarly shoreline and Lottie had been playing hide-and-seek with her brother. She gripped the steering wheel tighter.

They spotted Lowther Castle in the distance, sitting majestically among the trees. She'd never been there. This side of the Lake District was gentle and rolling, the dry-stone walls weaving across bright green fields for miles. Tourists rarely ventured over this way. Soon Graeme told her they were almost there. She'd never been to Bampton or Bampton Grange. The village itself was tiny and charming. Rolling fields surrounded stone cottages and the narrow roads were deserted. She imagined it must be hell for a journalist sniffing a story to be holed up here. The irony.

Graeme told her where to park. He looked about furtively.

'Does she have any idea who might want to hurt her, or who might have her laptop?'

'No. She just knows that whoever it is killed George and his work colleagues.'

'What makes her so sure?'

'Why don't you ask her yourself?'

He took a key from his jeans and walked down a pretty path to a cottage standing on its own. The garden was mature and well looked after. The curtains were closed. Inside, it was stuffy and warm.

'Graeme?' a female voice shouted down the stairs. It had an edge of panic: the woman was scared indeed.

'Yup. I've got Kelly with me.'

They heard footsteps, and a petite woman wearing sweatpants and a sloppy jumper padded down into the main reception room. Her face was fresh and she smiled warmly at Kelly, who offered her hand. Graeme said he'd put the kettle on.

'So, Tilly, we've been looking for you. You obviously thought you'd take matters into your own hands. I think my priority now that I know where you are is contacting Alexandros. We desperately need to talk to him.'

'He's shit scared. He's going to the family home up in the mountains. It was my idea. We said we'd Skype last night, but the connection was so bad we're going to try again today. I heard enough to know that he didn't go to the mountains yesterday because of his mother. He's going today instead.'

'What time?'

'I don't know.'

'Can you call him?'

'I can try, though he said he'd be driving.' She took out her phone and punched in a number. 'It's ringing out.'

'What has he told you about George and his colleagues?'

'Just that they were killed because the trials they were working on were reaching a stage that was viable.'

'What trials?'

'George had made himself an addict and was experimenting on a drug that could reverse the process.'

'Is this some kind of precious secret that is worth a lot of money?'

'It's not about the money, it's about the potential to disturb world economies, and George refused to sell it. They refer to it as Compound P, but I'm not entirely sure what it consists of. Alexandros was going to explain it all to me, but he's jumpy; he doesn't know who to trust.'

'Why did George pay you ten thousand pounds?'

'It was a deposit. He was going to pay me fifty grand on the publication of my article, which would have exposed something major. That's as far as he got. He was killed the night I spoke to him.' Tilly looked at her hands. 'Do you mind if I smoke?'

'No, go ahead.'

She fetched cigarettes and lit one, inhaling deeply. Kelly envied her and remembered how the first drag felt. She wouldn't appreciate it quite so much later when her hair and clothes reeked of the stuff.

'Graeme gave me a description of the men you saw in Portinscale. What was on your laptop?'

'Everything. My notes, my contacts, my ideas, names, profiles, bios: the lot. I'm devastated.'

'And you have no idea who's behind all this?'

'No. All George said was that some very powerful people wanted his work.'

'What about Alexandros? Why didn't he go to the police in London?'

'He thinks he has a better chance of staying alive in Cyprus.'

'Would you be happier if I arranged some kind of police protection for you?'

Graeme spoke. 'Nobody knows about this place, so it's like advertising something is here.'

Kelly had to agree with him. She didn't know what Matt would say about it, though, and she needed to keep Tilly on side.

'What do you think, Tilly?'

'I think Graeme's right. I feel safe here.'

'Right, Graeme, are you coming back with me?'

'I need to get my car, so yes please, I'll hitch a ride.'

Kelly made a note of Alex's mobile number and they left Tilly looking small and afraid. She would make sure that a patrol car from the closest station drove past more than their usual once a year.

# Chapter 39

Alexandros's mother followed him around the house talking at him as he tried to pack. She told him of his auntie's latest foot ailment, about the possibility of obtaining a rescue cat to replace the gaping hole in her heart left by Aphrodite, and about the layering of the perfect moussaka.

He'd persuaded her to close and lock both the front and back doors. She'd complained at first but he'd gone ahead and locked them anyway. He couldn't begin to explain his real fears. Not only would it scare her to death; she'd also probably tell half of Larnaca.

His anxiety was crippling and he felt like a sitting duck where he was. Tilly was right: he had to be careful. He hadn't even thought about the possibility of the military base somehow being involved, but they had police there who might already be looking for him. The endless scenarios in his head made him dizzy.

He trusted no one except himself. He'd even questioned if he should have faith in Tilly Knight. He went constantly back and forth in his mind about whether he should have confided in her, but then again, he didn't really know that much. He had no idea who had it in for George and his research project; just how valuable it was. George had never said they might be in danger.

The villa was deep in the Troodos Mountains, and his mother had refused to go with him. His instinct told him that it was only him they wanted – professionals would be quick and tidy – so he gave up trying to persuade her. In fact he felt guilty that every moment he stayed here was putting her in greater danger.

He smelled the pastries she had been making all morning. Sometimes she bought them from the bakery in Xylotymbou, but he preferred her home-made ones. She'd made boureki, and his stomach rumbled. He looked out of his bedroom window and gazed at the ocean. It was deep azure, and he could see boats and bathers enjoying the June sunshine. Below the window a car pulled up and stay parked for a few minutes. It had a British plate. Two white men sat in the front; they seemed to be having a heated conversation. One of them looked directly at Alex's window, and he darted behind the shutter, banging his head. It stung and he rubbed it. His room was dark, and outside the sun glared, so they probably hadn't seen him. He thought about his mother and ran downstairs to the kitchen. The back door was wide open. He slammed it shut and locked it, grabbing his mother's arm.

'Alex!'

'Shh!'

She continued to complain, but he forced her into the living room and sat her on the sofa, shushing her once more. He went to the downstairs shutters, which his mother kept closed at this time of the year to keep the house cool, and peered through them. The car was still there and the two men were pointing at the house. Then suddenly there was a squeal of tyres and they pulled away. Alex's head screamed with fear. He explained to his mother that she had no choice but to come with him. She became upset. He apologised but was just as firm, but she refused to leave.

He swore loudly in English so she couldn't understand, then reverted to his native tongue to try again. He told her they were in danger. He told her that some men knew he was here and wanted to kill him. That did the trick. She said she needed to pack and he gave her five minutes. If the pair in the car had been checking the location, it probably meant they'd come back at night.

Since he'd been on the island, Alex hadn't shaved, and now he grabbed a baseball cap, plopping it onto his head, as well as taking sunglasses, and a bandana for round his neck. His mother fussed around and he could hear her on the phone. He groaned inwardly and wished he'd never come here in the first place. He turned off all the electrical sockets, except the fridge, and checked that the windows were secure. He'd leave the back door unlocked so that when they came back they would cause no damage. It would be clear that no one was home.

He jogged upstairs to see if his mother was ready and found her sitting on her bed crying into her phone. He realised that he'd screwed up badly. He willed himself to think, but his thoughts were confused. He had no idea who to turn to, and only the villa seemed like a safe option. He made a decision and found a suitcase in his mother's wardrobe. He stuffed some items into it and slammed it shut, then took his mother by the arm and virtually carried her downstairs and out into the sunshine. He helped her into his pickup, then went back inside for his own luggage. Closing the door behind him, he jumped into the driver's seat, starting the engine too enthusiastically and scaring his mother.

She cried all the way to the Troodos Mountains.

The roads were quiet, and Alex drove with the windows down. To foreigners, June on the island was as hot as a furnace, but to a local, air con was only required when the mercury topped forty-five degrees, in August. He played music to distract his mother, but all he could hear was her wailing. Eventually he put the windows up so people wouldn't think he was kidnapping her.

All the way, he kept vigilant. He stared at every driver, examined every face, and watched the traffic to see if he was being followed. He forced himself to smile and tap the wheel so he didn't appear nervous or jumpy, but inside, his guts were mush.

His mobile phone rang, but he ignored it.

## Chapter 40

Kelly drove to Eden House. She was keen to brief her team for the first time in a week, and the thrill of the chase was evident in the office, despite it being Saturday. As far as she could make out from talking to DS Kate Umshaw, they'd made the most of her short sabbatical and set about proving themselves to their absent boss. Kelly was impressed. During an investigation, there were certain milestones that guided the whole thing forward. Sometimes, like false summits on a mountainside, they could follow leads for weeks and end up having to reverse and start again. But today felt good. The investigation was well oiled, and besides, she'd missed her team. She went into the incident room and strode to the front desk. Emma was having a well-earned day off, while Matt was expecting to attend via video link.

'Well, you lot look like you don't need me around here.' It was true: they all appeared busy and focused until they realised that their boss had just walked in; then they stopped what they were doing and greeted her, saying they'd forgotten the time and asking her how London had been. There was a low hum of excitement as they waited their turn to bring her up to date with what they'd been working on. It touched her and she felt like she really belonged. She noticed that this was happening more and more lately. Coming back to Johnny, coming home to her team, and later she'd see Ted. It felt right.

It was good to be back. The air was different from London, and not only that, the change of pace was welcome. There was less of a rush to get results and move forward. It wasn't that there was no urgency here; it was just that the self-imposed pressure was removed. Of course they wanted to find answers for those who loved George Murphy and his colleagues, but there was also a harmony that was lacking in the huge glass buildings of the capital. Kelly embraced it all and took a deep breath. Last night Johnny had asked her if the big city had retained its lure for her, and she'd emphatically told him no.

She logged on to her computer and Matt's face appeared. She introduced him to her team and began to lead the meeting, hoping he wouldn't butt in too much. Matt looked tired and she guessed she did too. Her team responded well to him, because he was good at his job and asked all the right questions, and after an initial nervousness, everyone soon relaxed.

'The white van angle is promising,' Kelly said, 'and we're still on the lookout for this man.' A photograph of Leo Brown came up on the large whiteboard shared by all their personal computers and screens, so that Matt could see. The mug shot supplied by the parole officer was unflattering. Kelly usually found that if something walked like a duck and talked like a duck, it usually was a duck, and Leo Brown was their strongest lead yet. But they couldn't find him. 'He should know by now that he's wanted for questioning.'

'The aunt is unconvincing and I've put her under surveillance,' Matt said. 'How did the interview with Graeme Millar go?'

If her team was puzzled, they hid it well. She hadn't informed them of Matt's suspicions. They also hadn't witnessed a suspect coming in to be questioned.

'He gave me the details of Marine Light Nautical. An old sailing pal of his is keeping his ear to the ground for the antique shell. Also Tilly Knight is with him and she's been in touch with Alexandros Skarparis. If I can persuade him to go to the military base in Cyprus then we could get him back here, but I haven't spoken to him yet. Apparently he's as jittery as she is and he's gone to a pad in the mountains. I'll speak to him later. Tilly's hotel room here has been broken into and I've got a description of two men; also her laptop with all her work on George has gone.'

'What did George tell her?'

'Nothing that implicates anybody in his death, apart from saying that his research into addiction was valuable to some powerful people. He was testing himself as a lab rat: hence the cocaine in his system.'

'Anything concrete?' Matt asked.

'No.'

Matt rubbed his eyes. Kelly moved on.

'Will, anything in the financial files of Allerdale House?' Will Phillips and Rob Shawcross had been given the task of trawling through the late peer's papers.

'The payments to George Murphy, and also the running of the Montague Club.'

The Montague Club had popped up when they were trying to find Sebastian. The elite postcode was enough to indicate the value of such a place, which turned out to be a sumptuous private club owned by the Montague-Rolands for decades. Matt had obtained a warrant for a full membership list; however, these private clubs, nestling behind the hustle and bustle of Mayfair, promising anonymity from prying paparazzi, were notoriously secret, and it might take more than simply looking through a register. Some members were probably completely off the record: celebrities and the mega rich, even royals.

'Does George Murphy strike any of you as the kind of man to hobnob with wealthy men in dinner jackets?' Kelly asked.

Matt remained silent, watching her. Everyone else shook their heads.

'Me neither, but it turns out he's a life member of the Montague Club. As is the CEO of Ravensword, Philip Tooting.' Kelly brought up Tooting's photo along-side George's on the whiteboard. 'He's an arrogant man and I'm not letting him off our radar just yet. George I can kind of understand, because he and Lord Allerdale were both champion rowers for Cambridge, though in different decades. From what we can make out about Allerdale, though, he was a bit of a philanthropist, and that's the opposite of Tooting, who's about as capitalist as they come. There's an annual rowing alumni dinner at the club; this year's was on Wednesday just gone.'

She let the information sink in.

'Matt, I asked DC Shawcross to create a matrix of names covering Ravensword and the Montague Club, using the lists you supplied.' For all his charm, Rob Shawcross was a certified nerd, and it came in handy. 'I'll bring it up. One name has popped up.'

'I can see that. Who's Christopher Slater?' asked Matt.

'He's a non-executive director at DEFRA,' Kelly said. 'His background is in global companies – no surprise there. All four NEDs at DEFRA have similar backgrounds: basically, they work for massive companies, then retire with golden handshakes and become advisers to government departments, on handsome salaries. It's all above board. Every state office has them. They work part time, enjoy huge benefits and status, and still get paid.'

'Nice work if you can get it. What's he got to do with Ravensword?' Matt asked.

'He's an ex-CEO. Resigned after the colantropine scandal. He also held positions in alcohol and tobacco firms, and the oil industry, and returned to pharmaceuticals before moving to advisory and charity work.'

'Jesus, they all look after each other, don't they?' Matt's voice dripped with disgust. 'And he's a member of the Montague Club?'

'Yup. And of the Cambridge rowing alumni,' Kelly added.

'Cosy,' Matt said. 'I can easily get hold of a guest list for Wednesday night.'

Kelly had expected that.

'It's not a solid lead – some old rich dudes getting together to chat about how good life is and smoke cigars – but I agree it looks bad. We'll have to be watertight on this one. The Montague Club has an army of lawyers; we've already had dealings with them for demanding the members' list. Everything – and I mean everything – has to be checked in duplicate and triplicate before we go around accusing civil servants of anything.'

'He's not a civil servant.'

'What? I thought you said he worked for DEFRA?'

'Non-executive directors are advisory; they come from business backgrounds, not ministerial.'

'Is that important?' Matt was curt.

'Not really. It's just—'

'Can you call me privately, DI Porter?'

He logged off. Kelly looked at her team, who sat in shock; they'd never seen their boss treated in such a way.

'I guess that means the meeting's over. We've all got plenty to do, and I've got the narcotics team to meet at Allerdale House. Keep up the good work, everybody. Rob, carry on digging about the membership. Will, call Lord Allerdale's solicitors, will you? See if they can't be persuaded to answer a few very straightforward questions and stop wasting everyone's time.' As an afterthought, she turned around. 'Find out if they're the same solicitors used by the Montague Club, or if they're affiliated.'

She went back to her office and dialled Matt's number.

'That was unprofessional,' she said.

'I had all I needed. Your team are doing great work, Kelly. Don't take things personally.'

His tone galled her. He was right: being face to face was so much easier. This way he could manipulate her every word.

'We've found Leo Brown.'

Kelly forgot Matt's rudeness. 'Where?'

'In one of his aunt's warehouses, along with half a million quid's worth of rowing kit. The aunt's in custody too. She's a hard-old hag. Hasn't said a word. Leo's coming down from a high, so he's jittery as anything.'

'That's brilliant! Has he said who hired him?'

'Whoa, slow down, we haven't even started the tough love yet. I'm making him sweat. We got a warrant for her office and found a Glock nine-millimetre.'

'Bloody brilliant!' Kelly clenched her fist.

'You could have stayed in London and been in the thick of it.'

She didn't bother answering. 'I'll ring the Montague Club for the guest list for Wednesday. I wonder if George was going to attend.'

'I still think I should come north to see where it all happens. Up there in the sticks.'

She hung up. She couldn't work out if he was winding her up personally or professionally. Was he trying to trip her up? Surely not. Undermine and embarrass, maybe. She shook her head. 'Wanker,' she said under her breath.

She found the number for the Montague Club and was put through to the bursar. She explained that as part of their ongoing inquiry, she needed to see the guest list for the Cambridge rowing alumni annual dinner. The man wasn't sure about what to do, so Kelly reminded him that the club's owner, Sebastian Montague-Roland, was happy for them to request the list, and that though she appreciated the need for discretion, this was a police inquiry, and they had secured a warrant. It was a tiny white lie: in fact warrants had to be so specific that a guest list was entirely different to a members' list, but she knew they'd soon get one anyway, unless the army of lawyers intervened. She needn't have worried. The man acquiesced quickly and she gave him her email address.

'Did you know George Murphy?' she asked.

'Yes, madam, I did. He'd been coming here for years, but not so much since Lord Allerdale's death, rest his soul.'

'How did the club mark the passing of a distinguished member who was so close to the previous owner?'

The bursar's voice dropped. 'Well that's the thing. They didn't. I think it was a tricky subject. I heard he was murdered; it would be terrible publicity for the club.'

'And do you think the late Lord Allerdale would have agreed?'

There was a pause.

'No, madam, I don't.'

'Thank you.'

The bursar was as good as his word, and an email came through ten minutes later. Kelly stared at the guest list and shook her head. George's name was crossed out; he'd been due to sit at the same table as her band of merry men, led by Sebastian Montague-Roland (who didn't row, and hadn't attended Cambridge). She tapped her foot on the chair leg and wrote some notes on a diagram. HOLMES used a very similar methodology: a series of spider diagrams with connections and patterns in different colours. Kelly preferred to draw her own models. They usually ended up the same as the HOLMES ones, but that wasn't the point. She wasn't doing it to see if she was right; she was doing it to visualise all the moving parts, to commit them to the part of her brain that took notice of what her hands did. To understand the information, one first had to own it, and it was very difficult to get excited about something that had been churned out by a computer. Christopher Slater was on Sebastian's table, as well as a serving colonel called Benjamin Dansford. She'd heard the name before but she couldn't place when or in what context. She wondered if he'd come up in one of Johnny's tales.

Matt called again and she toyed with ignoring him: the thought was childish but totally understandable, given his behaviour. She answered curtly.

'Kelly, I've just had a call from the military police at Dhekelia garrison. Whoever you spoke to at the MoD did as you asked and sent somebody to Alexandros's address, but there was no one home and they've tried several times.'

'He told Tilly that he was going to the mountains, to a villa; can they get hold of any relatives who might know where that is? Whose jurisdiction is it?'

'Local Cypriot. The military police are merely offering help because he was wanted for questioning here.'

'I wonder where Colonel Dansford is stationed currently, and if he ever served in Cyprus. If so, he might have some old pals still there.'

# Chapter 41

The Montague Club was quiet, but then it usually was unless there was an event taking place. It was the type of place that could cater for lots of people without seeming to ever be crowded. There were busy parts to it: mainly the rooftop bar, frequented by celebrities. But if one wanted solitude, it was readily available.

Philip Tooting mulled over the information he'd been given on Kelly Porter. She was like a terrier: fierce and loyal. She had a reputation for not giving up. But she also suffered the malfunctions of the midget canine: rashness and stubbornness born from a romantic sense of entitlement. He'd had several terriers himself, and they were good pets. He had come to the conclusion that Kelly Porter would fight to the death, but she'd also probably be stupidly brave. She could be tricked.

His heels clacked on the tiles as he was shown to a private dining room. Slater and Dansford were waiting for him, and the Colonel looked as though he was inebriated already, despite it being only mid-morning. Christopher rolled his eyes.

'Gentlemen. We have a problem.' Philip didn't even sit down before beginning to speak. He nodded to a waiter, who scuttled off to fetch a cigar and his favourite brandy; if Churchill could do it, then so could he. He couldn't smoke the cigar inside the room, but the balcony was welcoming and comfortable. No one complained if a whiff of smoke came in with a breeze. Things had been much easier when Alan was alive: George would do anything for him. But with the old man out of the way, George had been left vulnerable.

'This is getting too hot for me, Philip,' Christopher interrupted. 'I never signed up to be exposed to this level of invasion. I've had the Permanent Under-Secretary asking me about my membership. It's technically none of her business, but when pushed on how the information came to her attention, she was cagey and evasive. Someone's talking and I don't know if it's the police or Sebastian himself. If your buffoon of a soldier had handled things better, Benji, we wouldn't be in this mess.'

The Colonel took a large sip from the glass of red wine that had arrived on a silver platter. 'Now, now, gentlemen, we can all point the finger. Yes, Cumbria was handled badly, but that can't be undone. Using scum always has its disadvantages, but we also know that our options are limited when dealing with the matter of dirtying one's hands. We had a problem and that was eliminated. Unfortunately it was messy and one got away. It simply means that we now have another problem, but it's not insurmountable. The stakes just got higher. I want to talk about making life difficult for a few members of the police force.'

'You can't play that game, Philip,' Slater said, the colour draining from his face. 'We should cut our losses, tie up the loose ends, tidy up after ourselves and get a good solicitor. This will be my last time at the club. I have to put some distance between myself and certain familiar faces.

I'm withdrawing. I've always made absolutely sure that nothing leads to me directly.'

'I know, Christopher, and that's why you can't bail out now. Besides, your salvation is what you have on the dame. You could put her away for years, though she'd still squeal. If you didn't want to be muddied, you really should have found a different line of work by now, my friend. Even you leave a trail.'

Slater looked at Tooting, and beads of sweat began to form on his forehead.

'Besides, how will you explain to your wife that you can't go to Barbados this year? I've always got on so well with your family, Christopher. It would be with a heavy heart that I would have to explain your role in the messy deaths of some employees of mine. But I'm sure I could arrange some personal support for them.' He smiled and picked his teeth with a wooden pick from the silver pot that sat on a low table, next to olives, peanuts and some sort of sweet crisp.

'*You* are going to blackmail *me*?' Slater's eyes widened.

'Oh Christopher. Your hands are so dirty, you'd better be careful wiping the tears away; you might catch a nasty illness. Benji, are you still awake?'

'Yes, Philip.'

'I want you to find someone we can rely on; not one of your washed-up soldiers but someone who costs a little more. Get to the little scrapper and shut him up. Those holding cells can be violent places if one has to share with someone volatile with a desperate family on the outside.'

The Colonel fiddled with his tie. Slater paced up and down.

'What about Cyprus, Benji?' Tooting asked.

'I'm on it. I've got a few favours owed there. It hasn't been confirmed yet.'

'Well bloody hurry it along, man! I suggest we give the investigation somebody closer to the deceased to toy with. After all, Sebastian harboured a virulent jealousy towards George, especially once he found out that he was to look after his money until he proved himself capable of fucking a woman and providing heirs of his own. He's tried to slow the solicitors down, but I think we should do the opposite.' Everybody knew that Sebastian was beholden to Philip until he could get his hands on his grandfather's money. But then perhaps he'd be a liability.

'That's it. That's what we go with.' Slater was animated. Philip found it amusing that only a minute ago he'd been threatening to walk out on them. Now he was back on board simply because a fall guy had been provided to cover for him.

Philip nodded. 'What about the journalist. Why can't we find her?'

'She's vanished. She was snooping around asking questions. We had eyes on her but she got spooked. She was with a man. Graeme Millar. The same one who found George's body.'

'What? I'm not going to ask about your sources, Christopher, but are they accurate?'

'Watertight, Philip. Benji knows the guy.'

All eyes fell on the Colonel, who had got up to smoke a cigarette on the balcony. He stopped when the name came up, and turned to face his co-conspirators.

'The link is tenuous. I served for five minutes with him in the same garrison when I first met Brown.'

'Before or after Brown shagged your daughter?'

'Fuck off, Christopher.' The Colonel turned back to Philip. 'I don't know what he's doing in Cumbria. He was a fine soldier but not a career one. He was Brown's platoon commander.'

'I'm not feeling this,' Philip said. 'It's a little convenient, isn't it? How much do you trust Brown? I think he's set you up, Benji.'

The Colonel shook his head. 'No chance. It's pure coincidence. And he won't have given the police anything. Same for Auntie Brenda – she's got balls bigger than Churchill's.'

'You seem remarkably calm, I'll give you that. And no result in Cyprus either? Who are you hiring, monkeys?'

'I've had a lot on my mind. They'll find him.'

'Splendid. Make sure they do. Is the journalist talking to police?'

'We don't know,' Slater replied.

'Why not?'

'She's not on the system.'

'But you had her computer checked?'

'It's theorising mostly, no names.'

'Good. Let's eat. I'm ravenous.' Philip ended the conversation as waiters carrying silver platters came into the intimate dining room and began setting places and removing lids. He had ordered a lavish brunch of smoked salmon, toasted rolls, cold meats, kippers and fruit. There were jugs of freshly squeezed juice, and champagne should anyone wish to partake. It was a banquet fit for three conspiring males intent on getting away with murder. Philip slapped butter on a roll and layered it with smoked salmon. The noises of men eating greedily filled the room and they all stopped talking.

By the time they'd finished, a good forty-five minutes later, sentient acknowledgement of what they contemplated had been side-lined. The Colonel and Philip went on to the balcony to smoke, and Benji swayed a little.

'Why can't we just have this fellow Millar followed?' Philip asked.

'I am.'

'Good man. Who are you using?'

'Sebastian told me about a private detective who works out of Lancaster. I contacted him and gave him the details. He informed me that Millar drove well out of his way to visit a cottage in the middle of nowhere three times in as many days. Each time he went in, he had a thorough look about first.'

'Your man must be good.'

'Apparently Sebastian used him to check out a few things after his grandfather died, and he impressed him.'

'What does it take to get past an army man, Benji?'

'Millar only served for a few years; he's gone soft.'

Philip puffed on a £40 Arturo Fuente Opus X cigar. He kept a box of Gurkha Black Dragons at the club for special occasions only; today wasn't one of those. He glanced at the Colonel, who looked green.

'Good God, man, cut down on the Malbec, will you? You're no use to me when you're a gibbering piece of jelly. Sort yourself out.'

'Yes, Philip. I wanted to thank you for the lawyers. Both those rape charges have been dropped.'

'Marvellous.'

Philip contemplated the Colonel. He knew that if push came to shove, Slater would squeal like a girl should he be caught red-handed, but Benji would go to his grave with his secrets. And that was exactly what he was relying on. He needed a slick operation. A pool of reliable people, like the one who'd taken care of Professor Cooper: speedy, sanitary and meticulous. He'd already prepared the necessary documents to entrap Slater, who wouldn't work for DEFRA for much longer, that was for sure. Benji was a more personal attachment, like one of his dogs.

'It's fantastic up here, Philip.'

Philip looked beyond the balcony and wondered what his friend was referring to. The London skyline was unimpressive from this side of the city, and little could be made out apart from rooftops and the honks of traffic. Perhaps he meant the whiff of luxury coming up from the streets of Mayfair, somewhere he could never envisage gracing as a mere colonel. He might expect the odd invitation to a reunion at the Cavalry and Guards Club, but that was about it.

'Do me a favour, old chap.' Benji always talked like the public schoolboy he was.

'What's that?'

'Look after my family.'

'Now, now, we'll have none of that talk, Benji. Go and sleep it off; some of us have work to do. Don't let the bastards grind you down, old man. There's always a solution. Get your man up north to see if he can find the journalist, sort out Cyprus, and then we're all done. I'll make sure the detective doesn't get too close.'

The Colonel tottered drunkenly towards the balcony door. He swayed past Christopher Slater, who rolled his eyes again, and out into the hallway, where he made his way towards his room. Philip came back in.

'Fucking liability. I always said that, Philip.'

'All right, Christopher, calm down, you'll give yourself a nose bleed. Will you ask your damned contact to find out something personal about this detective? Let me down and I'll know it was lack of effort, do you understand? Meanwhile, I'll sort the solicitors.'

'Of course, Philip. I'll see you tomorrow.'

Philip left the room and headed straight to the car waiting outside to take him to his flat in central London. He'd had enough of the club. He'd speak to Sebastian in good time.

# Chapter 42

Leo Brown stared at his hands, then sat forward, resting his elbows on his knees. He'd been left alone and was being brought a coffee. He was trying to keep still, because he knew he was being recorded. He didn't want to give away anything through his body language that could incriminate him later. He had a story and so far he'd had the balls to stick to it. They were going easy on him: he was a professional police interviewee and knew these things. They were waiting to pounce, he could feel it. He intended to give them a few nuggets and play their game. Auntie Brenda would have said nothing apart from 'no comment'.

He was being interviewed by two coppers and they took turns asking him the same questions over and over again, but in different and sometimes conflicting ways. He knew they were trying to catch him out, and it was a clever tool. Lies took effort and were very complicated to get right, whereas the truth was easy to remember because it was indisputable. But he hadn't given them enough to pull apart. Yet. He was getting tired and thirsty, and he longed to lie down. He was also desperate for a smoke. A joint or a puff of a pipe would hit the spot.

Over the years, he'd been questioned hundreds of times about various misdemeanours, and he'd grown to despise the police. They were just ordinary men and women with a job to do, hopeful that the people they dragged in to question and intimidate were scared of the law. He was no longer scared of the law. In fact, he actually quite liked prison. It was like the army: it required no effort and zero responsibility, and he could easily get his smack. He'd read somewhere recently that soldiers who'd been kicked out for drugs offences were being let back in; they must be desperate. The idea that anyone could be expected to do what he'd had to do in Northern Ireland and not snort coke was a fucking joke. He also didn't fancy running any more. The people he worked for on and off were scarier than a little piece of ass in a black and white uniform. He yawned. They couldn't get him in here.

The dynamic duo came back in and resumed their tedious questions. They switched on the microphone, giving mundane administrative details first.

'Leo, do you recognise this vehicle? For the purposes of the tape, suspect is being shown evidence number LB/01.'

Leo looked at the photo of the white van.

'I think I want a lawyer.'

–

The detectives sighed. Time was of the essence in any interview, because they had only a limited period of time to hold somebody before they had to let them go. Anything not forensic, or not corroborated by a witness, counted as merely circumstantial, so they either needed a suspect to crack or for the lab results to arrive quickly. As somebody who'd been on the wrong side of the law, Leo Brown would know this, as well as their limits concerning interview protocol.

The vehicle in question still hadn't been located. By now, it could have easily been stripped of its plates and spray-painted, or even torched in some field. The plates caught on CCTV were different to those that Graeme Millar had reported on the van parked in Portinscale, but Millar had remembered one small detail that linked the two: the graffiti scrawled in the filth on the back. It matched what one of George Murphy's neighbours had reported about the van parked outside his house. The graffiti was memorable; it read: *I wish my wife was this dirty.* Then underneath, in a different style: *She was last night.*

One of the detectives read the words out to Leo, who smirked back at them.

'Leo, the ballistics team have come back to us, and the Glock found at your aunt's place matches the murder weapon used to kill George Murphy. For the purposes of the tape, the suspect is being shown evidence number LB/02.' It was a photograph of the Glock, next to a crushed slug. Leo wondered if the pellet had stayed in George's brain. If it had, it was bad luck.

'No comment.'

'Do you keep in touch with any of your army pals, Leo?'

'I said I want a lawyer.'

'Sure, but we may as well have a chat while we find you one.'

'Nice try. No comment.'

–

An officer came into the room and passed a piece of paper to one of the detectives. They smiled at one another and

Leo watched them. He knew the look: they had something. He yawned again.

'We've had some lab results sped up in your honour, Leo. Do you want to know what we've got?'

He sat up straight and rubbed his face with his hands. 'Sure, why not?'

'Your fingerprints were found inside George Murphy's house, as well as in the downstairs toilet at Allerdale House, on Derwent Water. Now can you tell us why that might be? Cumbria's a long way from home. And why would you be in George Murphy's house? You've told us you didn't know him.'

Leo's head dropped and he racked his brain for a way out, but none came. The only way to salvage anything was to massage a bit of a story around the truth, and hope for leniency due to his statement. He hadn't shot the guy. Nor had he rowed him over to the boatyard. He wasn't about to go down for murder.

But he didn't want to sell out the man who'd thrown him a lifeline if he could help it. He searched his memory, trying to find a different name, examining all the ones he'd come across over the years in an attempt to protect the person who'd recruited him in the first place. Integrity was something that had been drummed into him in the army, but it had become a joke. Loyalty was another thing entirely. Loyalty meant dying for somebody. He wasn't sure if he was ready to do that yet, though, and he kept his head in his hands as he searched long and hard for an answer.

'Give us something, Leo. This is bigger than you. Tell us who hired you to go up to Cumbria to make it look like a burglary.'

So they thought the burglary was part of the rig.

He remembered a drunken conversation he'd had one Sunday afternoon in a pub in Islington, ten minutes from his aunt's shop. He'd sunk pint after pint, with his old company commander pouring his heart out to him. It had been an odd sensation: his idol and mentor breaking down in such a fashion, reversing the roles of superior and soldier. It had grabbed Leo and galvanised his allegiance. His commander had told him about the hole he'd dug himself into, and how he was terrified of his wife finding out and leaving him, taking the kids, the house and his future. The man had given his entire life to the army, and in return he had ended up with shitty accommodation, a bitter wife and a pension that would barely cover the food bills.

He had asked for Leo's help, and Leo had readily agreed. It was the steadiest job he'd had in years, and it enabled him to get away from the clutches of his aunt. It also enabled his boss to send his kids to private school, spoil his wife and renovate a crumbling seventeenth-century cottage in Wiltshire, though he still had dead eyes, and a growing layer of fat bubbling around his girth.

A visit to the cottage in Wiltshire popped into Leo's head. There'd been other men there, one of them a slick dude in a suit. If he could drop the names, it might divert the police for a while; maybe enough time to warn the man who'd been like a father to him.

He looked up. 'What's in it for me?' he asked.

'We could find out about a plea arrangement, but with no guarantees. Do you know what that involves?'

Leo nodded. Of course he knew what it involved. The alternative was to run scared for ever, knowing that one day they'd get him, and it would probably be one of the guys he'd worked alongside that they'd send. He preferred to take control, even if that meant disappearing with a new identity; it was better than ending up with a bullet in the brain, dumped naked in some boathouse.

He made up his mind, and the officers glanced at one another, sensing as much. If he was to blow the whistle, he'd need to make it convincing.

'I didn't kill George Murphy.'

The pair sat up straight and waited.

'I can tell you who I worked with and I can identify three of them.'

He reeled off dates, jobs and names, but held back on those he genuinely liked. It was rare in the business, but it did happen occasionally.

'We need to know who is at the centre of the arrangement. Who's in charge? There's always a boss.'

Leo looked down at his hands.

'I overheard a conversation between two people, but I only got one name.'

The officers waited.

'Slater.'

The interviewing officers repeated it, making sure it was clear for the record, and moved on.

'Tell us what happened on the second of June.'

# Chapter 43

'Why aren't you updating HOLMES, Kelly? I knew this would happen! This investigation cannot work if you go off on your own and make decisions without me.'

'I update you pretty much hourly.'

'It's not enough. Why isn't the information about Slater on the file? Brown gave his name, clear and simple, but it doesn't cross-reference with the Montague Club membership because you didn't update it.'

'For God's sake, Matt. Calm down. Listen. I think we need to take this to the chief commissioner. This involves a whole host of very rich and powerful people. Don't you think it odd that whoever is behind this knows pretty much what we're doing; in fact they seem ahead of us sometimes.'

'So what?'

'So what? Come on! This is above my pay grade, and yours. They were all supposed to sit together at the dinner and George was due to be there too. Montague-Roland didn't mention this little detail and neither did Tooting. Do you really want to march into a government minister's chambers and arrest an adviser? If the press—'

She heard him sigh. 'Technically the Murphy killing is Cumbria territory, so you'll have to go through the proper channels, and I'll do the same for Emily and Mike. We'll need concrete evidence.'

'I know. I definitely don't want to make any premature moves. Slater's offices are on your patch; could you stretch to surveillance?' she asked.

'I can do that. Meanwhile will you update bloody HOLMES?'

'I really don't want to.'

'What? Tell me what you're thinking. I can hear your brain from here. I should never have let you go.'

Kelly ignored the comment. 'We're talking huge money here. You know that Philip Tooting's basic salary was one point two million last year, and that's nothing compared to his share options and benefits, not to mention his freebies. His bonus in March was three million, and most of that was invested abroad. His company turns over billions of dollars per year. Why would he not mourn the death of a man he shared cosy dinners with? George's name was scribbled out and no one at that event paid their respects or made a speech in his honour. Why? What was the neurocellular lab working on that was so threatening? I thought antidepressants and the like were worth billions – as would be a cure for addiction – so what's the problem? What did they do wrong?'

'Are you suggesting we create an elite investigation?'

'Yes. If it goes on to HOLMES, everybody from Hendon to the Hebrides will know within hours.'

'Now you're pointing the finger at the Met? For God's sake, Kell. Hang on.'

'Haven't you listened to anything I've said? How do we know that more agencies aren't involved? Who else knows about it at DEFRA? How deep does this go? Is it a World Health Organisation issue?'

'You're joining dots that haven't been drawn yet. It's a fatal flaw in police work.'

'Don't you dare make this about me! Tilly Knight spoke to George once, and we traced that call from inside Allerdale House. How did anyone else know she was involved?'

'So you're pointing your finger at my team?'

'Would it hurt to check file activity from those not necessarily tasked with the finer details?'

'Inside my office?'

She could smell his indignation but she had to know.

'Give me some evidence and I'll take it to the commissioner,' he said at last.

'How long?'

'Twelve hours.'

'And it stays off HOLMES?'

Silence.

'There's more,' she said.

'I'm all ears.'

'I spoke to the MoD again after what you told me about the military police not being able to get hold of Alexandros. Tilly can't get hold of him either and they were supposed to Skype to exchange documents. Alexandros Skarparis went off radar hours after a conversation I had with a brigadier at the MoD.'

'Now you expect me to believe the army is involved?'

'No. Well, kind of. I'd asked the brigadier to do a bit of digging to see if he could get someone from the Dhekelia base to visit Alexandros. He said he'd pass it on to someone else at the MoD. After Alex's disappearance, I called him back and asked him who he'd contacted.'

'You've got balls, I'll give you that. What did he say?'

'He sighed and said he was very busy, but he gave me a name.'

'And that name means something?'

'It does indeed. He's a colonel who's another one of Sebastian Montague-Roland's mates, and he was sitting right next to Sebastian at the dinner. That's not all. A long time ago, he was Leo Brown's commanding officer.'

'I'll have it put to Brown; meanwhile I'll get the alumni party in for interview.'

'No. That will let them know we're on to them, and with their money and resources, they could set about destroying evidence…' She fell silent.

'What is it?'

'Miranda Cooper.'

'What about her?'

'She was calling me the night of the crash. She'd just been sacked.'

'You think she had something to tell us?'

'I wonder if her office has been cleared out yet.'

'I'll send someone.'

'And I'll ask Graeme Millar about Leo Brown.'

'I really think it's time I came up to Cumbria.'

'No! You can't do that.' She tried to compose herself.

'I have more than fifty super-capable officers working round the clock on every single London lead, I think it's time I saw where it all started. Meanwhile I'll set up surveillance on DEFRA.' He hung up.

Kelly banged her phone against her head. Fuck. A thought occurred to her and she called him back.

'So soon? I'm just booking my tickets.'

She ignored him. 'Can you put the DEFRA surveillance on HOLMES?'

He agreed, and she ended the call. She toyed with the idea of going back to London on Monday to prevent him coming, but he was bull-headed and she knew she couldn't stop him. But she also realised that she couldn't avoid him.

She went back to her computer screen and studied the information she'd collated over the last few hours. She decided to take a break and spend some time searching the social media accounts of the Montague Club and its various members. Tooting's wife's Instagram page threw up a few interesting photos. The woman was immaculate, and whilst Kelly acknowledged that such accounts were by no means a true reflection of real life, the lifestyle displayed there was opulent to the extent of being obscene. There were photographs of yachts, designer clothes, exotic destinations, flash cars and a woman seemingly doing very little, and never with her husband. Kelly did a few calculations in her head and figured that Philip Tooting might well be able to afford such a grand lifestyle. She wondered if Christopher Slater's wife enjoyed the party life too, or the wife of a colonel, who should be able to afford jack shit.

Slater's wife posted pictures of her house and lavish gardens. Kelly knew that a non-executive director working for a parliamentary under-secretary might earn six figures, but she was curious as to how he sustained clear personal wealth beyond that sum. Perhaps he had other clever investments. Perhaps not.

She quickly called Johnny and asked him how much he reckoned a colonel sitting at a desk in the MOD, close to retirement age, might take home, then she searched for the man on Facebook. It was all there in his profile: the name of his wife, and pictures of their three children, who, it appeared, all attended expensive schools. She knew that the army paid school fees, but only if the children boarded because the parents were overseas. Quick phone calls confirmed they didn't.

The photographs posted by the Colonel and his wife were fairly standard – summer holidays, meals out and the like – but the children were a different matter altogether. A picture of a business-class seat on an Emirates flight stood out, as did several references to their horses. It was a red flag, and she dug deeper and deeper into the lavish world of the pals who graced the halls of the Montague Club.

At last she rubbed her eyes and stood up to stretch her legs. Something else was on her mind and it wasn't the inquiry. She needed to explain to Johnny that the SIO currently making his way up to Cumbria was more than an ex-colleague.

# Chapter 44

Christopher Slater took a cab to a bar in central London. It was near Victoria station and as different to the Montague Club as it could be. He'd felt queasy since speaking to Philip last night. He went over and over the details in his head: Benji, drunk, making rash decisions that came back to haunt them all. It was all his fault: *you pay peanuts, you get monkeys*. They were supposed to be clean, set up, staged, untraceable. Instead they were sloppy, rushed, lacking in sophistication and verging on the embarrassing. Philip had looked him dead in the eye when he'd said that everyone left a trail.

Even him.

He racked his brain to find an answer to the question that had been bugging him ever since: what did Philip really have on him? It was in Philip's own interests to clean up after both of them. Christopher had sent no emails, no texts or letters, and nothing existed – as far as he knew – with his name on it. But what if Philip had an insurance plan and was closer to Dame Charlotte than he let on? Christopher's relationship with the senior civil servant had begun in Kabul, where he'd arranged lucrative security contracts for the embassy. He'd supplied the companies and the ambassador had endorsed them. Simple. He'd also been responsible for introducing her to Philip, and he knew for a fact that she had generous share options with Ravensword, just like he did. Benji preferred cash, and that was what would get him caught in the end. But Christopher cared not for Benji or Charlotte Cross. The only one who could hurt him was Philip.

Philip was a classic psychopath, as most of the best CEOs were. Christopher had met thousands of them. He called them the 'black hearts'. As an ex-CEO himself, he was always being sent articles on the prevalence of psychopathy in the City. It was generally dismissed as complete bollocks. The press enjoyed the shock and awe for five minutes and then everybody went back to business.

But Christopher had seen first-hand how Philip Tooting operated. The man was so lacking in empathy or normal human compulsions that he was capable of anything.

He'd had a wretched childhood, with a father who beat him and a mother who would rather drink than protect her boy (Christopher had looked him up using his ministerial access to medical files). The chip on one of Philip's shoulders was bigger than the demon sitting on the other one. Christopher had even discussed it with Robyn Hastings, his boss. Lesbians were very good at spotting alpha males and megalomaniacs. He hadn't seen Robyn since their little squabble over her girlfriend and her dirty hands. It was everybody for himself now, and he knew that Philip would have a plan.

He'd tried Sebastian's private phone with no joy, and Philip wasn't answering either. Both went to voicemail, and he imagined the two men together, plotting the downfall of the rest of them. Benji, however, did pick up, slurring his words.

'Where are you?' Christopher asked.

'At the club, why?'

'I'm out.'

'Good for you, where?'

'No, I'm out. Finished. I don't want anything to do with it any more. Have you seen Sebastian?'

'No.'

'Is he not at the club too?'

'I have no idea.'

'What are you doing, Benji? How can you simply get pissed when everything is falling apart?'

'Oh don't be so dramatic!' The words were barely audible and it made Christopher even more nervous. Benji's drinking had escalated lately. He was constantly blotto, and Christopher knew why: he couldn't accept what he knew was coming.

He felt the same way himself.

He went to the bar and ordered a pint of bitter, despite the hour. He gulped half of it down in one. Drinking solved nothing, he knew that, but he needed to think. He had no power over what Philip did or didn't have. He had more on the dame than anyone, so if he were to go down, she would plunge further, but that was no consolation.

He thought about his wife and kids and understood why men committed suicide, taking their whole families with them.

Calm down! He willed himself. Pull yourself together! You've never been caught before. He silenced his worries, finished his pint and went for a walk to clear his head.

It was when he stopped to buy a sandwich that he spotted the car. He'd been in enough precarious parts of the world to know a tail when he saw it, and this one wasn't very good: they must be police. He broke out in a sweat and decided to test them to be absolutely sure.

If they were spending money on surveillance, it meant two things: they thought it important, but they didn't have enough to arrest.

Oh Christ.

He went inside another shop. The silver saloon was still there when he came out. He doubled back, walking past it and looking in the window. Two men sat in the front chatting to one another. It didn't fool him. He pretended to make a call on his mobile and the car began moving again, but this time it carried on and out of sight.

He breathed a little easier; perhaps he'd been mistaken after all.

He walked back towards Victoria, deciding to take the Underground this time. Nobody could follow him down there. He spotted the car again and froze.

It wasn't a mistake.

His heart beat double time and he sprinted across the road into the station, stumbling over a small child, who screamed. He didn't hang around to be berated by the mother. All the time he was looking over his shoulder.

He got through the barrier and sprinted to the nearest platform. He had no idea where he was going, just that he needed to get out of central London. Once he'd caught his breath, he discovered that he'd got on a District Line train travelling east. He noticed a woman opposite staring at him and thought he must look disconcerting: suicide bombers sweated before they detonated, didn't they? He smiled.

By the time they reached Mansion House, he could take the woman's stares no longer and disembarked. He walked aimlessly, heading wherever his feet took him: anywhere he wouldn't be recognised. He tried Philip's phone again, and this time he answered.

'Philip, I was followed. It's the police, I know it. It was an unmarked car with two personnel—'

'Christopher, Christopher! Calm down, for goodness' sake. Go home, go to the golf range. Make love to your wife, I don't know, take her to dinner. Relax! They've got nothing, I tell you, nothing. My laundromat is very reliable, you know. There's nobody and nothing that can be traced to you. Only your own mistakes can do that. How long have you known me?'

'I don't know, twenty years?' His breathing was slowing.

'Put things into perspective, man. Get out of London and away from back-stabbing, blood-sucking civil servants; the mere sight of them makes me think they're plotting. Enjoy your money, book a holiday. Do you think I would be so stupid as to compromise us? We always said that if any shit hit the fan, the dame would take the fallout: she's the one who's fiddled the system for thirty years, not us. We merely oiled the wheels and supplied the chemistry. Stop panicking.'

'Yes. Of course. God, I thought they had me. You're right.'

'All law enforcers need solid evidence, now more than ever, and if they don't have it, the case will never see the inside of a courtroom. But you have to hold your nerve, Christopher.'

'Yes. I will.'

'I know you will.'

They hung up. Christopher saw that he'd walked to the river, and he thrust his hands in his pockets and shook his head, embarrassed at what an idiot he had been. Going home was just what he needed; he'd spent too much time in the city recently. His phone buzzed in his pocket and he pulled it out and looked at the screen.

It was his contact inside the Met.

# Chapter 45

Kelly stared at her computer screen. A text from Matt informed her that he was on a train travelling north. She groaned inwardly: he hadn't wasted any time. She was desperate for distraction and to avoid the problems of the moment; she wanted to be anywhere else right now, and was thankful that she was meeting Ted and Johnny for a quick lunch, though she wasn't hungry.

She called Tilly Knight to see if she'd got hold of Alexandros. Tilly told her that she had, and that he'd taken his mother to the villa in the mountains, but before he left, he'd seen two men watching his house. No one outside of the Met knew that Skarparis was in Cyprus, except the brigadier and the colonel at the MoD.

Kelly went next door to talk to Rob, mainly because she couldn't sit still, but also to ask if his matrix had thrown anything else up.

'Those solicitors are digging their heels in,' Rob told her. 'I've spoken to our legal department, and special warrants apply to disputed wills. It's complicated, that's all, and might take a bit more time. If they were amenable, it would take minutes, but they're making us jump through every hoop.'

'I wonder why they would do that. Surely they wouldn't be that awkward by choice. Do solicitors have solicitors?'

Rob laughed. 'Yes! Can you believe it?'

'Who are they? Can you find out who else they represent? I'm popping out to sort Mum's house. I'll be about an hour.'

She walked into town and saw Ted standing outside a sandwich shop. He looked like any other smart, respectable gentleman and she felt affection inside her chest. Before she reached him, Johnny arrived and she watched the two men embrace. They laughed at a shared joke and Ted put his hand on Johnny's shoulder. She stopped walking. Her throat constricted and the unexpected wave of emotion overwhelmed her. The two men in her life, waiting for her arrival; decades and lives apart but together because of her. She composed herself and went to greet them.

Ted kissed her on her cheek and Johnny on the lips. It always amused her to see him in an urban environment because he stuck out like a sore thumb, with his flip-flops (albeit an expensive leather pair), shaggy hair and tanned skin. She'd never envisaged ending up with such a man, and she hadn't really stopped to ponder his attractions. She walked in between the two of them and hooked her arms through theirs. She could swear that Ted stuck out his chest a little.

'In here?' she suggested. It was a small, locally run bakery that did fabulous baguettes. They went inside the shop and chose lunch to take away.

Wendy's keys were due to be handed over in two weeks' time, but there were various items that still needed to be moved out. Nikki had already trawled through the property, taking what she wanted to remember her mother by, but Kelly had avoided it. Ted had said he'd go with her, and finally they'd found time. Not going in alone appealed to Kelly, and she felt better equipped with the two men by her side. It wasn't that she was in danger of breaking down; it was more that she didn't know how she'd react to being inside the lifeless property without her mother in it. She was scared of the silence more than the threat of hysterics. In a way, she wished her sister would turn up and throw things, bemoaning her misfortune. It would offer a diversion from the realisation that soon they wouldn't be able to visit their childhood home. When she considered it properly, though, she knew that she wanted her last experience of the tiny terrace to be peaceful.

They drove in silence and the reason for their gathering sat heavily inside the car, their delight about seeing one another fading. Johnny munched hungrily on his ham and cheese baguette, while Ted ate an oat biscuit. As they approached the street, familiarity mixed with strangeness swept over Kelly. Even the facade of the house looked different. Her stomach churned over and Johnny reached from the back seat to squeeze her shoulder. Ted took out a handkerchief and dabbed the corners of his eyes.

Johnny got out of the car first and closed his door. Kelly turned to Ted.

'I wish you'd got back together earlier and enjoyed more time.'

'You have no idea how much I agree with that,' he said. His eyes were red and she reached out to take his hand. Johnny waited outside, allowing them to take their time. Finally they got out of the car and Kelly found the keys.

Once inside, she instantly wanted to run away. The smell was the thing she hadn't expected. It was her mother – her hair, her perfume, her clothes: her whole memory was etched into the fabric of the place. She put her hand up to her mouth and turned away from Ted and Johnny. Her eyes took in the furniture and trinkets still standing in their places. She saw nothing obvious that she wanted to keep: just everything.

'I don't know what to take.' It was a simple statement.

'You said you might pack everything and take your time with it,' Johnny said helpfully. 'You can keep it at mine until you're ready to decide. It's maybe too early.'

'When do you hand over the keys?' Ted asked.

'Two weeks.' She turned away from them, predictably unexpected tears stinging her eyes.

'That's plenty of time to arrange packing and removal. If you're not ready to part with any of it, then keep it, like Johnny said. I've got bags of room as well.'

She smiled at both of them.

'Take anything you'd like, Ted. It's what she'd want.' She left them, heading for the stairs.

The smell was stronger as she walked into her mother's bedroom. Her hairdryer was still on the dressing table, and a jacket sat on the back of a chair. Her purse was on the bedside cabinet, as well as a whole array of pills, none of which had saved her in the end. It had been almost six months, but it still looked the same.

Kelly knelt beside the bed, because she didn't know what else to do.

Why had she left it this long? Nikki had taken what she wanted. Kelly felt the familiar pang of self-reproach. Without Mum, there was no point in seeing her sister.

The last time they'd been together, Nikki had questioned why Kelly was hanging about with an older man, making a fool of herself, taking him everywhere with her; insinuating some kind of fling with Ted. No doubt Dave Crawley would be sitting in her house right now, given a hero's return, and they'd be discussing how Kelly had stitched him up. Leave them to it, she thought.

She buried her head in the duvet and took in the strong aroma of a woman who had died far too soon. She felt a hand on her shoulder and looked up into Ted's eyes. She hadn't heard him coming up the stairs and she didn't know how long she'd been there, on her mother's bedroom floor. Her vision was blurry and she knew she was crying, but she was making no sound. He struggled to kneel down and sit down beside her, holding her in his arms. It was one of the most pleasant places she'd ever been. They stayed like that for long minutes and Kelly allowed herself to be weak for a moment. Inside his embrace was an unconditional place that she rarely encountered, and the succour was overwhelming.

When she pulled away, it was with a feeling of renewed strength and energy, and she made her mind up that she would phone the removal company and get everything packed up. If she got rid of it all now, she knew she'd regret it. She had room at home to store it all, as well as Johnny and Ted's offers should there turn out to be too much. She'd been warned by the removal company that people often underestimated what lurked inside the cupboards and drawers of a house inhabited for generations and virtually untouched.

'Is there anything you'd like?' she asked Ted.

He shook his head. 'She's in here.' He pointed to his chest. 'I'm afraid you're going to have to help me up, though.'

Kelly smiled and did as he requested. 'I can't get rid of anything yet.'

'Good idea. It can't be rushed.'

'Thank you for coming with me.'

'Not at all. You're working hard – you always work hard – but you need to take care of yourself too. And him down there…' he pointed to the floor. 'He's a good man, and he loves you, Kelly. I should know.'

She smiled. 'I know. Come on, let's go downstairs. Wait a minute, there was a photo on her dressing table… Look, here it is. That's me, I must have been three months old. Would you like it?'

Ted looked at her and his mouth opened, but no words came out. It was something that Kelly was unfamiliar with: a pathologist being lost for words. At last he nodded.

'Good.' She walked out of the room and went downstairs to Johnny with a lighter heart. She reckoned she could leave now without regret, and she looked around for one last time. The keys would be handled by the estate agent and the packing company she'd spoken to had said they'd probably only need a day to get everything ready for storage.

She went to Johnny and allowed him to hold her. Ted came downstairs and she smiled at him over Johnny's shoulder.

'Can I drop you home, Ted?' She was more than happy to drive him back to Keswick.

'No, I'm seeing an old friend in Penrith; you can take me back into town. What are your plans?'

'My colleague from London is on his way here. I don't really know why he's coming – I don't need him here – but I've got to get back to work.'

They left the house and Kelly locked the door. She took a deep breath and they got back into the car. She still had no interest in her baguette.

After they'd dropped Ted back to the centre of town, Kelly delayed turning the engine back on. Johnny asked about her visiting colleague. Her heart rate elevated and she looked out of the window.

'I would have thought he was better off in London, from what you've said. Is it normal for the Met to send coppers to the sticks?'

The phrase jolted her and she heard Matt's voice.

'I think he's trying to wind me up. The thing is, we were seeing each other for a while, before I came here, before I met you...' Her voice was nervy, but Johnny's face showed no sign of change. She sensed herself blushing and her hands shook, even though they were gripping the wheel tightly.

'And this week was the first time you'd seen him since?'

She nodded.

'And he's working the same investigation?'

Another nod. She stared ahead. The traffic slowed.

'Is there something you want to tell me?' He got straight to the point.

'I think he thinks I've still got feelings for him. But I haven't. I can't stand him.'

'Something must have made him believe that's the case. Did something happen in London?'

'No!' She said it far too quickly.

'You spent almost a week with him, and you never mentioned it.'

'I didn't know he'd be the SIO!'

'God, he must be so pissed off that he let you go.' He smiled at her and took her hand. 'Why are you so nervous?'

'I thought you'd be…'

'What? Jealous?'

'Aren't you?'

'A bit, but I also love you. He's coming here?'

She nodded.

'Can I meet him?'

'Oh no!'

'Why? I can wind him up. Is this the one who stabbed you in the back?'

'Same.'

'Now I get it. You were sleeping with him. No wonder it hurt.'

She looked away.

'So you're not tempted to move back there?' he asked.

'Is that what you were worried about?' She looked back at him.

He stared down at his hands. She brushed hair away from his eyes and leant over to kiss him. Three years ago, she'd thought Matt Carter was 'the one'; now it was difficult to believe that she'd settle for less than what was right in front of her.

'Do you want me to beat him up?' Johnny smiled broadly and winked.

## Chapter 46

The white van, with the graffiti still scrawled on the back of it, had been found in London. It had been pulled over for having a number plate hanging off. Upon further inspection, it was revealed that the number was fake and that it was partially covering the genuine one. The vehicle wasn't registered, but the occupants had been detained under caution and the plate had been put through the PNC. They had a match and they had three more suspects. One of them had mentioned Leo Brown, who'd already mentioned the three of them in interview. Things were falling into place.

They could prove that the van had visited both George and Alexandros's houses, and the graffiti on the back matched Graeme Millar's sighting in Portinscale. Soil analysis from the tyres would make it watertight, but that would take time. Fingerprints and DNA had been taken from the three occupants of the van and were being fed through the national database. They were also fed into HOLMES, in the hope of finding a match from evidence gathered at one of their sites of interest. The three men were interviewed at a station in Shoreditch. Each of them was pointing the finger at the other and trying to wriggle out of giving straight answers to straight questions. It was customary to expect this kind of behaviour from groups brought in together: each wondering what the other was saying and shaping their answers to come across in the best light, whilst damning their mates.

CCTV footage showed the three of them in the van near George's house, and a neighbour had positively identified them from photographs shown to her by a patrol unit. Pieces were falling into place, but for the investigation to move forward, they needed to find something on the big boys. Brown and the three thugs in custody were mere cogs in a wheel. Matt kept a close eye on the interviews by audio and video as he sipped a coffee on the train.

The first hint that they were close to something was when one of the suspects admitted to seeing a gun. The interviewing officers nailed him down, sensing an unravelling. Each interview was linked by audio and video to the SIO and Hendon.

'Tell us exactly what happened.'

They'd been questioned for five hours, and fatigue was setting in.

'I didn't do nothing, I swear. I had no idea what we were going for.' It was a usual response.

'Where were you going to do nothing?'

'Up north.'

'Specific?'

'The lake. I can't remember the name, I was no good at geography, but it took ages to get there. We stayed in a guest house in this tiny town.'

'Who drove?'

'Ken.'

'Kenneth Chubb? For the tape, I'm showing the suspect a photograph of Kenneth Chubb.'

He nodded.

'For the tape?'

'Yes.'

'Was the town Keswick?'

'Yeah, that's it. They speak funny up there, couldn't understand a word.'

'Carry on.'

'We got there Friday but I did nothing until Sunday. I went and got fish and chips and sat in a few pubs. They told me to go with them on the Sunday and we drove into the arse end of nowhere. It was pitch black. But I saw that Leo had a gun. He always carries one, man.'

'For the purposes of the tape, the witness is being shown evidence number LB/02. Was it this gun?'

'No idea. It was dark.'

'The witness has not positively identified the weapon. Was it a handgun, though?'

'Yes.'

'So it could have been this one?'

'Yeah.'

'Did you notice anything particular about where you were?'

'Leo saw the boathouse and said we should look around, but Denny said we had to stick to the house. Me and Leo were to wait outside. Ken went in with Denny.'

'For the purposes of the tape, can you identify Denny Tapps as the man who was arrested with you this afternoon? For the purposes of the tape, I'm showing the suspect a photograph of Denny Tapps.'

'Yeah.'

'What happened next?'

'Me and Leo went to the boathouse and it was unlocked. Leo said the kit was worth thousands, so we started loading it into the van.'

'That must have taken some time.'

The man looked up to the ceiling, then covered his face with his hands.

'We heard a shot.'

'What type of shot?'

'A gunshot.'

'From where?'

'Inside the house. Denny came out and said he needed help, and Leo went inside. They were in there ages and came out with something wrapped in sheets.'

'And I'm guessing you knew it wasn't a teddy bear?'

The man shook his head.

'Yes or no, for the purposes of the tape.'

'No, I didn't think it was a teddy bear. Denny said he'd been told to take it away from the house; he said he was going to row it over to the other side of the lake.'

'So we've established that whatever was in the sheets wasn't a teddy bear. Is it likely that it was the body of George Murphy, who had just been fatally shot inside the house?'

The man nodded.

'For the tape.'

'Yes.'

'Then what?'

'Denny took Ken with him and they were gone ages. We had plenty of time to load the dinghy on the trailer and get it hooked up to the van.'

'Did you at any point challenge what you had seen or heard?'

The man hung his head. 'No.'

'From start to finish, how long were you at Allerdale House?'

'Three hours maybe.'

'Did anyone else go into the house?'

'Leo went in for a piss.'

'When Denny and Ken got back from rowing across the lake, did they have the sheets?'

The man thought about this. 'Erm, they had a black bag. I guess they could have been in there.' That would explain why nothing had been found at the scene.

'What happened then?'

'We drove back to London.'

'What did Denny do with the black bag?'

The man thought again. 'I fell asleep. It's a long way up there, man. We stopped at a petrol station and I remember him stuffing the bag in a bin.'

'Do you know which petrol station?'

'No.'

'Are you absolutely sure? Was it on a motorway?'

'Nah, I can't remember.'

'Bullshit,' said Matt as the train sped north.

# Chapter 47

Kelly stood at her office window and stared out. She'd looked up Lord Allerdale's voting history for the House of Lords and sure enough, he'd voted against any progressive homosexual legislation. Next she'd called Alexandros Skarparis in Cyprus to inform him that two intelligence officers were on standby to travel to his villa and escort him to Akrotiri military base, where he and his mother could board an RAF flight to Brize Norton.

'It's the only way,' she said. 'We can protect your mother.'

That sold him, and he told her the location of the villa. She wasted no time and informed her contact at Ayios Nikolaos intelligence wing, avoiding going through the MoD.

Matt would be arriving soon, and Eden House was the last place she wanted to be. He'd called from the train to give her an update. Christopher Slater had left the city for the weekend, and had been tailed to his pad in Surrey. Sebastian Montague-Roland was attending meetings in London until eleven this evening, but had agreed to speak over the phone to detectives at five o'clock. He'd been curt and warned them of harassment. Another army of lawyers had descended on the switchboard at Hendon and had informed the SIO that for Mr Montague-Roland to be interviewed – informally or otherwise – they'd need to charge him with a crime. They couldn't. Yet.

Kelly was knackered and dejected, and wanted to take the afternoon off with Johnny. She wished she was in a position to accept his valiant offer to rough up Matt, but knew it was a chivalric gesture only.

Rob came excitedly into her office holding a printout. It was a welcome diversion.

'I've got the scientific formulas back from George's USB.'

'And?'

'It sets out a model for a cure for addiction.'

'Isn't that what they were working on in the Ravensword lab anyway? Addiction, mental illness and so on.'

Rob looked deflated. 'It's not the same at all.'

'Really?'

'Really.'

'I'm sorry. Come on, tell me then.' The apology was genuine. She realised she was wound up like a coil over Matt arriving, and she'd been short with her colleague.

Rob took a pen and a large piece of paper from a board, and began to explain to her how George was working on the theory that addiction wasn't a disease or a condition, but a miswiring as a direct result of the toxins ingested, effectively turning the whole theory on its head.

'Why does that matter?'

'Because the whole world wants us to believe that it's an affliction with no cure.'

'Are you telling me that George actually found a cure?'

'That's what the scientist who translated this told me. She was very excited. However, after the initial euphoria died down, she told me that it would be bad news for the company. Then she became cagey.'

'Why bad news? Surely something so genius is a cause for celebration?'

'She said something about losing revenue from drugs used to treat addiction. I guess what she was trying to say is that it has the potential to impact global economies.'

'Of course it would.' That was just what Tilly Knight had told her. They needed to get Alexandros here as soon as they could, and she willed the operation two thousand miles away to go smoothly. She went to her computer and googled some figures about legally prescribed addictive drugs: antidepressants, barbiturates, benzodiazepines and methadone. In the US alone, methadone prescription and the treatment surrounding it was worth $43 million per year.

'And that's not mentioning the illegal trade, which could grind to a halt with a drug like this,' she whispered out loud. 'It could be an effective political tool against South America.'

Rob cottoned on to her train of thought. 'And Afghanistan.'

'Alexandros told Tilly Knight that George wasn't a coke addict; he was experimenting on himself.'

An update on HOLMES interrupted them: Miranda Cooper's computer was found to be still in her office, and had been seized. It was currently being scoured by experts. Kelly raised her eyebrows to Rob, who turned towards a noise at the door.

'A visitor, boss.' DS Umshaw poked her head around Kelly's door. Kelly set her face into as warm a welcome as she could muster. Matt was standing in the doorway, smiling.

Kelly introduced her colleagues and took him around the office, introducing him to other members of the team, who'd already had the pleasure of meeting him on screen. She could see him scowling a little as he took in the silence, the calm, as well as all the scribbles on the whiteboard.

'I think I'll hold a brief now to get up to speed. We've had some more developments.'

'I know, we've been keeping up to date.' Kelly spoke with irritation.

The team stopped what they were working on and looked at their colleague from the Met. He strode to the front of the room and began barking out information. Kelly could see that they were struggling with his style, but they did their best to second-guess when he paused for effect or when he expected an answer. He spoke rhetorically a lot of the time.

'The DNA on the plasma inside the shower unit is a billion-to-one match with George Murphy.'

He paused and looked around at the team.

'Why aren't you using iPads?'

Kelly spoke for them. 'Our briefs are usually in real time, face to face, DCI Carter. We check the computer information regularly but use briefs as an opportunity to swap ideas and chew things over, as it were.' She smiled. If her team questioned her use of his title rather than 'guv' or 'boss', they didn't show it.

'Right. Excellent. Have we pieced together who George might have had contact with up here?' Kelly knew he'd been thrown off guard, but she was enjoying watching him struggle, even if no one else could see it.

'DS Umshaw?' Kelly said. Kate was shaken from her reverie and began to speak.

'We have a pretty solid timeline of events leading up to the murder. He regularly went to the small shop in Portinscale, and on Sunday morning he was reportedly in very good spirits. He also shopped in Keswick; we have CCTV of him entering several clothes shops and a fishing tackle shop.'

'Have we examined who else was in the premises at the same time?' Matt asked.

'Yes, sir. On one piece of footage he's seen paying at the counter and two men are standing behind him. One of them is Leo Brown.'

'What's the date?'

'Saturday the first.'

'So they were sussing him out. It proves planning and premeditation. Good. Feed that to the interviews in Shoreditch.'

Kelly nodded. She followed his gaze and saw that he was studying her whiteboard.

'I see your drawings replicate HOLMES well. Who's the artist?' he asked.

'Me,' Kelly said. 'Every time HOLMES updates, I add a new picture. We like it.'

There was a slight shift in the atmosphere, and Kelly filled the chasm. 'I'll log on now and we can get back to work. My team has been working flat out and I'd like to allow them to go home soon so they can have some kind of weekend.'

Matt gawped at her, but thought better of complaining. They finished up the brief and he expressed his satisfaction that they were all singing from the same song sheet. Kelly stifled her annoyance that he'd ever doubted it.

'Is Allerdale House far?' he asked. 'I'd like to see where it happened.'

Kelly breathed a barely perceptible sigh of relief.

'Can I have a volunteer to accompany DCI Carter to Allerdale House?' She was aware that their Saturday had dragged on, and she was expecting most of them in tomorrow. Emma would be back then, but it was Kate's turn to have some rest and recuperation; she'd also said Will could have a break.

'I'll go.' It was Kate who spoke, and Kelly smiled to herself. Matt would have to be on his best behaviour. She caught his glare out of the corner of her eye, but she gave him no opportunity to speak privately to her before Kate had her bag ready to leave.

'I'll call tech to ask if they've found out what was on Miranda Cooper's computer yet– if anything,' Kelly said. She watched them leave, then made the phone call.

Miranda had been very clever indeed. Tooting, in his arrogance, hadn't bothered looking around her office, and Matt had secured a warrant to have her computer taken away. Yesterday evening – the evening of her death – the professor had downloaded a file using an unusual icon. As Kelly stared at the image sent to her, she recognised it as the coat of arms of the Montague-Rolands.

Ted's call jolted her; she thought it apt considering his love of heraldry. She asked him what he knew about the Montague-Rolands.

'You still working on that case?'

304

'I am. Why is it that all the gentry around here have secrets?'

'It's part of the job description. I met old Lord Allerdale once. He was a keen hunter back in the day. He owned most of the land behind Cat Bells. Did you find out what happens to it all now?'

'Not yet. I get the impression that whatever Alan Montague-Roland wanted, it didn't go down too well. Thank you for earlier, by the way. It meant a lot. I'd been dreading it. It's hard to let go.'

'I know. Look, Kelly, I was calling for a reason. I've been thinking. I wanted to ask you if I should go ahead and arrange for you to meet your half-sisters.'

Kelly was floored. It was certainly a distraction, but perhaps not quite the kind she was after.

'Wow. Do they know?'

'Not yet. But I think that if you were to meet, you would all be rather fond of one another.'

'What about Mary?' She wasn't sure what his ex-wife would think about it.

'The girls are adults.'

'Right. Well, yes. If they agree. Why not?'

He rang off happy and Kelly stared at the phone for a few minutes before another call came in and claimed her attention.

# Chapter 48

Philip Tooting loosened his tie and poured a glass of wine, taking it on to his terrace overlooking the Thames. The view took in Tower Bridge, and that alone doubled the price tag compared to properties further down the river, out of sight of the prestigious landmark. His wife had no idea that he owned it. Not that she cared; she had plenty of places to go should she desire it. The only reason they weren't divorced was because of the cost. Separation would be ludicrous and financially disastrous; why pay solicitors when they could lead their lives independently, still benefiting from their wealth?

A call came through to his private work phone and he saw that it was his secretary, so he answered. She informed him that Miranda Cooper's computer had been taken away by the police. Ravensword worked round the clock – weekends meant nothing – but Philip had never set foot in the place on a Saturday as long as he'd been there. His secretary worked one weekend out of every four, though, and she'd witnessed the police coming and going.

A sensation began to form in his abdomen, one that he hadn't felt for a very long time. He asked her to go to the computer in his office and check when it was last logged on to. She was the only person who was allowed to touch it.

'What's the password this week, sir?' she asked.

He blushed, though she couldn't see it. 'Peasants.' He recalled crying the word out loud to Miranda as he came inside her, unable to keep the magnificent sense of power and domination from his voice. He changed his password from time to time, but he kept going back to that one; it held a resonance for him that he found hard to explain. He'd come from nothing and made himself what he was today, unlike ninety-nine per cent of the population, who sponged off everyone else.

'Right, sir… You last logged on at six fifteen yesterday evening. Wait a minute, nobody was here then.'

'I know I wasn't.'

'Oh.'

'What time did you leave?' he asked.

'Six o'clock, sir.'

'Bitch.'

'Sorry, sir?'

'Nothing.' He hung up.

Suddenly the view of the ancient waterway wasn't so appealing. He went inside and closed the door, gulping his wine as he went. Miranda was nothing if not technically competent. It had to have been her, but why? Revenge, of course.

He placed a call to his firm of solicitors and instructed them to release the original terms of Alan Montague-Roland's will to the police.

As he paced up and down, Christopher's words popped into his head. He racked his brains, trying to recall what he'd stored on his hard drive. In a word: everything. If Miranda had done what he thought she had, he was screwed.

He logged on to a personal iPad and searched BA flights to Buenos Aires. He had business dealings there, but more importantly, he owned a pad in Mar del Plata. Extradition from South America was unlikely. He placed the glass on the side and rubbed his eyes; he couldn't believe he was thinking like this.

There was a flight at 9.50 p.m. from Heathrow, but it was delayed by half an hour; he could still make it. The screen showed that there were several spare seats in business class. He purchased a return ticket – it was quicker – and went to his bedroom to pack. Everything he needed was in the flat. As he opened his suitcase, he ran through calculations in his head about what sums he had in which country, and how easily they were accessed. He thought about Miranda rooting around in his office, smiling to herself when she guessed his password correctly. It was she who'd encrypted all his files and created the bulletproof system, which was why he'd used his work computer to store it all on.

In his haste, he knocked a bowl off the bedside cabinet and it smashed on the polished tiled floor. He stepped on a shard of glass as he fastened his bag, and swore. Blood soaked through his sock. He stripped it off and hopped to the bathroom. The cut wasn't deep, but the bleeding wouldn't stop. He found a bandage in a cabinet and wrapped it tightly around his foot. But now he had blood on his shirt, so he went back to the bedroom to change. His phone buzzed and he ignored it. There'd be no pleasant exchanges now.

He wondered idly if the detective in Cumbria was at this moment reading the information stashed away over years of careful calculation and risk, her hand over her pretty mouth, wondering who to arrest first. Maybe she didn't work weekends; perhaps Miranda had her own passwords and the files hadn't been accessed.

He stopped. Miranda had had no idea she was going to die. She could easily have stored the information on a USB stick, taking it with her to bribe him with later: that was more her style. He'd made her angry, but he'd seen in her eyes that she still lusted for him. He'd grown bored with her before and she'd changed his mind, parading in front of him in various revealing outfits, but until yesterday, he'd never gone so far as to sack her.

He caught his reflection in the mirror and smiled. His teeth were perfectly straight and white, thanks to expensive dental work; his skin was tanned from golfing holidays and business trips to exotic resorts; his laughter lines pointed upwards, and his jaw was strong. He smiled again. He took his time checking his bag, then called a limousine company to take him to the airport.

## Chapter 49

Back at Eden House, Kelly read through documents downloaded and sent to her from Miranda Cooper's computer. The folder with the Montague-Roland crest as its icon contained fifty-three separate files, dating back six years. She shook her head: she'd need an army of staff to read the stuff. At Hendon, five officers were able to work on the same documents, taking ten each. Still, she had to start somewhere.

She opened a file titled 'The value of alcohol'. It was dated 2012 and detailed the revenue from alcohol sales in the UK and the cost of treating alcohol-related illnesses on the NHS. The figures were staggering. The government made £10 billion a year from alcohol tax revenue, but only paid an estimated £3 billion in medical care. Kelly had no idea how the figures were calculated, but there was a breakdown of costs relating to kidney failure, heart disease, various cancers and liver disease.

Next she looked at a document titled 'Drug industry value by country'. Scanning down, she read that a conservative estimate of the value of the global illegal drug industry was around $360 billion, half of that generated in South America, with cocaine coming in at $130 billion alone, and heroin at $110 billion. In the 2000s, ninety per cent of the cocaine coming into the US was from Mexico.

It was calculated that $64 billion worth of illegal drugs went from Mexico to the US annually. Kelly noted with dismay that Afghanistan had supplied a staggering ninety-three per cent of the world's heroin in 2014.

Next she read about the GDPs of the major drug-producing countries and realised that the global illicit drug trade kept economies afloat. Somewhere in her memory she already knew that, but now it seemed important.

A World Health Organisation report from 2015 drew a bleak and depressing picture of the face of global addiction and what the richest countries on earth were doing about it. She stopped reading. Of course a pharmaceutical giant such as Ravensword would be interested in all of this. She felt foolish. Her shoulders hurt and she had a feeling she was going around in circles, but she read on. This morning Matt had given her twelve hours to find something tying the Montague Club men together. So far she'd found nothing.

She opened another file. It was another WHO document, this time from 2016, but she noticed that it was addressed to DEFRA and the Department of Health. She looked up the names of the relevant secretaries of state and their senior civil servants and jotted them down. A series of diagrams stared back at her and she considered closing the file without further investigation, but the way they were set out, as well as the handwriting accompanying them, made her stop. She'd seen the formulas before: yesterday, when Rob had been updating her on the USB found in George's car. She poked her head around the door of the incident room and asked him to bring up the scientific calculations they'd sent off to be examined. They matched. She had something linking Tooting to George, but then he was his employer, so it still proved nothing.

She went back to her screen and found herself staring at a remittance payment. It was from a private Ravensword expense account, signed by Tooting, paying an outstanding mortgage with the Halifax. Kelly squinted. She was sure it must be an anomaly. She checked again: it was definitely a residential mortgage for £375,000 on an address in Wiltshire, in the name of Benjamin Dansford. Butterflies vibrated in her stomach.

Next she brought up an expense account for the Montague Club and found further evidence that the relationship between the men was more than casual. Tooting regularly entertained at the club, and kept details of expenditure; a quick check confirmed that he was reimbursed for his efforts through a private member's account: Sebastian's. She also noticed that there was a record of his guests, with dates.

She needed Rob, and called him into her office. She showed him what she'd found and he whistled. Philip Tooting had entertained the permanent under-secretaries of both DEFRA and the Department of Health at the Montague Club.

'And look at this,' Kelly said. He leaned over her desk and she pointed to the screen: it was a list of Ravensword shareholders, and Dame Charlotte Cross, Permanent Under-Secretary at the Department of Health, was on it.

Her phone rang. It was a secretary at the firm of solicitors in London that Rob had been dealing with. When Kelly ended the call, she looked at Rob, puzzled.

'What?' he asked.

'The solicitors who were making our life a misery over Lord Allerdale's will: they're sending it over now.'

'Really? Change of heart?'

'Or finally realising that legally they have to?' They both shrugged.

She opened her inbox; the will had already been sent. She clicked on it and read the opening page. '"Last will and testament of Alan Montague-Roland… settled under terms of absolute secrecy." Is that a *thing*?' she asked Rob, who shrugged again.

'I suppose you can get anything made legal if a solicitor signs it.'

They returned to the computer screen.

'No way.'

They both stared at the page.

## Chapter 50

Kelly called DS Umshaw and requested that she bring DCI Carter straight back to Eden House. Meanwhile she collated information from the officers tasked in Hendon and fed it into a cross-referencing model created by Rob. He'd asked her why she didn't want to feed it through HOLMES, and she'd told him the truth: she thought that someone on the inside was feeding information to whoever was behind the murders.

Matt strode into the office with Kate Umshaw rolling her eyes behind him.

'Why doesn't anyone lock doors around here? It's virtually asking for trouble.'

Kelly ignored his dripping condescension and retorted with the possibility that in this case it might actually have been deliberate. Sebastian Montague-Roland might not have been there when his grandfather's friend was murdered, but he knew about it and might actually have ordered it.

'George was the trustee of Alan Montague-Roland's will,' she told him.

'Go on,' Matt said. Quiet now.

'I think what Graeme Millar told me might have been true: old Lord Allerdale was a raging homophobe. He was disgusted with his grandson, who is gay, and cut him

314

out of his will. The whole lot was to be controlled by George – which explains how he was able to keep funding his lab – until Sebastian married and had children. Heirs. Which will never happen.'

'But the payments to the lab stopped.'

'Because there was provision in the will. George no longer needed bank transfers. Lord Allerdale gifted him three million in cash. It must be in a separate account.'

'I thought you said Sebastian didn't contest the will?'

'No, it was the solicitors who instructed it: the same ones who represent both the Montague Club and Philip Tooting. Lord Allerdale made him executor three years ago.'

'And they won?'

'It's still being contested, though they originally said it was settled – that was off the record, and they've got amnesia over that bit now. They obviously smudged the timeline so that potential investors that Sebastian was lining up didn't get cold feet and pull out once they learned he was broke.'

Matt allowed the information to sink in. 'Great work, DI Porter. Can we have a word?'

Kelly looked at her team and they took it as a sign to get back to work. 'Once we've secured arrest warrants, we can call it a day. I want you to go home and get some rest. I'm afraid I might need some of you tomorrow as planned. I'll let you know.'

'Yes, boss.'

Kelly took Matt into her office. Before he could speak, she asked him if he'd looked into a leak at Hendon.

He nodded. 'I've got someone I trust completely having a nose around staff sheets, job uptake and log-on hits on the PNC. He did call me when I was on the train and I intended to check it out this afternoon.'

'It's this afternoon now, Matt.'

'I know.'

'It's difficult to swallow?'

He nodded.

'Have you got a name?'

He nodded again. 'I don't know for sure, but I told the DI who's doing the digging to look into his background. He's a young sergeant who was overlooked for the detective route. I told him he needed more experience. He's logged on to the PNC way more than he should be for his grade. He's been in the office every day, and... You know you asked me to put the DEFRA surveillance on HOLMES?'

She nodded.

'It worked, apparently. He's not been in since. I'll call Hendon now and see if they've traced his desk phone calls.'

'Thanks, Matt.'

'He's throwing a good career away; he'll get hammered if it's true.'

'Is it too soon to question him?'

'Probably not, but I'll get his phone log back first. My DI has tried to make contact.'

'I hope your journey wasn't wasted. It looks like you'll be better off in London after all. I can clear up here.'

Matt looked at her. 'It's never a waste to see a crime scene. It is beautiful up here. I can see why you like it. Is Umshaw a handful?'

'Erm, no, not at all, she's an asset.'

'I found her uncompliant and stand-offish.'

'Matt, that's how you find most people. We don't kowtow up here. It's all quite informal.'

'I've noticed.'

'We get the job done.'

'I can see that. Let's have a look at those documents. I want to see something that an interviewer can use before I order the arrest warrants. I can't go waltzing into the Department of Health getting it wrong. For that, I'll need the commissioner's approval as well, and it's Saturday, he's probably on the golf course.'

'Surely you have emergency access?'

'It can be arranged. The important thing is that we're right.'

'OK, look. This is Dame Charlotte Cross, Permanent Under-Secretary at the Department of Health, KCMG.'

Matt raised his eyebrows.

'She has an illustrious past, once holding the position of Her Majesty's Ambassador to the Islamic Republic of Afghanistan.'

'Jesus, Kell.'

She let it go.

'That's only the beginning. There are pages and pages of dossiers and articles about the value of illegal and legal drugs to governments, especially the UK and US. Dame Charlotte authorised a study into the collapse of the Afghan economy when the US destroyed the poppy fields in the early 2000s, and the subsequent investment in the country that led to a revival of farming and a resumption of the opiate trade. It now accounts for something like ninety per cent of their GDP. The same is true in Mexico and Colombia, parts of Central America and the Golden Triangle between Laos and Vietnam.'

Matt watched her.

'Now look. There's a projected timeline for the analysis, testing and production of a drug that is referred to over and over again as Compound P. That's what Tilly Knight told me about, but she didn't know what it was.' She opened a new file. 'This is Dame Charlotte's correspondence with Christopher Slater, who, after the colantropine affair, took on several grey roles in large companies before finding himself an adviser to a board working for the UN on the impact of the opium trade in Afghanistan. After that, he got a position in a US pharmaceutical company and then turned up on the staff of Permanent Under-Secretary Robyn Hastings at DEFRA. By the way, Robyn Hastings and Dame Charlotte Cross have both been to the Montague Club recently, and wrote on government-headed paper to thank the man who invited them, Philip Tooting. Philip has been nothing if not thorough in keeping records, should he need them.'

'Why would he be so stupid?'

'Well, I suppose you've got to keep this lot somewhere, and he wouldn't want his wife finding it. Tooting's secretary said that Professor Cooper set up a private computer in his office. She remembers it well because it was not a standard Ravensword model.'

'So why sack her? That's asking for trouble, given what she knew.'

'She might not have known the extent of it, but went looking after she was sacked.'

'Clever woman.'

'But she paid with her life.'

'It looks that way. We still haven't found the driver of the Ravensword lorry, so it will be difficult to prove.'

'I think we've got more than enough to bring in Tooting.'

'I agree, but it will probably be taken off us.'

'I know.' Kelly spoke with resignation. She hoped they would be able to stay in charge of some elements of the inquiry, but something involving government departments, civil servants and MoD personnel was bound to be given to at least a superintendent.

'We need to start work on our case to put it to the commissioner.'

'How do we split it? This lot will take us until the small hours. What if George was willingly involved in all of it and got burned?'

'Possible. Let's find out.'

Matt's phone buzzed with a call from the station in Shoreditch where the three suspected accomplices of Leo Brown were being held.

'We have another witness mentioning Colonel Dansford, and also an admission that they spoke to some guy who rowed up to the beach at Allerdale House.'

'Corroborating what Graeme said?'

'Yes.'

Kelly was elated to hear any shred of evidence that Graeme might be telling the truth.

'But they also said that the old man – positively ID'd as George Murphy – was not alone. He was talking to another man much younger than him. It's enough. I'm sending units to the lot of them.'

'Did they have a name?'

'No, but they gave a description.'

## Chapter 51

Colonel Dansford replaced the receiver. He knew he was intoxicated; that was how he'd existed for the last twenty-odd years. He'd begun to drink too much in the army, as a subaltern. Everybody did it: port after dinner, tequila in the officers' mess, and all-night benders in between weeks of exercises with no sex or booze in sight. It was a slippery slope and a common one.

He knew Leo Brown wouldn't be able to keep his mouth shut for ever, even if Philip thought someone could get to him on the inside before trial. He was doomed. His career was over and his reputation would be ruined. He'd been taken for a fool while Philip, he knew, would have a Plan B. Unfortunately he'd had first-hand dealings with the dirty end of the business. That was his role: the doer, the fixer, the recruiter.

It had always suited him. That was what he was good at: getting people to do stuff. And he knew a lot of rogues, usually stationed around army bases. Brown was fairly innocuous in the grand scheme of things. Some of the contacts he'd found were machine-like psychopaths, willing to kill anything that moved for five thousand quid.

That was the other problem: he'd grown sloppy with money. It came and it went, and he hadn't taken Philip or Christopher's advice and been tidy. They were always telling him to launder his earnings and take care the dots didn't join up, but he was an army colonel! He was useless on the outside in the world of business affairs. He was institutionalised, but he couldn't imagine rotting away in a cell for the rest of his days without a good bottle of red.

He cared not a jot should he sully the reputation of the club. He'd just ordered another bottle of Gevrey-Chambertin to his room, and he could barely sign the chit, his vision was so blurred. It had been a long old descent into full-blown alcoholism, until one day he woke up and reached for a glug of red before he got out of bed. Of course, it didn't help that he had it readily available wherever he went, on tap, on chit, for a favour. He drank more of it than water or tea.

There was a loud banging on his door and it made him drop the whole bloody bottle onto the floor. Luckily the cork was shoved in the top from his last slurp (habit) and it had bruised his toe but he hadn't lost a drop. The banging came again. He ignored it.

'Colonel Dansford.' He recognised the voice as the porter on duty. 'Sir, if you're in there, we've been asked to confirm your presence at the club. Somebody is trying to reach you.'

He looked over to the door and then walked to the window. His room faced the square, but he could see nothing. He squinted and fought with the sash window, which budged a little.

The knocking came again.

'Sir, it's the police. We don't want a scene.'

The Colonel stopped fighting with the window and stared blankly out of the window. It had always been a dream; a stupid *Boy's Own* dream. He realised at that moment that he'd made nothing of himself; all he'd managed was to do a few people's dirty washing. He walked to the door and hissed, 'Good God, man, I'm half naked. Give me a minute, will you!'

'Of course, sir, but we don't want any fuss. With respect, Colonel, you need to get dressed.'

He walked away from the door muttering to himself, close to oblivion. As he took the cork out of the bottle and swigged it back, he caught a reflection of himself in the mirror. He'd never really been vain, but one day he'd tried on an old dress uniform and hadn't been able to fasten it. Now he looked at his gut and his shiny face and his dead eyes and it saddened him. He opened the bedside cabinet drawer and took out an old service revolver that he'd come across when he'd been in charge of logging kit back in after a tour to Iraq. It was easy to massage the figures before the age of barcodes and snotty upstarts who did everything by the book. The thing might not even still work. That would be the final insult, he thought as he opened the chamber. There were three bullets in there and he couldn't remember for the life of him when he'd put them in. It was a weighty piece of kit. Some soldiers brought Afghan rugs back from tour, others broke marble off Saddam Hussein's bathroom walls. He'd brought an old friend.

He lay on the bed and took the bottle in his other hand. Outside his room, he heard footsteps and conversation: they'd come back. A loud bang resonated around the room.

'Colonel! They're coming in now. It's most unsatisfactory, sir, but we had no choice. Are you dressed?'

He closed his eyes and drained the bottle of wine, tipping it until the last drops trickled out: it was damn fine. Then he put the muzzle in his mouth and aimed it slightly upwards: not that he had much brain left now that it had been turned to liquid mush, thanks to some fine vintages.

He squeezed the trigger.

# Chapter 52

Tilly sighed and switched off the TV. Graeme hadn't called her and she had no idea what he was up to. She'd stared out of the window, watching for his car, and seen a police squad car drive past. It made her feel safe and slightly more confident. Kelly Porter had been as good as her word. She had promised to protect Alexandros too, and Tilly wondered if he was on the British army base yet.

She hadn't experienced such boredom for years. She'd always been active. Even as a child, she couldn't sit still, always wanting to dance, climb or run. Journalism suited her because of the erratic hours and the chance that she could be called to cover a story at any moment. She could find herself standing in the freezing cold watching fire-fighters deal with a factory blaze, or be woken up to rush to the scene of a major crime. She went from one location to another, interviewing, listening, and gathering nuggets of information from the public. She met with hostility, resentment, abuse and even violence.

She'd cut her teeth at a north Hertfordshire local news-paper that published once a week and was distributed for free, moving to a daily in Nottingham. Homesick and missing the stories a big city brought, she moved back to London and started out on her own. It paid the bills – just – and she dictated terms and conditions. It was just as widely varied (abortion to the price of French cheese), but without the constant threat to her safety. She almost laughed out loud at the irony. She'd never been in so much danger as she was now. Or at least that was what Graeme believed. Her own conviction was wearing thin.

The long hours of not being able to go outside made her mind wander, and she itched to do something. She knew Graeme didn't want her sneaking out for a cigarette, even if she checked up and down the road first, but she hated smoking indoors. She craved nicotine and was finding that the reduced opportunity to smoke made it worse. She filled the hours writing notes and formulating a story around what she knew, but she couldn't do that all day and all night; it was mentally impossible. She'd also had enough of catch-up TV and box sets. She remembered most of what was on her laptop and kept busy trying to write it all down.

Graeme had told her that no one knew about this place. If that was the case, then no one in the small village would recognise her. She'd promised him over and over again that she wouldn't stray outdoors, but this afternoon she'd broken that promise and gone out of the back door, over the stone wall and into the adjoining field. She'd found a beck at the edge of the field and had taken her shoes off and paddled in the water, sucking deeply on a cigarette and watching the clouds change shape. It was blissful.

Cumbria smelled different to London. The air was thin and sweet, not heavy and murky. It smelled as though it was doing her good just by surrounding her. Her skin felt fresher and her head clearer. After her paddle, she'd lain on the lush green grass for a while, staring up at the sky and smoking two more cigarettes. She thought she must have dozed off, because she woke with a start. She got up quickly, slipping her shoes on, and scurried back to the house, where she realised that in her excitement she'd left the back door open.

She pulled it closed and locked it behind her, swearing under her breath.

The cottage boasted a large, well-stocked wine cellar, and she perused the contents and selected a bottle to open with her early dinner. Graeme had said he'd be back, but if he didn't answer his phone then she couldn't exactly go after him. She'd already called Kelly Porter, who'd said she'd check in with him and get back to her.

Tilly was used to cooking for one, and though she didn't do it all the time, occasionally she would prepare an intricate meal from scratch. She looked in the fridge and found lamb chops and salad bits and bobs. She searched for some mint sauce and some yoghurt to make a quick sauce. The smell of the chops cooking filled the small cottage with the promise of comfort, love and satisfaction. There was nothing quite like the smell of grilling meat. She poured herself a large glass of red wine and went to get the fire prepared. She'd only been here two days, but it felt like a week.

The other difference between north and south, she'd noticed, was the temperature. In June, London sweltered and commuters melted, but here, where the air was crystal clear and the mountains cast shadows, the evenings were cool and a fire was welcome. Graeme had made one every night. She remembered how to do it from watching her dad. Mum had wanted to close the chimney and buy a fancy flame-effect gas fire, but Dad wouldn't hear of it. Now Tilly lit the newspaper and it caught the kindling with a satisfying sizzle. She placed the guard in front of it and went to check the lamb.

She made what she called an interesting salad; in other words, not just lettuce and tomato. She found fennel, which she sliced thinly, a bag of pine nuts and some raisins. She tossed it all together with a grated carrot and some balsamic dressing and went to put a log on the fire, now that it had settled. Graeme had wired up a Sonos speaker to his Wi-Fi and she searched for some soothing music. With a bit of luck, the lamb and the wine would make her drowsy. It was her first night alone in the cottage; the other two, she'd had Graeme by her side, even if he had come back late from drawing up plans at Allerdale House.

She heard a sound outside the back door. It sounded like a bottle toppling over. She'd seen cats around the garden, and sometimes perched on a wall when she looked out, so she dismissed it. However, it made her want to check all the doors again and peek out of the window to see if Graeme's car was back. She felt a little foolish, but it couldn't hurt. She tested the lamb and turned off the grill. While the meat rested, she went upstairs and checked the window locks as well. All was secure and she came back downstairs. When she reached the back door, she felt like peeking out, just to look at the stars, but she decided against it and pushed on the handle. It was secure.

She finished her meal alone and took her plate to the sink, which was scrupulously clean and tidy: the cottage had been bleached to within an inch of its life since she'd moved in. She drained her wine and stared at her phone, jumping when she heard the same sound outside the back door again.

During the day, there was plenty of noise from tractors, sheep and cattle. But at night, the countryside was as still as a graveyard. She went to the back door and unlocked it. The only thing that would still her mind was checking for herself whether a pesky cat was toying with the recycling. She opened the door, but saw nothing in the back yard. There was no cat. There were, however, two wine bottles on the floor that must have been blown over by the breeze. She tutted and stepped outside to pick them up.

# Chapter 53

An unmarked car left Agios Nikolaos intelligence station and headed for the Troodos Mountains, escorted by two military police in another vehicle. They estimated they'd be there in just over an hour.

British soldiers always struggled in the summer heat, and the men in the first car turned the air conditioning up to maximum. The military bases couldn't afford air conditioning in most of the quarters, and the luxury of the cool car was satisfying. They chatted amicably, discussing the football season that had ended last month with Manchester City winning the FA Cup.

'You're an armchair supporter,' one jibed. 'You can't support a team where you don't live.'

'You don't live there either.'

'I'm on operations! It doesn't count.'

'Operations, my arse. You're an analyst. Don't tell me you got the Iraq medal for sitting in a chair in a listening station?'

'Fuck off.'

It was ordinary banter.

'Who are we getting?'

'A witness in a British case. He's wanted back.'

'So he bolted?'

'He's a Cypriot national working in London.'

'Big case?'

'No idea. All I know is we need to get him to Akrotiri for the last flight to Brize Norton.'

His partner looked at his watch. 'Doable.'

'And his mother.'

'Why his mother? Is she a witness too?'

'No idea.'

The officer looked in his rear-view mirror and watched the car behind. The RMPs looked serious and bored.

'Did you ever consider the military police?'

'Nah. All that abuse. Worst job in the army.'

'How did you get into intel?'

'Transferred from the infantry when I was at Chicksands.'

The car belted out cold air and a few drops of icy water fell from the air-conditioning unit down the dash.

'It's getting hot out there.'

Their surroundings grew greener as they left the desert-like conditions around Nicosia and entered the fresher mountain terrain. They followed their instructions and drove deep into a forest. The mountain road wound up and up and they talked about skiing at the army station up here.

'It's all right can't complain. Three runs isn't much, but it's one of the only places in the world where you can ski in the morning and sunbathe in the afternoon.'

'Wait, you missed the turning.'

'Did I?'

'Yeah, I'm sure that was a sign to the village.'

'Right, I'll back up.'

The RMP vehicle pulled up as they stopped and wound the windows down, allowing the heat to rush in. They explained what they were doing. The RMPs rolled their eyes as if the two intel officers were incompetent. They reversed and took the correct turning. A few minutes later, they pulled up outside a modest villa that you would definitely miss if you didn't know what to look for, hidden away from the tiny track.

They parked in front of a large garage, and all four men got out. The RMPs carried weapons with the safety on. They had been warned of a moderate threat. They walked up to the front door and rang the bell, then knocked on the solid wooden door. All the shutters were closed.

There was no answer.

The RMPs set off around the building, banging on doors and windows as they went.

Nothing.

Round the back, there was a pool and a pool house, which was open. They went to knock on the glass screen, pulling back when they heard the sound of growling.

Three wild dogs were gorging on two bloated bodies. The first man inside retched and coughed as he cocked his weapon.

'Jesus! Get down!'

The Intel officers darted for cover inside an outdoor kitchen and hid behind the counter. The two RMPs radioed their base at Dhekelia, but not before firing their weapons to scare off the dogs. The animals whimpered away, but hung about in the yard.

The RMPs walked closer: one spoke into his radio. 'One deceased male. Thirties. Dark hair. Resembles Alexandros Skarparis. One deceased female. Sixties. Resembles Rosa Skarparis.'

The intel officers poked their heads above the counter.

'Don't worry, apart from these two, I think we're alone. We'll check the house. Looks like business has been taken care of. I'm sure we won't find anyone still here.'

The first intel officer looked at the corpses. He was no expert, but they hadn't been dead long. The dogs had taken a few chunks, but they were recognisable. It was a sobering sight. He looked straight into the eyes of the woman, and wondered if she'd suffered.

All the conversation in the car seemed suddenly irrelevant as he remembered how his companion had said they should eat a good lunch before setting off to the mountains. He shuddered to think that that two-hour delay might have been the difference between life and death for the mother and son on the floor in front of him.

He shut the pool house door to make sure the dogs couldn't get back in, and sat down outside. The image of dead bodies surrounded by pools of their own blood, being gnawed on by wild dogs, was something he hadn't signed up for.

## Chapter 54

Graeme took Kelly's call just before five o'clock. He'd had to cover for two members of staff who were sick. He itched to get back to Tilly, but Kelly said she'd sent a squad car earlier and everything seemed fine. She agreed to send another one and knock this time. Meanwhile Graeme called the cottage. Tilly sounded miserable.

'I keep hearing noises out the back.'

'What type of noises?'

'I don't know. I went out to check, but there was nothing there.'

'Don't do that. Kelly's sending a car. I'm sorry I left you all afternoon. I need to drive to Allerdale House, just to collect a file of drawings that I can work on tomorrow; it's my day off and I intend to spend it with you.'

'Studying drawings?'

'It's better than being on your own. This might all be over and we could go out.'

'Did Kelly say that?'

'No, but it can't go on for ever, can it?'

'I tried to call Alexandros again, but it went dead.'

'The line to Cyprus is crap. Keep trying. Use the landline; don't waste your mobile bill.'

They hung up.

He closed up the marina and drove to Allerdale House. Sebastian had given him the code to get in through the gate, and he pressed it into the pad. The gates opened and he drove through. The view of the lake took his breath away, despite having seen it many times before. It was the way the gardens sloped down to the beach, and the view of the water in the distance so private and untouched. He wondered idly who took care of the gardening.

As he opened the back door, he heard voices. He stopped and listened, wondering if somebody had let themselves in without permission. He'd promised to let Sebastian know if anyone came and went without his say-so.

'Who's there?' He heard a voice shout from upstairs. He was sure it was Sebastian, and thought it odd that he hadn't informed him that he'd be coming up from London.

'It's just me,' he called back. 'I came to get some drawings I left here.'

'Graeme?' Sebastian appeared at the top of the beautiful double staircase. He was dressed in a robe, and the top of it was open.

'I'm sorry I disturbed you. I'll get my file and go.'

'Wouldn't you care to join us?'

Graeme didn't know how to respond. Hadn't he made it clear he wasn't interested? Another man appeared behind his boss, dressed in a similar manner. He'd walked in on a love tryst. He looked at his feet. 'I won't be a minute.'

He walked through to the orangery, where he knew he'd left the file of ideas. He picked it up and turned round. Sebastian was standing at the foot of the stairs holding an old rifle. Graeme dropped the file.

'What the fuck?'

'Graeme, I can't have anyone know I'm here.'

'I won't tell anybody! Put that thing down! Jesus, is that from the Napoleonic War?' He hoped humour might calm the man. He glanced upstairs. The other man was now fully dressed and descending the stairs. Graeme knew this wasn't a good situation to find himself in. He had two opponents, and one of them had a gun. He had no idea what they were up to and why they didn't want to be found.

'I have no interest in who you choose to take to bed, Sebastian. I'm not about to out you.'

Sebastian laughed. 'This isn't about being outed, you imbecile.'

'I don't really want to know what it's about. Seriously, though, that thing looks like it could backfire: I've seen it happen before. Is that your grandfather's hunting gun?'

Sebastian looked at the weapon and Graeme knew that he was mulling over the consequences of the thing going off in his hand.

'You pay my wages,' he said. 'Why would I betray you? I don't know what this is all about, but I have no intention of mentioning anything to anybody. You have my word.'

'Don't believe him.' The other man spoke. He looked like a man in control, and much more handy than Sebastian. If they were having an affair, that wasn't the full extent of their relationship; he looked more like a bodyguard. He and Graeme eyed each other.

'Look, why don't I simply vanish and forget I saw you? You're on your own property; it's none of my business.

Actually, that detective in charge of the inquiry into what happened here has been asking around after you. Is it her you're avoiding?'

Graeme was stalling for time, but he had no idea if it was working. He could see that the man behind Sebastian wasn't armed. Sebastian looked as though he'd never fired a shot in his life, and it was virtually impossible to hit a moving target even if you were well trained.

'When are you going to start locking your doors?' He tried humour again, and prayed that the orangery's outer door was unlocked. Sebastian looked down at the rifle, then turned and said something to his lover.

Graeme took his chance and made a grab for the orangery door; it *was* unlocked. He raced through it, the force of his exit making it crash back on its hinges. He heard glass shatter; he also heard a very loud gunshot and thought he'd been hit. His legs felt like jelly, and he dived over a bush and onto the gravel beyond it, smashing his chin and scraping his hands. But he wasn't thinking about anything except getting away, and he didn't look back.

He ran towards the water, having no other option, and dived in just as he heard another shot. His lungs screamed and he felt pain in his back; whether it was from exertion, fear or a lead slug, he didn't know. He spotted a boat about twenty yards off the beach and swam underwater as far as he could. When he surfaced, the man on deck – he recognised him as Horace, a local out on a fishing trip, no doubt – stood up and waved his newspaper at him.

He had virtually no breath left, and as he reached the boat, he went under again. The cold burned his skin and he felt himself weakening.

'Start the motor!' he shouted, not knowing if he could be heard or if he was just gurgling water. But then he heard the engine cough into life, and Horace reached over the side to pull him up.

'What the hell do you think you're doing?' he said. 'What was all that bloody noise? It woke me up, that's for sure.'

'Gunshots, Horace. Now get me out of here.'

## Chapter 55

The patrol car was already at Eamont Bridge when it got the call. No one had told them to use sirens. It was a routine call to a woman on her own: a potentially important witness intimidation case. They sped through the countryside at a good pace, slowing down only to negotiate tight bends. The driver was adept at throwing his vehicle around roads framed with sharp dry-stone wall edges, and he navigated with expertise, but the passenger still held on to his roof strap.

When they arrived in Bampton, the village was deserted, and they carried on to the tiny hamlet of Bampton Grange, searching for the house in question. The only light was from a few tiny orange slits behind closed curtains and blinds, and they struggled to locate the address. They checked their navigation equipment and found that they were on the wrong side of the road. There seemed to be nothing out of the ordinary at all. No barking dogs, screaming arguments, or drunken yobs. It was just black and silent.

They got out of the vehicle and approached the door. One of the officers knocked. There was no answer. He knocked louder, then spoke into his radio.

'Patrol 357, no answer at property, repeat, no answer at property. Going round the rear of the residence.'

Round the back, they found a different scene. There was smashed glass, and the door was wide open. Inside, the property was in darkness.

'Proceed with caution,' came the instruction.

'Is anybody there?' one of the officers shouted. 'Tilly?'

They looked at one another and stepped inside. The first officer switched on a light. The other held up his hand and shook his head. He spoke urgently into his radio.

'Patrol 357, request for support. Evidence of violence.'

His colleague made his way cautiously into the living area. As he reached the bottom of the stairs, a cry could be heard above him, and he took the steps in twos. His colleague swore: it was a blatant procedural error, but in the heat of the moment, few men could ignore a woman in distress, and they all knew it.

'Patrol 357, urgent request for support.' He gave the address again and continued his search of the downstairs. A figure emerged, rushing down the stairs; the PC swung around a fraction of a second too late and was caught by a fist in the face. It startled him, but he was incapacitated for only a half a second before he gave chase. He was the quicker of the two, and the man hadn't made it out of the back door before the officer was on top of him, using his specialist training to disable him and cuff him. He left him on the floor, face down, while he took to the stairs to assist his partner.

There was another scream, and he rushed into the bedroom to find a woman being held by a second man, who was brandishing a knife. His partner was negotiating with him calmly.

'Come on, pal. You're already going down for breaking and entering; you don't want to go down for anything else.'

'Fuck off, mate. You need to let me past.'

'You know I'm not going to do that.' He spoke into his radio, whilst holding up his hand in a peaceful gesture. 'Patrol 357, request hostage negotiator.'

'You don't need one of those, mate. Just let me past with the girl and I won't hurt her.'

'I can see she's hurt already.' The woman was bleeding from a cut on her head, and her clothes were roughed up and in disarray. 'Miss… is it Matilda? Tilly?'

She nodded.

The man tightened his grip on Tilly's neck and held up the knife. The second officer shifted in the doorway and caught her attention. He held her gaze while his partner continued to speak to the man.

'You're not going to get past us. It's over, pal.'

'Don't "pal" me, you fuck.'

'It's gone wrong. Whatever you were planning to do, it's not going to work. You might as well accept it and take the lesser charges. I don't know what you want with the young lady, pal, but she's—'

'I told you, don't call me pal!' The man's physical demeanour changed into pure fury, and the PCs watched as Tilly slipped beneath his grasp, making herself into a tight ball at his feet, and elbowed his crotch. The man yelped and the officers sprang into action. One grabbed Tilly and dragged her away; the other took the full force of the intruder, who swung the knife into the air and brought it down hard. The PC groaned and cried out.

'He got me, Steve.'

'You bastard!' The PC who was unharmed lifted his truncheon and brought it down with full force on the head of the man who'd stabbed his friend and colleague. The man slumped and fell to his knees, then face first onto the carpet. They were taught where to hit someone on the head without causing permanent damage, but it was a risky manoeuvre and only used in emergencies. The officer cuffed the guy, then rushed to his friend. Tilly was cowering in the corner of the room.

'Did it go into your stab vest?'

'No, it missed and went through my jacket.'

'Fuck, let's see… Patrol 357, officer down! Repeat, officer down!' In the distance, they could hear sirens.

The injured officer clutched his side. Blood was seeping into the carpet beneath him, and both men realised it must be a deep wound.

'Get a medic!' Steve screeched into his radio. 'Mate, I'll be back in two seconds. I'm going for the first aid kit.'

He ran down the stairs and out to his patrol car, grabbing the kit they all carried. It was more sophisticated than the ones you could buy in a chemist's, but it wasn't designed to save a life if an artery had been punctured. All he could do was his best. He ran back up the stairs to where his colleague was slumped on his side. The floor was sticky with blood, and the PC was pale and drowsy.

'Stay with me, mate! Look at me! MEDIC! MEDIC!' he screamed into his radio.

The sirens grew ear-splitting and stopped outside. Steve had no idea who to thank: God, or the skill of the driver, or the forethought of the desk operator who had sent a patrol car with a medic. He almost sank to his knees when he saw the green overall rush past him with a huge case. All he could do now was watch as the medic stripped his friend's clothes and examined the wound.

'Hold here, now!' the medic commanded. Steve knelt and did as he was told. The medic got out what looked like a sewing kit and gave the wounded officer a shot of something before setting to work.

Steve looked away.

He swore he could hear a chopper.

# Chapter 56

Kelly put one hand over her eyes and turned towards the car window. She couldn't sit around at Eden House waiting to see if the injured officer pulled through. Graeme Millar had reported what had happened at Allerdale House, and she and Matt were on their way there behind several patrol cars and two armed response vehicles. Graeme had warned them of the volatility of the old weapon, and they couldn't be too careful.

She knew that Sebastian could have left by now, either by car or boat. The mystery man was a new one, but he could easily have a playmate from London that they knew nothing about. Their digging had been focused on George, Ravensword and the lab research, rather than the disgruntled disinherited grandson.

'It happens. You're not responsible,' Matt tried to reassure her.

'Yes I am. I allowed myself to be persuaded that the risk to Tilly was one-dimensional. I underestimated a direct threat.'

Matt looked at his iPad. 'Colonel Dansford has shot himself at the Montague Club. He's dead.'

Kelly looked up. It was as much a confession of guilt as anything else.

'Personal reasons?' she asked sarcastically.

'Come on, Kelly. We've got work to do. Chin up. We're almost there. Tooting's gone off the radar, but we'll find him. It'll take a little longer to get an arrest warrant for our senior civil servants. We don't want any mistakes.'

Kelly knew he was right. It could take weeks to put together a watertight case pointing at senior members of the Home Office and beyond. They didn't even fully understand yet where the illegal activity began and ended.

Units from Keswick were on standby to support them at Allerdale House, but not before the ARVs arrived. She didn't want any other casualties. They used blues and twos, and it was exhilarating speeding down the A66 with anticipation burning inside them. The ARV commander would take charge of the initial securing of the property. They intended to clear every room before allowing other personnel inside. Kelly wished at moments like this that she could rush into buildings herself and point a gun at somebody who dared to exist in a twilight world of thuggery, threatening and harming others with impunity.

Cars moved aside for them. Kelly alerted the Derwent Water coastguard and instructed them to clear the lake, sending warnings to all registered boats in the area. Matt liaised with London and received updates from the squad cars approaching the home of Christopher Slater, as well as that of Colonel Dansford's widow. Descriptions and alerts had been sent to all units across the capital and beyond, as well as airports and motorway patrols with the ability to track number plates. Tooting owned three cars and had a driver who ferried him around in a Mercedes. All four vehicles had been entered into the combined alert.

They had a hit from CCTV on the A4 out of London towards Heathrow. A quick check confirmed that Philip

Tooting was planning to leave the country on a BA flight to Buenos Aires. The unit deployed to the airport was instructed to procure airport staff cooperation and take Tooting by surprise. A senior manager at the airport contacted BA, who agreed to position the flight as delayed so that Tooting stayed in the business lounge.

Kelly glanced at Matt's iPad and saw that he was watching five separate frames on the one small screen.

An alert popped up on his phone.

'Christ.'

'What?' Kelly turned to him.

'The PC injured at Graeme Millar's cottage. He died in the air.'

'Fuck.' She spoke in a low whisper. 'Wasn't he wearing a stab vest?'

'Yes, but the knife came in the side, under his arm. It went into his brachial artery.'

Kelly stared out of the window into the blackness and they drove on in silence.

'Do we know the suspects? Are they talking?' she finally asked, after clearing a lump in her throat. Both men apprehended at Graeme's cottage had been taken to Kendal for questioning.

'Not yet.'

The cars sped through the gloom of the falling night and Kelly felt nauseous. She hadn't eaten properly in days and the fatigue was kicking in; it would soon be replaced by adrenalin, but until then, the motion of the car made her drowsy.

They turned off to Portinscale and made their way to the private lane that led to Allerdale House. Suddenly the car jolted forward and made a brutal emergency stop.

Kelly's head swung forward and then backwards, banging on the rear rest and coming to a stop. Her neck screamed in agony. Matt put his hand out to her.

'Sorry, ma'am,' said the driver. 'Obstruction ahead.'

They listened on the radio, nursing their whiplashed necks, as the two ARVs apprehended a car containing a driver and a passenger.

'Police! Hands on the wheel! Stay inside the vehicle, do not move your hands!'

They saw high-visibility jackets up ahead and the glint of weapons pointing at the vehicle. The driver was unknown, but the passenger was positively ID'd as Sebastian Montague-Roland. Both men were arrested and read their rights. Neither made a comment.

The ARV commander informed Matt and Kelly that they could leave their vehicle, and they did so, rubbing their necks gingerly.

Sebastian Montague-Roland looked shaken but still arrogant as he sat in the back of one patrol vehicle; the second man, whom neither Kelly nor Matt had seen before, sat in another. They were to be taken to Eden House for formal interview. Meanwhile, she and Matt would accompany a search of the escape vehicle as well as the property to see what they could find. A forensic team had already been called.

## Chapter 57

Christopher Slater was sound asleep in his sprawling six-bedroom home in Surrey. His wife had been roused by bright lights and shouting outside. She'd assumed it was drunks or other such riff-raff and had gone along the first-floor landing to see if their children were home. She still called them children, though they were both in their late twenties. Still using their parents' house as a free base between jobs and partying. Mrs Slater didn't mind.

Now, as she peered out of the window after confirming that both the children were in their rooms, she saw police cars parked in the drive, with officers and dogs swarming around. She shook her husband.

He'd taken sleeping pills and was difficult to rouse. He'd come home late smelling of booze, and they'd argued.

A loud pounding at the door scared her, and she shook her husband more determinedly. The boys padded half asleep through to their parents' room.

'Mum? What's going on?'

'I have no idea. I'm sure it's a mistake.'

Finally Christopher woke up, though he was incomprehensible for the first few minutes. The sleeping pills and the booze made him sound like an idiot. He scrunched his brow. The continued banging pierced his

347

thoughts and a voice booming through a loud hailer made him sit up alert and fully awake.

'Christopher Tarquin Slater! Answer the door! This is the police! We have a warrant for your arrest!'

The boys looked at their mother and then their father.

'What on earth is happening?' Mrs Slater asked.

'I have no idea. You stay here. I'm sure it's a mistake.' Christopher stood up and started getting dressed. 'I'll go and see what's going on.'

He knew exactly what was going on, but he didn't have the courage to tell his family: to prepare them. Instead, he left the room knowing that he wouldn't see them again as a free man. He couldn't look at his boys.

He went downstairs and opened the front door.

'What the...' His voice tailed away as he came face to face with two heavily armoured police officers. Both were over six foot tall and neither smiled at him. 'Look, chaps, I think there's been a mistake.'

'Are you Christopher Tarquin Slater?'

'Well, yes...'

'Turn around, sir. We're arresting you on suspicion of being an accessory to murder, fraud and corruption. You have the right to remain silent...'

He was shoved roughly around, facing the interior of the lavish house that had been his family home for eighteen years. His wife came to the top of the stairs and gazed at him questioningly. He looked away.

The cuffs that were snapped on to his wrists were cold, hard and very tight. He winced. He was marched out of the house towards a waiting car, and as he looked back at the house, he saw at least five officers entering it, flicking lights on and moving equipment into place.

He'd never felt so scared in his life. His thoughts whirled. Had Benji been arrested too? And Tooting? He tried to stay calm. As they drove away, he could feel the blood throbbing in his hands.

'What is this about? Why are those officers going into my house?'

'We've got a search warrant, sir.'

Christopher closed his eyes. He had no idea where he was being taken or exactly what he was accused of. They'd mentioned murder and fraud in the charge.

All would be well. Philip's lawyers would see to it.

# Chapter 58

The delay to his flight was only a minor irritation, and Philip sat back with another glass of champagne. The business-class lounge wasn't what it used to be; anyone could come in here now if they had enough Air Miles. They even served Prosecco. His wife called, and he decided to answer it in case it was something important about work or the grandchildren.

'Philip, the police have been looking for you: at the club, here, at the flat in London.'

'How do you know about the flat in London?'

'Oh come on, Philip, I know about everything. That's not important. Why do they want to speak to you?'

'I have no idea.' The creeping feeling returned under his ribs and he glanced around the lounge, but no one was taking any interest in him.

'Where are you?' asked his wife.

'I've just been to the gym. I've been on the rowing machine. I'm knackered, actually, I'm—'

'I suggest you get back here as soon as you can. They've been calling all your numbers.'

'I don't keep work phones on me at the weekend, you know that.'

'I gave them your private number.'

'They haven't called it.'

He glanced over at the receptionist behind the desk: she was speaking into her phone. One look his way told him what he needed to know. He hung up on his wife and looked at his watch, then gathered his things and made his way to the exit from the lounge. He was too late. Uniformed police entered through the double glass doors and blocked the way.

'Mr Philip Tooting?'

'That's my name.' He straightened his tie and tidied his jacket over his arm.

'We're arresting you on suspicion of murder, conspiracy to murder, fraudulent activity and perverting the course of justice.'

'Well, I… This is ludicrous.'

A burly officer approached him and turned him around. His laptop case and hand luggage fell to the floor, along with his jacket. He struggled and complained, but the officer was firm and he heard the sound of handcuffs. His wrists were restrained and the cuffs locked tightly before he was marched out of the lounge.

People stared. Some took photographs. Others pointed.

Philip's cheeks raged red as he was paraded through the terminal building towards a private customs area. He was escorted through a search station and towards some service entrance doors, where three police cars waited. They'd sent the fucking cavalry.

He went over the charges in his head. He couldn't think who he'd be accused of murdering: he'd never got his hands dirty. Nor could he think of one single link between him and Benji that would lead him to be accused of conspiracy to murder. The fraudulent activity was an open book. As soon as these oafs released him and he was sitting in front of somebody in a suit and a tie, he'd call his solicitor and secure his release.

## Chapter 59

Matt and Kelly entered the interview room. This was the first time in three years that they'd interviewed a suspect together, and it felt odd to her.

So much for her weekend with Johnny.

Sebastian Montague-Roland sat tight-lipped and straight-backed. He looked proud and defiant, but also innocent and lost. They confirmed details for the tape and began the process of trying to get to the bottom of what role he had played in the whole affair.

'You were there when it all happened, weren't you, Sebastian?'

'I beg your pardon?' He'd waived his right to a lawyer, saying that he'd done nothing wrong. It was an unusual choice: high-profile suspects usually had a solicitor ferried to the interview room quicker than the coppers got there. Kelly carried on regardless, expecting him to change his mind.

'We have a witness statement from another suspect, who has admitted to being present at Allerdale on the night of the murder of George Murphy. He says that a man matching your description was seen talking to George in the orangery.'

'As if he could see me from there.'

'From where? How do you know where he was standing?'

Sebastian put his head in his hands.

'Do you know any of these men?' Kelly spread out photographs of Leo Brown and the other three men who were in custody in London. They'd charged Denny Tapps with the actual murder.

'No. I never got involved with any of Philip's thugs.'

'Philip's thugs?' Kelly and Matt exchanged glances.

'You mean you think this was all me? My God! I'm just as much a victim as George!'

'Could you explain?'

Sebastian sighed and hung his head. 'Grandfather was old school.' He looked between them and to the uniform at the door. 'I'm gay, and my grandfather was devastated. So much so that when Philip threw oil on the flames, he changed his will.'

'What did Philip do?'

'He showed him photos.'

'What photos?'

Sebastian glanced again to the policeman at the door.

'Of me at the Montague Club with various lovers. The same room was always booked for me, you see, and I had no idea. My grandfather was furious. He called me an animal. I was lucky to have anything put in trust really.'

'We've read the will. Why did your grandfather think you might decide to marry and settle down?'

'He saw homosexuality as a disease that could be cured. I promised him it was a passing thing.'

Kelly felt sympathy for the man in front of them, but it still didn't explain what had happened to George.

'Why were you at Allerdale House on Sunday the second of June?'

'I was negotiating with George. He understood my predicament and appreciated the unfairness of it all. Philip didn't want George having any of my grandfather's money because it would weaken his hand when he came to force George to hand over whatever he was working on.'

'Did you know that the men who turned up were there to kill him?'

Sebastian hung his head again. 'No, but I realised it after I'd heard what happened.'

'And did George know he was in danger?'

'I tried to get him to leave with me, but he was stubborn and proud. He didn't believe anybody would sully Grandfather's memory.'

'So when did you leave?'

'After I saw the men go. They really did say that they were surveyors. George had mentioned that Grandfather wanted to renovate the place but was too old. We discussed a leisure complex. I thought he'd called a firm of surveyors, and I guess he thought I had.'

'And you lied to us because…?'

'Philip still has footage of me.'

'I see.'

'Why was there no tribute to George at the alumni dinner on Wednesday?' Matt threw in a hardball.

'It wasn't discussed. I don't have the authority to…'

'Or the courage?' It was cruel but true. 'You're scared of Philip?'

Sebastian looked away. 'Not scared, more beholden. I don't want those pictures reaching the newspapers. My family is landed, titled and rich; it would be a juicy story for the gutter press.'

'And your companion?'

'He's a waiter at the Montague Club. I thought we could move away together. I never imagined that anyone would turn up at Allerdale House looking for me.'

'But you gave Graeme Millar a bloody job!' Matt raised his voice. 'Why? Wasn't that a little risky?'

Sebastian blushed. 'Graeme is a trustworthy man. I needed a local and I thought those thugs could turn up any time.'

'Have you ever handled a weapon before today?'

'Not that type of weapon.'

'It's really not the time for jokes.'

'Well when is it the time? I've lied to the police, I've been arrested, my grandfather thought I was depraved, I've been disinherited—'

'Actually, Sebastian, we located George's will. It would seem that he wanted to do the right thing by you and didn't entirely agree with your Grandfather. He had it amended just before he died. It states in an emergency clause that if he dies before you, the estate reverts to you in its entirety. It's a bitter sweet discovery, given what happened.'

'Are you toying with me, Officer?' Sebastian asked seriously.

'Nah, mate, we're not,' Matt said. 'But you're still under arrest for obstructing the course of justice and using an illegal firearm with intent to maim and kill.'

'I never meant to hurt Graeme! It would have been a fucking miracle had I hit him.'

'You can tell that to your lawyer. We'll keep you in a cell here until your hearing tomorrow, and then you'll probably be moved to Haverigg Prison to await trial. Unless you use your new-found wealth for bail, of course. You know, it would be an honourable gesture to donate some of that cash to the families of Emily Wilson and Mike Hudson.'

'Who?'

'George's colleagues who were murdered. Do you know anything about that?'

'No.'

'What was discussed on your table at the alumni dinner?'

Sebastian looked nonplussed. Matt sighed and referred to his notes.

'You were sitting with Philip Tooting, Christopher Slater and Colonel Benjamin Dansford.'

'The same table that George was supposed to sit on, but his name was scribbled out,' Kelly added.

'I find those things a mighty bore, to be honest. What Philip says generally goes in one ear and out of the other.'

'Why do you suppose Colonel Dansford committed suicide earlier today?'

'What?'

'We've got Slater in custody. Were you privy to the instructions to execute George and his colleagues?'

'No!'

A uniform entered the room and asked if he could see Kelly outside. She excused herself and closed the door behind her.

'Ma'am, we've received a message from the army base in Dhekelia, Cyprus. Alexandros Skarparis and his mother are both dead. Their bodies were found this afternoon. They were shot.'

'Oh no.' Kelly put her hand to her mouth. She went back into the room and beckoned Matt out.

'What is it? You look ashen.'

'Alexandros and his mother have been executed. Gunshots. We were too late. I think we have enough on Sebastian to let him sweat tonight. I want to know what Tooting and Slater have to say. Someone needs to pay for this, and with Dansford dead, I can see the others walking away because there's no way to prove their hands were dirty. I also want to send officers to Cyprus. I don't trust the army to get to the bottom of this.'

'That'll take time.' Matt's phone rang. He listened, nodded and thanked the person on the other end.

'Lights still burning in Hendon?' Kelly asked. He smiled and nodded.

'One of the vehicles coming in the other direction when Miranda Cooper's car was crushed by the Ravensword lorry had dash cam. We've got a picture of the driver.'

She gave him a high five. Some good news was welcome.

'We can't let these bastards walk, Matt.'

'I know. Kelly, you look knackered. Why don't you go home. I've got this. We're as far as we can be at the moment.'

'What about the interviews of Tooting and Slater; we need to get to them before their lawyers get them released.'

'Let me worry about that. Even if I was in London, I'd still do it by video link.'

'Where will you sleep?'

'There are cells underneath this place?'

'You can't do that,' she protested.

'I'm joking. I've booked a hotel over the road – the Castle.'

'Twat.'

'Thanks, Kell.'

She glared at him. She was desperate to go home and pour a glass of wine. Emotion welled up inside her, and she didn't want Matt to see her cry. She walked away and called Johnny on the way to her car. As soon as she heard his voice, she let everything out: the copper at the cottage in Bampton, Alexandros and his poor mother, Emily, Mike…

'I'll go to yours now. Josie has a friend over,' he said.

She hung up and found a tissue in her bag.

# Chapter 60

In Hounslow, as Matt watched via direct screening, Philip Tooting replied 'no comment' to every question posed to him, at the encouragement of his lawyer.

In Camberley, Christopher Slater was leaking like a faulty tap, giving so much away they could barely keep up. None of it was on Tooting. Instead, it focused on Dame Charlotte Cross. The commissioner informed Matt that he'd be separating the inquiries, and from now on, he himself would be heading the investigation into the conduct of the Permanent Under-Secretary.

Matt leaned forward and spoke to a closed-network microphone connected to the interviewing officers questioning Slater. 'Ask him who his contact is at the Met.'

'I don't know what you're talking about.' Slater was trying to play them and assume the role of master puppeteer; dictating what information he should concede. Matt told the officer what to say next.

'A mobile telephone found during a search of your property in Ascot, Surrey, revealed that an officer from the Metropolitan Police called your number, and received calls from you, twenty-three times over the past two weeks. Can you explain why that might be?'

Matt couldn't imagine how shitty it had been for the officer who'd been tasked with dragging the sergeant in for questioning at Hendon, but the grim job had been carried out and it hadn't taken long to establish sufficient evidence for a charge. He'd lose his job, he'd go down for sure, and he would probably never be trusted again. Idiot. Whatever the benefits, it was never worth it.

Matt left Slater's investigation and turned back to Tooting's.

'Tell him that Ravensword have frozen his assets while they conduct a private investigation into abuse of company finances.'

For once, Tooting didn't comment; not even to say 'no comment'. Both Tooting and the solicitor next to him shifted slightly in their seats: Philip had chosen to use a Ravensword solicitor to represent him.

'Tell the solicitor sitting next to him that he might want to call his boss – who is awake and expecting his call – to clarify whether he is to remain as Mr Tooting's counsel tonight.'

At 1 a.m., both interviews were suspended and the suspects sent to cells to mull over their futures.

Matt checked on the status of Tilly Knight, who'd been taken to a local hospital. He thought he might take a wander over there. Sleep was out of the question, and he was curious to meet Graeme Millar. He turned off the monitoring equipment in the office at Eden House and looked around. This was Kelly's empire, and he was envious of her. It was intimate, three-dimensional and real. Not that he disliked his own job – far from it – but this had the feel of an old-school investigative environment where officers chased leads and pulled in suspects face to face. He had to admit that his role in London could be soulless.

He grabbed his jacket and asked the staff downstairs at the front desk how he could get to the hospital. They arranged a car and he was soon on his way.

The town of Penrith was non-descript, he thought, and it was bloody cold despite the season. He arrived and found the relevant ward. He'd checked ahead that Graeme Millar was keeping a vigil on his new squeeze and had bedded down in the visitors' room. He spoke to the sister in charge briefly and was told that Tilly was stable, with minor injuries: mainly shock and bruising. He was taken to the guest area and found a man dozing on an armchair, covered in a blanket. He stirred and sat up.

Matt held out his hand. 'DCI Carter. I'm heading the investigation into Tilly's assault.'

Graeme took his hand. They sized each other up.

'I should never have left her,' he said.

'We all say that.'

'Do you know what happened to the policeman who was injured? I've asked here but no one will tell me.'

'He died, I'm afraid.'

'Jesus. Poor bloke.'

'And all for someone who wasn't really involved,' Matt added.

Graeme screwed his brow. 'Who? Tilly?'

'Yes. I was led to believe she didn't know who was behind George's murder, so whoever was sent after her was there on a very slim chance. Do you know what was on the laptop that was taken?'

'No. Only that it was her work.'

'Good job up at the big house, by the way. We took Montague-Roland in for questioning. Why do you think he allowed you access to the house? Wasn't it risky?'

'I don't know. He wouldn't be aware how well I know Kelly and Johnny. He also needed a local, and I know the area.'

'Who's Johnny?'

'Kelly's other half.' Graeme watched the DCI when he said this, and wished for some reason that he hadn't.

'Has Johnny some relevance to the investigation?' Matt asked.

'No. I teach them both to sail. But Sebastian wouldn't know that.'

'The men you saw hanging around the house: could you ID them from some photos for me?'

'Sure.'

Matt reached into his case and took out photographs of the suspects being held in London. They were in no particular order. Graeme positively ID'd Denny Tapps and Ken Chubb, then stopped on the photograph of Leo Brown.

'You know him?'

'Yeah, he was one of my young soldiers in the army. He's involved, is he? He was always up to no good.'

'I think you know the answer to that, Mr Millar. What about this one?' Matt showed him a photograph of Colonel Dansford.

'Dansford? Is he still serving? Jesus, he looks as though he's put on a few stone.'

'He committed suicide this afternoon.'

Graeme stared at him wordlessly.

'It seems odd to me that no one ever saw George on the lake. He was spotted in a few shops and remembered fondly by the woman who owns the little shop in Portinscale. You work on the lake every day, and sail past the big house, but were unaware that anyone was there. You never saw a chimney smoking, lights burning or cars coming out of the lane; yet you did row up to the beach and saw several men up to no good, but failed to report it.'

'No wonder Tilly came up here to hide rather than trust you lot. You finished?' Graeme asked. The two men held each other's stares. Matt broke away first.

'Any idea where I can find this Johnny character?' he asked.

'You'll have to ask Kelly. Goodnight.' Graeme walked out of the room.

Matt left the ward and found the car waiting to take him back to his hotel opposite Eden House. He checked the investigation notes one last time before nodding off on top of the double bed, fully clothed, an empty beer bottle by his side.

## Chapter 61

Kelly felt like her head was stuck to the pillow when her alarm woke her at seven o'clock on Sunday morning. Johnny lay beside her, wide awake.

'How you doing?' he asked. She'd been a mess last night. It had all come out, in an ugly, jumbled torrent of tears and snot. Johnny had listened; he'd held her and put her to bed. He hadn't tried to solve it or make it all go away. He'd put no pressure on her to pull herself together or do anything other than melt down and burn out. It had felt good, but now, trying to muster the energy to face the chief constable and turn up for a day's work filled her with dread. Her head was thick and her body ached with fatigue and exhaustion.

'How bad do I look? We'll take it from there. Pass me a mirror.'

'I wouldn't do that if I were you.'

'Is it that bad?'

'Nothing a strong coffee and some eggs won't sort out. And loads of make-up.'

'Thanks.'

'How about we take some time off? I can arrange for Josie to go to her mum's and we can go somewhere remote.'

'But we've got our main holiday at the end of the year.' They'd talked about taking a sailing trip along the Florida Keys for her fortieth and his fiftieth, though nothing had been booked yet.

'I don't think that's going to come quickly enough.'

She thought about it, lying back on her pillow and yawning deeply. He had a point. When she was away, even if it was just on the boat on the lake, out of mobile phone reach, she did unwind. The commissioner in charge of Hendon had already said that the inquiry was being divided. Their side of things – the murders of George and his associates – was almost wrapped up.

'Why don't you have a look while I'm out? Are you on call today?' she asked.

He nodded. 'I'll drive you in. Pick you up later too. How long will you be there?'

'It all depends if we can get confessions wrapped up and a likely case for the CPS. Things might heat up if any new information comes to light. We know who did it; we've got the fall guys in custody. But we don't know exactly who ordered it. Remember that colonel you told me about? Leo Brown shagged his daughter at Catterick.'

'Dansford?'

'Same. He shot himself yesterday.'

'Fatal?'

Kelly nodded, and sat up to stretch.

'Christ. Why?'

'Well that's it, I'm not sure, but without him, it'll be harder to pin down who did what.'

'So he was definitely involved?'

'Up to his eyeballs. But he'll take his contacts to the grave.'

366

'Come here.' He took her face between his hands and kissed her. Her body was willing her to stay in bed and phone in sick, or pretend to be invisible: anything to not leave.

'Have you checked on Graeme?' she asked, pulling herself away.

'I was going to do that today. Is the girl all right?'

'Tilly? She's going to be OK. My mission today is making the bastard who stabbed the officer talk.'

Johnny took her hand. 'Why don't you have a shower and I'll do breakfast. When do you want to leave?'

Thirty minutes later, they were in Johnny's car on the way to Eden House. When they got there, Kelly sighed and swore.

'What?' Johnny asked.

'That's Matt.'

Johnny looked to where a man was standing on the red stone steps outside the office. He pulled up and Kelly opened her door. The man stared at him. Johnny smiled and waved.

Kelly turned to him and widened her eyes. 'Stop it.'

Matt came towards the car. 'Morning, Kelly.'

'Matt, this is Johnny. Johnny, Matt.'

Johnny reached across and held out his hand. Matt shook it.

'Call me when you want a lift,' Johnny said, and Kelly shut the door, watching him drive away.

She and Matt entered Eden House in silence and took the lift up to her floor. She would only call her team in should she need them. Coordination with London would allow her to make that decision later.

Matt spoke first. 'Did you sleep?'

'Like the dead.' She regretted the choice of phrase. 'Too well.'

He updated her on what had come in overnight, and they had a brief argument about him not going to catch up on sleep. The commissioner wanted an update at 9 a.m., and Kelly's chief constable would sit in.

'Good news,' Matt said.

'What's that?'

'We arrested the guy caught on the dash cam driving the Ravensword lorry that killed Miranda Cooper.'

'Confession?'

'Yup, his prints and DNA were all over the lorry, and he had no alibi.'

'Randomly thought he'd take her out, or an order?'

'Came from Dansford.'

'Shit. His suicide could derail the whole fucking thing.'

'What about Cyprus?'

'No leads so far. If that was Dansford too, it could be serving personnel on the military base there.'

Matt agreed but it also meant another battle with red tape: this time, the MoD.

'Has Dansford's house been processed?' Kelly asked.

'Yup. There was a whole team crawling all over it. They're still there. The wife has been put up in temporary accommodation. A bereavement officer is with her. We'll ask the commissioner if we have enough to keep Tooting, Slater and Montague-Roland in custody.'

'By 9 a.m.?'

'Knowing Commissioner Pickford, she'll have been up all night working every possible angle. She won't let the death of an officer go. It's a shit thing to say, but it could turn out to be our trump card. There's too much at stake, and it's likely the press will have her head if she ignores the web behind it all.'

They made coffee and set up their equipment. There was a perceptible silence and Kelly looked at Matt.

'Boyfriend?'

'Yes.'

'Rugged.'

'Yup.'

They went back to what they were doing.

At 9 a.m. sharp, the chief constable of Cumbria Constabulary came on line and on screen, along with the commissioner of the Met. Kelly and Matt were ready and sat side by side, prepared to fire what they knew at the pair of senior officers with the power to proceed or limit.

'Could you convey my condolences to the family of the PC who lost his life?' The commissioner spoke first, and the chief constable assured her that her thoughts and sympathy would be passed on formally. 'He leaves how many children?'

'Two, ma'am.'

'Carter? Porter? What have we got?'

They started at the beginning. Each knew the facts of the case intimately without once glancing at notes. They spoke in turn, supporting and corroborating one another, for a full hour. Finally they referred to the potential involvement of senior civil servants.

'I've got a meeting booked with the Foreign Office this afternoon,' the commissioner said when they'd finished. 'They've taken an interest in the formula for Compound P. I see the Home Secretary after that: he's in a hurry to weed out any wrongdoing and release a statement to the press. He's making one concession, and it was on the basis that I confirm the scale of involvement with private business. That is that Charlotte Cross will be stripped of her damehood and arrested at home rather than at work, pending questioning. The prime minister is being briefed later today. Good work, you two. Carter, I suggest you get back to London. Porter, there's a job for you at the Met if you want it.'

'Thank you, ma'am, I've already left once. I'm quite happy where I am, thank you.'

They ended the call.

'I think that means you can go home,' Kelly said.

'I've already looked: there's a train at just after 1 p.m. to Euston. I'm glad I came to see where you hang out.'

'Can I buy you an early lunch before you go?' she asked.

# Chapter 62

*'Compound P has the potential to change the modern world. It could save millions from the misery of substance abuse and destroy drugs cartels overnight, destabilising economies reliant upon that trade. But therein lies the problem. A drug with the power to transform one of the richest countries on earth into the poorest could become a bargaining chip for those who have wanted control over those regions for decades. And the cycle of abuse is thus transferred from the impact of addiction on modern society to the subjugation of whole countries. Who wins?*

*'Well, the politicians of course. And Big Pharma.*

*'The cost of producing the drug, along with the necessary development procedures from review, testing and endorsement, could cost the joint government venture tens of billions of dollars, but the results would surely be worth it.*

*'For now, we have been assured that Compound P is being investigated purely for research purposes. Meanwhile, George Murphy and his colleagues can finally be laid to rest. The body in* The Lady of the Lake *baffled*

*investigators earlier this year, but now the truth behind the development and procurement of Compound P – long George Murphy's wish – has been revealed.*

*'In the latest twist, the five largest pharmaceutical companies in the world have all given public statements about the non-viability of Compound P. They say it can't be manufactured; that the chemistry behind the formulas being worked on by George Murphy simply doesn't add up. The human brain cannot be manipulated into thinking it doesn't desire a substance. However, a Cambridge University professor has controversially stated otherwise. He thinks it could work. The professor was unavailable for comment tonight.*

*'This is Tilly Knight, for the BBC's special edition of* Science World.'

Johnny switched off the TV.

'She's good.'

'She's covering the trials next week,' Kelly said.

Six men, including Philip Tooting and Christopher Slater, were due to stand trial at the Old Bailey for the murders of George, Emily, Mike and Alexandros.

Nothing had been reported about Charlotte Cross's spectacular fall from grace, and Kelly could only speculate why. An internal board of inquiry first had to establish if there was a case to investigate; only then would criminal charges be pursued. Tilly Knight wasn't privy to the details of the police investigation, or the documents found on Miranda Cooper's computer, and so no one but the officers closely linked to the case were aware of its depth.

The trial of Miranda's murderer had taken place in late June and had lasted one afternoon. The killer had been sentenced to eighteen years.

Sebastian Montague-Roland had accepted a plea bargain and a suspended sentence in return for testifying against Tooting and Slater. Work had begun in earnest at Allerdale House, with Graeme dishing out the extensive work to grateful local contractors.

The house was now kept locked.

Johnny and Kelly raised their glasses of red wine to their impending holiday. Preparations and paperwork had prevented them from escaping sooner, but it was only three weeks now until their joint birthday trip to Florida. Graeme had crammed in some extra sailing lessons for them, and they'd hired a vessel out of Key West. They were to fly into New Orleans and make their way down there by car.

The doorbell rang and they put their glasses to one side as Kelly went to welcome their guests.

Ted stood in the doorway, flanked by two women around Kelly's own age. All three of them smiled broadly. Kelly stepped aside to let them in, and one by one, they were introduced.

# Acknowledgements

There are so many people who have contributed to making this series special. Thank you to my agent, Peter Buckman, for your never-ending encouragement, wisdom and faith. Also Laura McCallen and the whole team at Canelo for your passion and meticulous attention to detail. That includes Jane Selley for your incredible copyediting and Tom Sanderson for the stunning cover.

I'd like to thank Jim Armitage, my scientist friend and awesome football coach to Freddie, for your brilliant input on the pharmaceutical process.

For their fascinating insight, Harry Chapfield, Cumbria Constabulary (ret'd), Inspector Paul Redfearn, London Met Police, and DI Rob Burns, Beds Police.

To the lemons: you keep me laughing, my dear friends.

To Mike, Tilly and Freddie, I love you so much; your love and support keeps me going x

Do you love crime fiction and are always on the lookout for brilliant authors?

Canelo Crime is home to some of the most exciting novels around. Thousands of readers are already enjoying our compulsive stories. Are you ready to find your new favourite writer?

Find out more and sign up to our newsletter at canelocrime.com